ASSASSINATION

"But first," said Admiral Canaris, "there is another project I would like you to work on, one in which Emil has expressed personal interest."

"Emil" was the Abwehr code name for Hitler. Niedersdorf sat down, waiting. Canaris lit another cigarette, then spoke in a quiet, musing tone. "What would be the effect on the war situation if Roosevelt, Churchill and Stalin were assassinated?"

The question, with its enormously wide and complex implications, startled Niedersdorf. He replied slowly and cautiously, shaking his head, "It would require a complete analysis to estimate the full scope and nature of the effect, Admiral. It would vary among the different nations, of course. . ."

The admiral sat up. His voice was crisp and firm. "We have a Fuehrerbefel, an order direct from Emil, to prepare an assassination plan. We must consider the national capitals too secure for such a plan to succeed, so it will be predicated on travel abroad by the target individuals."

"Stalin never travels abroad, Admiral."

Canaris lifted his eyebrows, smiling faintly. "Among the communications between Washington and Moscow that we have intercepted and decoded, there are many from Roosevelt importuning Stalin to meet with him. Since Stalin needs the material the United States is providing, eventually he will agree. It is unlikely that Roosevelt will travel to the Soviet Union, or he would already have done so. They will undoubtedly meet elsewhere, and Churchill will be there when they do."

Niedersdorf nodded musingly. "When will you need this plan?"

"By the end of the week."

Also by Aaron Fletcher:

OUTBACK
THE CAPRICORN PEOPLE
LOVE'S GENTLE AGONY
FLAME OF CHANDRAPORE
RENDER UNTO CAESAR
THE HOMECOMING
THE MICROWAVE FACTOR
ICE PICK
THE RECKONING

PROJECT JAEL

Aaron Fletcher

A LEISURE BOOK

Published by

Dorchester Publishing Co., Inc.
6 East 39th Street
New York, NY 10016

Printed in the United States of America

And Jael went out to meet Sisera, and said unto him, Turn in, my lord, turn in to me; fear not. And when he had turned in unto her into the tent, she covered him with a mantle.

And he said unto her, Give me, I pray thee, a little water to drink; for I am thirsty. And she opened a bottle of milk, and gave him drink, and covered him.

He said unto her, Stand in the door of the tent, and it shall be when any man doth come and enquire of thee, and say, Is there any man here? that thou shalt say, No.

Then Jael took a nail of the tent, and took an hammer in her hand, and went softly unto him, and smote the nail into his temples, and fastened it into the ground: for he was fast asleep and weary.

So he died.

Judges, 4:18-21

PROJECT JAEL

PROLOGUE

WHEN THE CALL from the hotel desk woke Callaghan, it took him a few minutes to wake up completely. His jet lag, still lingering after a full day, was worse at two o'clock in the morning.

The electric razor that was supposed to operate on fifty-cycle current ran too slow. Shaving with a disposable razor, he nicked himself. Then, when he was ready to leave, he remembered the cigarettes only at the last moment. They were Camels, hard to find in London. He put the carton in his topcoat pocket as he went out.

George Conley was waiting for him in the lobby, sitting in an armchair and reading a newspaper. In his early fifties, Conley was a large man with a ruddy, fleshy face and eyes that could be either blue or an icy shade of slate gray. With something of the military officer as well as something of the policeman about him, he was a senior operations staff officer of MI-6, the British Secret Intelligence Service.

Conley folded his newspaper and put it in his trench

coat pocket as he walked toward Callaghan, his burly presence a stir in the early morning stillness of the wide, dim lobby. Their friendship spanning years, Conley's handshake was warm and firm. "Charles, it's bloody good to see you again," he said heartily. "It's been far too long."

"Indeed it has, George. You certainly look well."

"All the parts are hanging together, even if I am getting a bit baggy. I'm damned sorry to have you up at this hour, Charles. But it's a long drive, and he likes to receive visitors during the morning."

The pronoun was almost capitalized the way he said it; the man to whom he referred was a legendary figure in the Western intelligence community. Callaghan smiled and shrugged. "No problem, George. I've always wanted to meet him, and I was very pleased when I received your message. I certainly appreciate your taking me."

"It's my pleasure, Charles. I see you have the American cigarettes for him, so let's be on our way. I have a car outside." He smiled as they walked toward the front doors. "I was absolutely delighted to hear that you were being assigned here as station chief, Charles. That's quite a promotion, isn't it? And every other chap I've known in that post has been at least ten years older than you are."

"I've been with the Company nearly twenty years now, which is more seniority than most have at my age," Callaghan replied. Then he laughed. "And I'm supposed to have an inside track here. Ever since you pulled the chestnuts out of the fire for me in Iran during the Khomeini takeover, I've been known at Langley as an Atlantic man."

Conley laughed too, shaking his head. "That was only a small return for the times you've helped me, Charles. But if being well regarded has anything to do with it, you are an Atlantic man. And if it comes down to choices, I am as well. When you get settled in, I'm certain that we'll have very good cooperation where our bailiwicks meet."

"There's no question about that. Monday is my official date of arrival, so I'll get started then on finding out where the strings are and which ones have knots in them. I checked with your section yesterday, but they said you weren't available."

"Yes, I would have come to see you last night instead of sending a message, but I was doing some tidying up. I've been elsewhere for a time."

His choice of terms subtly indicated that his absence, involving some sensitive matter, was not open to discussion. It created no awkwardness between them; their friendship was based on a mutual understanding of its limitations. Their conversation continued, each of them in turn asking about the other's family as they went down the wide steps at the front of the lobby and out through the front doors.

Light drizzle was falling outside, blending with thin spring fog to make pearly, luminescent halos around the lights on the hotel marquee and the street lamps. The car, a dark Jaguar sedan with bulky lines of understated luxury, gleamed wetly at the curb in the hotel loading zone. As they got into the car, their voices and the slam of the car doors were loud in the dark stillness of the deserted street.

The drizzle turned into rain as they drove toward the

motorway, the clicking of the windshield wipers punctuating the burble of the powerful engine and the hissing of the tires. The lights bordering Hyde Park flicked rapidly past along Park Lane. Conley was a fast, aggressive driver.

On the motorway leading north out of London, the car bored past other traffic droning along in clouds of mist. Conley and Callaghan continued talking, reminiscing and discussing friends; but their conversation kept returning to the purpose of their trip. "He's a sort of emeritus director now," Conley said. "But he keeps his hand in very firmly, and he receives a few visitors."

"No one really retires from the game, do they?"

Conley chuckled and shook his head. "No, I suppose not, Charles, and him least of all. And he gets what he wants, of course. When your father had that heart attack, he had me make arrangements through your people for full reports. How is he now?"

"Amazingly well, considering that he still drinks like a fish and smokes like a furnace. He's a part-time consultant with NSA now, and he still gets out to Langley occasionally."

"He'll want to know all about your father. He's always been very fond of him."

"The feeling is mutual, to say the least. My father often talks about when they first met in Teheran, during the war. That was his first assignment after he joined the OSS. He told me once that the action floated by the Germans to assassinate Roosevelt, Churchill, and Stalin at the Teheran Conference amounted to considerably more than what was released to the public."

Conley nodded emphatically. "Indeed it did, Charles. In fact, it was a very close thing."

"That's what my father said, but he also said that he was only on the sidelines. During the war, all the action that amounted to anything in Teheran revolved around the MI-6 residency."

"Yes, that's right. The military was involved in that particular action, because the Germans put quite a lot of effort into it. But the residency was the focus."

"Has he ever told you about it?"

Conley laughed, shaking his head. "No. To say that the man is a sphinx is an understatement. However, other things occurred at about the same time that had a great influence on my life. I didn't understand what was happening, of course, because I was only a boy. But I started probing into them in later years." He began to say something else, then hesitated and changed the subject, nodding toward the back seat. "There's a flask of coffee back there, Charles. Pour us a cup, if you would."

The abrupt end to the conversation indicated that it had touched on a sensitive subject. They fell silent for a few minutes as Callaghan poured the coffee. It was strong and black, its nutty scent blending with the varnish and oiled leather smells of the car as steam wafted up from the cups.

They were speeding along a deserted stretch of the motorway, the headlight beams cutting through the darkness and rainfall mixed with wisps of fog.

Conley drained his cup, then sighed musingly. "It isn't that security is involved, Charles," he said. "The Teheran action was a long time ago, and you're hardly an outsider as far as the Service is concerned. But the fact of the matter is, a lot of family skeletons clatter about rather loudly in that old closet. However, you're a very close friend and more or less a member of the family, and it's an interesting story. So I'll tell you about it, but I'll ask you to exercise due discretion."

"Yes, of course."

"Would you pour me another shot of coffee, please? As you'll see, it took me quite a few years to piece it all together. But we have a long drive ahead of us, and it will fill the time."

Callaghan opened the thermos bottle again and refilled the cups. Conley relaxed in his seat, sipping his coffee and collecting his thoughts. Then he began speaking. As he talked, Callaghan analyzed what he said in terms of its source. It was an automatic reaction, a point of view developed from force of habit; product without its provenance was useless.

The sources of parts of the story were obvious. Conley had full access to the MI-6 archives. He had been stationed in Germany and had worked with the BND at a time when many of its operatives were former members of the German intelligence services of World War II, giving him an opportunity to learn that side of it. He also knew and had talked with others who had been present and involved in one way or another.

Other details seemed to derive from personal sources of his own, possibly his mother's letters and other papers; or perhaps she had kept that bane of intelligence operations, a diary. Some of the story was a web of supposition woven over gaps between facts, but it was informed supposition. As well as anyone could, Conley knew the people who had been involved, knew what they would do under given circumstances.

The circumstances had been the upheaval of World War II, with its turbulent events and the often brutally harsh methods necessary to keep abreast of those events. Callaghan refilled the coffee cups when they became empty, listening to Conley as the car raced along the motorway through the dark, rainy night.

PART ONE

November-December, 1942

CHAPTER ONE

THE SLAP OF cards and a thin, wavering whisper from a radio carried along the hall from the guard post to Niedersdorf's office. The radio was tuned to Radio Berlin, which was ending its broadcast day with the recording of Maria Von Schmedes singing "Another Beautiful Day Draws to a Close," as it did each night. It was midnight.

The noise from the street had died away hours before. Few ventured through the darkness of the blackout and the winter weather gripping Berlin to the Tirpitz Ufer, a stone quay between the Landwehrkanal and the Tiergarten. Fewer still came to the gray, anonymous building at 72-76 Tirpitz Ufer. To those who worked there it was the Fuchsbau, the Fox Lair. To others it was the headquarters of the Abwehr, Military Intelligence.

Hours had passed while Niedersdorf pored over stacks of files, collecting information for an analysis he had been ordered to prepare of an incident that had electrified the headquarters: Kondor, the Abwehr network of agents centered in Cairo, had suddenly folded and ceased all radio transmissions.

The chief of the Abwehr, Admiral Wilhelm Canaris, had ordered Niedersdorf to analyze the extent of the loss and possible causes for it. The first part of the analysis had been simple, a piecing together of frantic, fragmentary reports from independent agents in Alexandria and other places. Kondor was a complete loss; all the operatives and their contacts had been arrested.

The second part had been elusive, but Niedersdorf had found clues during hours of searching through files. Facts innocent in isolation but suspicious in combination had formed into a conclusive answer on how Kondor had been destroyed.

Chairs scraped at the guard post along the hall, the guards standing at attention; then footsteps came slowly along the hall. Canaris stepped into the doorway, a spare, middle-aged man in an impeccably neat uniform. His thin, ascetic features were shadowed by his cap visor from the dim light that gleamed on the admiral's braid on his overcoat sleeves.

Niedersdorf pushed his chair back and stood. "Good evening, Admiral."

"Good evening, Franz," Canaris replied in his soft voice, smiling. "Are you to be commended for diligence, or chided for unwillingness to brave the cold and go to your quarters?"

"Perhaps something of both, Admiral. I have been working on the analysis on Kondor."

Canaris took off his cap as he walked into the office, his white hair slipping down on his forehead. His finely etched features expressionless, he pushed his hair back and tucked his cap under his arm as he took off his gloves. "Have you unraveled the mystery for us, Franz?"

"I have found a satisfactory explanation, Admiral.

There is evidence that the network was infiltrated."

Canaris nodded impassively, turning back to the door. "Come to my office and we will discuss it."

Niedersdorf followed Canaris out into the cold, drafty hall. The light from the guard post was dim, casting a soft gleam along the hardwood floor and leaving deep shadows beside ornate pilasters that stood between the tall, heavy doors and reached up into the darkness of the high ceiling. Niedersdorf and Canaris went into the Admiral's office, their boots stirring loud echoes in the stillness.

Canaris turned on a lamp on his desk, then went to a cabinet in a corner. The lamp made a pool of light around the desk, the corners and high ceiling of the room lost in thick shadows. Behind heavy blackout drapes covering the tall windows, panes rattled in the wind keening around the building. The admiral opened the cabinet and took out glasses and a bottle. "Will you join me in a drink, Franz?" he asked.

"Yes, Admiral, thank you. Did you and Frau Canaris go to the opera this evening?"

"Yes, and it was enjoyable enough. It dispelled some of the gloom resulting from my visit to OKW this afternoon."

The admiral's voice was faintly derisive as he referred to High Command Headquarters, making Niedersdorf feel uneasy. Having been assigned as chief of staff of the Abwehr a few weeks before, Niedersdorf had found the admiral to be cordial, with a talent for inspiring loyalty; but Canaris was also an enigmatic man, with dangerously iconoclastic attitudes. He returned to the desk with two glasses and handed one to Niedersdorf as he lifted his. "Your health, Franz."

"And yours, Admiral."

Niedersdorf sipped the liquor. It as Steinhäger, rather than whiskey, gin, or one of the more unusual liquors that the admiral kept in the cabinet. Canaris unfastened his overcoat and sat down behind the desk, motioning to a chair. Niedersdorf sat down as he began telling Canaris about the clues he had found in the files and his conclusions on what had happened in Cairo.

The intelligence network had expanded rapidly during the past months, at a rate that in retrospect was suspicious. Another suspicious fact was that a new British MI-6 resident had arrived in Cairo a few weeks before the expansion of the network had begun.

In addition, a message to Lutz, the Abwehr resident in Cairo, had referred to the expansion of the network and warned him to thoroughly investigate agents before recruiting them. There was also a report from Lutz on the interrogation of an Arab named Astafan, a British agent who had been detected and captured. The interrogation had established that the British only suspected the existence of Kondor.

Astafan had been captured and interrogated three days after the warning had been sent from Berlin. The British resident had obviously known about the warning, either through interception or from a source within Kondor. He had prepared Astafan in advance, then had planted Astafan on Lutz in order to give him a false sense of security. Kondor had been skillfully infiltrated, then destroyed.

Canaris was silent for a long moment after Niedersdorf finished, his expression inscrutable as he looked into a dark corner of the room. He took out a box of cigarettes and lit one, shrugging as he exhaled. "Lutz was a good operative, but he was outmatched," he said. "Now we must do what we can to recover ourselves. Our comrades on the Bendlerstrasse are making the most of this at OKW."

The admiral's whimiscal reference was to the Sicherheitsdienst, Foreign Intelligence, located on the Bendlerstrasse. Niedersdorf took a drink from his glass, nodding. "The SD always makes the most of our difficulties. We can move independent agents to Cairo and reconstruct the network, and there are other things we can do. I'll include recommendations in my report on Kondor, if you wish."

"Do, and we'll discuss them with the staff," Canaris replied, standing. "Field Marshal Rommel depends upon us, and we must have another network in operation as soon as possible. I want to finish with this, because we have other matters to deal with." Crossing the office, he stood in front of a large map of the world that covered most of a wall. "When I was at OKW this afternoon, I was briefed on a plan that is being developed to interdict the flow of materiel to Russia."

The admiral's soft voice was almost lost under the moaning of the wind around the building. Niedersdorf stood up and stepped over to the map. "Will we be involved, Admiral?"

Canaris nodded, pointing to Iran on the map. "The plan is to close the North Sea routes; then the only remaining route to Russia will be through the Persian Gulf and along the Trans-Iranian Railway. We're to send in sondercommando platoons to sabotage the railway."

"Do you wish to have the sondercommandos controlled through a local agent in Iran, Admiral? Mueller, the Swiss, is in Iran. We also have Moltke in Northern Iran, and others we could use."

Canaris shook his head. "No, I would rather keep

Mueller separated from this, and Moltke has more than enough to do in recruiting among the Poles the Russians are deporting. I see no reason why the platoons can't operate independently."

"Nor do I, Admiral. If they do, though, perhaps they should be commanded by officers."

"Yes, perhaps so," Canaris agreed, walking back to his desk. "We have few sondercommando officers, but that will be a difficult mission. I would like you to go to Lake Quenz and select the platoons, because our comrades on the Bendlerstrasse will also be sending in sabotage teams. This is a rare opportunity to demonstrate the superiority of the sondercommandos over the SD forces. But first, there is another project I would like you to work on, one in which Emil has expressed personal interest."

"Emil" was the Abwehr code name for Hitler. Niedersdorf put his empty glass on the edge of the desk and sat back down, waiting. Canaris lit another cigarette and looked away for a moment in silence, then spoke in a quiet, musing tone. "What would be the effect on the war situation if Roosevelt, Churchill, and Stalin were assassinated?"

The question, with its enormously wide and complex implications, startled Niedersdorf. He replied slowly and cautiously, shaking his head, "It would require a complete analysis to estimate the full scope and nature of the effect, Admiral. It would vary among the different nations, of course. . . ."

His voice faded as he saw that Canaris was not listening. The lamp on the desk highlighted the planes of the admiral's thin features and made dark shadows in the hollows of his face. He puffed on his cigarette, lost in thought. The wind moaned around the building, making the blackout drapes sway; the cigarette smoke around the admiral's head swirled in the cold draft sweeping through the room.

Then the admiral sat up, visibly collecting his thoughts. His voice was crisp and firm. "We have a Fuehrerbefel, an order direct from Emil, to prepare an assassination plan. We have also been ordered to collaborate with the SD in this matter, so our present requirement is for a working plan to use in discussions with them."

"Based on how large a force, Admiral?"

"A single platoon, trained and equipped for assassination. We must consider the national capitals too secure for such a plan to succeed, so it will be predicated on travel abroad by the target individuals."

"Stalin never travels abroad, Admiral."

Canaris lifted his eyebrows, smiling faintly. "Among the communications between Washington and Moscow that we have intercepted and decoded, there are many from Roosevelt importuning Stalin to meet with him. Since Stalin needs the materiel the United States is providing, eventually he will agree. It is unlikely that Roosevelt will travel to the Soviet Union, or he would already have done so. They will undoubtedly meet elsewhere, and Churchill will be there when they do."

Niedersdorf nodded musingly. "When will you need this plan?"

"By the end of the week. I will have our liaison arrange a meeting with the SD, and I would like you to accompany me to the meeting."

There was a note of dismissal in his voice; Niedersdorf stood up. "Very well, Admiral. I will have the plan ready by Friday morning."

Canaris nodded, puffing on his cigarette. Niedersdorf

turned and walked toward the door, then Canaris spoke again. "Franz, you failed to mention the name of the new British resident in Cairo while we were discussing Kondor. Do you know his name?"

Niedersdorf stopped in the doorway and turned back. "The name in the files is Keeler, Admiral. When I was first assigned here, I saw that name several times while I was familiarizing myself with past operations. But I haven't researched it in the dossiers of enemy intelligence services. It could be a cover name."

Canaris smiled, shaking his head. "No, that is his real name."

"You are familiar with the man, Admiral?"

"Yes, indeed," Canaris replied, laughing dryly. "And when you have been here longer, you will be familiar with him as well. We have quite a large dossier on Keeler in central records. You should get it and study it thoroughly at the earliest opportunity."

"I shall, Admiral. Good night."

Canaris nodded and puffed on his cigarette, still smiling whimsically as Niedersdorf went out.

CHAPTER TWO

A CHEAP LITHOGRAPH scenic hung on the wall in the small, cramped office in an attempt to simulate a window and dispel the feel of being underground. It failed; the cement walls and ceiling seemed burdened by the yards of earth overhead, while the air from the ventilation system had the dank, moldy smell of a cellar. The woman behind the desk was middle-aged and heavyset, wearing a gray cardigan with a gray dress. She looked up interrogatively as he stepped into the office and closed the door.

"I'm Keeler."

Her eyes opening wider, she smiled as she stood up. "Oh, yes. I'm Miss Davis, Mr. Keller. Mr. Beamish has been expecting you, sir. I'll let him know that you're here."

"Thank you."

She crossed the office and opened the door, looking into the inner office and murmuring. A chair scraped, then Beamish pushed past the woman and bustled out, balding, pudgy, and rumpled. His effusive smile failed to reach his eyes; his eager handshake was limp. A froth of spittle gathered at the corners of his mouth as he talked rapidly. "Well, well, here you are, Keeler. It's been a while, what? But you haven't altered a whit, have you? Well, come on in, come on in."

They went into his cluttered office, Beamish closing the door. He waved to a chair as he stepped around the desk and sat down. "That was a good show in Cairo, what? Set them on their arses, didn't you?"

Keeler unfastened his trench coat and put his hat on the edge of the desk as he sat down. "Things worked out fairly well there."

"No, everyone knows it was more than that, Keeler. And I'm more than pleased to have you in my section, because I'm short of effectives. These wartime augmentees are driving me bloody mad, you know. Well, I was told you finished up with Snively a few hours ago, and I was hoping you'd stop by before we packed it in for the day. . . ."

His voice faded into an expectant pause. He continued smiling brightly, his eyes hard and staring. Keeler looked back at him in silence for a moment, then spoke: "I went to see my tailor."

"You did? Well, I didn't know, and I was wondering what I'd say if someone asked me where you were. Will he be able to see you? But I expect tailors find ways to get around the shortages and see to their regulars, don't they? Have you been renewing any acquaintances?"

"I've been staying at Dandridge House, if that's what you mean."

"Aye, that's what I mean. Wanting a bit of companionship and what goes with it is only human, but one can't be too careful, can one? Well, I'm sure this transfer will be no trouble for you. I work for Willoughby, just as Snively does, and we're set up the same."

"Very well."

"If you can do for me in Iran what you did for Snively in Egypt, then Bob's your uncle. And we'll get along famously, I'm sure. All I require is that the job be done by the rules."

"Very well."

"Things might be a bit muddled in Iran, but I'm sure you'll have them in hand promptly. A chap named Nicholson has been resident there for a good while. He's gone a bit unsteady, so we're bringing him in off the street before he starts breaking eggs. The other two will remain. They're wartime augmentees, but I'm sure you'll manage with them."

"Very well."

"I'll let Archives know that you'll be down tomorrow morning to look at the files on Iran, and we'll have your brief together on Monday. And you're to see Willoughby tomorrow afternoon at one. You will remember to be there promptly at one, won't you?"

"Yes."

"I'm sure Willoughby only wants to congratulate you on the good show in Egypt. But while you're there, he might mention your final report on that station. Snively sent copies of it around, and I've been looking through one. A few things in it caught my eye. . . ."

His voice fading, he wiped saliva from the corners of his mouth with the back of a hand as he separated a copy of the report from other papers on his desk. Corners were turned down on some of the pages. He opened it to one of them, then looked at Keeler with his beaming smile, his eyes glassy and penetrating.

The office was silent except for the sigh of the ventilation system, Keeler looking at Beamish. Keeler took out his cigarettes and lit one. Beamish pushed an ashtray over to the edge of the desk. The silence continued for several seconds, Keeler taking a drag on his cigarette and Beamish's smile unwavering. Then Beamish spoke again: "A few things in your final report caught my eye. . . ."

"What?"

"What, you say? Well, the business concerning this agent Astafan, for example. One could gather that some are under the impression that you may not have had authority to run a full cipher. That you tipped him over without proper sanction, so to speak." He thumbed through the report to another page with its corner turned down. "And concerning this man Zehedi. It does seem a bit odd to have a courier who works as a driver for the Soviet embassy, doesn't it? That could leave the impression that you may have been running an action on the Bolshies, couldn't it? But that would have been outside your brief, wouldn't it?"

"Shall I go over the report with you?"

Beamish shook his head rapidly, smiling widely and pushing the report aside. "No indeed, Keeler. What you did when you worked for Snively is between you and Snively, isn't it? And perhaps Willoughby as well, what? No, I only wanted to chat with you and have a word with you about our arrangements. I won't keep you if there's anything you want to do."

Keeler stood up, picking up his hat. "I'll go see my father."

"Your father? Aye, one should keep in touch with the family. I won't keep you, then. And I'll let Archives know that you'll be down tomorrow at eight. You will try to be here promptly at eight, won't you?"

"Yes. Good afternoon."

Keeler put out his cigarette in the ashtray and picked up his hat. Beamish looked up at him with a wide smile, his eyes cold and probing. Keeler turned and went out. The woman in the outer office looked up from the papers on her desk, smiling. Keeler nodded to her as he left the office.

The corridor, a cement tunnel, was painted the same dull green as the offices. It stirred with activity, people with folders and stacks of papers moving quietly between offices along it. A fireproof door at the end opened onto a small landing, where staircases illuminated by bulbs in shatterproof glass covers went down to deeper levels and up to the street level. Keeler climbed the stairs leading upward.

The door at the top opened into an office with stained plaster walls and battered ministry furniture. A man at the desk by the door pushed a register and pencil toward Keeler as another sitting by the door on the other side of the office glanced up from his newspaper. Keeler found the line on the register where he had signed in, wrote the time in the last column, then crossed the office and went out the other door.

The hall outside the door was wide and lofty, the main corridor in the east wing of the Ministry of Public Works Building. Its tall pilasters and high plaster ceiling, stained with age, were cracked from nearby detonations of bombs. Typewriters clattered in offices along the hall. The cold draft sweeping through the hall smelled of rain on cement, exhaust fumes, and of smoke from the bombing.

Wide steps led down from the imposing entrance of the

building to the sidewalk along Haymarket, near its corner with Pall Mall. As the light faded into wintry dusk, the streets were filling with the first trickle of the evening exodus from shops and offices. The atmosphere was one of siege, combined with a grim, unyielding grip on a semblance of normalcy. Familiar advertisements hung on boards covering broken display windows; people queued for buses on corners by sandbagged entrances to bomb shelters. Taxis drove along the street, one swerving to the curb when Keeler waved.

Keeler's father lived in Aldersgate, on a quiet street lined with identical brick row houses. His knock on the door was answered by the housekeeper, a heavyset woman in a tight black dress. Her face, framed by hair dyed deep, flat black, was large and round, with pinched features crowded together in the center. She forced a smile, opening the door wider. The entry was dim, with a familiar, stale odor of old books.

The housekeeper closed the door. "This is a surprise, but then we never know when to expect you, do we? Your brother, Reverend Evan, always lets us know in advance. It would appear harder for him to plan ahead than it would be for you, what with him being in the Army and all, wouldn't it? All the same, I'm sure the vicar will be pleased to see you. You seem to be keeping well."

"Yes. How are you?"

"Oh, one year is much the same as another to me. I've buried two husbands, and I daresay I could outlive two more if I had the patience to try. Sit in the parlor, and I'll tell the vicar you're here."

"Thank you."

"He's much the same as he was, in the event you're

interested. He spends most of his time in bed, and we have him where his study used to be. But that's where we had him the last time you were here, wasn't it?"

"No, he was upstairs."

"Then I must be thinking of when Reverend Evan was here. My word, I don't know how I could confuse you with him. Well, we have the vicar where his study used to be so he won't have to use the stairs."

As the woman walked away, moving ponderously along the dark, narrow hall, Keeler went into the front room. Damp and cold, it had the static, lifeless feel and musty smell of having been unused for years. It was cluttered with furniture, pictures, and ornaments, filled with memories that whispered across the years. Keeler sat in a chair by the cold fireplace and lit a cigarette.

A photograph of Keeler's half-brother was in the center of the mantel, his clerical collar looking out of place with his uniform. Smoking his cigarette, Keeler glanced around at the other pictures. Then he tossed the cigarette into the fireplace and stood up as the housekeeper came back down the hall. The woman took his hat and put it beside the empty calling card tray on the table in the entry, then they walked along the hall.

"You'll be careful not to upset the vicar, won't you?" she said. "It could bring on a bad spell, and the doctor we have now isn't the best. Doctor Richardson was inducted into the Army, like most of the others. Like almost everyone, as far as that goes, and I expect you get some queer looks going about in mufti, don't you? But you will be careful not to upset the vicar, won't you?"

"Yes."

They stopped at a door. The housekeeper opened it and walked into the room, her smile wide and her voice loud and cheerful. "Here you are, Vicar. Here's Mr. Frank, come to visit with you."

The poster bed was alien to the room, the covers clashing with the paneled walls. Keeler's father, propped up against pillows, closed a thick book and took off his glasses as Keeler crossed the room. An aged man, his taut pale skin was almost translucent over the angular bones of his face, while his pink scalp showed through his thin white hair. His bloodless lips were set in a thin, impatient line, his eyes smoldering.

Keeler shook the old man's limp hand and spoke first. "How are you?"

"By God's grace, as well as anyone could expect," the old man replied in a hoarse, strong voice, glaring at Keeler. "You appear to be thriving in this time of iniquity, when the forces of evil are writing a dark and bloody chapter in the history of mankind."

"I'm well enough."

The housekeeper smiled brightly, nodding. "Isn't this ever so nice, Vicar?" she said. "We weren't expecting anyone, and Mr. Frank comes to visit with you. I'll go make a cup of tea, and you can have a nice chat." Her smile faded as she turned to Keeler. "You can sit over here, where it won't bother the vicar's breathing when you smoke. We don't have ashtrays, but you can use this dish on the table and I'll swill it out later. Well, I'll go make that cup of tea, then."

She went out, leaving the door ajar. Keeler unfastened his trench coat as he sat down and lit a cigarette. The old man moved things on the night stand to make room for his book and glasses. Then he spoke in a curt voice: "Have you heard from Evan, then?"

"It's been a while."

"He was promoted to regimental chaplain."

"Yes, I heard about that."

The old man's skeletal, veined hands plucked at the bedclothes, his eyes moving up and down Keeler. "And you aren't in the Army yet? I thought this was what you'd been waiting for all of your life."

"I'm still with the Foreign Office."

They fell silent for a moment. Keeler took a drag on his cigarette and flicked ash into the dish. The old man's breathing became labored as he glowered at Keeler. He spoke again, his voice louder. "They certainly look after their own, don't they?"

"I don't know what you mean."

"You know full well what I mean!" the old man shouted, suddenly livid with rage. "They send others to the slaughter they started, but never their own! And they continue to call themselves the Foreign Office, do they? I'm amazed at such temerity, considering that they've contrived to plunge the world into mass slaughter once again! We who sought peace were swept aside, and your warlords have free rein once more!"

The tirade ended, his voice becoming shrill and penetrating on the last words. Then he burst into a spasm of hoarse coughing. Clutching his chest with one hand, he reached over to the night stand and poured something into a glass from a bottle. The housekeeper's heavy footsteps came back along the hall, stopping outside the door.

The old man drank from the glass and drew in a deep, gasping breath, controlling his cough. He put the glass back on the night stand, knocking it against other things as his hand trembled. The housekeeper's footsteps went back along the hall to the kitchen. Keeler took a drag on his cigarette and looked out the window.

Rain made streaks in the sooty grime on the panes. The wall around the back yard was topped by broken glass set in cement. A single, stunted tree stood in the yard, its naked, spindly branches reaching up into the gathering dusk. Keeler put out his cigarette in the dish and lit another one as the housekeeper came in with two cups of tea.

"Here we are, a nice cup of tea," she said cheerfully. "Having a nice chat, are you? I've stirred yours, Vicar, and don't let it get cold. And here's yours. Well, I'd best draw the drapes. We can't forget the blackout, can we?" The room became dark as she closed the drapes. She turned on the light and walked back toward the door. "If you want anything, Vicar, just ring your bell. I'll be right out here where I can hear, so ring your bell if you want me for anything at all."

She went back out, leaving the door ajar. Keeler moved the cup of tea aside and flicked the ash of his cigarette into the dish. The old man took a drink of his tea and put it on the night stand, the cup rattling on the saucer. Then he spoke in a low, grudging tone. "Will you be here long this time, then?"

"A few days. Is there anything you need?"

"I do very well on my own, thank you. You look like you've been in the sun a lot, so you must have been abroad."

"Yes."

The old man waited for further comment. Then he spoke again. "A few weeks ago, I saw Richard Naseby, the past rector of St. Albans. He asked me what you do in the Foreign Office, and I didn't know what to tell him."

"I'm a passport control officer."

"What does that entail?"

"Having to do with documentation."

"You're a clerk, then, is that it?"

"That's near enough."

"Don't you have any friends from school or college who can help you find something more useful to do?"

"It satisfies me."

"And clerking in the Foreign Office keeps you out of the Army?"

"Evidently."

The old man's breathing started to become labored again. He looked away, controlling it. A car passed along the street in front of the house, the distant sound of its engine carrying into the silent room. Keeler put out his cigarette in the dish and stood up. "I'll be off, then."

The old man looked up at Keeler as he stepped to the side of the bed, then he lifted his hand. Keeler shook his hand. "Goodbye."

"Goodbye."

Keeler walked toward the door. The old man put on his glasses and picked up his book from the night stand. He cleared his throat, making a sound as though he were going to say something. Keeler stopped and looked back. The old man thumbed through the book, looking for the page he had been reading. Keeler turned back to the door.

The housekeeper sat on a chair outside the door, knitting. She put the knitting in a bag by the chair and followed Keeler along the hall to the front door. Keeler put on his hat and took out the envelope containing the money and ration coupons. He put it on the calling card tray as the housekeeper opened the door. "Goodbye. Come again when you can," she said.

"Yes, I will. Goodbye."

CHAPTER THREE

THE AIR RAID warning sounded while Sheila Conley was on a bus, talking to an older woman seated by her. The woman seemed disposed to listen, Sheila was so involved in what she was saying that the bus had jerked to a stop before she became aware of the sirens. Their low moaning escalated to a battering scream as people scrambled off.

Pencil beams of searchlights probed at the clouds, dimly illuminating the dark street with thin, grayish light reflected by the overcast. Sheila tried to stay beside the woman as people crushed in around her, but she and the woman became separated. She clutched her shopping bag and walked along the sidewalk.

The people on the sidewalk scattered into side streets and went to shelters, the howling of the sirens drowning their voices and footsteps. Sheila saw the sandbagged entrance of a shelter ahead. Unable to penetrate the clouds, the searchlights began going out. Thick darkness closed in as Sheila wrapped her arms around her shopping bag and ran the last few yards.

The shelter was a small one, with a single wooden bench. An old man in a local defense volunteer's helmet was on the near end of the bench, a woman with a child next to him. Sitting beside her was another woman, then three middle-aged workmen and a man wearing a topcoat and bowler. The man in the topcoat, unusual because he was in civilian clothes but young enough to be in the military service, stared at Sheila.

Sheila gave him a warning glare as she stepped to the end of the bench and sat down. Sheila was an attractive woman, but it had been a wearily familiar joke among her family that she would never stop talking long enough for a man to propose marriage. Then she had met George Conley, a man with a tolerant, imperturable good nature. He had often been less than completely attentive when she talked, but he had never ignored her. In return, she had given him her love and undivided loyalty.

Ignoring her glare, the man in the topcoat still stared at her. He had unpleasant features, a pale, sallow face and thick, moist lips that looked bright red in the dim light. "You're very pretty to be out by yourself," he said.

Sheila bristled, glaring up at the man. "The reason I'm by myself is because my husband is in the Army," she replied acidly. "That's far more than can be said for *some* men of his age who are still skulking about in civilian clothes."

The man shrugged off the rebuff. "I have a medical deferment," he said nonchalantly. "But while it keeps me out of the Army, it doesn't interfere with anything I want to do. Do you still live in Cheapside?" he asked, referring to her accent. "I have some friends who had to move away because of the bombing."

"It's none of your affair where I live!" Sheila snapped. "I want naught to do with you, and if you're wise you'll leave me be."

The man continued smiling, his eyes deliberately moving up and down her. "I'm only trying to be friendly. I have friends in the Army, and they find plenty of opportunities to have a good time. I'm sure your husband does as well, so there's no reason why you shouldn't. You could make things pleasant for yourself."

"And you can get a *real* medical deferment instead of having to bribe some doctor as foul as yourself!" Sheila shouted, her temper exploding. "And I'm the one who'll give it to you, you slimy bugger! I'll not listen to the likes of a swine such as you talking about one who's in the Army and fighting for his country!"

The man recoiled, his face flushing with embarrassment as he glanced at the others. The old man on the opposite end of the bench leaned forward and frowned at Sheila. "Here, now, what's all this? I'll deal with it if someone is bothering you, but I'll not have such foul language in here."

"You'll have something you'll like less than that if you give me any bother!" Sheila retorted. "I'm not in such a state that I need the likes of you to help me, so you keep out of it!"

"Bloody hell," one of the workmen groaned. "She's started the bloody Bow Bells ringing, and I'd as lief take my chances with the bombs as stop here and listen to this."

"Aye, I'm cockney, and I'm bloody proud of it!" Sheila barked, glaring at the workman. "If you've a mind to leave, no one's holding you. And if you've a mind for trouble, I'll see to you when I've sorted out this sod here!"

As the workman looked away, muttering under his breath, Sheila turned to the man in the topcoat. "I don't want your foul breath on me, you blackguard," she said softly, glowering at him. "So you move over and give me room. And if you say another word to me, you'll rue the day that the old sow who whelped you gave you life."

The man's face was crimson as he looked away and edged away. Sheila picked up her shopping bag and put it on the bench beside her. Trembling with anger, she drew in a deep breath and released it. The sirens had stopped howling. The people in the shelter who had been talking were now silent. And they were hostile.

Then they began talking again, speculating about where the bombs would fall. Sheila's anger slowly faded and left a bitter, hollow ache within her. She felt isolated and lonely, the atmosphere in the shelter oppressive with animosity directed toward her. Tears began burning in her eyes. She blinked them away, steeling herself against the temptation to yield to the weakness they represented.

She yearned to talk to someone, to release the flood of words dammed up within her. Sometimes she wished she were a mute. The inexhaustable wellspring of words within her had always been a curse, making her vulnerable and exposing her to ridicule. It was even worse during times of stress. And with her husband in the Army and her son evacuated from London, she lived in almost constant stress.

Filling pages in her diary offered a form of relief. Writing letters were an even more complete means of relief; she wrote several to her husband each week. She began planning a letter in her mind, choosing subjects and what she would say about them.

The child along the bench wailed and wept in fright.

The woman holding the child murmured soothingly, the others talking quietly. The old man at the end of the bench stood up and stepped to the shelter entrance, listening for aircraft engines.

Keeler heard the aircraft engines at high altitude to the southeast, a distant whisper of sound. A tense, steely quiet had settled when the screaming of the sirens had faded into plaintive moans and died away. Keeler's footsteps echoed along the dark street as the grinding rumble of the aircraft engines gradually became louder.

The taxi driver had pointed and shouted over the sirens about a shelter when he had let Keeler out. Keeler had paid him and walked away. He had continued walking as the streets emptied of people and became quiet. He was accustomed to streets that were quiet and empty of people.

An anti-aircraft battery at a distance down the river began firing, whacking rhythmically, blindly at the sound of the engines. Others around the docks, then nearer batteries began firing. The first bombs fell, dull thuds of incendiaries south of the river. Then there were rapid spurts of sound as incendiaries rained down.

The red glow of flames reflected by the clouds dissolved the thick darkness around Keeler. As the feeble light in the deserted street grew brighter, hues of crimson tinged with yellow, the sidewalk and the nearby buildings became visible. Then high explosive bombs began falling, aimed at the fiery glare of the flames through the clouds. They detonated with deep, reverberating booms that sounded like kettledrums.

A stick of bombs scattered, the series of explosions marching north of the river, each one louder and closer.

The last one, scant blocks away, detonated with a shattering blast of noise and a shock wave that made the sidewalk heave as a hot breath of concussion pushed along the street. The ringing in Keeler's ears faded into the frantic clanging of bells—a fire brigade rushing along a nearby street. He stopped in a doorway and lit a cigarette, then walked on.

At the next intersection, a small, wizened old man in an air raid warden's helmet leaped out of a doorway. He looked up at Keeler in astonished indignance and shouted over the roar of the bombs and the pounding of the anti-aircraft batteries, pointing to a shelter entrance on the corner. Keeler tossed his cigarette into the gutter and walked toward the shelter. The old man trotted back to his doorway.

A faint gleam of light from a tiny bulb illuminated the short tunnel at the bottom of the steps, flickering as bomb blasts shook the shelter. Several people sat on the single wooden bench. A woman cuddled a whimpering child and talked to it in a resolutely cheerful tone. Grimy, weary workmen leaned against the sandbagged wall and dozed. An old man wearing a local defense volunteer helmet sat on the near end of the bench.

The old man started to wave Keeler toward the other end, then frowned suspiciously and stood up. "I'll have a look at your identification, if you don't mind, sir."

Others glanced up as the old man squinted at Keeler's Foreign Office identification in the dim light. Then, the old man nodding and touching his brim of his helmet, Keeler moved on. A young woman at the end of the bench bristled in readiness for a confrontation if he crowded her, the man next to her giving her more than enough room.

Keeler brushed against the shopping bag on the bench beside her as he sat down. Her head snapped around angrily.

A subtle chemistry stirred between them, an electric tension of sexual attraction and something more. The woman was strikingly beautiful, in her early twenties, and wearing a cotton smock under a drab, shapeless coat. Her frown faded, her large blue eyes becoming wide. She flushed hotly, an involuntary smile tugging at her lips, then she pulled the shopping bag closer to make room for him as she looked away.

Keeler glanced at her as her eyes darted toward him. She blushed again and quickly looked away. A wedding band glinted on her left hand as she pushed at stray wisps of short brown curls hanging out around the sides of the faded scarf tied under her chin. She displayed the ring, holding it up like a talisman to ward off evil influences as she glanced at him once more and spoke.

"Knocking about twelve score to the dozen out there, aren't they? Did you have trouble finding shelter in the dark, then?"

Her accent was rich, thick cockney, and she had the cockney willful, belligerent self-assurance. Keeler nodded, taking out his cigarettes. "Yes. Cigarette?"

"No, thank you all the same. If you didn't know where the shelter was, you must not live nearabout here."

"No."

"And you're not in the forces? You're not a conchie, are you? No, I can tell you're not."

"I'm with the Foreign Office."

"Aye, you don't have the pansy look of a conchie. Or one of those who bribe some quack to get an unfit certificate. The Foreign Office, did you say? Well, fancy that. Who'd believe that I'd be sitting and talking to someone from the Foreign Office? What's your name?"

"Frank Keeler."

"I'm Sheila Conley, and I'm pleased to meet you. Keeler? Frank Keeler? Aye, haven't I read about you in the newspapers?"

"I think not. Do you live near here?"

"No, I live off Putney. I nicked off work a few minutes early to go shopping, and I was on my way home when the sirens went. The girl on the machine next to mine said there were shops on Newgate for the toffs where everything is off ration. . . ." Her voice faded as she glanced up at him once again. Too self-assured to be defensive over class distinctions, her apologetic smile was bright and natural as she continued talking. "But they're no different than other shops, so tomorrow I'll tell her that she's been spreading rumors. And lying through her teeth as well. But I'm sure your wife sees to shopping for you, doesn't she?"

"I'm not married."

Bombs fell nearby, jarring the shelter violently and making the light wink off and on. Sheila was silent for a moment. On the edge of his vision, Keeler saw her studying his face. He took a drag on his cigarette, looking down at her. Sheila turned away, her wedding band shining as she pushed at her hair. "Are you sure I haven't read about you in the newspaper?" she asked.

"I believe it's very unlikely."

"Oh, I think you're only being modest, Frank. But there's naught wrong with that, because most make too much of themselves. So you're not married, then? Well, fancy that. Where do you kip?"

"At Dandridge House at present."

"Dandridge House?" she sighed, clicking her tongue. "Blimey, that's posh, isn't it? Are you asked for your identification often?"

"Occasionally."

"They're just being nosy, Frank." She leaned forward and looked at the local defense volunteer, talking in a loud voice. "Every nosy bugger in London lined up when they were passing out helmets and armbands, because they just wanted to muck about in others' affairs." The old man pursed his lips and frowned resentfully, looking straight ahead, while the others pointedly ignored Sheila. She sniffed in satisfaction as she sat back. "It's no bloody good being walked on. You want to stand up for yourself a bit more, Frank. If anyone but a bobby asks for your identification, you should have a look at theirs as well."

"Perhaps so. You say you work?"

"Aye, well, everyone does now, don't they? And it isn't as though my Georgie doesn't provide, but with him gone in the forces and my little Georgie evacuated to Trews, it's no good sitting and watching my fingernails grow, is it? The odd shillings find a ready home as well. . . ."

Sheila continued talking, telling Keeler about her job at Grayson's Boot Factory. She also told him about a new machine she had been put on recently, how it had barely escaped damage from a bomb during an air raid the week before. Then she told him about her previous job at Battersea Power Station, a passing reference to friction between her and other women hinting at a series of brawls.

Keeler smoked and listened. He derived keen enjoyment from being with people who talked and provided full communication by themselves, being himself taciturn by nature. When the conversation was a simple outpouring of reactions, memories, and thoughts and not a blanket of sound to cover subterfuge, he found listening to others intensely gratifying. Sheila was superlative, a compulsive talker.

She was also bewitchingly attractive, exuding a compelling aura of nubile womanhood. Her earthy cockney accent and the chiming soprano of her voice were pleasant. Her blunt, direct personality was charming, her self-confidence appealing. She was also drawn to him, her eyes reflecting an inner struggle between her reaction to him and the loyalties represented by her wedding ring.

The hostile atmosphere between her and the others in the shelter isolated her and Keeler. It was as though they were completely alone, Sheila talking and Keeler listening, as one wave of bombers passed and another came. Sheila went from one subject to another, talking about women she knew at work, her husband and his induction into the Army, and about his relatives and hers.

Then she broke off, sighing. "But that's of no interest to you, is it? You're just being a proper gentleman, letting me natter on."

Her eyes begged him to want to listen. He did, shaking his head as he lit another cigarette. "No, I find it quite interesting. Do you consider the name Pelham unusual, then? I've heard it often, and I knew a boy at school named Pelham Harcourt."

"Aye, at Eton, or was it Harrow? You won't hear that name often amongst our lot, though. He was my mother's next to oldest brother, and he was a rum one from what I can remember of him. . . ."

She continued talking about her relatives until she exhausted the subject, then went on to other topics. Another wave of bombers came as Sheila talked about her childhood. Then she began on girls she had known at school, systematically relating all she could remember about each of them. Keeler smoked and listened silently.

When the all clear sounded, Sheila became silent and dejected, her eyes avoiding Keeler. He carried her shopping bag as they followed the others filing out of the bomb shelter. The overcast sky was bright with the light of fires raging out of control south of the river and around the docks. A strong odor of smoke, dust, and cordite hung in the air.

Sheila and Keeler stood outside the shelter, a tense silence between them. The street became quiet as the footsteps of the others faded. Then Sheila pushed at her hair and cleared her throat with a soft sound, reaching for her shopping bag. "I'd best be on my way."

"I'll take you home."

"Here, now, what's this?" she said, forcing a laugh. "You know I'm a married woman, Frank."

Her smile faded, her attempt at a humorous, bantering tone failing. She looked away, the ruddy light of the flames playing over her smooth cheeks and shining in her eyes. "It was ever so lovely having you to talk to," she murmured. "I can't remember anything as lovely, because you're so nice and all. But then we had to leave the shelter, and everything changed. Still, I don't want to just go one way while you go another."

She sighed, falling silent for a moment, then resumed talking. "I've seen tarts who consort with other men while their husbands are abroad," she said. "And I've had my say about them. Plenty of men have been around me as well with their shy grins, but as close as they've got to me is my hand across their chops. It's different with you, though, but at the same time it isn't different at all." She looked up at him, lifting her hands and dropping them in a gesture of resignation. "You're a great bloody help, aren't you? Well, come on, then."

They crossed the street and walked along the sidewalk, Sheila silent for a few minutes. Their footsteps echoing along the quiet, deserted street, they passed dark windows reflecting the fiery glow in the sky. Then Sheila began talking again, telling Keeler about other air raids she had experienced and other shelters she had been in.

A taxi driving through an intersection ahead of them stopped when Keeler waved. The driver, a cockney, discussed directions with Sheila in a virtually unintelligible exchange. Then she sat back in the seat, talking about the taxis that had been hired for her wedding, a taxi she had ridden in at a funeral, and other incidents involving taxis.

The taxi turned off Putney and wound north through the twisting streets, stopping at the entrance to a narrow, cobblestone mews. Keeler paid the driver and the taxi clattered away as Sheila took his arm to guide him. The cobblestones were slippery underfoot, and the darkness was impenetrable in the warren of tiny dwellings.

Sheila fumbled in her purse; a key rattled in a lock, then a door squeaked open. Keeler felt his way across the threshold and followed Sheila inside. Closing the door, she snapped a switch, then clicked her tongue in aggravation. "Wouldn't you know it—the electric's off! Just a mo."

A match box rustled, then a match flared and Sheila lit a stub of a candle. The weak, flickering light moved ahead of her as she shielded the flame with a hand and crossed the room. It was a one-room dwelling, its low ceiling, thick walls, and wide iron hinges on the heavy front door and lavatory door dating it far into the past. Things that she had made to hide the cracks in the walls and the shabbiness of the furniture gave it a cheerful, comfortable atmosphere.

Sheila put the candlestick on a table and knelt in front of a small fireplace. ''Don't look for the likes of Dandridge House in Coogan Mews, if that's what you were expecting,'' she said. ''Come on and sit down while I make a fire to take off the chill. Have you had your tea?''

''No.''

''Aye, well, I'm willing to share a meat pie if you're willing to chance that they're made of rats, as some say. Put the bag there.''

Keeler put the shopping bag on the table and sat on a kitchen chair by the fireplace. A cat mewed at the door as Sheila lit the fire. She went to the door and opened it. A thin, bedraggled alley cat ran in and darted to the fireplace. Sheila took a plate of scraps from a food safe and put them in a bowl on the hearth for the cat, talking about a neighbor's cat and other cats she had owned.

The fire dispelled the darkness and the chill, making the room warm and cozy. Its flickering light shone on Sheila's beautiful face and made highlights in her brown curls as she rattled dishes and divided a small meat pie and a can of beans between two plates. She put them into an old-fashioned warming oven built into the side of the fireplace, talking about the shops where she had bought the food.

As they ate, sharing a bottle of ale, Sheila talked about foods she preferred, those she disliked, and notable meals she remembered. When they finished, she took the dishes into the lavatory and washed them. Then her monologue died away as she sat on the other side of the fireplace and absently stroked the cat, looking into the fire. After a few minutes, she looked up at the clock on the mantel.

"It's just gone half nine, hasn't it?" she said.

Keeler glanced at his watch and nodded. "Yes."

"It's still quite early, isn't it? But it's good to make an early start on the dark mornings."

"Yes."

"I'll just have a swill and put on my nightie, then."

"Very well."

Carrying the candlestick across the room, she took a nightgown down from a hanger and went into the lavatory. The cat sat on the hearth and stared at Keeler through slitted eyes as he smoked and listened to the water running in the lavatory. It stopped, then Sheila came back out. Her face shone from being washed and her long nightgown trailed around her ankles. She looked vulnerable and virginal, her eyes avoiding him.

Keeler hung his suit coat and tie over his trench coat behind the door, then went into the lavatory. A razor, shaving mug, hair brush, and comb were placed neatly on a folded towel on a shelf by the sink, kept ready for her husband's return. She had told Keeler that her husband was in Egypt; he thought about the long, weary columns of soldiers he had seen there.

The fire had burned down when Keeler went back into the room. Sheila was in bed, turned to the wall. He blew out the candle, then took off the rest of his clothes and put them on a chair. The bed sagged under his weight, the soft, heavy bedclothes smelling of soap. As he put a hand on Sheila's shoulder, she turned to him.

At first she was nervous and tense with guilt. Their lack of familiarity with each other created an uncertainty that she met with her characteristic candor, pulling up her nightgown and positioning herself expectantly. The tension remained for a time as he held and kissed her until she began to relax.

She gradually responded as his caresses became more intimate, her mouth opening damply under his and her nipples becoming taut against his chest through her nightgown. Her slender body was warm and yielding against him, her skin soft and silky under his fingers. Caressing him and pressing herself to him, her sighs became soft moans and whimpers. She gathered her nightgown higher and wriggled out of it. Then she became impatient, tugging at him demandingly and pulling him over her.

The last trace of tension gone, a shuddering tremor raced through her as he entered her. She touched his face and shoulders with the tips of her fingers, her body lifting and moving as she murmured against his lips. Her breath caught in her throat in gasps as the sensations gathered momentum within her. Her lithe body moved more forcefully, thrusting at him in a hard, driving rhythm. Then her fingernails bit into his back and her legs clasped him as she surged in a convulsive frenzy of motion.

The wrenching spasms of ecstasy passed, bringing exhaustion and the mutual regard of well-matched lovers. Her satisfaction became relief that an essential ritual had been performed, establishing an intimacy that eliminated all barriers to what could be discussed. She began talking again, telling him about her trepidation on her wedding night, about hearing her mother and father in the act of sex, and about things women had told her concerning their husbands' sexual peculiarities.

As she talked, she slowly moved and tugged at him until they were in a comfortable, convenient position for her to talk and for him to listen. She pulled his head down to her shoulder and rested her cheek on his, her lips an inch from his ear. Their legs entwined, their bodies pressed together. She talked, and he listened.

When the ashes in the fireplace had settled and the room had become completely dark, mice scuttled about. The cat prowled in the darkness and attacked in lunges more felt than heard, mice squeaking and scurrying frantically. Sheila's breath was warm against Keeler's face as she talked, her voice softening to a drowsy whisper.

Slipping out of the variety of standard English she used for his ease of understanding, she lapsed completely into throaty, glottal cockney dialect. Words and occasional phrases were unintelligible as she continued talking. Keeler, listening to her, fell asleep.

CHAPTER FOUR

WILLOUGHBY WAS A thin, dapper man of middle age, but his sharp, aquiline features were unwrinkled and ageless. His eyes, the pale, icy blue of blind eyes, were as devoid of expression as his face. The top of his desk was bare except for a copy of Keeler's final report on his assignment in Egypt. As the secretary closed the door behind Keeler, Willoughby's head moved a fraction of an inch in a nod.

"Good afernoon, sir," Keeler said.

"Good afternoon, Keeler," Willoughby replied in his thin, dry voice. "Thank you for being punctual. Sit there, please."

Keeler sat on the chair in front of the desk and lit a cigarette. Opening a desk drawer, Willoughby took out a pipe and tobacco pouch. He held the pipe over the pouch and put pinches of tobacco into the bowl with careful, precise movements of his thin, white fingers.

"That was a good show in Egypt, Keeler."

"Thank you, sir."

"Where did you spend the night last night?"

"I met a woman and stayed with her, sir."

"I presume there is a connection between this woman and your conversation with Beamish in regard to the possibility of having another issue of ration coupons, is there not?"

"Yes, sir."

Willoughby struck a match and lit his pipe, then dropped the match into an ashtray in the desk drawer. He opened another drawer and put a pad and pencil on the desk. Keeler stepped to the desk and wrote Sheila's name and address on the pad. Willoughby took out an envelope containing several thick booklets of ration coupons and put it on the desk. Keeler put the envelope in his pocket as he sat back down. Willoughby glanced at the pad, then put it and the pencil back in the drawer.

The pipe made a soft, gurgling sound as Willoughby puffed on it in silence for a moment, then he began questioning Keeler about the agent Astafan. The questions substantially the same as those Keeler had been asked before in regard to the agent; he went through the same answers. Willoughby's tone and features revealed no reaction as he probed the subject for several minutes, then he shook his head.

"Keeler, the necessity of running a full cipher is not the issue. We are concerned with whether or not you had authority to do so. And there is no need to address the point of humanitarian considerations involved in the decision to tip over an agent to the enemy in the certain knowledge that he will be tortured to death. However, you do realize the repercussions that would occur if some untoward circumstance came to pass and made it a matter of general knowledge even years from now."

"Yes, sir."

"It is for that reason such an action is taken only after a

concensus is reached that the benefits outweigh the risks. Now, I've read the daily situation report in which you address the subject. In light of the knowledge that you ran a full cipher, it is possible to interpret your comment in the report as an intention to do so. Without that knowledge, the meaning of the comment is totally obscure.''

''It seemed clear enough to me at the time, sir.''

''If by that you mean to say that you didn't intend the meaning to be clear, Keeler, I quite agree. And you say that you hadn't been contemplating and making plans for some months beforehand to do this?''

''No, sir.''

''Then let us again go over how you found yourself in the fortuitous position of having an agent ready to run as a full cipher.''

''After I began training Astafan, I found out he had been running with the Free Egyptian Officer Movement, so I kept him outside and used him as a roustabout. We were just beginning to work on Kondor when he was recruited. All he knew was that we thought something was there.''

''Why did you keep him on your roll at all? If you considered him to be unreliable, why didn't you simply drop him?''

''He had found out a little too much about the operation, sir.''

Willoughby's cold, penetrating eyes bored into Keeler's for a moment. Then he looked down at his pipe, which had gone out. He struck a match and lit it again. Keeler put out his cigarette and lit another one. Willoughby puffed on his pipe as he changed the subject and began questioning Keeler about Zehedi, the courier who had also been a driver for the Soviet embassy. Keeler explained that

Zehedi had been hired by the Soviet embassy after he had been enrolled and trained as a courier.

"And you say the man didn't realize that he was being hired by them?" Willoughby asked. "Through what turn of events did that happen?"

"He lost his job with the removal firm, and the driver's union found him another. It was only when he was told to report for an interview that he found out the job was at the Soviet embassy."

"And you allowed him to go for the interview? Or didn't he see fit to consult you in regard to this somewhat startling development?"

"I was in Alexandria at the time, sir. He thought it would be suspicious if he didn't go, and he didn't have time to contact me."

"That seems too coincidental, Keeler. Judging solely by the facts, we have a choice of two explanations. Either through circumstances that would be comical if they were not so perilous, you had a courier who was hired by the Soviet embassy as a driver." He puffed on his pipe, his eyes on Keeler's as he continued in a quieter voice. "Or the man was in fact an agent, only listed as a courier. And for some reason known only to yourself, a point of conjecture which I find most alarming to contemplate, you planted an agent in the Soviet embassy."

"That would have been outside my brief, sir."

"Indeed it would have," Willoughby agreed in a soft, steely tone. "Indeed it would have, Keeler. But in any event, the man seems to have disappeared now, has he not?"

Keeler took a drag on his cigarette, nodding. "Yes, sir. His father died, and he went to his village to take care of his family."

"Again, that seems too coincidental, Keeler. The disturbing thing about all this is that it suggests you had your wicket bowled by the short notice on your transfer from Egypt, that you had insufficient time to tidy up private ventures you had undertaken."

"I put everything I did in my sitrep, sir."

"It would be futile to discuss that further, except to remark that any obscure comment in a daily situation report from you in the future will prompt an immediate request for full clarification. The fact is, your explanations are less than convincing. For example, you say that Astafan had found out too much for you to drop him. For him to have found out anything at all is amateurish and completely unlike you."

"It was a mistake, sir."

Willoughby puffed on his pipe in silence for a moment, then he nodded. "I'd prefer to consider all we've discussed as mistakes that won't be repeated, so I'll drop the entire matter." He took his pipe out of his mouth, his icy blue eyes on Keeler's. "Limit your activities to your brief and special instructions, Keeler. If you perceive a need for further action, then recommend it through channels. It will be undertaken if it is considered necessary, with measures that are deniable if it is against an ally. Do I make myself completely clear?"

"Yes, sir."

Willoughby picked up the report and put it in a desk drawer. "Have you had a look through the files on Iran?"

Keeler moved to a more comfortable position on his chair and relaxed, taking a drag on his cigarette. "I'm still in the process of going through them, sir. Things appear a bit disorganized there."

"The residency is a shambles, and you're being sent

there because it is becoming of more interest to us. Aerial reconnaissance shows that the Germans are expanding their shore installations at Narvik. The backroom people believe that is a preliminary to stationing more vessels there to cut off the flow of materiel to the Soviet Union. That being the case, the Trans-Iranian Railway will be a primary sabotage target.''

''Yes, sir.''

''Another concern is at Pahlavi, where the Soviets are sending out the Polish people they had in their internment and labor camps. A few of the Poles keep disappearing, and it is apparent that the Germans are recruiting them. It is only a matter of time until they begin showing up somewhere as saboteurs, so you'll want to look into that.''

''Yes, sir.''

Willoughby hesitated, thinking; then he tapped his pipe in the ashtray in the desk drawer and took out his tobacco pouch again. ''There's one other thing I'd like to mention. We have indications that a meeting between the Prime Minister, President Roosevelt, and Premier Stalin might possibly be in the offing.''

''They would meet in Russia, sir. Stalin won't venture out of the Soviet Union.''

Willoughby shook his head, putting tobacco into his pipe. ''It would be more accurate to say that he won't go beyond the protection of Soviet military forces. If you will, consider the fact that Roosevelt travels only by ship when going abroad for any considerable distance. In light of that, where do you think they might meet?''

Keeler nodded musingly. ''The only location that would satisfy all the requirements is Iran.''

''That's my conclusion, and President Roosevelt seems to have what amounts to an obsessive desire for such a meeting. Stalin appears cool to the idea in itself, but he does want increases in war materiel from the United States. And, of course, he wants a front opened in France to take the pressure off the Soviet armies."

"Is there any indication of an agreement on a meeting?"

Willoughby shook his head, striking a match and lighting his pipe. "It's pure speculation at this point, but such a meeting would be of transcendent importance if it did take place. We're forced to assume that the Abwehr and the SD would find out about it, and it would be very tempting for them." He shook the match and dropped it into the ashtray. "If an agreement for a meeting is reached, you will receive a special mission instruction."

"Yes, sir."

Willoughby sat back in his chair, puffing on his pipe. "Thank you for coming in. We probably won't meet again before you leave unless your new acquaintance proves to have unfortunate associations, and I'm sure you hope that is not the case as much as I do. So if I don't see you again, I wish you every success."

Keeler put out his cigarette in the ashtray by his chair as he stood up. "Thank you, sir. Good afternoon."

"Good afternoon, Keeler."

Keeler took his hat and trench coat from the rack as he went through the outer office. He walked along the corridor to the stairwell, then down the stairs to the Archives Section on the third basement level. When he pushed a button by the door, a woman came to the door and escorted him inside and along a hall to a reading room. Keeler lit a cigarette and sat down at the table as the woman pushed a metal cart stacked with file folders into the room and went back out, closing the door.

Having read part of the material during the morning, he put it aside and looked through the remaining folders. There were personnel files and dossiers on other intelligence agencies in Iran, as well as files on digests covering public affairs, political and economic factors, demographic statistics, and other data. Keeler took the folders off the cart and stacked them on the table, then began reading.

The Teheran station was small, with only five people assigned. Two were women, cryptography technicians. Clive Holcomb and Chadwick Meacham, the two operatives, were wartime augmentees and had worked as couriers and informants before the war. Meacham was forty and had more experience than Holcomb, who was thirty-two; but Holcomb's was the only one of the two files that contained favorable comments on his performance.

The most valuable agent controlled by the station was Erling Mueller, a Swiss double agent who worked under the cover of a merchant and importer. In a coup of coat trailing, he had been planted on the Abwehr resident in Geneva before the war, then had moved to Teheran. Left in place by the Abwehr when the Allies had moved into Iran in force, he had an established schedule for radio contacts with Berlin.

The digests on Iran reflected that the country was in turmoil. It was flooded with refugees—Italians exiled by Mussolini, Jews who had fled German-occupied Europe, and others. The merchant and professional class included Chinese, East Indians, Armenians, and a wide variety of other nationalities. The expatriate Poles being deported from labor and internment camps in Russia included a high proportion of women, children, and old people, who were being placed in resettlement camps.

The stack of dossiers on other intelligence agencies was small. The British Tenth Army chief of military intelligence was Colonel George Campbell, a former artillery officer. The American OSS residency consisted of a single operative, a man named Charles Callaghan. The NKVD residency was a large one, as they always were, with six operatives. The name of the resident, Andrei Vertinski, was vaguely familiar to Keeler.

When he finished reading the last folder, Keeler stacked the files back on the cart and pushed the bell button. The woman came and took the cart away, then returned and escorted Keeler back to the door. He went up the stairs to the first level and along the corridor to Beamish's office. At noon, he had gone to Dandridge House to pack a case with clothes and two bottles of Scotch a porter had obtained for him. Before going to see Willoughby, he had left the case with Beamish's secretary.

Beamish came out of his office when he heard Keeler in the outer office. "Well, well, here he is," he said heartily, his wide smile in place. "All through for the day, are you, Keeler? And you had your meeting with Willoughby, did you?"

"Yes," Keeler replied as he picked up his case and put it on the edge of the secretary's desk. "Will you have a drink with me?"

Beamish hesitated, looking in surprise at the bottle that Keeler took out of the case; then he nodded eagerly. "Aye, I don't mind if I do. By God, I didn't think there was any Scotch left in England! Get us some cups, Mabel. Did Willoughby have any questions, Keeler?"

"Yes. Bring yourself a cup as well, Miss Davis."

"No, thank you all the same, Mr. Keeler," the woman

replied. "Shorts go to my head. and I rarely have anything more than a glass of wine."

"Go ahead, Mabel," Beamish chuckled expansively. "You çan put water in it from the kettle. Well, we'll have your brief together on Monday, and I'll go over it with you, Keeler. Willoughby did say that he wanted me to make sure you understand what is on it and what isn't."

"Very well. Would it be possible to get two priority train passes to Trews?"

Beamish's eyes narrowed with curiosity. He glanced at the woman as she brought teacups and the kettle from a table in a corner, then he looked back at Keeler with his wide smile. "Two Trews? You wanted an extra issue of ration coupons, and now you want to go to Trews with someone?"

Keeler nodded, opening the bottle and pouring liquor into the cups. "Yes, on Saturday and return on Sunday. With a reservation for two at the railway hotel there on Saturday night. Cheers."

"Aye, here's your good health," Beamish replied, picking up a cup. "And yours, Mabel." He took a drink and sighed in satisfaction. "That's proper good Scotch, Keeler. Are you sure you have the right place? There's bloody naught at Trews, you know." He turned to the woman. "It's only a bit of a village, isn't it?"

She nodded, taking a cautious sip from her cup. "Yes, but it's very quaint and quite pretty. That's where a lot of the children were evacuated to. My cousin's children are there."

"Is that it, Keeler?" Beamish asked, laughing. "Going to see some little ones? Aye, I daresay we can get you some train passes."

Keeler finished the liquor in his cup and put the bottle back into the case. "I'm most grateful," he said, closing the case. "I'll be off, then. Good night."

Beamish and the woman nodded and replied as Keeler went out. A shift change of technicians was taking place, people streaming down the stairs as those who were leaving came up from the lower levels. Keeler stood in the line moving slowly up the steps, then signed out on the register as the guard looked through the contents of his case.

When he left the building, the parking lights on vehicles moving along the street were opalescent spots through the darkness, fog, and drizzle. The open square in front of the bombed-out Odeon Theater was completely dark and filled with people milling about and waiting for buses. Keeler called out Sheila's name. She replied happily, pushing through the crowd and hurrying toward him.

She had bought four shopping bags of food with the money he had given her. He carried two of them and his case, following her as she went to one side of the square to hail a taxi. In the taxi, Keeler opened his case and took a drink from the bottle. Then he sat back in the seat and relaxed, listening to Sheila. She talked about the first time she had tasted beer, about a bottle of whiskey her father had won in a raffle, and about liquor her parents had bought for her wedding. . . .

The sirens began howling as Sheila unlocked her door. She sighed in disgust, trying the light switch, then lit the candle and looked up at Keeler in its dim, yellow light. "We don't get as many bombs here as they do closer to the river," she said hesitantly. "But if you want to go to a shelter, there's one at the bottom of the street. . . ."

"I'd as soon stay here."

"Aye, I would and all," Sheila replied cheerfully. "Let me have those bags and your suitcase, Frank. I'll pour you a drink, and you can sit down while I make a fire. And I'll put your bottles on the floor over here so they won't get broken if we get a bomb nearby. . . ."

Her voice was almost lost under the screaming of the sirens as she talked and bustled about the room. He sat on a chair beside the fireplace as she poured Scotch into a glass for him, then knelt on the hearth and kindled the fire. As the fire blazed up, she began emptying the shopping bags. She had bought fish and chips to heat for dinner, as well as a wide assortment of other things that were unrationed.

The shrill sound of the sirens faded and Sheila's words became audible. She let the cat in and gave it a piece of fish on the hearth, talking about fish and chip shops, put the plates of fish and chips in the warming oven, then fell silent, kneeling on the hearth and looking up at Keeler. Turning back to the oven and closing the door, she spoke in a softer tone. "You'll be leaving soon, won't you?"

The subject had been avoided between them, a known but undefined menace. The firelight shone on her delicately-modeled, angelic face, its usual animation lacking as she waited for a reply. Keeler took out his cigarettes and lit one. "It'll be four or five days."

Sheila relaxed, the reply not as disappointing as she had feared. She pulled her chair closer and sat on it, dusting ashes from the hearth off her smock. "Aye, well, that's a lifetime nowadays, isn't it?"

"Perhaps so. I'd like you to write to me. There's an address in the city where you can send letters, and they'll be forwarded."

Sheila blinked in surprise. Then a pleased smile tugged

at her lips as she looked away and shrugged. "Aye, well, where's the sense in that, Frank? When you leave, it's best that we both put this behind us. I felt like a kept woman today, gadding about with my pockets full of money. And I'm already far too fond of you for my own good."

"I want to hear from you. I want to know what you're doing."

Her smile becoming wider, she looked at him from the corners of her eyes as she picked up a stick and jabbed at the fire. "Do you really feel that way about me, Frank? I fancied you might think I was only some tart to be forgotten as soon as you were gone."

"I think considerably more of you than that, Sheila."

"Well, I'll write to you, then." Her smile faded as she tossed the stick into the fire and sat back. "I never thought I'd come to this, though. My Georgie has been good to me, and I've never before so much as looked at another man. But I've never met anyone like you before."

"Aren't you going to join me in a drink?"

"No, love, shorts make me so giddy that. . . ." Her voice faded, then she shrugged as she stood up. "Oh, why not? You're ready for another, aren't you? I'll have a spot in a drop of water, then."

A distant rumble of aircraft engines vibrated the air as she went to the cabinet for another glass and took it to the lavatory to put water in it. She came back out and poured more Scotch into Keeler's glass, then poured a splash into hers. As the sound of the engines grew louder, anti-aircraft batteries fired in the distance.

The thudding of incendiaries blended with the pounding of the anti-aircraft batteries as Sheila talked about other bombing raids, telling Keeler about the death of her parents, the total destruction of the block where they had lived, and the lack of positive identification of bodies. When the first high explosive bombs began falling, she was talking about her agony of indecision before sending her son to Trews.

"We'll go there on Saturday," Keeler said. "You can spend Saturday and Sunday with the boy."

Sheila smiled sadly and shook her head. "No, we won't be able to, Frank. It's ever so difficult to travel about now, because all the seats on trains are reserved."

"We'll have priority train passes and reservations for the night at the railway hotel there. It's being arranged."

The house trembled as bombs detonated closer, the cat sitting up on the hearth and looking around in alarm. Sheila beamed ecstatically. "Truly, Frank? Are you certain? Oh, it'll be ever so lovely to see him! He's so young, and I'm ever so frightened that he'll forget me. And I have a ration coupon that I can use to get him some sweets!"

Keeler took the envelope of ration coupons from his pocket. He leaned over and put it on Sheila's lap, then took a drink from his glass as he sat back in his chair.

Sheila put her glass on the floor, staring at the ration coupons in astonishment. "Bloody hell! Where did you get all of these, Frank? They aren't dicey, are they?"

"No."

"Bloody hell," she chortled gleefully, thumbing through the booklets of coupons. "Would you look at this lot! And now I wish we'd gone to the shelter. I'm afraid a great, huge bloody bomb will fall on me and kill me before I can get to the shops and. . . ."

Her voice choked off as her smile suddenly disappeared. She looked down at the ration coupons, her eyes filling with tears and her lips and chin trembling. Then, tears spilling down her cheeks, she put a hand to her face as she leaned over and began weeping.

The house shook violently, bombs threatening a few blocks away. As smoke belched from the fireplace, the cat leaped up and darted under the bed. The window panes and things on shelves rattled. Something fell in the lavatory. Sheila's shoulders trembled as she sobbed. Keeler took a drag on his cigarette and a drink from his glass.

At last Sheila lifted her head, wiping her eyes. "I don't know what to say, Frank," she sobbed. "I don't know how to thank you, love."

Keeler leaned forward to hear her over the pounding roar of the bombs, then sat back. "Tell me what happened at your job today."

Sheila sat up in her chair, sniffling and wiping her eyes as she picked up the glass. Keeler tossed his cigarette into the fireplace and lit another one. Taking a sip from her glass, Sheila began talking about the day's events. Keeler listened as her voice faded in and out under the pounding thunder of the bombs.

She suddenly broke off and laughed as she pointed to the door. "Would you listen to that out there? And do you know what today is? A girl at the factory reminded me. . . ."

The deafening roar or a bomb exploding several blocks away drowned her voice. Keeler leaned toward her. "Pardon me?"

"It's Armistice Day!" she laughed. "Today is Armistice Day!"

Keeler nodded, taking a drag on his cigarette. The house shuddered and the overpressure forced smoke and soot out of the fireplace as sticks of bombs rained down, falling farther away. Sheila leaned forward and talked loudly so Keeler could hear her, telling him about Armistice Day celeberations she had attended as a child.

CHAPTER FIVE

VORCZEK AWAKENED TO the familiar sensations of frigid cold and gnawing pangs of ravenous hunger. The numbing fog of sleep was an escape; he tried to hold onto it, but it faded, full consciousness returning. The heaving motion had stopped and quiet had replaced the loud drumming of the engine. The barge had arrived. He opened his eyes.

The sun was a cold, bright disc behind a scum of high clouds covering the wintry sky. An old man lying against Vorczek had a sour, acrid odor, a stench that was almost lost in the miasma hanging over the mass of people crowded into the barge. The old man looked dead, his eyes dull behind slitted eyelids and his mouth gaping open.

An old woman with the man looked around through lank, greasy strings of dirty gray hair hanging over her face. A woman with a child was at the edge of the oily water puddled in the center of the barge, trying to push her way through the crowd to get out of the water, dragging the sodden bundle of rags covering her child.

Others stirred and looked around. They were ragged

and filthy, their eyes hollow and dazed in their haggard faces. Their movements were the painfully slow, economical motions demanded by the instinct for survival when the body is starved. The barge was beside a wooden pier, rocking in the water and thumping against the piles.

Heavy boots thudded on the pier, soldiers carrying cardboard boxes to the barge. Their uniforms were different from Vorczek's fading memories of Polish uniforms, far different from the hated Russian uniforms. They were unfamiliar, but there had been rumors that the camp at the end of the journey would be administered by the British.

Vorczek looked at the soldiers with remote, listless curiosity as they came along the pier. Then the boxes the soldiers were carrying and a ripple of movement among those on the side of the barge next to the pier suddenly had electrifying meaning to Vorczek and to others. The boxes contained food. The soldiers were starting to pass it out.

The stillness hanging over the barge dissolved into a bedlam of workless cries and a surge toward the gunwale below the pier. Strength flowing into Vorczek's limbs, he scrambled to his feet. Those in front of him were a yielding, shifting mass under him as he leaped, climbed, and kicked his way through them.

The soldiers hurriedly passed out loaves of bread and thick, heavy pieces of sausage to the forest of grimy, clawing hands. Vorczek used his greater height and strength, pushing to the gunwale and reaching up to a soldier. The soldier's face was blanched, his eyes mirroring horror. He handed a loaf of bread and a piece of sausage to Vorczek.

As he returned to safety, Vorczek protected the food with his body. Those unabl to reach the side of the barge snatched at the sausage and bread, but Vorczek shouldered and kicked his way through them. His strength fading when he reached his place on the opposite side of the barge, he lay down, panting breathlessly.

Then he began devouring the food, hot saliva filling his mouth and overflowing. The sausage was rich and greasy, smelling of garlic and other spices. The bread was crusty and soft inside, made of the best flour. As he bit off pieces and chewed rapidly, a surge of burning pain in his stomach warned him to eat more slowly.

The old woman held out a hand, whimpering. Vorczek hesitated, then tore off a piece of bread and gave it to her. She ate and put pieces of the bread into the old man's mouth. The woman with the child pulled herself closer to Vorczek, reaching out and begging in a wordless wail. He tore off a piece of bread and handed it to her.

The commotion on the other side of the barge faded as most of the people got food and sat devouring it. The soldiers brought more boxes and tossed food to those too weak to push into the mass of people at the side of the barge. Some lay motionless in the water in the center of the barge, unconscious or dead. Vorczek was uncomfortably full when he finished his food, a novel sensation.

Other soldiers in white coveralls carried stretchers along the pier and stacked them, while one brought a short ladder and lowered it into the barge. Two in Army uniforms walked along the pier, one an officer and the other a noncommissioned officer with sergeant major's chevrons. They were accompanied by a man wearing a brown uniform and a Red Cross arm band.

The Red Cross official, carrying a megaphone, lifted it and shouted through it in a clipped Warsaw accent: "Attention! Attention! I am Boris Koszanski of the Polish

Red Cross. This is Captain Avery of the British Army, who commands this camp! All able-bodied men among you who are between the ages of fifteen and forty-five are to be inducted into an army to fight the enemies of Poland!"

"We'll volunteer for your army!" a man shouted in reply. "We're more than ready to fight the whoreson Russians!"

"Silence!" Koszanski bellowed through the megaphone as chuckles and murmurs of agreement passed among the people in the barge. "You will not make provocative remarks about our allies! You are to be inducted into an army to fight against Germany! You will be severely punished if you make provocative remarks about our allies!"

Derisive jeers rang out among the people in the barge. The sergeant major, a tall, burly man with an intimidating demeanor, stepped to the edge of the pier. He glared down into the barge, his eyes narrow in the shadow of his cap visor and his thick mustaches bristling. Silence fell. The sergeant major turned away, motioning Koszanski to continue.

Koszanski lifted the megaphone again. "Attention! All men between fifteen and forty-five years of age will now leave the boat and line up on the dock. All others will remain in the boat until ordered to leave!"

Men began milling about, gathering at the foot of the ladder and climbing it. Pains from the unaccustomed feast of rich food stabbed in Vorczek's stomach as he stood up and walked toward the ladder. Others pushed in behind him when he joined the men crowding up the ladder. The pain in Vorczek's stomach intensified as he climbed. The wind was forceful out of the protection of the barge, sweeping across the gray, tossing expanse of the Caspian

Sea in icy gusts. Others were in pain as well, gripping their stomachs and swaying on their feet as Vorczek passed them and went to the end of the line.

The sergeant major shouted, repeating and mispronouncing a word in Polish. "Sit! Sit! Sit!"

The men began sitting down. Vorczek, shivering with cold, reached the end of the line and sat. The movement increased the pain in his stomach to a searing agony. He wrapped his arms around his belly, waiting for it to subside. Koszanski shouted through the megaphone at the women, children, and old people in the barge. They began climbing the ladder and straggling along the pier toward the shore.

The pain in his stomach fading, Vorczek watched the people climbing the ladder. There were hundreds of them, an entire train load from an internment camp at Krasnoyarsk in the Siberian Highlands. They had been at Guryev when the train bringing Vorczek and other men from the labor camp at Kirov had arrived there. He had eagerly searched among them, asking for word of his family. But none of them had ever heard of his father, mother, or sisters.

When people stopped coming up the ladder, soldiers went down into the barge. They helped some to ascent, then used the stretchers to carry those who were unable to walk. Some on the stretchers were dead, thin hands frozen in clutching gestures and worn, shabby shoes sticking out at awkward angles. When the last of the stretchers were finally carried away, the sergeant major shouted at the men in broken Polish to follow him.

The stomach pains began again and slowly diminished as Vorczek stood up and walked along with the others. Looking ahead, he saw a complex of large tents at the end of the pier. A road led to a flat expanse set back from the beach, where hundreds of tents stood in rows. Several hundred yards along the beach, an old sagging dock with boats tied up at it reached out into the water in front of a town that spread back toward rocky, barren hills on the horizon.

The line of men slowed at the end of the pier, entering the tent complex. Smoke smelling of burning hair and cloth was thick in the air. Soldiers assembled the men into four lines in front of long benches where other soldiers were cutting off the men's hair, acrid smoke billowing from the hair burning in nearby barrels. Vorczek's stomach pains began again; he gripped his belly and kept up with the man in front of him.

As a bench emptied of men, a soldier counted off Vorczek and the men in front of him, pointing to a bench. "Go! Go! Go!"

Vorczek and the others hurried toward the bench where soldiers with hair clippers stood, bits of hair clinging to their rubber gloves and white coveralls. They worked their clippers impatiently, shouting for the men to sit. As Vorczek found an empty place and sat down, gloved fingers gripped the back of his neck and pushed his head over a bucket half full of matted hanks of hair.

The toothed edge of the clippers bit into Vorczek's skin at the nape of his neck and moved rapidly up the back of his head and across the top to his forehead. Hair fell into the bucket, the clippers working across his head in swaths. The soldier gripped Vorczek's neck harder and turned his head. Vorczek winced as the clippers cut the fine, thin beard from his face. Then the soldier stepped back, waving and shouting.

"Go! Go! Go!"

Vorczek followed the men around another tent. Soldiers were shouting and pointing. On the other side of the tent, men were undressing and throwing their clothes into a pile. Soldiers picked up the clothes with sticks and tossed them onto a fire. Vorczek undressed, adding his worn, broken shoes and threadbare canvas shirt and trousers to the pile.

Following shouted orders, the naked men formed into a line straggling into another tent. Running water hissed inside and gushed out one side of it, forming a stream that ran down to the rocky beach. Vorczek trembled with cold as he joined the line of naked, shivering men, their eyes stark in their pale, beardless faces and ragged tufts of hair sticking up on their shorn heads.

As he went into the tent, the shock of the icy water spurting from overhead pipes almost took Vorczek's breath away. Men cursed and groaned around him, their wet, naked bodies pushing in on all sides. Vorczek took a bar of soap from a high wooden shelf and lathered himself as he was moved slowly along by the pressure of those pushing into the tent. His discomfort was almost overcome by the pleasure of feeling the grime of months washing away from his body.

Outside the tent, a pungent, penetrating odor of insecticide hung in the air. The men formed another line, still shaking with cold. A soldier at the front of the line held the nozzle on a spraying machine, while another pumped a handle to pressurize the machine. The one holding the nozzle shouted, "Arms up! Arms up! Arms up!"

Vorczek reached the front of the line and lifted his arms. The soldier sprayed Vorczek's armpits, then ran the nozzle around his genitals and soaked his pubic hair with the insecticide. It stung and itched as Vorczek followed the other men toward another large tent. A hubbub of impatient voices and bustling activity came from inside it. As Vorczek stepped into the tent, a soldier motioned him forward.

The soldier pointed to a board on the floor with lines on it, shouting, "Foot! Foot! Foot!"

Vorczek placed his foot on the board. The soldier looked at it, shouting something to another soldier behind a wooden counter. He reached into a box and threw a pair of boots on the counter as a soldier beside him added two pairs of socks and a canvas bag. Vorczek looked at them in wonder. The boots were new, made of costly leather, while the socks were of thick, heavy wool.

The soldiers shouting and waving, Vorczek took the things and moved on. As he walked along, other soldiers threw coveralls, underwear, a cap, and a heavy coat at him. The soldier at the end of the counter gave Vorczek a towel and a cloth bag filled with things, motioning him on to join the other men gathered at the rear of the tent, shivering and dressing.

All the expensive, durable clothes were new, with a rich feel and smell. The boots were by far the best he had ever owned, as was the heavy wool coat. Vorczek's stomach pains were only a minor discomfort by the time he was dressed, with the warm coat buttoned and the cap covering his head. Opening the cloth bag, he felt a novel sense of ownership as he looked at the toothbrush, toothpaste, razor, and soap in the bag.

The men formed into four lines outside the tent. At the head of the lines, soldiers who spoke heavily-accented Polish sat at tables and asked for names and other information. After their interrogation, the men moved on and the sergeant major motioned them to join the rows of men seated on the ground. As he took his place with the others, a soldier with a box under his arm gave each man two cigarettes and matches.

A truck rumbled along a road behind the tents, the bed filled with women and children in dark smocks and coats. The women, their heads shorn, held children with shorn heads; their hollow eyes stared at nothing. Other trucks passed, some filled with old people and others with more women and children. When the last man in line ahead of Vorczek moved away, Vorczek stepped forward, taking off his cap and bowing.

Papers on the table fluttered in the wind as the soldier shuffled them. He poised his pen, looking up. "Name!"

"Anton Vichai Vorczek, your honor. May it please your honor, I would like to ask if your honor has information on others who have—"

"I know nothing of what you speak! Age!"

"I will be twenty-two on my next nameday, your honor. I beg your honor's pardon, but I seek the know the whereabouts of my father, my mother, and my sisters. Their names are—"

"I know nothing of families! Speak with Red Cross about families! Place of birth!"

The soldier wrote on a paper, waving in dismissal. Vorczek hesitated, then bowed again and put on his cap as he walked toward the men seated on the ground. There was a movement along the shoreline. He glanced, then he stopped and looked. Two Russian soldiers were walking along the beach, laughing and talking.

Fiery, choking hatred exploded within Vorczek. Years had passed since the brutal, savage horde had poured into his village, but the memories of that time of terror remained etched in his mind with a raw, agonizing clarity, memories of the crumpled, bleeding form of his father after he had been beaten, of the screams of his mother and sisters as they were raped, of the cries of pain and anguish of others.

Russian soldiers had prowled among the crowds of villagers being herded to assembly areas, selecting women to rape and men to beat. Soldiers guarding the trains had amused themselves by ramming sticks between the slats of the railroad cars, laughing uproariously when someone screamed in pain. During overnight stops, they had dragged out young boys to torture into submission.

Vorczek's time in the labor camp had been years of starvation, abuse, and degradation. Any resistance or threat of violence to a Russian foreman had resulted in a severe beating or death. Those in charge of the labor camp had been brutal and sadistic. But the soldiers had been far worse.

The sergeant major was suddenly standing in front of Vorczek. His face was stern; his piercing blue eyes narrowed in warning. He pointed to the Russian soldiers with his quarterstaff and shook his head. Then he pointed to the men sitting on the ground and motioned Vorczek to join them.

The soldier with the box gave Vorczek two cigarettes and two matches. Vorczek had never smoked, but tobacco was a luxury so he lit one of the cigarettes and sat down. The smoke choking him, he coughed and cleared his throat. As he looked at the Russian soldiers again, he felt the sergeant major's eyes on him. He averted his face, puffing on the cigarette, and watched the Russian soldiers from the corners of his eyes.

CHAPTER SIX

THE RAW, BLUSTERY wind pulled at Ayoub's robes as he crept between the lines of tents, shivering with cold. His feet, bare except for his worn sandals, were numb. The cold made his ageing joints stiff, while his remaining teeth were sensitive to cold and ached with stabbing pains whenever he breathed through his mouth.

It was the kind of day that he normally would have spent in the warmth of his home or at a café in the town, but he had a reason to endure the cold. A new boy was at the Café Kosra, a young boy with a cherubic face, smooth limbs, and a mischievously inviting smile. He was Greek, which added an exotic piquancy to his physical beauty. The Café Kosra was crowded each night with men who came to watch him dance.

A single night with him cost an enormous amount, but money had lost all meaning to Ayoub in comparison with the boy. His desire for the youth had been obsessive since the first time he had seen him dance. While many others desired him and talked lustfully about him, few had enough money to spend a night with him. But more than enough money was potentially within Ayoub's reach.

Hidden pockets inside Ayoub's robes were filled with items to sell and trade—cigarettes, small bottles of vodka, religious medals, pictures of women in erotic poses, and other things. But they were useful only to give him a pretext to talk to the Polish soldiers, who had little money or anything else of value. He traded at a loss far more often that he made a profit. His money came from another source.

Helmut, a European who often visited the town, paid large sums of money for assistance in talking with the soldiers. Helmut was generous, but working for him was difficult and perilous. The officers and noncommissioned officers in the camp drove outsiders away. And Helmut's instructions had to be followed precisely. The one who had worked in the camp before Ayoub, having disobeyed Helmut's instructions, had disappeared.

Most of the soldiers were now marching on the parade ground. They would be dismissed at dusk and would go to their tents after eating, but that would be a poor time to approach them. Guards and noncommissioned officers patrolled the camp after the soldiers went to their tents, watching for outsiders and soldiers wandering about. And Helmut had told Ayoub to deal with the soldiers individually rather than in groups.

A few soldiers were always scattered through the camp on work assignments, and Ayoub had learned where they could be found. Some congregated at the hospital tent during the afternoon, where the medics sometimes gave them coffee. Now Ayoub crept along the rear of a tent across the street from the hospital tent, then knelt at a corner and peeked around it.

He quickly ducked back, crouching low to the ground.

An officer and two corporals stood in front of the hospital tent, talking. Ayoub's teeth throbbing with pain from his involuntary gasp of alarm, he took out a bottle of vodka and sipped it. When his teeth stopped aching, he leaned forward and peeked again. The officer and the corporals were still there, showing no indication of leaving. Ayoub sighed in disgust as he turned and crept away.

The mess tent, located on the far side of the camp at the edge of the wide field between the camp and the town, was another possibility. Ayoub worked his way toward it. The wide, straight streets through the camp were deserted. They were tempting, an easy path, but he would be visible for hundreds of feet if he took that route, so he slipped between the tents and darted across the streets.

The wind was more forceful at the edge of the camp, sweeping across the brushy, sandy field. The mess tent coming into view ahead, Ayoub approached it cautiously. Pots and pans clattered inside, and the British mess sergeant bellowed in broken Polish. No one was in front of the tent, or at the side. Ayoub knelt beside it, disgruntled. Then he heard voices behind it.

Ayoub crawled along the side of the tent and peered around the corner. He sat back and smiled to himself in satisfaction. Two men were peeling potatoes behind the tent, and Ayoub knew both of them. One was Josef Jankovic and the other was Anton Vorczek, one of Ayoub's best prospects. The two men looked up as Ayoub came around the corner of the tent.

"What do you want, Ayoub?" Jankovic demanded. "We have no money or anything to trade, and we've been told not to talk to peddlers. Our officer says there are German spies in the town."

Ayoub laughed and shook his head. "German spies?" he replied in heavily-accented Polish. "If the Germans are faring so poorly that they have need for such as me to be spies, they will be defeated within the week. I only wish to sit down out of the wind and rest."

"Give us a cigarette, then, or find somewhere else to hide."

Ayoub searched in his robes and took out a box of cigarettes as he sat down by the large kettle between the men. He gave each of them a cigarette, looking in the kettle. "It will take you many hours to fill this with potatoes," he said. "Why do you have to do this kind of work?"

"Because I made too many mistakes on the parade ground," Jankovic replied, feeling in his pockets for a match. "I'll never make a good soldier, like Anton."

Ayoub looked at Vorczek, smiling. "Anton is a good soldier?"

Jankovic nodded emphatically, striking a match and cupping it in his hands. "He is among the best. He learns faster than anyone else, but he isn't careful about other things." Having lit his cigarette, he leaned over to light Vorczek's. "He was going to be a corporal, but an officer heard him shouting an insult at a Russian. So now he will peel potatoes for a week, as well as remain a private."

Vorczek sat back, puffing on his cigarette. "I wish I could have done more than shout," he muttered darkly.

Jankovic frowned and shook his head in warning. "You may wish you had learned to hold your tongue. What you say could be repeated."

"Not by me," Ayoub said quickly. "We are friends here, and I dislike the Russians very much."

Jankovic drew on his cigarette, tossing a peeled potato into the kettle. "What did the Russians do to you, Ayoub?"

"They robbed me. Twice I went to their camp to buy and sell, and twice they took what I had and gave me nothing in return. I had heard that is how Russians trade, and now I know it is."

"Perhaps you cheated them, like you do us."

"No, no, I never cheat," Ayoub protested, laughing. "I only make a small profit so I can pay for my food and lodging."

Jankovic snorted skeptically as he picked up the bag by the kettle and stood up, dumping out the last few potatoes. "I will go and fetch another bag of potatoes, Anton. Don't let Ayoub cheat you out of your boots while I'm gone."

Vorczek smiled, tossing a potato into the kettle and reaching for another one as Ayoub laughed and shook his head. Ayoub waited until Jankovic went around the corner of the tent, then took out a bottle of vodka and offered it to Vorczek. Vorczek took the bottle and drank from it, then handed it back. "Thank you, Ayoub."

Ayoub smiled and nodded, tucking the bottle back into his robes. The preliminaries to persuading Vorczek to talk with Helmut had been completed during previous conversations. Ayoub had found something that Vorczek wanted, and he knew how to exploit it. Now they were alone for a moment, but Ayoub controlled his urge to rush into conversation; Helmut had warned him to sacrifice opportunities rather than stir suspicions. At last, Ayoub spoke in a tone of friendly interest: "Did you find out anything about your family, Anton?"

Vorczek sighed and shook his head, looking down at the

potato he was peeling. "I talked to a Red Cross officer, but he said their names are not on the lists of people who have come here."

After murmuring sympathetically, Ayoub forced himself to remain silent to avoid any indication of eagerness. Watching Vorczek peel the potato, he reflected that the young man fulfilled each of Helmut's requirements. He was thin from years in a labor camp, but he was tall and would be muscular when he gained weight. His blue eyes shone with keen intelligence, while his bold, strong features reflected a determined, aggressive personality. And most important of all, he had a burning hatred for Russians.

Another moment passed, then Ayoub spoke in a casual tone. "Perhaps I could help you, Anton."

Vorczek shrugged, tossing the potato into the kettle and picking up another. "There is nothing that anyone but the Red Cross people can do, Ayoub. They have the lists of names, and only they will know when my family comes here. *If* they come here."

"They have the lists," Ayoub agreed, choosing his words carefully. "They also have many things to do. Is it not easier for them to say that names are not on the lists than it is for them to look on many lists?"

Vorczek glanced at Ayoub, his eyes and face reflecting something more than the aggressive side of his personality; the potential for violence was just under the surface, guided by an astute, resourceful mind. He nodded tautly. "I thought about that," he muttered. "The Red Cross officer with whom I talked seemed too busy to bother with me."

"That might have happened," Ayoub said. "But I know a man who is very important, one who buys and sells things of great value. If he asked, he would find out the truth.'' He glanced around, then spoke in a lower voice. ''But you must tell no one about this man.''

''Why?''

''Because he feels as you and I do about Russians, and they feel the same about him. He comes here to buy and sell, but they would drive him away or possibly even put him in prison if they caught him.''

''Is he Iranian?''

Ayoub pulled the trailing end of his turban around the lower half of his face, moving closer to Vorczek. ''One can find people here from many places, Anton,'' he said quietly. ''This man was born in Switzerland, but he had lived here as a merchant for many years. And he likes Polish people, so perhaps he is part Polish.''

''How can he conduct his business if he comes and goes in secret? And how could he find out about my family?''

''Only the Russians must not know he is here, Anton. He can trust others, and he knows who they are. They include wealthy merchants in the town, as well as people in the Red Cross. If he wishes to find out about people on the Red Cross lists, he can do so very quickly. If you wish, I will take the names of your family to him. Then you can go and talk with him to see what he has found out.''

''Talk with him? I would be punished for leaving the camp.''

''Who would know? After the guards check your tent tonight, you could leave without being seen and meet me here. Then I will take you to the merchant.''

''Why must I talk with him? You could talk with him and tell me what he found out.''

''One does not treat this man in such a manner, Anton,'' Ayoub said patiently, shaking his head. ''He is a very important man, and very wealthy. You must be courteous if you want him to do a favor for you."

"Why would an important man do this for me?"

"As I said, he likes Polish people. He also dislikes Russians, and he is sympathetic toward those who have been mistreated by them. And who knows what other reasons he may have? I only know that he has done this before for men from the camp."

"He has?"

"Many times. If you will write down your name and the names of your family, I will see that he gets them. Then you can meet me here later and we will go and see him. But it should be tonight, because I am not sure of how long he will be here."

As he finished talking, Ayoub fumbled in his robes and took out a scrap of paper and a stub of a pencil. His hands trembled, and his mouth was dry. Clamping his lips closed, he held out the paper and pencil encouragingly. The paper fluttered in the wind. Ayoub's heart pounded as he waited.

Vorczek frowned musingly, seconds dragging by. Then, taking the paper and pencil, he began writing. Ayoub glanced toward the corner of the tent that Jankovic had gone around, struggling to keep from betraying his sense of urgency. Vorczek finally finished writing and handed the paper and pencil back. Ayoub tucked them into his robes as he stood up, repeating his instructions to meet him at the mess tent that night. Then he left, the wind whipping his robes, making them stream away from his legs. But he barely noticed the cold as he stumbled through the sandy soil toward the path to the town, chuckling exultantly. When one more soldier agreed to talk with Helmut, he would have enough money to spend a night with the boy at the Café Kosra. And if one of the soldiers accepted Helmut's offer, his bonus would be enough to spend several nights.

When Ayoub was gone, Vorczek thought of questions he should have asked. The explanation about the merchant was unconvincing. But Ayoub had always been a friendly old man. He had given Vorczek drinks of vodka and cigarettes, and he had been interested in Vorczek's family. He seemed harmless. But more than that, Vorczek wanted to believe the old man's story, yearning for contact with his family.

The gray, wintry daylight was fading into dusk when Vorczek and Jankovic finished filling the kettle and took it into the mess tent. The men filed in from the parade ground for the evening meal, filling the tent with a hubbub of voices and a clatter of mess kits. After they had left, the sergeant major and the Polish officers sat at a table in a corner and talked as they ate. When Vorczek and the other workers had eaten and cleaned up, the mess sergeant dismissed them for the day.

Vorczek went to his tent and sat on his cot, waiting. Men played cards and talked noisily for a time, then began going to bed. When the lantern in the center of the tent was extinguished, Vorczek took off his boots and lay under the blankets in his clothes. The conversation faded away into snores and heavy breathing. In a little while, the guards came in with a flashlight and shone the beam from one cot to another. Vorczek waited for a few minutes after the guards left, then pushed his blankets aside and sat up, reaching for his boots.

The darkness was thick, the gusty wind bitterly cold. Vorczek moved quietly between the tents, feeling for the ropes to avoid tripping. As he approached the mess tent, he circled around to one side of it, keeping out of the light streaming from the doorway. The sergeant major and officers were still talking inside, their voices a quiet murmur as Vorczek crept around to the rear.

He stopped behind the tent, thick darkness surrounding him, then whispered, "Ayoub?"

"Ai, you are here," Ayoub chuckled quietly, a few feet away. "You make little noise for one of your size, Anton. Come, he is waiting."

The old man took his arm and hurried him out into the field between the town and the camp. Ayoub was a dark shadow by Vorczek, shivering in the cold wind and puffing heavily as he stumbled along. Vorczek's boots sank into the sandy ground and scrubby growth whipped at the legs of his coveralls. They went through a shallow ditch, then felt the firm surface of a path underfoot.

The wind carried the smell of charcoal smoke and a blend of other odors from the town. Light gleamed dimly, the diffuse yellow glow of lamps shining through cracks in shutters. The smells became stronger and the lights brighter, then the outlines of buildings were vaguely visible against the dark sky as the path led into a street.

Ayoub stopped suddenly, speaking quietly in a sibilant, liquid foreign language. A man a few yards away replied as he approached through the darkness. Silhouetted momentarily against the light from a shuttered window, he wore robes. Ayoub talked with him in whispers, then there was a clink of coins exchanging hands.

"This man will take you to the merchant, Anton," Ayoub murmured, moving away. "Then he will bring you back here."

Expecting Ayoub to go with him, Vorczek started to object, but Ayoub had already disappeared into the night.

Vorczek turned to the other man. "Where is the merchant?" he asked.

The man laughed softly and replied in his own language, his tone apologetic. He took Vorczek's sleeve and tugged on it, making another comment. Vorczek hesitated, then he followed him.

The dark, narrow streets felt and smelled foreign. The atmosphere was alien, while the odors of the spices that blended with the scents of cooking food were strange to Vorczek. A jangle of discordant, tinny music came from a café at the far end of a street. Soft sounds of conversation and laughter filtered out of houses on either side.

The man led Vorczek into a dark alley, with walls closing in on both sides. The wind sweeping along the alley smelled of urine. Vorczek's guide felt his way along one wall and stopped at a door. He rapped three times, then twice more, tucked his robes around himself and sat down against the wall. The door squeaked open and a man looked out.

"Ah, please come in, my friend," the man said, smiling at Vorczek. "It is very cold tonight. Come in and warm yourself while we talk."

The dim light coming through the doorway was bright in the thick darkness. The man was large, dressed in European clothes and a long tweed topcoat, and he wore rimless glasses with thick lenses. His voice was jovial and his face was fleshy and ruddy—a Teutonic face. He spoke fluent Polish, with a hint of an accent that sounded German.

Vorczek stepped inside and the man closed the door. The place was little more than a hovel, a dwelling that had been vacant for a long time. A ragged mat over the single window moved in the draft, and the floor was littered with shards of broken earthenware and other debris. In a corner that had been swept out, a folding table and stools were set up beside a charcoal brazier. The coals in the brazier added a tinge of red to the yellow light from the lantern on the table.

The man motioned Vorczek toward the table. "I must apologize for receiving you in such poor surroundings," he said. "But Pahlavi offers little choice for temporary accommodations. Please sit down."

The corner was warm, flames playing over the coals in the brazier in the drafts from the wind moaning outside the house. Feeling uneasy in these strange surroundings, Vorczek sat down. He looked at the man as he sat at the other side of the table. "What is your name?" he asked.

"Please call me Helmut," the man replied amiably, taking out a notebook. "My friends call me that, and I trust we will be friends. Your name is Anton Vorczek, isn't it? And you wish to know about your family, whose names are. . . ." He thumbed through the notebook, then stopped at a page. "Radovan, Letizia, Zetta, and Ona Vorczek."

"Oza."

The man lifted his eyebrows and took a pen from an inside pocket. He changed the name, his manner grave and deliberate, then nodded. "Oza. Very well, I will ask again about her." He closed the notebook and replaced the top of his pen, shaking his head. "But as for the others, they are not listed on the records here."

Vorczek sagged with disappointment. "Then the Red Cross official with whom I spoke was telling the truth. I thought he might have been lying, not wanting to go to the trouble of checking the lists."

"Perhaps he was, but the names of your family are not

on the lists. I had someone look for them this afternoon." He put the pen and notebook away, then took out a box of cigarettes and a silver cigarette lighter. "But that isn't the end of the matter. Cigarette?"

Vorczek took one and leaned across the table as the man held out the lighter. He sat back, puffing on the cigarette. The man lit one for himself and put the cigarettes and lighter on the table. Then he shook his head as he drew on his cigarette and exhaled.

"That isn't the end of the matter," he repeated. "In two instances when I checked on relatives for friends, I found them listed at resettlement camps but not here. In other words, the lists here are not completely accurate. I will also check again for your sister Oza. If I find out anything, I will send you a message by Ayoub."

"Do you think they may be in a resettlement camp?"

The man hesitated, then shrugged. "Possibly, but I wouldn't want to give you false hopes, Anton. Do you know how many people the Russians seized and took out of Poland?"

"No."

"I don't either, and I doubt that even the Russians know the exact number. But the best estimate that can be made is three million."

"Three million?" Vorczek gasped.

The man puffed on his cigarette and exhaled with a sigh, nodding. "And thus far, the Russians have accounted for less than one hundred thousand. I will see what I can find out for you."

The light from the lantern glared on the man's thick glasses, turning them into opaque discs. Though his eyes were concealed, his attitude was sympathetic, suggesting that there was little hope. He took out a flask that had two small silver cups nested on top of it. Removing the cups, he placed them on the table and opened the flask.

"Are you German?" Vorczek asked.

The man smiled affably and nodded as he poured liquor into the cups. "Yes, so it would be wise not to discuss our meeting with anyone. It could cause you and possibly our friend Ayoub some difficulty, but it would make little difference to me. Only the one who brought you here knows where I am, and I will be gone shortly. But there is no reason why we can't be friends, is there? Here, try this cognac."

Vorczek took a sip from the cup. The cognac was good, smooth and warm as it trickled down his throat. He took another sip and puffed on his cigarette. "Are you a spy?"

The man sat up in astonishment, then laughed heartily. "No, no! I am not a spy, Anton. Do you think I brought you here to get information from you? What would you know that would be of interest to the German High Command, my friend? No, you are here because you wish to know about your family, and I wish to help you if I can."

"Ayoub said that you are a merchant."

"Yes, I am. I have been a merchant in Iran for many years. I have nothing to do with the war, except that I sometimes make arrangements to send men to Germany. Men who feel that Russia rather than Germany is their enemy."

"The Russians are my enemy, but I have heard that the German Army is in all of Poland now."

"Yes, the German Army has driven the Russians out of Poland, and Polish communists, homosexuals, and others are being sought out. But there will be peace and friendship between our countries when the war is won. Poland's enemy is Russia, not Germany. Don't you agree?"

"Yes, I do. You send men to Germany to be in the German Army?"

The man nodded. "I have sent many to the German Army, and a few have become sondercommandos. The training is very difficult, but one who is young and strong can succeed if he is very determined."

"What is a sondercommando?"

"The best of the very best," the man replied. He sighed, smiling wistfully. "They are members of the Brandenburg Division, which is assigned to military intelligence, and they are given only missions of greatest importance. Soldiers fight in divisions, but sondercommandos fight in squads and platoons. They go deep into Russia to strike terror into the enemy, to sabotage fuel depots, trains, bridges, and things of that nature. It is a great honor to be a sondercommando, Anton."

"And there are Poles among them?"

"A few are men who were born in England and in the United States of German parents, a few are Irish, and a few are of other nationalities. And yes, many are from Poland. Perhaps you might consider joining them."

Vorczek smoked his cigarette, thinking. He was bitterly disappointed over the lack of information about his family. Now it appeared that the main reason he had been brought to see this man was to hear about the sondercommandos. It was even possible that had been the sole reason, that the man had no sources through which to find out about Polish refugees.

But Vorczek felt no resentment. The man's glowing description of the sondercommandos was very intriguing. The thought of being able to spread death and destruction among Russians behind the lines of combat with the German Army was an alluring temptation, making him want to join them. But if he did, it would make him an enemy of the other men in the camp, his own countrymen.

Dropping the cigarette stub and stepping on it, Vorczek shrugged. "I will think about it."

"Yes, one should make a decision such as this only after long and serious consideration," the man replied promptly, nodding. "I want you to be certain in your own mind about what you wish to do. In the meantime, I will see if I can find out about your family."

"I am very grateful."

"You are more than welcome, my friend," the man said as he stood up. "Now you must return before you are missed. Here, take these cigarettes with you."

He pushed the box into Vorczek's coat pocket. Vorczek nodded and smiled. "Thank you very much."

"It is nothing, Anton," the man chuckled, putting a hand on Vorczek's shoulder as they walked toward the door. "You have my best wishes whatever you decide to do, but do not wait too long. As soon as there are enough men here for a regiment, you will be sent elsewhere. So make your decision soon, Anton."

"I will."

They stopped in front of the door, the man smiling warmly. "I have enjoyed our conversation tonight, my friend. And if you decide you want to go to Germany, send me a message through Ayoub. He knows how to contact me through the man who brought you here. But you must use only certain words so I can be sure that the message is from you."

"What should I say?"

"Tell Ayoub to inform Helmut that Anton is ready to leave. Only you and I will know those precise words. Can you remember them?"

"Yes, I will remember. I am to tell Ayoub to inform Helmut that Anton is ready to leave. I will remember."

The man smiled and nodded, patting Vorczek's shoulder, then he opened the door. The man sitting beside the door stood up as Vorczek stepped outside and the door squeaked closed, cutting off the light. The man took Vorczek's arm and led him through the impenetrable darkness of the alley, buffetted by the keening wind.

CHAPTER SEVEN

THE COLD, GUSTY wind stirred up dust on the parade ground as the men stood stiffly in a long line of platoons and swirled around the man who stood stripped to the waist with his wrists tied to a post at the front of the parade ground. The muscles in the man's bare, white back and arms knotted as he tried to keep from shivering with cold and with fear.

The wind blurred the words the Polish officer was shouting through a megaphone, making his voice sound wavering and distant. Private Kadlicek had struck a Russian soldier, the officer said. A summary court-martial board had been convened. Private Kadlicek had been tried and sentenced to twenty lashes.

A man behind Vorczek spoke quietly, his words barely audible over the wind and the officer's voice. An eyewitness to what had happened, he repeated substantially what Vorczek had heard others say. Kadlicek and the Russian had argued, which had led to a fight. The Russian had struck the first blow, then he had been soundly thrashed.

The Polish officers, including the one who was speaking through the megaphone, had come from the government in exile in London to train and command the regiment. None of them had ever seen a Russian labor or internment camp, but they had formed the court-martial board. They stood in line with the British captain and the sergeant major. A medic and a Polish corporal holding a whip were at the end of the line.

The officer with the megaphone finished pronouncing sentence, then turned to the British captain. Exchanging a salute with the captain, he stepped back into line with the others. A few minutes passed, then the heavy thumping of men marching in formation was heard. A contingent from the Russian garrison marched onto the parade ground, headed by an officer barking commands.

The formation halted and the officer beckoned a large, burly soldier out of the ranks. The soldier followed the officer as he walked toward the captain and the others. The captain stepped out of the line and spoke with the Russian officer. Their voices were inaudible, but the substance of the conversation was clear from the Russian officer's gestures. He wanted the soldier he had selected to wield the whip.

An angry mutter passing through the platoons subsided as the captain firmly refused. The Russian officer, a large man, stepped closer to the captain and talked in a loud, angry voice, but the captain was unintimidated. The Russian officer stamped furiously back to his men, the soldier following him.

The captain returned to the line and motioned to the sergeant major, who saluted, then stepped smartly to the post where Kadlicek was tied, followed by the medic and the corporal who took their places on either side of Kadlicek. Then it began, the sergeant major counting the strokes in a loud voice that resounded across the parade ground as the corporal swung the whip.

The first blow left a long, red weal across Kadlicek's shoulders, the whip striking with a meaty thud. The second left a welt just below the first one. The muscles in Kadlicek's arms and back became rigid as he gripped the post tightly. Tendons standing out in his neck and his face twisting with pain, he bit his lower lip to keep from crying out.

The sixth blow drew blood. Kadlicek slumped and hung from his wrists, bright rivulets of blood trickling down his back. The captain's voice rang out sharply. The sergeant major wheeled on the corporal and castigated him in a shrill, enraged voice. The corporal's face blanched and he stood stiffly at attention.

The Russian officer shouted impatiently. The captain ignored him, calling to the sergeant major and pointing with his quarterstaff. The sergeant major motioned to the medic, who bent over Kadlicek and looked at his back. The medic helped him to his feet and placed Kadlicek's hands on the post so he could grip it. Then the flogging resumed.

Kadlicek screamed on the twelfth blow. The hoarse, ragged cry was torn from him against his will, his face contorted in agony. Dark streaks appeared on the legs of his coveralls as he urinated, writhing with pain. A murmur of satisfaction passed among the Russians. Kadlicek sagged and hung limply from his wrists. The impact of the whip made his body bounce against the post.

At last it was over. The medic and sergeant major untied Kadlicek and the Russians marched off the parade ground. One of the Polish officers summoned men from a platoon to carry Kadlicek away. The officers spread out among the platoons, resuming drill practice. Vorczek's platoon was made up of men assigned to work details. A corporal dismissed them to return to their duties.

The men around Vorczek muttered among themselves as they walked along the street through the tents. Vorczek turned off the street, wanting to be alone, and headed toward the mess tent, stepping over tent ropes and pegs. His scalp felt tight. Burning nausea churned in his stomach. He breathed heavily, as though he had run a long distance.

A movement ahead caught his eye—a robed form slipping from the rear of one tent to another. Recognizing Ayoub, Vorczek hesitated for an instant, then began running toward the old man. Ayoub fled, weaving and darting rapidly between the tents. Vorczek raced after him with long, pounding strides.

Ayoub squealed in fear as Vorczek caught the back of his robes and jerked him to a standstill. Then his fright changed into surprise as he recognized Vorczek. He grinned, gasping in relief. "Anton! When I heard you, I thought you were one of the officers or corporals. Here, Anton, have a cigarette and. . ."

"No, I do not want a cigarette," Vorczek interrupted brusquely. "I want to send a message to Helmut."

Ayoub's eyes widened with alarm. He glanced around, hissing in warning. "Quietly, Anton! Speak very quietly of this. Others may hear you, and it would cause great trouble. Here, calm yourself and have a drink of vodka."

"I do not want a drink of vodka, Ayoub. I only want to send a message to Helmut. Inform Helmut that Anton is ready to leave."

"Inform Helmut that Anton is ready to leave," Ayoub

repeated slowly. Then he smiled and nodded. "I will tell him, Anton. But now you must calm yourself and not do anything that will bring attention to you." His smile widened and became gleefully triumphant as he patted Vorczek's arm. "You must keep yourself in readiness. It will only be a day or two until Anton will leave."

CHAPTER EIGHT

THE TIRES GROUND through ice and frozen snow in the gutter as the Mercedes stopped, waking Niedersdorf. The faint glow of the dashboard disappeared as the driver turned off the lights and the engine. Niedersdorf sat up wearily in the darkness and felt for the small box on the seat beside him. The driver got out of the car and came around to open the rear door, ice and snow crunching under his boots.

Niedersdorf put the box under his arm as he climbed out of the car. "Take my luggage to my quarters and leave it with my orderly," he said.

"Yes, Colonel. Shall I return here and wait for the colonel?"

"No. I will call for a car when I'm ready to leave."

The driver clicked his heels together and closed the door. Niedersdorf crossed the sidewalk and felt for the steps, then began climbing them. The driver got back into the car and started the engine. The red glow of the tail lights dimly illuminated the steps and the wide double doors at the top of them. The car pulled away, moving slowly along the street with only its parking lights on. Niedersdorf pushed the bell button.

A panel in one door slid open and the heavily-filtered beam of a flashlight shone on Niedersdorf's face. Then the panel closed and the heavy door opened with a ponderous groan of hinges. Niedersdorf stepped into total darkness. The door closed, then the duty officer turned on a lamp on the desk in the corner of the entry.

The duty officer bowed stiffly. "Good evening, Colonel."

"Good evening. Is the admiral still in?"

"Yes, Admiral Canaris is in his office, Colonel."

Niedersdorf signed the register, then crossed the entry toward the stairs. His footsteps echoed hollowly across the wide, dark entry, loud in the late night stillness. The light from the lamp on the duty officer's desk faded, then the dim light from the guard post on the first landing became visible, faintly illuminating the stairs.

He climbed the stairs slowly, wearily. The trip he had just finished had been a long one, as well as one that worried him. Ten days before, Canaris had give him the tickets, passes, and other documentation for the trip, along with a page of instructions. The first instruction had been to memorize everything on the page, then burn it. Three hours later, he had been on a train to Frankfurt.

In Frankfurt, he had gone to the address he had memorized and found the woman and children described in the instructions. The woman had spoken German with a French accent and the children only French, which had been omitted from the description. Their bags had been packed, ready for the long trip by train—west to the French border, southwest across occupied France, then south across Vichy France and into Spain.

The trip had been boring, the woman wary and the children terrified of him. Shortly before crossing the Spanish border, he had changed into civilian clothing, as directed. All the documentation was in order and they had passed through the checkpoints without delay. In Madrid reservations had been made at the Hotel Continental.

An hour after they arrived, the man mentioned in the instructions had arrived, obviously the woman's husband and the children's father. He had given Niedersdorf the box to deliver to Canaris, which had been omitted from the instructions, and he had spoken German with a distinct English accent, a further fact that had not appeared in the instructions.

Niedersdorf had heard rumors among the Abwehr headquarters staff that Canaris and the head of British MI-6 had private channels of communication, as well as a gentleman's understanding on matters not related to the war effort. Niedersdorf had ruthlessly squelched the rumors; the results would be cataclysmic if any hint spread outside headquarters. But the trip that Niedersdorf had just completed seemed to substantiate the rumors.

The guards on each landing stood up as Niedersdorf climbed the stairs. When he reached the top floor, he walked along the hall and went into his office. The heat had been turned off during his absence, and the air was cold and stale. He hung up his overcoat, put his cap and gloves on his desk, then carried the box along the hall.

The admiral's office was dark except for the lamp on the desk, its light gleaming on the admiral's white hair as he pored over a stack of papers. He looked up when Niedersdorf rapped on the door jamb, straining to see into the darkness. Then he smiled. "Franz! Come in, Franz, come in. You have returned sooner than I expected."

Niedersdorf walked into the office and bowed. "Good evening, Admiral. Yes, I had good connections on the return journey."

"You must be very weary, and I'm pleased that you came by tonight to see me. Were you successful?"

Niedersdorf nodded, placing the box on the admiral's desk. "Yes, all the instructions were carried out, Admiral. And the man who met the woman and children asked me to bring this to you."

Canaris stood up, looking at the box with a musing smile. Then he took a letter opener and began sawing at the tape on the box. "I do hope this is what I think it is," he said. "Was the trip uneventful?"

"The only thing worthy of note is that I was delayed upon coming back into Germany. I believe it was a check by the Gestapo."

Canaris shrugged nonchalantly, tearing the tape loose. "Himmler's bees will buzz about, looking for something to sting or for something sweet to take back to the hive, won't they? But they were wasting their time. And the man arrived promptly?"

"Yes, Admiral. He was as described in the instructions, with the additional characteristic that he spoke German with an English accent."

Canaris stopped working with the tape and looked at Niedersdorf with an inscrutable expression. Then he smiled. "Or Irish, Franz?"

Niedersdorf blinked, then smiled and nodded. "Yes, or Irish. I wouldn't be able to distinguish between the two."

"Nor would I, Franz," Canaris chuckled cheerfully, opening the end of the box. He sighed with pleasure as he took out two bottles. They were liquor bottles, without labels or any other identification. "Ah, this is very good,

Franz, very good indeed," Canaris said happily. "It has been far too long since I've tasted Scotch. I'm sure you would enjoy some refreshment, so I'll pour us each a drink." He carried the bottles to the cabinet, glancing over his shoulder. "I missed you more than usual this time, because we have been quite busy."

"Has the plan for the deployment to Iran been completed, Admiral?"

"Yes, all is in readiness," Canaris replied, opening one of the bottles and taking glasses from a shelf. "We are waiting to dispatch the platoons in conjunction with the beginning of the naval offensive in the North Sea. But in order to reach an accommodation with our comrades on the Bendlerstrasse, we had to make a concession that I dislike. The SD had an agent in a village near Tabriz who will act as the contact for their teams, but they wanted an alternate. I had to agree to let Moltke function in that capacity."

"That could be extremely dangerous for Moltke. SD operations are often very insecure."

"Yes, but he is only an alternate, and it is unlikely that he will be used. Their agent in the village has been there for years, and he should last through this operation. We used your suggested list of personnel for our platoons, even though Colonel Lahousen maintains his objections about sending officers."

"I agree with him from the standpoint that we can hardly spare the officers. We have far too few in the Brandenburg Division."

Canaris nodded as he walked back across the office with the glasses. "We have, and I've been giving that matter some thought. The problem, of course, is that very few Wehrmacht officers can complete the sondercommando training. An obvious solution would be to send some of our most promising men to the officer training academy. I discussed that with General Keitel a few days ago."

"What was his reaction, Admiral?"

"Naturally, he has strong reservations about sending foreign-born personnel to the academy, and most of our best men are foreign-born. But he stopped short of refusing to consider it, and we will discuss it again." He handed a glass to Niedersdorf and lifted his. "Your good health, Franz."

"And yours, Admiral," Niedersdorf replied. He tasted the liquor, then swallowed it grimly, keeping his features neutral. It had the bitterness of whiskey, with an unpleasant, smoky aftertaste.

Canaris took sips from his glass as he sat down, savoring the taste. "How do you like it, Franz?"

"It is quite good, Admiral."

Canaris chuckled wryly, shaking his head. "Franz, your ability to dissimulate suffers when you are weary. Would you prefer Steinhäger?"

"No, thank you, Admiral."

"Perhaps you will develop a taste for it," Canaris said cheerfully, sitting back in his chair. "But bear in mind that it is a taste that is difficult to indulge just now. Moltke has become very efficient, and several more recruits from Pahlavi arrived at Lake Quenz while you were gone. Most of them will be unable to complete the training, of course, but we should be able to get one or two sondercommandos from them. And we also had some bad news from Iran."

"Bad news, Admiral?"

"Yes. Keeler is the British resident there now."

Niedersdorf winced, taking another drink of the Scotch. "How reliable is the report, Admiral?"

"Completely reliable. It came from Mueller in Teheran."

"That is bad news indeed, but it should be some time before Keeler has a network organized there. They have been of no trouble at all to us, so he will have little to work with at first."

"Yes, we will have a period of time in which to warn our active agents and take over precautions," Canaris agreed. "But that period will be limited, considering that we are dealing with Keeler."

Drinking the last of his Scotch, Niedersdorf struggled to keep from showing his distaste. Canaris took a sip from his glass and smiled at Niedersdorf as he picked up his cigarettes from the desk. "I know you must be very tired, Franz, so I won't keep you. Thank you very much for delivering the Scotch so promptly. It has ended an otherwise dreary day on a very pleasant note."

"I am gratified that I was able to please you, Admiral," Niedersdorf replied. "I will come in early tomorrow morning and review everything that took place during my absence. Then I will be ready to work on any special projects you may wish to assign me."

"It would probably be best if you worked on the other plan we prepared in collaboration with our comrades on the Bendlerstrasse," Canaris said, lighting a cigarette. He separated one paper from the others on his desk and glanced over it. "The assassination plan. Emil has reviewed our draft plans and the memos of our meetings, and he has approved them. We are now ready to proceed to a final plan."

"A contingency plan?"

"Yes, to be implemented if any of the three target individuals travel abroad and we become aware of it within sufficient time to take advantage of the situation. We will designate sondercommando personnel by numbers and qualifications only, then select the individuals to deploy when and if the plan is implemented."

"Very well, Admiral, I will begin work on it tomorrow. Do you wish to assign a code name?"

Canaris puffed on his cigarette as he looked off into a dark corner of the room. He exhaled the smoke slowly, his lips pursed in thought. Then he nodded. "We will designate it Project Jael."

The name had a soft, liquid sound, unlike the usual code names which were resounding, warlike titles drawn from Teutonic legend and history. Niedersdorf hesitated, then nodded. "Very well, Admiral. May I ask the origin of the code name?"

Canaris glanced up at Niedersdorf, then looked away as he chuckled dryly. "It is a literary allusion of sorts, Franz."

"I see," Niedersdorf said, his understanding no more complete than before. "I will begin work on Project Jael tomorrow, then." He bowed and turned toward the door. "Good night, Admiral."

Canaris puffed on his cigarette and nodded, still smiling. "Good night, Franz."

PART TWO

March-June, 1943

CHAPTER NINE

VORCZEK SWUNG HIS arms stiffly and dug his heels into the ground as his platoon marched across the parade ground. Buds made a tinge of pale green on the bare limbs of the mountain birches along the edge of the parade ground behind the reviewing stand. The spring sunshine was warm, but the breeze brushing Vorczek's face had a crisp feel of the snow on the peaks of the Alps towering in the background.

Three other platoons marched across the parade ground ahead of his. Two months before, at the start of primary training, there had been eight. Over one hundred men, having failed the training or given up under the grueling pressure, had been sent to the Wehrmacht. Now the time had come for the final and most drastic reduction in numbers.

The commander and senior noncommissioned officer of the primary training camp stood on the reviewing stand. Vorczek could see the roofs of the upper camp on the slope rising behind them. It was the home of the Brandenburg Division, where the advanced training was conducted. Of the one hundred men in the platoons, ten would go there and ninety would be sent to the Wehrmacht.

The sergeant barked commands and the platoons halted in front of the reviewing stand. Silence fell, the men standing stiffly at attention. Vorczek's right shoulder ached from a fall on the obstacle course, while his left temple throbbed from a hard blow during hand-to-hand combat training. Other scrapes and bruises twinged, but he was barely aware of the pain, wondering if he would be one of the ten who were chosen. That was the only thought among all of the men; the tension was almost palpable.

As the commander and the senior noncommissioned officer of the upper camp approached, Vorczek looked at them from the corners of his eyes. He had seen Major Buehler before from a distance—a tall, heavyset man. His decorations and badges were bright against the dull gray of his tunic and jodhpur trousers, his knee-length boots gleaming. A monocle shone dimly in the shadow of the high peak of his cap.

The master sergeant with Buehler, also a large man, was named Kosanovic; he was Polish. About forty-five, with gray hair and deep creases in his stony face, he was a veteran of years of service in the Polish Army. An Iron Cross hung at his throat, and sondercommando and parachutist badges were among the decorations he wore.

Buehler returned the salutes of the two on the reviewing stand, climbing the steps. Then he glanced at the platoons.

"Stand at rest."

His deep, curt voice carried along the line of platoons. Vorczek relaxed and the men around him moved and sighed audibly. Buehler and Kosanovic talked with the other two men for a moment, then Buehler stepped to the edge of the reviewing stand. He looked back and forth along the platoons as he began talking: "I can accept only ten men for advanced training. All of you are good men, and it was very difficult for us to make a decision. There is no reason for shame in not being chosen."

The atmosphere crackled with tension as he glanced over his shoulder at Kosanovic. The master sergeant took out a piece of paper and handed it to him. Buehler adjusted his monocle as he turned back and looked at the paper. "Those whose names I call will leave the ranks and form a line by the reviewing stand. Breunner!"

There was a muffled exclamation of triumphant glee and hurried footsteps. Breunner rushed forward and stood stiffly at the end of the reviewing stand. He attempted to keep his expression neutral, but his face was crimson and a jubiliant smile kept breaking through.

"Feeney!"

Feeney raced forward and slid to a stop by Breunner, his round, freckled face beaming. Buehler lifted his eyebrows as he looked at the list, then motioned to Kosanovic. The master sergeant stepped forward and told Buehler in a murmur how to pronounce the name.

"Drzewiecki!"

He mispronounced it anyway, and Kosanovic chuckled a comment as Drzewiecki ran forward to take his place. Then Buehler called out other names, most of them German and an occasional name of another nationality. Vorczek listened numbly, a cold, hard knot forming in his stomach.

"Vorczek!"

It took Vorczek a long, dragging second to react. Then exultant joy exploded to life within him. The sergeant in front of the platoon glanced back and nodded in congratulations. Vorczek grinned at him happily and ran forward to join the others at the end of the reviewing stand. He took his place in line, his elation still growing.

When the last man had been called, Vorczek felt the eyes of the ninety men remaining in the ranks on him and the other nine. Then Buehler dismissed the platoons and they marched away, the sergeants barking orders. The four men on the reviewing stand walked down the steps and exchanged salutes, then the commander and senior noncommissioned officer of the primary training camp left.

Kosanovic stood at one side while Buehler talked to Vorczek and the other men about the training at the upper camp. He explained that their initial training would consist of instruction in weapons, tactics, and academic subjects. After that, they would be eligible for deployment on combat missions, as well as for temporary duty with the Wehrmacht and Luftwaffe to attend special courses of training in demolitions, radio operations, parachuting, and other things.

Buehler took his monocle from his eye and a handkerchief from his pocket. "When I spoke to the others, I did so in a way to encourage them to be good soldiers," he continued, polishing the monocle. "And they will, because they are good men." He tucked the handkerchief back into his pocket and fitted the monocle over his eye, glancing back and forth at Vorczek and the other men. "But you are the best. Two hundred came here, and ten remain. Apply yourselves to your training accordingly."

He walked away, exchanging a salute with Kosanovic. The master sergeant snapped orders and formed Vorczek and the other men into a squad. Then they marched across the parade ground and along the road through the camp to get their belongings from the barracks. Trucks were waiting as those who had not been chosen quietly and listlessly gathered up their things, preparing to leave.

Vorczek collected his belongings and rejoined the squad outside the barracks, then they marked up the road with Kosanovic. The upper camp came into view, looking like an alpine village. The headquarters was the only building that was remotely military, with a flagpole in front of it and the flag waving lazily in the breeze. A bronze statue of a sondercommando stood before the flagpole, a bronze plaque on its base listing the names of sondercommandos who had been killed in combat.

The other buildings along the neat, tree-lined street looked like chalets, with thick log walls and sharply-pitched roofs. A ball field, parade ground, and small arms range were in an open, level valley at the end of the street. Men in black sondercommando fatigues were playing ball on the field. Others walked along the street and went in and out of the buildings in a subdued bustle of activity.

Civilians did the detail work at the camp. Two old men were sweeping the street, while others piled crates and emptied garbage cans at the rear of the dining hall. A civilian was in charge of the supply building where sondercommando uniforms were issued to Vorczek and the others.

They went next to a classroom, where Kosanovic introduced a stout, middle-aged woman with stern features as one of the instructors. She issued textbooks, notebooks, and German dictionaries in the native language of those who did not speak German. Vorczek signed for his, then looked through the mathematics textbook in apprehension as he waited.

The billets were small chalets with private rooms on each side of a central hall. Vorczek carried his things into his room and put them away. The room was luxurious, the late afternoon sun shining through the window and gleaming on the paneled walls where pictures hung. The Brandenburg Division insignia was in a frame above the desk.

The dining hall was a large room with a quiet, serene atmosphere. Windows along one side overlooked the forested slopes of the mountain and the shimmering blue expanse of Lake Quenz below. Chandeliers hung from the high beamed ceiling, and the walls were decorated with flags and other battle trophies captured by sonder-commandos.

The food was delicious, but Vorczek found the camaraderie even more satisfying. Kosanovic sat at the table and talked with Vorczek and the others about the training schedule as they ate. Officers sat with enlisted men at other tables. Formal terms of address were used, but the men were more friendly than military in attitude.

Kosanovic dismissed Vorczek and the others after they had finished eating. As they returned to the billets, men were gathering in front of a training building that was used at night as a motion picture theater, while music came from the canteen. Corporals and sergeants walked along the street toward the road to the town, their badges and boots gleaming.

The other nine men in the squad went to the canteen and the theater. Vorczek was tempted to go with them, since the entertainment was a luxurious novelty. But he was worried about the complexity of the textbooks, so he sat down at his desk and began looking through them. Darkness fell and the camp became quiet as Vorczek continued to study, thumbing through his dictionary to translate unfamiliar terms.

Footsteps came along the hall; doors opened and closed. Then Vorczek's door opened and Kosanovic looked in. Vorczek pushed his chair back and stood up. The sergeant glanced at the books on the desk as he stepped into the room, a clipboard under his arm. "You didn't want to go to the canteen or to the theater, Vorczek?" he asked.

"Yes, but I thought I should look at my books. . ."

His voice faded, Kosanovic frowning and shaking his head over the reply in Polish. "Speak only in German, Vorczek, as I did," the sergeant ordered firmly. "Speak in German, and think in German." His frown faded and he smiled faintly. "You should be able to by now. I understand that you studied your German textbook every night while you were in the primary training camp."

"Yes, I did. How did you know about that, Sergeant Kosanovic?"

"We find out all we can about the men there so we can make the right selections," Kosanovic replied. His smile became more friendly, then he chuckled. "And it attracts attention when someone sits in the latrine for hours each night. But you have your own room now, so you won't have to go to the latrine to have light to read."

"I will need to work very hard," Vorczek said, looking at the textbooks. "I only went to a village school, and I don't know if I will be able to do as well as I should."

Kosanovic nodded confidently. "You will. All the men here are those who excel, but you have something extra. You're the type of man who strives to push a step ahead of others. That is why you studied your German textbook at night, and that is why you're here instead of at the canteen or the theater." His eyes narrowed, and he tapped on his clipboard to emphasize his words as he continued. "When we were selecting the men in your squad, I told Major

Buehler that you would do better than the others. I don't like to be proven wrong, Vorczek."

"I will do my best, Sergeant Kosanovic."

Kosanovic grunted and nodded in satisfaction, taking a large envelope from under the papers on his clipboard. "That is all I ask. I have something here that will help you." He opened the envelope and took out a photograph. "I'm sure you know who this is."

The photograph was grainy and slightly blurred, a copy of another photograph. Vorczek took it, puzzled. "Yes, of course, Sergeant Kosanovic. But how will this help me?"

"It will remind you of why we are here, Vorczek."

Vorczek looked at the photograph again, then slowly nodded. "Yes, it will. Thank you, Sergeant Kosanovic."

Kosanovic nodded and slapped Vorczek's shoulder, then turned to the door and went out. It was quiet after his footsteps faded along the hall, the radiator under the window clicking softly and the breeze stirring the trees outside. Vorczek looked at the photograph for a long moment, then went to his locker. Opening the locker, he pushed the edge of the photograph under the molding at the top of the door.

He returned to his desk and began leafing through a textbook. Then, the photograph drawing his attention again, he looked at it. It was on the edge of the light from the lamp on the desk, barely visible. But the features were engraved in Vorczek's memory—the thick mustache, narrow eyes, and sardonic half-smile. In Russia, that face had stared down from buildings, factory walls, and every other place where a poster could be hung. The photograph was of Josef Stalin.

Training began at seven, after reveille and breakfast.

The morning was taken up by classes in mathematics, history, geography, and astronomy. After lunch, there was a class in tactics and logistics for small forces operating in hostile territory. The rest of the day was devoted to basic weaponry that would eventually range from arms up through heavy machine guns and mortars. The classes ended at six in the evening.

While the others went to the canteen and to the theater, Vorczek sat at his desk and studied his notes and textbooks. The language remained a problem. Many words used in the classes were technical terms that were unfamiliar to him, and he could read German only with difficulty and frequent reference to his dictionary.

The material being taught was even more of a problem. The instruction in tactics, logistics, and weaponry was easy for him, but that in the academic subjects assumed a higher level of education than he possessed. The men returned to the billets when the theater and canteen closed for the night, but Vorczek still sat at his desk for hours, laboriously reading the assigned pages in the texts. And still the instruction the following day seemed to have no relationship to what he had studied the night before.

By the fourth day, Vorczek felt he was being inundated with unrelated bits of information and falling further behind each day. He was numb from lack of sleep, staring at the picture of Stalin to stir his hate and keep his mind alert when he studied. His desire to do better than the others now seemed hopeless. He had an agonizing sense of being on the verge of losing his opportunity to avenge what the Russians had done to him and his family. Everything that mattered to him was gone—his family dead or lost, his village destroyed, his country ravaged. The Brandenburg Division had the potential of becoming an anchor in his life, something meaningful to him. Sondercommandos were a closely-knit brotherhood linked by a common bond that was symbolized by the sondercommando badge. He had to have that badge.

Others in his squad also had difficulty with the training, but they were reluctant to forego their entertainment. The entire camp assembled on Saturday, and Buehler and Kosanovic sat at a table in the headquarters and counted out money as men saluted and signed the payroll. Vorczek received eighteen marks, more money than he had ever possessed. His squad was free until Monday morning at reveille, and the other nine men left the billets in a noisy group as Vorczek sat down at his desk to continue studying.

Then, at a point when the situation appeared hopeless, it changed. He was suddenly fluent in German. The long hours of study had yielded results. The instructions also took on concrete purpose. Mathematics became the means to measure distance with a theodolite, or to calculate the trajectory of a mortar round. It combined with astronomy into ground navigation, and history and geography became geopolitics.

Achieving momentum in the classroom work took a supreme effort, but it was easy to maintain after it was done. Vorczek reviewed past material and learned it thoroughly, then read ahead in the texts, forging past the others in his squad. When several of them began asking his advice and seeking his help in some of the subjects, he found himself exercising an increasing degree of leadership as he helped them.

In the labor camp, Vorczek had often found himself taking the initiative and making suggestions when others had been uncertain about what to do. The same thing had happened at Pahlavi, almost resulting in his promotion to corporal. It happened again now. Instructors began leaving Vorczek in charge when they were absent from the classroom, and he gradually emerged as the leader of the squad.

Kosanovic began asking Vorczek about the squad and discussing the progress of individuals with him. Beuhler, frequently greeting a few men when he came in the dining hall during meals, began nodding to Vorczek. When tests were administered at the end of the fourth week of training, Vorczek's scores were well above average. At the reveille formation the following morning, Buehler called Vorczek out of the ranks and handed him a set of lance corporal badges.

On the following Saturday, there were an additional five marks in Vorczek's pay. Vorczek returned to the billets then, taking out his books as the other men prepared to leave for town, laughing and talking as they tramped along the hall. Then quiet settled, Vorczek working at his desk.

Heavy footsteps came along the hall an hour later, stopping outside Vorczek's door. Kosanovic opened the door and looked in. "What are you doing, Vorczek?" he asked.

Vorczek pushed his chair back and stood up. "I'm working on a map, Sergeant Kosanovic."

"When is it due?"

"No date has been set. The instructor said to study it and be prepared to discuss it, and she would set a date later."

"In that event, you should go to town and have a few beers, Vorczek. It doesn't happen very often, but you will probably be promoted to corporal when you finish training. You're doing everything I expected and more, but you also need to relax occasionally."

His tone was friendly, but there was a firm undercurrent in it. Vorczek nodded. "Very well, Sergeant Kosanovic."

After Kosanovic had left, Vorczek gathered up the papers and books on his desk and put them in his locker. Then he took out his tunic and cap and put them on as he went out. He walked along the street through the camp to the road leading down the mountain to the town. The road was deserted. It curved and twisted down the mountain through the thick forest, the only sound that of birds in the trees. The trees thinned out and disappeared near the foot of the mountain, then the sunshine down on vineyards on each side of the road. The town spread back up the slope from the blue expanse of the lake, a jumble of sharply-pitched slate roofs along a maze of ancient, narrow streets. The other men in Vorczek's squad had talked about the Gasthaus Lautzen, a place frequented by men from the camp, but Vorczek was unsure of where it was located.

Stopping at an intersection where the narrow streets went off at odd angles, Vorczek saw a gasthaus on a corner across the street. It looked clean and quiet, set back from the main flow of traffic. The apartment above it had ornate shutters on the windows and flower boxes on the windowsills. Vorczek walked across the street toward it.

The doorway and ceiling were low, and it was cool and dim inside. There were no customers. The only person in the front room was a young woman drying glasses behind the bar. Vorczek closed the door and took off his cap as he went over to the bar. The girl, about eighteen years old, was very pretty. Her long, thick blond hair was pinned on top of her head, and she had a full, shapely figure.

Her eyes moved up and down him quickly as she smiled in greeting. "Good day. Would you like something to drink?"

"Good day. I would like a glass of beer, please."

She finished wiping a glass and filled it, then picked up the mark he put on the bar, dropped it in a coin box under the bar, and placed his change in front of him. Then she began wiping another glass, glancing up at him from under her lashes and lowering her eyes again.

Vorczek took a drink from the glass, smiling at her. "Do you work here all the time?"

"Herr Koehler, the owner, is my father. I only help with the work occasionally. You are from Poland, aren't you?"

"Yes, but I am a citizen now. My name is Anton Vorczek."

"Mine is Frieda."

"I am very pleased to meet you."

Frieda smiled and nodded in reply, wiping another glass. After a moment passed in silence, she glanced up at Vorczek and looked back down at the glass. She seemed wary rather than aloof, carefully weighing how he acted and looked, what he said. Sipping his beer, Vorczek started to speak again, then a door behind the bar opened.

A short, stout man with features that remotely resembled Frieda's came through the doorway, carrying a keg of beer. His neutral expression changed into a suspicious frown as he glanced between Vorczek and Frieda. He slid the keg under the bar and turned to Frieda as he straightened up. "If that is all of the glasses, Frieda, you can go upstairs now."

"There is another tray of glasses in the kitchen. This is Lance Corporal Vorczek, Father."

Vorczek put down his glass and bowed. Koehler

grunted, looking at Vorczek narrowly. He dusted his hands together and hesitated, glancing from Vorczek to Frieda again, then went back through the door. As his footsteps faded, Vorczek spoke quietly. "Your father doesn't want me to talk with you, does he?"

Frieda smiled and shrugged. "What father wants his daughter talking with soldiers he doesn't know? But most of the soldiers go to the Gasthaus Lautzen. Is that where you go most of the time?"

"I have never been there. This is the first time I have been to town since I came here, because I work very hard on my training."

Frieda looked at his badges again, surprised. "You are a lance corporal and you haven't finished your training?"

"I am progressing very rapidly."

"You must be. And if you continue working that hard, you may be promoted to corporal."

"Yes, Sergeant Kosanovic said I may."

Frieda smiled and nodded, looking back down at the glass she was drying. She suddenly seemed more congenial and inviting, her smile coquettish. She was a beautiful girl. The laces on her bodice were taut from the pressure of her large, thrusting breasts. Her dress hugged her tiny waist and flared out over the smooth, full curves of her hips. Her lips looked moist and soft.

Vorczek took a drink of beer, smiling at her. "Would your father let me come and see you if I asked him?"

Frieda shook her head doubtfully. "I don't think so, but you should ask *me* first. Why do you want to come and see me?"

"Because you're very beautiful, and I like you."

Frieda glanced at him in appraisal again. Vorczek searched for more persuasive phrases, then stopped himself as she pursed her lips musingly and looked away. She pondered for a moment, then leaned toward him. "I'll introduce you to my mother," she said softly.

"Can she get your father to let me come and see you?"

"Yes, if she approves of you. If you get to know her and my father, we can go walking together."

A tinge of a flush rose to her cheeks as her eyes danced, her tone suggesting that going walking together was a euphemism for something far more intimate. Vorczek put his hand over hers. "Will you introduce me to your mother today?"

Frieda glanced at the doorway behind the bar, pulling her hand from under his. She nodded. "Yes. She enjoys playing bezique. Do you know the game?"

"No."

Frieda took his glass, refilled it and looked through the doorway for her father as she returned. Waving the money away as Vorczek started to take more from his pocket, she reached under the bar for a deck of cards. She began shuffling the cards, smiling up at him. "I'll teach you how to play bezique," she said. "We don't have much time, so you must pay close attention. And the first thing you must learn is to always let my mother win."

Vorczek laughed and nodded. "As a soldier, I know that small defeats are sometimes necessary to win the greater victory."

Freida flushed again as she nodded, smiling, then began dealing the cards.

CHAPTER TEN

KEELER LIT A cigarette as he walked out onto the road. The stark, harsh light of the early morning sun made every stone and clump of brush in the barren landscape stand out in sharp relief. The dirt road was a narrow, rutted shelf on the side of a steep mountain, disappearing around sharp curves a hundred yards away in each direction. On the horizon to the north, the craggy mountains along the border between Turkey and Iran were etched against the morning sky.

As he stood and looked around, Chadwick Meacham, one of his two operatives, walked out onto the road. Meacham's beefy, sagging face was bleary with sleep, and his suit and topcoat were rumpled. He yawned, hitching up his trousers over his bulging stomach. "It's very clear and sunny this morning, isn't it, Mr. Keeler?"

"Yes."

"Yes, it is indeed, isn't it? Well, if our man's coming, he should be along just directly, shouldn't he?"

"Yes."

Meacham smothered another yawn and rubbed his face,

the stubble on his heavy jowls rasping against his palms. "Well, I'll just go and stir Charles out, shall I?"

"Very well."

Meacham turned and walked back into the hollow at the side of the road. It was a caravanserie on a trading route that had been in use at the dawn of recorded history, carved into the mountain by the erosion of eons and finished off by nameless laborers centuries before. A large Army truck, an olive drab Chevrolet staff car, and a jeep were parked at the rear of the hollow, looking rudely modern in contrast to the ruins of the shelters and animal pens made of native stone and sun-dried bricks.

Soldiers moved around a fire on one side of the hollow, putting away their bedrolls and heating water to make tea. Campbell, the Tenth Army intelligence officer, sat by a fire on the opposite side. His ruddy face was pouchy and lined with sleep and he rubbed his eyes and brushed at his thick, white mustaches.

Meacham went to the staff car and pounded the rear door with a fist, shouting, "Wake up, Charles! You can't sleep all bloody day!"

The door opened and Callaghan got out, smiling sleepily. The American OSS resident in Teheran, he was a tall and deceptively awkward-looking man who moved with lithe, athletic ease. "Goddamn, Chad," he groaned. "If you knew how my head feels, you wouldn't do that."

"Aye, well, it'll serve you right for tippling too much, won't it? In England, we call that knocking someone up, you know."

"Yeah, I know. Just for the hell of it, I'll put in my report that I got knocked up on this trip. I'll let you know what they say."

Meacham laughed heartily as he and Callaghan walked

toward the fire where Campbell sat. Najafi, an Iranian police sergeant from Teheran, was asleep in the rear of the jeep. He stirred as Meacham and Callaghan passed, then settled himself again. Galzinski, a young Polish lieutenant, was bundled in blankets, asleep in the bed of the truck.

Campbell folded his blankets, talking with Meacham and Callaghan as they sat down by the fire. Keeler took a drag on his cigarette and tossed it away, then joined them.

"This is the big day, Frank," Callaghan said.

Keeler nodded, sitting down by the fire. "Yes."

"I'd sure like to know how you went about tracking all of this down," Callaghan said. "But that's just wishful thinking, and not a request for information. I know you can't reveal your sources and procedures. You certainly put all the pieces together, though."

"The game's yet to be bagged, old chap," Campbell said doubtfully. "Still and all, this reflects more insight and more of a professional touch than the man you replaced could have managed, Keeler. Have you been with MI-6 for a good many years, then?"

"Yes."

The colonel nodded, waiting for a further comment. Keeler took out his cigarettes and lit one in silence. There was an awkward pause, then Callaghan slapped his hands against his thighs as he stood up and looked around. "Who's for an eye opener?" he asked cheerfully. "I believe I have another jug in the trunk of the car."

"I wouldn't mind sweetening my tea with a drop," Meacham replied, then he glanced cautiously at Keeler. "But perhaps it would be best for me to forego it. I'll want a clear head, won't I?"

"I will too," Callaghan laughed, walking toward the staff car. "But I won't have it until I've had a drink."

Campbell leaned toward Keeler and spoke quietly as Callaghan walked away. "Did I get on touchy ground, Keeler? I didn't think how long you've been with the Service would be secret."

"It isn't."

Campbell nodded, brushing his mustaches with a finger. "Yes, well, I didn't think so. . . ." His voice faded as he waited for a reply. Then, Keeler remaining silent, Campbell cleared his throat and brushed his mustaches again as he looked at the other fire. "Well, the men have finished making tea, it appears."

Two soldiers approached, carrying tin cups and an aluminum kettle. Callaghan rummaged in the trunk of the staff car and took out a bottle of whiskey. Najafi sat up in the rear of the jeep, looking around sleepily, then climbed out. Galzinski jumped down from the bed of the truck, yawning and stretching as he walked toward the fire with Callaghan and Najafi.

The soldiers filled the cups with black, unsweetened tea, then Callaghan passed the bottle around. Campbell poured a substantial amount of whiskey into his tea, and Keeler poured an ounce into his. Smiling in satisfaction, Meacham poured several ounces into his when the bottle was passed to him and Najafi and Galzinski each followed suit.

Keeler smoked and drank his tea, listening to the conversation between Meacham and Callaghan. Callaghan had obtained the truck, staff car, and jeep from the American garrison at Tabriz, but security precautions had prevented his revealing the true reason the vehicles were needed. He told Meacham the story he had concocted and Meacham roared with laughter as he took gulps from his cup.

The sergeant major in charge of the soldiers walked over from the other fire and stamped his feet as he saluted Campbell. "Sir, request permission to have the men serve up their morning rations, sir!" he barked in a blurred rush of syllables.

Campbell glanced at his watch and turned to Keeler. "According to your calculations, the convoy should be along any time now, shouldn't they, Keeler?"

"Yes."

Campbell looked at the sergeant major. "Have the men wait a bit, Sar' Major. Perhaps we can get the job done first."

The sergeant major stamped and saluted again, then marched back to his men. Campbell took a drink from his cup and brushed his mustaches as he looked at Keeler. "I hope this won't be a waste of time, Keeler. You do realize that it entailed no small difficulty to get that platoon of soldiers from their company, don't you?"

"Yes."

"The brigadier said that you're to have full cooperation, and you may be sure that you'll have it from me. But I'll look a proper fool if we return empty-handed, won't I? Are you reasonably sure that the man you're after will be along here directly?"

"Yes."

"Well, I trust you're right. It did strike the brigadier odd that you'd worry about a few Polish soldiers disappearing when saboteurs are raising hob all along the railway, and I can't but agree with him. But back to front or not, he said that you're to have full cooperation. And I will cooperate, but I do have more to do than chase about on. . . ."

He broke off as a shrill electronic squeal came from a backpack radio across the hollow. The radio operator ran to the set and silence fell as the man spoke into the handset. Then he lifted the pack and slid an arm through one of the straps, the long antenna swaying.

The radio operator ran across the hollow, calling to Campbell. "The lookout has spotted a convoy, sir. Do you want to speak with him?"

Keeler turned to the radio operator as Campbell hesitated. "Ask if one of the vehicles is a dark green, five ton Mercedes, the bed covered with canvas."

The radio operator put his arm through the other strap and settled the pack on his back, talking into the handset. He listened, then nodded to Keeler. "That's the third one in the convoy, sir."

Keeler turned to Campbell. "That's our target."

"By God!" Campbell exclaimed triumphantly, standing. "Are you certain? We'll soon set him to rights, then! Sar' Major, get your men sorted out, and send the sharpshooter over here!"

The sergeant major roared orders, galvanizing the soldiers into a scrambling bustle of activity. Callaghan ran toward the staff car as Najafi and Galzinski headed for the jeep. Meacham looked around excitedly, gulping down his tea and whiskey. A young corporal carrying an Enfield with a telescopic sight trotted over from the other fire.

Campbell beckoned the sharpshooter. "Step on over here, lad. You know what to do, don't you? Try not to kill him, because Mr. Keeler here is interested in having a word with him. Take your shot as soon as the last vehicle in the convoy comes around that curve down there, because that'll be our signal."

"Yes, sir."

"Get up on that cliff, then, and do us a proper good job." He turned to Keeler as the corporal sprinted away. "Keeler, it would be best if you and the other non-combatants stayed here until we get the convoy stopped and the guards on it settled."

"No, I'll get behind that fall of rock just along the road."

"Very well, but you're at your own risk, you know."

Keeler nodded, taking a drag on his cigarette and tossing it into the fire. He walked toward the road, Meacham following him reluctantly and Callaghan close behind, carrying a Browning submachine gun. He loaded a clip into it as they walked along to a jumble of rocks that had slid down the steep bank at the side of the road.

The sharpshooter climbed over a boulder on the bluff overlooking the road, then disappeared. Keeler sat down on a rock out of view from the road.

Campbell led the soldiers along the road, the sergeant major sending them off the side of it in twos and threes. Rocks tumbled into the gorge below as the soldiers climbed over the edge of the road and concealed themselves.

The jeep pulled to the edge of the hollow and stopped out of view from the road. Silence settled, broken only by the chugging of the idling jeep engine. A hawk circled high above, riding the updrafts from the rugged, mountainous terrain. A breeze moved along the road and stirred puffs of dust, carrying with it a distant sound of roaring engines.

The sound gradually grew louder. The trucks climbed the steep grade on the other side of the curve, engines laboring and transmissions scraping. The volume of sound grew to a blaring roar as the trucks filed around the curve.

The sharpshooter's Enfield fired with a shattering clap. Brakes squealed and tires slid on the road. Guards on the trucks fired wildly, thinking they were under attack by bandits. The jeep skidded onto the road and raced toward the trucks, Galzinski driving as Najafi leaned over the windshield and shouted through a megaphone. A soldier in the rear of the jeep trained a mounted machine gun on the trucks.

The jeep's windshield exploded as a bullet struck it. The jeep slewed sideways and stopped, Galzinski sliding down in the seat. Najafi ducked and screamed through the megaphone. The machine gun thundered in bursts, spewing brass. Soldiers along the road fired into the air. As the gunfire from the trucks died away, Keeler leaped out and ran toward the trucks which had halted in a ragged line, guards jumping down from them. Sporadic shots rang out. Campbell bellowed a warning at Keeler from the other side of the road. Footsteps pounded behind him, then Callaghan ran past him. A bullet struck the road a few feet ahead, kicking up a plume of dust. Callaghan's submachine gun roared as he fired into the air.

The wind pulled Keeler's hat from his head and whipped his trench coat around his knees. A guard stood by the first truck, fingering his rifle uncertainly. Keeler hit the man with his shoulder and knocked him sprawling. A cluster of guards standing by the second truck scattered as Keeler leaped onto the running board of the third truck and jerked the door open.

The driver cowered against his door in terror. The

passenger was a heavyset man in European clothes and a tweed topcoat. He sagged forward, blood welling from a hole in the shoulder of his topcoat. Keeler seized his collar and jumped back, dragging him out of the truck. Rimless eyeglasses with thick lenses fell off as the man tumbled out. Keeler knelt over the man, prising his mouth open and groping in it.

But he was too late. Tiny shards of glass were in the saliva. The teeth pressed Keeler's fingers with a pulsing pressure as convulsive quivers passed through the man's body and his limbs jerked. A strong, bitter almond-like odor came from the mouth. Keeler stood up, taking out his handkerchief and wiping his hand.

Meacham ran up with Keeler's hat, puffing heavily. He and Callaghan looked at Keeler interrogatively. Keeler glanced at them and shook his head as he put his handkerchief away and took his hat. Meacham grunted in disappointment; Callaghan sighed and looked away. Soldiers swarmed around the trucks, assembling the guards and drivers.

Campbell walked around to Keeler. "Is he alive, Keeler?" he asked.

"Not for very long," Keeler replied, taking out his cigarettes. "The sharpshooter is to be commended for an excellent job. But I was too slow in getting to the man, and he took cyanide."

"By God, he did, didn't he?" Campbell murmured in wonder, looking down at the man. "Can you fathom someone doing such a thing?"

Keeler nodded as he lit a cigarette. "Yes."

Campbell blinked, looking at Keeler. Then he cleared his throat and brushed his mustaches as he turned away. "Aye, well, he's been dealt with, and that's the main thing, isn't it?'' He stepped to the rear of the truck and frowned as he looked in. ''You get out of there! Galzinski, come over here and take charge of these traitors! Keeler, do you want to let the rest of the convoy go on?''

''I'll have a look at them first. Najafi, get this driver out of here and tie him, then come with me and translate, if you would.''

Najafi climbed into the cab of the truck and dragged the driver out. Six Polish soldiers clambered down from the bed of the truck, their faces transfixed with fear. Galzinski and two others shoved them along the road toward the caravanserie. The dying man's muscular contractions became hard, driving spasms, his limbs stirring dust on the road. Then the movements diminished and stopped.

Callaghan and Meacham took pictures of the man's face with pocket cameras; then Callaghan turned to Keeler. ''Can you tell me his name and what service he was with, Frank?''

''Rulen Moltke,'' Keeler replied, taking a drag on his cigarette. ''He was an Abwehr operative. Meacham, you know what to do.''

Callaghan laughed as Meacham nodded in glum distaste. ''I'll give you a hand, Chad,'' he said. ''And I'll even flip a coin with you to see who pulls his shitty drawers off him.''

Meacham smiled weakly as they began dragging the body to the edge of the road. The driver stood beside the truck and shivered in fright, his thumbs tied together behind him. Gagging sounds came from his mouth as Najafi tied a cord tightly around his neck and to a slat on the bed of the truck, then followed Keeler along the road to the first truck in the convoy.

All of the guards were mercenaries who had been hired

by the drivers for the trip. Most of them had rusty, decrepit weapons that dated back to World War I, but nine had new Mauser model 98 carbines and two others had new Walther P-38 pistols. Najafi took those with the new German weapons to one side to question later, then translated as Keeler questioned the drivers and checked the papers and cargoes on the trucks.

The only connection between the trucks was the fact that they were traveling in convoy for mutual protection. Nothing was unusual about any of them except the fifth one in line, which looked suspicious. It was battered and rusty, but in excellent mechanical condition, with new tires. The cargo included crates of pottery, two bales of camel hair, and other miscellaneous items of relatively modest value, but the driver had hired a large number of guards.

The truck was en route from Teheran to Diyarbakir, the papers listing a firm in Teheran as the owner. Keeler was familiar with the firm. It was a front for an Arab named Rashid al-Kharis, one of the major drug dealers in Iran. The name had come to Keeler's attention when he had heard that Kharis had collaborated with the Germans in the past. Kharis was also connected with a Kashgai tribe located north of Teheran, providing him with a private army.

The driver's eyes were keen despite a smooth, fawning smile as Najafi translated questions and replies. Keeler took a drag on his cigarette as he asked another question: "Where is the heroin hidden?"

Najafi translated the question into Pharsi. The driver replied in a protesting voice; then Najafi translated the reply: "I know nothing about heroin. I have only the goods listed on my papers."

"You are lying," Keeler said. "I will ask the question again. If you lie again, I will have the soldiers unload the cargo and search it for contraband. Where is the heroin hidden?"

Najafi translated, the color draining from the driver's face. He fumbled in his sleeve, moving closer to Keeler and Najafi, then turned his hand toward them, displaying a thick roll of bills. Najafi looked at the money, then at Keeler. Keeler shook his head. The driver glanced around and spoke in a soft whisper, Najafi translating.

"I never load all my cargo at the same place. Most of it is loaded at a warehouse on Sahyun Shamra, but for the camel hair I go to the meat market in the main marketplace. And I go after dark."

Keeler took a drag on his cigarette, nodding. The meat market was in a corner of the main marketplace where spaces were owned by several dealers. It was a strange place to pick up bales of camel hair, and it also closed at sundown. But the information fit with other facts Keeler had acquired.

He had routinely investigated a chemist named Erasmo Biehler, who was employed as a butcher at the meat market. Nothing about him had been unusual, except that he was an educated man working at a menial job. But the meat market would provide perfect cover for a laboratory where heroin was made from opium. It appeared that Kharis owned a shop in the meat market, where Biehler worked as a chemist rather than as a butcher.

"A European works at the place where you load the camel hair," Keeler said. "A small man who limps and has a beard."

Beads of sweat stood out on the driver's face as he nodded and whispered affirmatively. Keeler handed the papers back to Najafi, who returned them to the driver and deftly plucked the roll of money out of the man's hand. The driver smiled and nodded in relief as he put the papers in his pocket. Keeler walked back toward the third truck, Najafi pocketing the money and following him.

Meacham and Callaghan had finished stripping the body and were wrapping it in a blanket. The clothing was folded, the contents of the pockets piled by it. The passport was Swiss and the wallet contained cover identifcation that matched it. Several keys were on a ring with what appeared to be a good luck charm, old and worn down to a metal disc.

The thick eyeglasses were rolled in a handkerchief. Meacham had used grease from a truck axle to take fingerprints on a sheet of paper that was folded under a pocket flask with silver cups nested on it. There was an ink pen, a silver cigarette lighter, a thick roll of Iranian money as well as ten of the heavy gold coins that German operatives used for paying those who were reluctant to accept paper money.

Keeler glanced through the things, then turned to Callaghan. "Did you get a look at everything, Charles?"

Callaghan laughed dryly as he knelt to help Meacham gather up the clothes. "You bet I did. This might be the only chance I'll ever get to see a real German operative."

Meacham guffawed, and Keeler smiled as he turned and walked toward the guards with new German weapons. Najafi followed him and summoned the first guard with an impatient wave, one who had a Mauser carbine. Keeler questioned him about it, Najafi translating. The man said he had bought the carbine in Sarbandan, a large village a few miles from Tabriz, but he knew nothing about the man who had sold it to him. The others told the same exact story.

When the convoy drove on along the road, the noise and activity subsided. The soldiers began opening tins of rations as Meacham, Callaghan, and Campbell sat around their fire. The six Polish soldiers sat beside the Army truck in the caravanserie under guard. Najafi pushed Moltke's driver down to a sitting position at the edge of the road in front of the caravanserie, then went to the jeep. Keeler sat on a rock a few yards away and lit a cigarette.

Najafi returned with a night stick and a length of thin, strong cord that was knotted at half-inch intervals. He put them down by the driver, then folded his arms and looked into the distance, motionless and impassive. The others began eating, talking quietly and watching Keeler. A soldier took food to the Polish prisoners, then asked Keeler if he wanted to eat. Keeler shook his head.

The driver became more nervous as the minutes dragged by, looking up at Najafi and murmuring questions in a quaking voice. Najafi ignored him. Keeler finished his cigarette and tossed it away, then began the interrogation. The driver had been under surveillance, and Keeler knew a lot about him. He began with what he knew, and the driver began lying. Keeler lit another cigarette and nodded to Najafi.

Najafi used the night stick, the driver writhing and squealing in pain. The Polish soldiers stopped eating and watched, appalled. Others craned their necks and stretched, watching. The driver began screaming shrilly and throwing himself from side to side. Keeler nodded to Najafi. The policeman straightened up and stepped back.

The driver curled on his side on the road, quivering and moaning. Najafi straightened his cap and dusted his uniform, then folded his arms and looked into the distance again, waiting. Keeler finished his cigarette and waited for a moment, then began the interrogation again. The driver lay on his side, whimpering replies. He was still lying. Keeler nodded to Najafi.

Najafi used the knotted cord. Centering it on the man's forehead, he tied it firmly and slid the night stick under it at the back of the man's head. Then he spun the night stick, tightening the cord. The man jerked up to a sitting position, his eyes bulging. Then he began shrieking and drumming his heels against the road.

The man's hoarse screams of agony resounded in the hollow and stirred echoes from nearby hills. Dark streaks of urine spread down his trousers. Vomit spewed from his mouth. Then he went limp and sagged. Keeler nodded to Najafi. The policeman released the pressure on the night stick and let it unwind, untied the cord and took it off the man's head.

When the driver was able to talk, he told what he knew. And having worked for Moltke for months, on the inside and at the hub of Moltke's operation, he knew a lot. Keeler pieced together each step of recruiting the Polish soldiers and transporting them to Turkey to be flown to Germany, filling blank gaps in what he already knew.

Keeler asked about Sarbandan, where the guards on the trucks had obtained new German weapons. The driver replied in a quavering, breathless whisper, Najafi kneeling by him and listening closely as he translated. The man had driven Moltke to Sarbandan on two occasions. Moltke had visited a merchant named Faraj. The driver described Faraj, and his description matched that of the one who had sold German weapons to the guards. He described the place where Faraj lived, as well as an oilcloth-covered package that Moltke had brought back after the first visit. Keeler exhausted the subject and expanded the interrogation, searching for other information of value.

And he found it. Money had been passed through the courier network from Berlin for Moltke to deliver to agents, but Moltke had been ill. The driver, having acted as the courier, knew the contact procedures for every Abwehr agent in Iran.

One was located in Abadan. The drop was a niche under a tombstone in a graveyard, a wreath on the grave the alert signal to notify the agent to check the drop. The agent was a sleeper, inactive and waiting for when he was needed. Three drops had been made in Teheran. One had been to Mueller, Keeler's double agent with the Abwehr. Another had been to the owner of an apartment building, a man named Abolfazi. The recognition signal was a specific way of asking about an apartment. The third had been to a blind drop in the railway station, the alert signal an envelope sent through the local mail. The driver was unable to remember anything about the envelope except the fact that the name on it had been European.

Keeler explored other avenues but learned nothing more of value. The man's presence of mind returning, he frantically searched for other things to tell Keeler. It became repetitious. Keeler dropped his cigarette and stepped on it as he stood up, nodding toward the edge of the road. Najafi gripped the man's shoulder and pulled him along.

The man went limp, shrieking and wailing. Najafi seized his collar and dragged him through the rocks and dust. The man screamed frantically, then his screams were drowned by the sharp report of Najafi's pistol. Keeler walked toward the fire as Najafi pushed the body off the edge of the road and followed him.

Meacham had been drinking more whiskey, his eyelids heavy. Callaghan's features were expressionless, while Campbell frowned at Keeler in stern disapproval. The stew in the kettle by the fire had dried. Keeler poured tea into a tin cup and sat down. Najafi spooned lumps of stew into a mess kit and sat down, eating hungrily.

"You don't fancy anything to eat, Keeler?" Campbell remarked. "I've never been one for eating in the day, and that business with that poor driver took away the little appetite I did have. I shouldn't think that I'd have much of an appetite for a week or more, if I were you. You'll want to go to that house you mentioned when we return to Tabriz, won't you?"

"Yes."

"The men and I will secure it for you first, in event of any difficulty with guards and such. I may as well have the men get ready to leave. It'll be dark by the time we get there."

Keeler took a drink of tea and nodded toward the Polish soldiers. "I'd like to question them before we leave."

Campbell frowned and nodded cautiously. "Very well, but you will bear in mind that they're military prisoners, won't you? I have six of them now, and I want to have six when I get back to Teheran. Further, I won't countenance having them bashed about."

"I believe they'll answer my questions readily enough."

Still frowning, Campbell grunted and nodded as he brushed his mustaches. Callaghan suddenly burst into howls of laughter at what Keeler had said, slapping his knees. Meacham blinked drowsily and looked at him, then began laughing, as did Najafi and Galzinski. Campbell relaxed, chuckling wryly.

"By God, I'll bet they *do* tell you all they know, Frank," Callaghan said, chuckling as he picked up the whiskey bottle. "*I* sure as hell would. Do you feel like a drink?"

"No, thank you."

Callaghan took a swing from the bottle and puffed on his cigarette. "That sure was a smooth operation, Frank," he said. "You must have agents planted everywhere, and I wish I had the same. Would you care for another drink, Chad?"

Meacham glanced at Keeler and shook his head. "No, the sun is hardly over the yardarm yet, is it? But thank you all the same. You must have a few agents here and there, Charles."

"Damned few, and only in Teheran," Callaghan replied, offering the bottle to Campbell. The colonel poured whiskey into his cup as Callaghan sat back, looking at Meacham. "My ambassador controls my kitty," he said. "I don't have enough money for very many agents."

Meacham clicked his tongue and shook his head in solemn, alcoholic sympathy. "Oh, that's no bloody good, is it? Ambassadors have no grasp at all of intelligence operations."

"Mine just keeps telling me not to cause any trouble. I have one or two agents who should be on the inside of things, but I'm not getting much from them. This one guy I have on my roll gets in and out of everything repairing clocks, but he's not giving me anything but chicken feed. And he's a pain in the ass to work with, because he doesn't speak English and he insists on working through a cutout. But I don't mind the cutout too much, because I think the son of a bitch is a queer."

Meacham laughed, and Campbell snorted in disgust as he handed the bottle back. Keeler lit a cigarette, listening to the conversation. Callaghan's description fit a clock-maker in Teheran named Pourzand, who was Bergian and spoke no English, and who was homosexual. Keeler had considered enrolling him as an agent, then had dismissed it.

Pourzand was an NKVD agent. Vertinski, the NKVD resident, would be understandably irate if he found out that Pourzand had also enrolled with Callaghan. But the NKVD was notoriously stingy with money, while Pourzand was apparently a man of negotiable loyalties, as many agents were. Keeler took a drag on his cigarette and a drink of tea, as Meacham and Callaghan continued talking.

CHAPTER ELEVEN

MEACHAM'S ADENOIDAL BREATHING was loud in the stillness, and Callaghan a silent presence beside Keeler as they stood in the shadows and looked across the dark street. The pale light of the moon dimly illuminated the brick wall on the other side of the street. Shadows moved along the wall—soldiers silently creeping into position.

The guard at the foot gate scuffled with a soldier, then howled in pain. His outcry triggered a growing volume of noise that swelled into an uproar. Soldiers flowed through the gate, their boots pounding along the walk to the house. Lights came on. A door splintered with a rending crash. Women screamed and men shouted in alarm. Campbell and the sergeant major bellowed orders.

Keeler crossed the street and went through the gate and along the walk with Meacham and Callaghan. The shattered remains of the front door hung from its hinges. Soldiers dragged a protesting man around the veranda from the garage and took him inside. Keeler followed them into the front room which was crowded with soldiers and the household staff, the women weeping and the men looking around in fright.

Campbell pushed through the people toward Keeler. "Everything is secure, Keeler," he said. "I'll have some men with you and take my prisoners to the stockade at the garrison. We can meet later at the officers' mess."

"Very well, but don't wait for me. I may be a while."

"You'll be a bloody good while if you're not there before I leave. I'm for a good supper and something to take the dust out of my throat. What do you intend to do, Callaghan?"

"I'll tag along with you, George," Callaghan replied. "We can go in the jeep and leave the staff car for Frank and Chad."

"Aye, there's a good idea," Campbell said. "Sar' Major, detail a corporal and five men to remain, and we'll be on our way."

The sergeant major stamped and saluted. He selected the soldiers to remain behind, then he and the other soldiers followed Campbell, Callaghan, and Galzinski out. Najafi herded the servants into a corner of the front room as Keeler and Meacham went to the garage at the side of the house.

Keys on the ring that had been in Moltke's pocket fit the sedan in the garage. Meacham unlocked the doors and trunk, then took out the seats in the car. He prodded them with a screwdriver and searched the car as Keeler went over the garage walls, looking for hidden compartments where documents or equipment could be stored. They finished, finding nothing, then went back into the house.

It was fundamental tradecraft for operatives in enemy territory to maintain cover in their household, and Moltke had. Sitting at the table in the dining room, Keeler questioned the servants through Najafi while Meacham prowled in the study off the front room. Each related the same story; they believed Moltke had been a merchant.

Najafi took the last servant back into the front room, then returned to the dining room. "I have noticed that the furniture here is very valuable, Mr. Keeler," he commented, smiling widely.

"How would you get it back to Teheran?"

"I would dispose of it here. That would take two or three days, but the police captain expects me to return with you. If he believed that it was necessary for me to remain here for a few days. . . ."

He hesitated expectantly. Keeler nodded. "Very well, I'll tell the police captain that you will return within four days. Will you be able to get back to Teheran on your own?"

"Yes, I have ways," Najafi chuckled. "And naturally, I expect to pay a commission for your trouble. . . ."

Keeler shook his head, taking the key ring from his pocket and removing the car keys from it. "No, but I want everything left alone tonight. These fit the car. As always, Najafi, I want you to forget what I discussed with those I questioned today."

"I have already, because it never means anything to me," Najafi replied as he took the keys. "I will take the servants to the police station and make arrangements to have them held until I finish my business here. I will see you in Teheran in four days, Mr. Keeler."

"Very well."

Najafi smiled happily as he went back into the front room, where he barked orders at the servants, herding them out of the house. Keeler searched the drawers and doors in the buffet, then pulled the buffet away from the wall and looked behind it. He walked around the room and looked behind the pictures on the walls. Next he went into the study.

Meacham was opening drawers and piling folders and ledgers on the desk. Keeler took a stack of folders and glanced through them. They appeared to be filled with cover material that Moltke had accumulated in his role as a merchant; but the Abwehr occasionally communicated in various codes with agents through their cover addresses.

Keeler put the folders aside and picked up a ledger. "We'd better send all this to London so the technicians can sift through it. One of those cartons out in the garage will do to box it up for now."

Meacham went out as Keeler leafed through the ledger and returned a few minutes later with a cardboard carton into which he began piling folders. Keeler went into the front room. The soldiers lounged on the couch and chairs, talking quietly. Keeler went to the liquor cabinet in a corner and looked in it.

He turned to the corporal. "I won't need you any longer, Corporal. If you wish, you and your men may take this liquor and share it with the others."

The soldiers scrambled to their feet and collected around the cabinet, rattling the bottles as they eagerly gathered them up. After they left, talking and laughing happily, a steely quiet settled over the house. Keeler looked through the bookshelves, then went through the drawers in various tables.

Meacham came in from the study with the carton, stopping short and staring at the empty liquor cabinet in dismay. "I say, wasn't there a bottle or two in that cabinet, Mr. Keeler?"

"I gave it to the soldiers. Take the car and set up Ahmagian for a meeting, if you would."

Meacham nodded glumly as he put the carton on the couch, then left. Keeler finished searching the front room and walked along the hall to the rear of the house, his footsteps echoing. He searched the kitchen and the servants' quarters, then went to the master bedroom.

A chinoiserie cabinet against the wall beside the night stand had a strong lock on the door, which a key on Moltke's ring fit. After hesitating a long moment, Keeler took the key out of the lock without opening the door; it had been too easy. He went back along the hall and through the front room, around the veranda to the garage. After gathering up a handful of small tools, he reentered the house and returned to the bedroom. Keeler dug at the thick coatings of lacquer on the back of the cabinet with a screwdriver and pried up a panel. Taking the lamp from the night stand, he put it beside the cabinet, then put his eye to the crack behind the loose panel. No wires or springs were attached inside. He slid the screwdriver into the crack and removed the panel.

An Afu radio set, standard equipment for Abwehr and SD operatives, was inside. The cabinet door was armed with a cyclonite bomb that had a spring-loaded percussion detonator, its trigger on the inside edge of the door. A swivel lever kept the trigger from engaging the spring if it was depressed when the door was opened no wider than an inch, giving enough room for one familiar with the arrangement to reach in with a finger deactivate the device.

Meacham returned while Keeler was removing the detonator. He walked along the hall and started to pass the door, then backtracked. "Have you found something, sir?"

"Yes—his wireless. Is Ahmagian set up?"

"Yes, sir. Shall I help you there, Mr. Keeler?"

"No, it's armed with a bomb, and I'd rather handle it by myself."

Meacham walked rapidly back along the hall as Keeler put the detonator aside, then opened the cabinet door. A standard Abwehr code book was under the radio set, along with schedules for contacts with Berlin. Keeler put them and the radio set on the bed, looking around. The floor, of smoothly finished stone blocks, was the only potential hiding place in the room. Keeler took out the silencer for his automatic and began crawling, tapping the floor with it.

When a block beside the wardrobe rang with a hollow sound, Keeler carried over the lamp and tools. Lifting one side of the block, he peered into the crack. The lamp revealed a trigger poised to catch a ring at the top of a spring. Keeler reached in with his screwdriver and pushed the trigger aside, then lifted the block.

After disarming the bomb, he removed the contents of the hole underneath. There were bundles of Iranian bank-notes, as well as a bag containing dozens of heavy gold coins. Taking out an oilcloth-covered package at the bottom of the hole, he unwrapped it. It was the package that Moltke's driver had described, containing an SD code book, a contact schedule, and two frequency crystals for an Afu radio set.

The facts fit together into a cohesive whole as Keeler examined the package. Faraj, the merchant in Sarbandan, was an SD agent and the contact for the SD saboteurs who were operating along the Trans-Iranian Railway. The

Abwehr had apparently agreed to let Moltke act as an alternate SD contact, and Faraj had provided him with the necessary materials. Faraj was the weak link, the one who had exposed everything through pilfering and selling SD weapons.

Keeler went to the door and called to Meacham, telling him to go to the garage for another carton, then opened the bag containing the gold coins, distributed them between the pockets in his suit jacket and trench coat, then threw the bag under the bed. A moment later, Meacham came in with a carton, and saw the things on the bed.

He stopped, lifting his eyebrows in surprise. "By God, he had some money, didn't he? And isn't that an SD code book, Mr. Keeler? What's an Abwehr operative doing with an SD code book?"

"It appears that he was an alternate contact for the SD saboteurs."

"Indeed? London will be pleased that you turned this up, won't they? We could have Mueller monitor the frequency with his set, and that would give us a good line on them, wouldn't it?"

"That's a possibility. Their primary contact is a merchant in a village near here, and we may also get a line through him."

Meacham nodded, putting the things into the carton, then picked it up and followed Keeler out of the house. The staff car was at the curb in front of the foot gate. Meacham put the carton in the trunk with the carton of folders and ledgers, then got into the driver's seat as Keeler sat down in the back.

The street was silent and deserted as Meacham drove along it. He slowed at an intersection, turning onto another street where the walls were lower and in need of repair, pocked with crumbling holes in the glare of the headlights.

The pavement became rutted, the walls disappearing. Packs of stray dogs lurked in shadows and prowled around piles of rubbish. The buildings were multistoried, dilapidated old structures of wood and sun-dried brick. Beggars emerged from alleys and doorways, ragged forms wailing and reaching out to the car as it passed.

Farther along, beyond the slums, the street was wide and smooth. Lights in shop windows and signs over restaurants and nightclubs glowed brightly. Cars were parked at the curbs in front of them, their drivers clustered together chatting, waiting for their employers to emerge from dining and dancing. Pedestrians walked along the street—Arabs in robes, Iranians in seedy European clothes, and soldiers in uniform.

The street became dark and quiet again as they entered the business district of the city. The car passed a mosque buried in the shadows of a wide square, then drove through streets of tall office buildings. Meacham switched off the headlights at a dark intersection and turned onto a side street. The moon shone down between the buildings, dimly illuminating the street as Meacham drove slowly in low gear. He took his foot off the accelerator, letting the car coast to a stop in front of a building. A shadow emerged from a dark doorway and crossed the sidewalk to the car. Ahmagian, an Armenian and a grossly overweight man, made the car sag as he clambered in. Wheezing and puffing he settled himself in the seat, smelling of garlic and attar of roses.

"Good evening, Mr. Keeler," Ahmagian whispered in French.

"Good evening, Ahmagian."

"Were you successful in intercepting the German operative?"

"Yes."

Ahmagian murmured in satisfaction. Then, as Meacham pulled away from the curb, Ahmagian began relating miscellaneous information he had gathered. An effective agent, he had played a key role in tracing Moltke's activities; but he also had the typical agent's fascination with trivia. Keeler lit a cigarette and sat back, listening absently.

Meacham swung the car around in a full turn at an intersection and let it coast to a stop at the curb, then turned off the ignition and settled himself comfortably. Impressed by Keeler's personal visit, which was rare, Ahmagian embellished what he had to say and made it last. Keeler finished his cigarette and tossed it out the window, then lit another. He began listening to Ahmagian more closely.

". . .The district governor frequently complained about the Russian soldiers," Ahmagian was whispering. "Then he died just after a secret visit by Doctor Grotesmann, the director of the hospital in Teheran. My informant said that those who are troublesome to the Russians often become ill and die after visits by Doctor Grotesmann."

"Does your informant know Doctor Grotesmann well?" Keeler asked.

Ahmagian hissed affirmatively. "Very well indeed. His brother was a porter in the doctor's house in Teheran, and he knows many things about him. He said that Doctor Grotesmann was a communist in Holland many years ago."

Keeler took a drag on his cigarette, thinking about other reports he had heard—that Grotesmann frequently visited the Soviet embassy, while personnel often visited the hospital. Keeler had attributed it to the fact that there was no resident doctor at the embassy; but the pattern of contact was the same as that between operatives and an agent.

Ahmagian's sibillan whisper resumed, mentioning that an additional operative had arrived at the NKVD residency in the city. The same thing had been related by other agents, which puzzled Keeler. SD and Abwehr sabotage teams were slowing traffic on the Trans-Iranian Railway, which would logically concern the Soviets. But the locations where NKVD operatives were arriving had no relation to the railway, and he could think of no other reason for an increase in Soviet interest in Iran.

Ahmagian related what he had heard about local political intrigues, sexual activities of local politicians and other notables, and similar gossip. When he finished, Keeler handed him an envelope of money. Ahmagian fingered the money in the darkness, chuckling in satisfaction. "Now that the German operative is disposed of, do you have another assignment for me, Mr. Keeler? Or should I merely keep you informed of developments in general?"

"Have you heard of a man in Sarbandan named Faraj?"

Ahmagian was silent for a moment, then wheezed and grunted affirmatively. "Yes, he is a merchant. And I have heard that he has been coming to Tabriz during the past weeks to buy fresh vegetables, cheeses, and other food. But he is not a food merchant."

"It could be that the food is for some of the Germans who are sabotaging the railway."

"I will make enquiries and see what I can find out, Mr. Keeler. I should have some information by the time I make my next report, but I will need to hire more men if you wish to have Faraj watched."

Keeler took a drag on his cigarette and tossed it out the window, then leaned forward and tapped Meacham's shoulder. "Do so, and be certain that they are reliable. When I receive your report giving their names and other pertinent information, I will increase your money to pay them."

Meacham sat up and started the engine. The car moved slowly away from the curb and along the dark street, then coasted to a stop where the Armenian had got in. Ahmagian opened the door and squeezed out of the car, whispering in farewell. Meacham drove on along the street. He switched on the headlights and accelerated at the next intersection, turning onto the street that led to the garrisons.

The garrison area, on the edge of the city, was divided into three sections. The American section was a sprawling, brightly-lighted expanse that had been bulldozed flat and covered with equipment staging yards, vehicle parking areas, and Butler hut compounds. The Russian section was silent, dark, and fortress-like behind its tangle of high barbed wire fences and looming guard towers, while the British section was a melange of temporary buildings and previously existing structures.

The duty officer in the headquarters summoned the security officer, a young lieutenant who was awed by Keeler's identification. He sealed the cartons from the trunk of the car with tape, then unlocked a vault in the basement and stacked them there. Keeler and Meacham went back out to the car and drove on.

The officers' mess was in a graceful old dwelling that had dozed through decades as a country home on the outskirts of Tabriz until the war had come to Iran. The common room was quiet and almost empty, a few officers sitting at tables over drinks. A radio behind the bar was tuned to the BBC; the thin sound of music carried across the room. Campbell, Callaghan, and Galzinski were at a table in a corner.

Campbell waved and shouted as Keeler and Meacham entered. "Come on over, then! By God, we were about to give you up! Waiter! Waiter! We'll have some service over here, if you please!"

A waiter slid off a stool at the end of the bar and walked toward the table as Keeler and Meacham crossed the room. Campbell's ruddy face was flushed; Callaghan's grin was wide and relaxed. Galzinski sat tilted to one side, his eyes dazed, his eyelids heavy, and his face slack.

Meacham chuckled, looking at the empty glasses and bottles on the table. "It appears as though you've been busy," he commented. "Are you sure they have anything left?"

"If they don't, they can fetch more." Campbell laughed boisterously. "Here, sit down, sit down. What'll you have? They have some good ham sandwiches if you're hungry, and I expect you are."

"I'm bloody famished," Meacham said. "I'll have two ham sandwiches and a double whiskey. No, bring *two* double whiskeys and save yourself a trip. It appears that I have some catching up to do."

"You do indeed," Campbell chuckled. "What'll you have, Keeler?"

"A sandwich and ale, please."

"Is that all? Not very thirsty, are you? Bring the rest of us the same again. Are you having another, Galzinski?

Speak up, man. Well, bring him one, and someone else will drink it if he doesn't." As the waiter walked away, Campbell turned back to Keeler. "You were a long time, Keeler. We were just discussing getting back, weren't we, Callaghan?"

"Yeah, I have the guys over at the airfield standing by on our takeoff time in the morning," Callaghan replied. "Do you have to meet with anyone, Frank, or would you like to leave early tomorrow?"

"I'm finished here."

"How about seven, then?" Callaghan asked, looking around the table. "That would get us back to Teheran with plenty of the day left."

"That's none too early for me," Campbell said. "I've always been an early riser, I have. From when I was a lad."

Callaghan nodded, pushing his chair back. "I'll go give them a call and set it up for seven, then."

He walked toward the bar as the waiter returned with a tray filled with drinks and plates of sandwiches. Meacham downed one of the whiskeys and ordered another. Keeler began eating a sandwich.

Callaghan returned to the table, taking a drink from his glass as he sat down. "It's all set up for a seven o'clock takeoff," he said. "We're to be there at six."

"That's very good," Campbell replied. He took a drink from his glass and turned to Keeler. "I went to headquarters and used their secure telephone to call my people and the brigadier, Keeler. The brigadier was most pleased with the way things turned out. Most pleased indeed."

"Very well."

"He asked me to extend to you his most sincere congratulations for an excellent piece of work. And he asked me to find out from you when we might be able to expect something of the same on these saboteurs who keep blowing up the railroad tracks."

"I don't know."

"Aye, well, you can understand his position, can't you? Everyone up the chain of command screams to heaven when the trains are delayed. And when there's a delay because of those bloody saboteurs, he has me in and goes at me like a sergeant major going at a private with dirty boots. You can see what's involved, can't you?"

"Yes."

"Now that man you killed today was luring off Polish soldiers, which certainly can't be allowed. All the same, with no disrespect to Galzinski here or to his countrymen, we have divisions of Polish soldiers, don't we? But we have only one railroad, don't we? Now when will something be done, Keeler? A week? Two weeks? A month?"

"I don't know."

"Aye, well, I'll do what I can to pacify the brigadier. And I'll try to keep him from writing a strong complaint through channels about our intelligence support. But I can put him off for only so long, Keeler."

"Very well."

Campbell took another drink and started to speak to Meacham, then turned back to Keeler. "Incidentally, my people had word on that soldier in Egypt you were asking about—Corporal George Conley. It seems that he was killed in action."

The man was Sheila's husband; when she had mentioned in a letter that it had been a long time since she had received a letter from him, Keeler had made an enquiry through military intelligence channels. The sandwich was suddenly dry in his mouth. He took a drink of ale, then pushed the glass and plate away, reaching for his cigarettes.

Sheila's letters, two and three arriving each week, ran to twenty pages or more. And they were precious to him, evocative of Sheila. She leaped from one subject to another, but guilt was a constant undercurrent—guilt over taking the money he sent, guilt over the extra ration coupons that were mailed to her in plain, brown envelopes, guilt over the myriad of ways in which she was unfaithful to her husband.

And she would suffer an agony of guilt and anguish when she heard about his death. She would also suffer it alone. Keeler replied to her letters, but was unable to write more than a bare acknowledgement. It was impossible for him to help her deal with her grief and guilt. He could make arrangements to have the extra ration coupons sent but, he could not provide what she needed now.

His hand brushed his keys as he fumbled for his cigarette lighter. He took them out and looked at the fob they were on. Sheila had bought it for him in Trews, when he had taken her to visit her son. On one side was a replica of a statue in the town square in Trews, on the other the city arms and motto. It was cheap and gaudy, a souvenier stand trinket.

And it was priceless.

Suddenly, it reminded him of something he had seen recently. He thought for a moment, then took out the keys that had been in Moltke's pocket. The fob Sheila had given him was very similar in size and shape to the worn, scratched metal disc that was on Moltke's key ring.

He became aware of the silence at the table. Everyone

was looking at him. Campbell had asked him something. He put the keys back in his pocket and lit a cigarette. "Pardon me?"

"I asked if he was one of your people working under cover," Campbell replied. "Or was he a friend?"

"Neither."

Campbell nodded, blinking and brushing his mustaches. He glanced around the table, then back at Keeler. The silence was becoming distinctly uncomfortable. Then the waiter came to the table with a whiskey for Meacham, creating a diversion. Meacham took the drink and ordered another. Campbell and Callaghan drained their glasses and also ordered more drinks. Keeler took a drag on his cigarette and stared down at the table.

He became aware that time had passed. His cigarette had burned down and gone out. He put it in the ashtray and lit another. The others around the table were talking and the radio behind the bar was playing. The music had a wavering, distant sound, the station fading in and out. The conversation around the table was also indistinct to Keeler, as though it were reaching him from across a vast distance.

CHAPTER TWELVE

"CORPORAL ANTON VICHAI Vorczek! To front!"

Kosanovic's stentorian voice rang out across the parade ground. Vorczek stepped out of ranks and marched along the line of platoons. The men stood stiffly at attention, a mass of uniforms on the edge of his vision. It was Saturday afternoon, the entire division having assembled after being paid. Buehler and Kosanovic stood in front of the reviewing stand with Colonel Franz Niedersdorf, chief of staff of the Abwehr.

Vorczek faced right when he reached a point parallel to the reviewing stand, then marched toward the three men. Niedersdorf was tall and thin standing beside Buehler, the breeze stirring the wings of their jodhpur trousers. Vorczek halted and saluted. Niedersdorf returned his salute. Buehler adjusted his monocle and unrolled the accolade, then read it aloud in a booming voice that echoed across the parade ground.

The grandiose and flowery phrases were unrelated to Vorczek's memories of what had happened. The opposing force had been larger than anticipated. The immense complex of petroleum tanks at Lenkorov had been beyond the hill and the battle line. With the other squads pinned down, there had been only his. When the sergeant in command had been killed, he had reacted to the situation and taken over.

Buehler finished reading. Kosanovic opened a velvet case and held it out to Niedersdorf. The colonel took the Iron Cross out of the case and stepped to Vorczek, fastening the ribbon around Vorczek's neck. He turned back to Kosanovic, took the set of sergeant badges, and handed them to Vorczek.

Then his sharp, pale features relaxed in a wintry smile as he put out his hand. "Congratulations, Sergeant Vorczek."

"Thank you, Colonel Niedersdorf," Vorczek replied, shaking hands.

They exchanged salutes again, then Vorczek marched back to his platoons. Buehler dismissed the formation and the ranks dissolved into a milling crowd. Men gathered around Vorczek to congratulate him while others hurried toward the road to town. Niedersdorf, Buehler, and Kosanovic passed the crowd, the two officers returning salutes, and walked toward headquarters.

Niedersdorf's presence was usually the signal for a flurry of activity. He frequently came to the camp to pick out personnel for special missions and to observe combat exercises, but there had been no alert when he had arrived this time. He had come to present the decoration to Vorczek and to review training records, also bringing with him two notices that the headquarters clerk had put on the bulletin board.

One notice was puzzling. It was an order for all personnel of Polish birth to assemble in the theater at eight the following morning; official reference to the men's origins was unusual. The other was a notification that the Brandenburg Division had been allocated a vacancy in a class at the Wehrmacht officer training academy, for which Niedersdorf would interview applicants. That notice had caused jocular banter among the men about who might aspire to be an officer.

Lieutenant Fremmel, the officer who had commanded the mission to Lenkorov, congratulated Vorczek and walked through the camp with him. They were joined by Oberg and Neumann, the other two junior officers in the division. Fremmel commented admiringly on the mission: "You certainly deserve that decoration and promotion, Sergeant Vorczek. But for you, those petroleum tanks might still be there."

"It appeared that the regiment was being replaced at that garrison, sir," Vorczek replied. "Everyone agreed that we found far more soldiers there than anyone had expected."

Fremmel grimaced and shook his head. "Bad luck isn't an adequate reason for a failed mission. No reason is adequate."

"And now you'll learn about that and other unpleasant facts, Sergeant Vorczek," Oberg laughed. "As a sergeant, you'll have a whole squad to worry about instead of only yourself. But you'll also have more money to spend on the girls at the Gasthau Lautzen, of course."

"The Gasthaus Lautzen?" Fremmel exclaimed in mock reproach. "You don't know Sergeant Vorczek very well, do you? He has a girlfriend in town."

"And her father owns a gasthaus," Neumann added. "So why would Sergeant Vorczek want to go to the Gasthaus Lautzen?"

Oberg laughed and nodded. "Why indeed? A girlfriend whose father owns a gasthaus? Does she have a sister, Sergeant Vorczek?"

"No, sir." Vorczek chuckled, saluting as he turned down the path to his billet. "And I'd better get right down there before you become too interested in her!"

The officers laughed, returning his salute and walking on. Vorczek went into his billet and down the hall to his room, where he took off his tunic and hung it up to pin on the new badges. A picture of Frieda was on his desk, one that had been taken about two years before. It was a picture of her as a girl, because she had changed into a woman only recently.

One reason for the change was also the reason for her father's distrust of soldiers. Her baby was a year old, a boy. Frieda and her mother had watched Vorczek closely the first time he had seen the baby. When he had displayed no unfavorable reaction, he had passed the test. Frieda had become passionately affectionate toward him, her mother had become friendly, and her father had become less suspicious.

Putting on his tunic and cap as he went back out, Vorczek met Kosanovic on the way to the dining hall. They walked together, Kosanovic congratulating Vorczek and nodding in satisfaction as he looked at the new badges on Vorczek's tunic. Then Vorczek asked about the purpose of the meeting of all personnel of Polish birth the next morning.

Kosanovic shrugged and shook his head. "Perhaps they want to ask our permission to make Saint Stanislaus Day a German national holiday," he joked. "I know no more about it than you do, Vorczek, except that Colonel

Niedersdorf brought a film from Berlin that he wants shown. What do you think about the other notice?"

"About the officer training academy?" Vorczek laughed. His smile faded as he looked at Kosanovic. "Are you serious, Sergeant Kosanovic?"

"Of course I'm serious, Vorczek!" Kosanovic snapped impatiently. "Have you thought about it?"

"No, I haven't. I couldn't be an officer, Sergeant Kosanovic."

"Why not?"

Vorczek searched for words, then shrugged and shook his head. "Simply because I couldn't. There are many reasons."

As they stopped in front of the dining hall, Kosanovic glanced around, then turned back to Vorczek, speaking quietly. "I'll tell you something that I don't want repeated," he said. "Four men have talked to Colonel Niedersdorf about it, and they were all turned down. He wants someone who is young, intelligent, and aggressive. You may be the one he's looking for." He turned and walked toward the dining hall. "Think about it, Vorczek," he said over his shoulder.

Vorczek walked on along the street, unconvinced by what Kosanovic had said. A high level of camaraderie existed between the officers and men in the Brandenburg Division, in sharp contrast to the Luftwaffe base where he had gone for parachute training. But there was also a barrier that consisted of more than military rank. All the officers he had met were native-born Germans, well-educated men from established if not wealthy families, a class apart. He was accepted as an equal in the Brandenburg Division, and Frieda and her family regarded him favorably because he was her best prospect. But among Germans at large, the attitude toward him was different.

The Koehlers were preparing for the Saturday night crowd when Vorczek reached the gasthaus. Frieda was drying and stacking glasses behind the bar, while her parents worked in the kitchen. She smiled ecstatically when she saw his new badges, but evaded his eager hands and pointed to the kitchen in warning. They went into the kitchen, where her parents beamed, all smiles as they congratulated him warmly.

"Things are certainly different now," Koehler said, puffing on his pipe. "During the last war, I was in the Army for three years before I was promoted to lance corporal."

"Anton is a sondercommando," Frieda replied. "Sondercommandos aren't like ordinary soldiers, and someone who has the Iron Cross should certainly be at least a sergeant."

"And you mustn't say things that can be construed as criticism of the government, August," her mother added, rattling glasses in the sink. "We are family here, but others might hear you and report you to the authorities."

"Let them report those who complain about the beer I am given to sell," Koehler grumbled, walking toward the cellar door. "I suppose I'd better bring up another keg for tonight."

Vorczek followed him. "I'll help you carry it up, Herr Koehler."

"Don't get your tunic dusty, Anton," Frieda said. "You promised to go to town with me and buy me some ribbons, remember?"

Nothing had been said between them about ribbons; it

was just an excuse for them to be alone. Koehler stopped at the cellar door, looking over his shoulder with a frown. Frieda's mother looked at her husband. There was a momentary silence, then Koehler grunted and started down the steps. Frieda and her mother relaxed and smiled as Vorczek followed.

The baby was in a crib in the kitchen and Frieda was upstairs when Vorczek and Koehler came back up with the keg. Two early customers had arrived, and Koehler talked to them and filled their glasses with beer. Vorczek put the keg under the bar, listening for Frieda's footsteps. When he heard her come down the stairs, he dusted his tunic and went into the kitchen.

Frieda, wearing one of her best dresses, was tying a scarf around her hair. She crossed the kitchen and said to her mother, as she knotted the scarf and adjusted it, "Anton and I would like to walk along the lake after we go shopping."

Her mother stacked glasses on a tray, glancing from Frieda to Vorczek with a conspiratorial smile. "Very well. If it is after dark when you return, come in the back door so your father won't see you. I'll look after Johann and put him to bed."

Frieda nodded, leaning over the crib to kiss the baby, then Vorczek followed her out the back door. In the alley behind the gasthaus, Frieda glanced around as she stepped behind a shed beside the back door. Then she smiled up at Vorczek. Taking her in his arms, he kissed her hungrily. After a moment, she wriggled out of his arms, giggling. Then they walked sedately along the alley to the street.

They strolled along the narrow, cobblestone streets through the town and looked in shop windows. The time passed slowly for Vorczek. At first, Frieda's obviously extensive sexual experience had filled him with jealousy. But she had repeatedly promised that there would be no one else but him in the future, and her highly-developed skills and wanton, totally uninhibited enjoyment of sex made their moments alone very exciting.

At dusk, they walked out of the town along a road that wandered through fields by the side of the lake. The yellow lights glowing in houses along the road became more scattered, and Vorczek lifted Frieda over the gate across a path. They walked down to the lake through a grassy field dotted with groves of trees that were dark masses in the moonlight. Frieda took his hand and drew him into the shadows.

The night was warm and the grass was soft and fragrant as they lay facing each other under the trees. Frieda always took the initiative and set the pace between them, bending him to her will. And the progression was always painfully slow, prolonging anticipation until it became torture. Now only their hands touched, her fingers caressing his as she talked softly. Her voice was a husky, sultry whisper in gutter language, a stream of obscenities describing her body and his and what they were going to do. She unfastened her dress and put his hands on her breasts, her fingers placing his and indicating where to apply pressure. Then she began unfastening his clothes.

Her hands touched and stroked as she moved closer and whispered against his lips. The touch of his hands made tremors race through her body, her lips became damp against his. Her breathing quickened, her hands caressing him urgently. The flow of coarse words continued and became muffled as her tongue touched his and darted into his mouth.

She pulled away from him, then stood over him as she undressed. Her soft body was alabaster white in the moonlight, the dark spots of her nipples and triangle of pubic hair standing out in sharp contrast to her milky skin. She unfastened her hair and let it fall down her back as she posed and moved provocatively, displaying herself. Then she knelt by him and finished undressing him.

He grasped her when he was naked, trying to pull her to him, but she twisted away and pushed him down on the grass. Then she bent lower, stroking him with her long, silky hair. Her lips and fingers thrilled him and her breath tickled as she murmured what she was going to do. She delayed tantalizingly, then he became tense as the damp warmth of her mouth enfolded him.

She moved slowly and deliberately, holding her hair to one side so he could see her. Her fingers touched and pressed skillfully, making the sensations more intense. As his body arched up, she stopped and sat up, tossing her hair back. then she stood up and stepped astride him. Kneeling and grasping him, she guided him into herself.

He responded involuntarily when they touched, lifting his hips and pressing into her moist body. Her fingernails dug into his stomach as she hissed angrily, and he forced himself to relax again. Moving her hips from side to side, she continued lowering herself, folding her legs and sliding down onto him. Then, her full weight resting on him, she reached for his hand and pulled it to her.

She guided the movement of his fingers, sighing in pleasure. Her lips parted as her head tilted back, her sighs becoming whimpers. The tips of her fingernails pressed his hand, the signal for more rapid movement. Her features tensed and she stopped breathing. A keening sound came from her throat. She shuddered, catching her breath with a deep gasp, then her breasts heaved as she slumped and panted breathlessly.

A tortured need for release gripped him, a need she kept deferring. She put her hands on his chest and braced her arms, then lifted and lowered herself on him. When he strained toward her, she stood up. Kneeling on the grass, she wriggled her hips in invitation. She guided him into her and moved with him, twisting and writhing in front of him as she whimpered. Then she pulled away again.

She lay on her back, her thighs spread open as he lowered himself onto her. Her mouth opened under his as she moaned, surging up to meet him. Their bodies clasped together and moved in a frenzy, spasms gripping her again. She slipped from under him, denying him release yet again. Then, pushing him down to the ground and bending over him, she eased his torment with her lips and fingers.

A cool breeze stirred and blew off the lake, making them shiver as they lay in each other's arms. When the lights in the houses along the lake began going out, they dressed and began walking back. Vorczek held her and fondled her until they reached the edge of town, then she pulled away and walked demurely beside him.

They had spoken indirectly about marriage, but Frieda had always kept the conversation from becoming specific. Vorczek, knowing she and her parents regarded the idea with favor, believed that his promotion would make a difference. It did. This time Frieda allowed the conversation to run its course as they stood in the alley behind the gasthaus.

"I love you, and I was hoping you would ask me," she

said. "But will you make me send Johann away? He's a good Aryan and they would take him at one of the camps for children, but I love him."

"No, I won't make you send him away," Vorczek replied, laughing. He pulled her closer. "I want you to keep him."

"But he would still be without a name. . . ."

"Isn't there a paper a man can sign to declare a child his? I will do that, then he will have my name."

"Would you do that, Anton?" she gasped in delight. "Would you really do that for me?"

"Yes, of course. But we shouldn't delay, because I don't know when I will be sent on another mission or how long I may be gone."

"I will tell my parents tomorrow, then you can talk to them," she sighed happily, putting an arm around his neck and pulling his lips down to hers. She slid her other hand down, caressing him through his clothes. "Every time we go to bed, I will make you very pleased that you are married to me, Anton," she murmured against his mouth.

Vorczek held her tightly, kissing her passionately, until Frieda pulled away reluctantly and stepped to the door. She looked through the glass to see if her father was in the kitchen, then waved to Vorczek as she quietly opened the door and went inside.

He walked along the alley to the street, glowing with satisfaction. The total upheaval in his life was past. The Brandenburg Division had failed to fulfill all of his expectations, but it provided purpose. Similarly, the Koehlers were motivated by self-interest. But they were a family, and Frieda would be his.

Others straggled up the road to the camp along with

Vorczek, all of them Poles, returning early because of the meeting the next morning. Vorczek walked along the street to his billet, then went to bed. Men continued returning to the camp, their voices faintly audible in the quietness of the night as Vorczek went to sleep.

The next morning, Vorczek woke thinking of Frieda and of what he was going to say to her parents. He went to the dining hall for breakfast, then to the theater, joining the men who were gathering around the door and going inside. The crowd grew and became noisier as the men laughed, talked, and speculated about the purpose of the meeting.

Kosanovic arrived, his stony features set in rigid lines of contained rage. Men standing around the door spoke to him, but he only glared. They quickly and quietly took their seats in silence. The headquarters clerk followed Kosanovic into the theater, carrying a film reel can. He threaded the film into the projector as Kosanovic closed the drapes and turned off the lights.

The projector chattered, numbers flashing on the screen as the speakers hissed and crackled. Then the film began. The scene was of officers and men in Wehrmacht uniform walking around large holes in the ground, conversing and pointing to the holes. A man's voice came from the speakers speaking in a crisp, precise Berlin accent, explaining what was going on.

Soldiers of the German occupation forces at Katyn, a village west of Smolensk, had discovered what appeared to be a mass grave. When the commander of the occupation forces had ordered an investigation, several more graves had been found where Polish Army officers had been buried. The commander had reported it to Berlin. A team of officers had been sent to investigate and had discovered more mass graves.

Berlin had requested an international investigation through Red Cross channels, offering safe conduct and accommodations. The Soviet Union had ignored the request and the United States and Great Britain had declined to participate. The Polish government in exile in London had demanded an investigation. The Soviet Union had severed diplomatic relations with the Polish government.

There were closeup views of burned-out machine gun barrels found in the graves, as well as of the Russian manufacturer's stamp on them. There was evidence of futile resistance, decomposed hands clutching fabric, pieces of Russian uniforms, and shots of disabled heavy equipment that had been used to dig the graves, then abandoned nearby, all of Russian manufacture.

The men were shown vast fields covered with thousands of decomposed bodies in tightly-spaced rows. The insignia on the uniforms were those of the command elements of various corps and armies, the cream of the Polish Army. The massacre and mass burials had occurred during the first days of the German-Russian partition of Poland. The bodies had been examined in order to collect data that could be used for identification and was turned over to the International Red Cross. Then they had been reinterred with military honors.

The film ran out. The lights came on. Kosanovic and the clerk turned off the projector and rewound the film. The chatter of the projector, the rattle of the film can, and their footsteps were loud in the stillness. Men silently stood up and filed out of the theater.

Vorczek went to his billet and sat on his bunk, numb with seething, choking rage. A recurring thought kept running through his mind. Sergeants commanded squads, which were occasionally deployed into Russia on limited missions. But only platoons commanded by officers were sent on extended missions behind the battle lines in Russia. The barrier that stood between him and the officer corps was unchanged. But now he had a reason to break through that barrier, a reason that burned within him.

He opened his locker and took out his brushes, brushing his uniform and boots. Then he left the billet and walked along the street to headquarters. The clerk was typing at his desk in the outer office and three junior officers were sorting through training records at a long table.

The officers looked up from the records as Vorczek entered. One of them spoke. "What do you need, Sergeant Vorczek?"

"I wish to speak with Colonel Niedersdorf, Lieutenant Fremmel."

The other officers exchanged a glance as Fremmel crossed the room to Kosanovic's office. Kosanovic came out and went to Buehler's office as Fremmel returned to the table. Shortly thereafter Kosanovic came back along the hall. He glanced at Vorczek's uniform and boots, motioning him to come forward.

Vorczek marched to Buehler's office. Niedersdorf was at Buehler's desk, poring over a stack of training records, while Buehler sat in a chair by the desk. Vorczek stepped into the doorway and rapped on the doorjamb. Niedersdorf looked up from a folder and nodded. Vorczek marched into the office and stopped in front of the desk, saluting.

Niedersdorf returned his salute. "What do you wish to talk to me about, Sergeant Vorczek?"

"I wish to apply for officer training, Colonel Niedersdorf."

Buehler made a sound of satisfaction, taking his monocle from his eye and a handkerchief from his pocket. Niedersdorf reached for a small stack of records at one side and separated one folder from the rest. Vorczek read his own name on the folder as Niedersdorf opened it. Buehler breathed on his monocle and polished it, watching Niedersdorf as he leafed through the folder, glancing over the pages, then looked up at Vorczek. "Sergeant Vorczek, officer training would be far more difficult than the training you have already completed, and in a different way. In addition, it would be to your disadvantage that you are not German born. Do you understand?"

"Yes, colonel Niedersdorf."

"We have been allocated a vacancy in a class at the academy through a special arrangement between Admiral Canaris and General Keitel, and we hope to have more vacancies in the future. It would be calamitous for the Brandenburg Division if the first person sent to the academy was unable to complete the training. Do you understand?"

"Yes, Colonel Niedersdorf."

"Despite all the difficulties that you would face, you believe that you would be successful?"

"I know I could, Colonel Niedersdorf."

The colonel looked down at the folder again and turned another page, musing. Then he turned to Buehler. "Do you recommend Sergeant Vorczek for officer training, Major Buehler?"

"Without reservation, Colonel Niedersdorf," Buehler replied promptly, fitting his monocle back on his eye. He tucked his handkerchief into his pocket and sat back in his chair, nodding. "Sergeant Vorczek was identified as one of our most promising men when he was in primary training. He has more than fulfilled that promise."

Niedersdorf turned another page in the folder and glanced over it, then pursed his lips and looked out a window across the office as he pondered. At last he nodded and closed the folder. "Very well. Have your clerk assist Sergeant Vorczek in completing a formal application, Major Buehler. When I return to Berlin, I will take it with me and forward it to the Wehrmacht." He turned, looking up at Vorczek. "Do not fail us, Sergeant Vorczek."

"I will not, Colonel Niedersdorf."

CHAPTER THIRTEEN

MEACHAM CRANED HIS neck and looked across the table at the folder in front of Keeler. "Is that more on the Jankowska woman that you have there, Mr. Keeler? We have quite a lot on her now, don't we?"

Keeler nodded, thumbing through the pictures and papers in the folder. The woman in the photographs was young and slender, with beautiful features and long, thick blond hair. The man with her in two of the photographs was several years older and an inch shorter than her. He was Erling Mueller, Keeler's double agent with the Abwehr.

Mueller had hired the woman as a maid shortly before Keeler had arrived in Iran. The information in the folder, accumulated since Keeler had found out about her, constituted an exhaustive investigation. Nothing in it suggested that Celise Vassilievna Jankowska was anything other than a young, well-educated woman from a moderately wealthy family that had been swept up in the turmoil of the German-Russian partition of Poland.

"If she's a maid, then I'm the Duke of Bedford,"

Meacham chuckled, nudging Holcomb with his elbow. "And I can't blame Mueller, because she'd turn anyone's head. What do you think, Clive?"

Holcomb was Meacham's opposite, a thin, intense man with dark hair and nervously energetic mannerisms. He looked up from his writing pad and nodded. "She's very attractive, no doubt about that. What did you get on her, Mr. Keeler?"

"A reply to our query to the resident in Cairo. He found some soldiers in one of the Polish regiments who had been tenants on her family's properties. They said substantially the same as all the others."

Holcomb lifted his eyebrows and shrugged, lighting a cigarette. "An agent does complicate his cover when he has a woman living with him, but it seems certain that there's nothing suspicious about her. And Mueller does seem determined to keep her, doesn't he?"

Keeler nodded, glancing at the clock on the wall of the small basement room as he closed the folder and put it aside. "Is that part of the sitrep you're working on there?"

"Yes, sir. It's part two."

"I'm doing part three," Meacham said. "I'm down to the section on personnel, and I'm listing that new courier that Ahmagian enrolled."

"Let me have the material for part one, if you would."

The daily situation report was submitted in an undeviating format, divided into parts that were subdivided into sections. Part one of the report was current operations; the first section was presently devoted to the SD saboteurs who were attacking trains on the Trans-Iranian Railway.

Meacham and Holcomb separated folders from the stacks in front of them and handed them across the table.

Keeler looked through them, picked up a pencil and pulled a writing pad closer, then began writing.

The three SD teams operating in Northern Iran had been reduced to two several weeks before, when a regiment from the Russian garrison at Tabriz had attacked and destroyed one of them. Mueller had been intercepting their transmissions by monitoring the frequency of the crystals that had been in Moltke's house. A team had requested a munitions airdrop, then had been attacked by the Russian regiment at the airdrop rendezvous.

The incident strained coincidence, but Keeler knew of no other explanation. There was no conceivable way the information could have come from Mueller. It was unlikely that the NKVD had the SD frequencies and codes, but it was at least possible that the regiment had discovered the SD team while on maneuvers in the barren wilderness.

The other two teams had changed frequencies, but Ahmagian had established surveillance over Faraj. The merchant procured fresh foods and other things for the teams; and with Tuetonic, methodical regularity, the saboteurs were meeting with Faraj on the first and third Sunday of each month. The pattern was almost complete, numerous options on how to attack and destroy the teams becoming evident.

Keeler loosened his collar as he continued writing. The basement room was hot, a floor fan droning uselessly. A woman at the desk on the other side of the room turned the fan to direct part of the air flow toward her desk. She was small and bird-like, her gray hair in a tight bun and rimless glasses perched on the end of her thin nose. Meacham looked up and frowned over his shoulder.

The woman glared at Meacham over her glasses, daring him to comment then turned to Keeler. "It's less than an hour until the scheduled time to begin transmitting the sitrep, Mr. Keeler."

"Very well, Mrs. Biddle. Are you through with that part, Meacham?"

Meacham nodded, shuffling pages from his writing pad together. He handed them to the woman. "Just put what's on the back of this page in between pages three and four. That's easy enough, isn't it?"

"It is for you as long as I'm the one doing it, Mr. Meacham," the woman replied acidly. "And I'm less likely to make mistakes that aren't my fault if I have it in proper order and all at once, of course."

"If you'll bloody tell me how to write it all at once, I'll be pleased to do it. Otherwise there's no point in complaining, is there?"

"I've asked you not to use profanity when you speak to me, Mr. Meacham. And I'm not one to complain, but I can think of much worse things to do. Constantly imbibing the demon rum, for example."

Holcomb suppressed a smile. Meacham turned back to the table and muttered under his breath as Mrs. Biddle crossed to the racks of cryptograph equipment against the wall. She flipped switches and opened a panel, then leafed through a thick book to find the settings for the encoding wheels for the day.

Meacham gathered up a stack of folders on the table, standing up. "Shall I do part four, Mr. Keeler?"

"If you wish. Be sure and put in the listing the Army gave us to plant on Berlin through Mueller."

Meacham took the folders to a file cabinet, returning to the table with another stack and sat back down, opening one of the folders. "From the looks of this listing, it appears that an offensive in the Mediterranean is being planned, doesn't it?''

Keeler glanced up from his pad and nodded noncommittally. Meacham sorted through the folders and began writing. Holcomb finished part two of the report and gave it to Meacham, then took the folder containing the station roll from a file cabinet and began making up the list of contacts scheduled for meetings that night.

The room was filled with noise as Mrs. Biddle operated the keyboard on the cryptograph equipment, encoding parts of the report. Wheels clacked and whined as they spun, while keys slapped against paper in rapid, staccato bursts, printing encoded five-character groups.

When part one of the report was finished, Keeler handed it to Meacham, then took the list of contacts scheduled for meetings that night from Holcomb, lighting a cigarette and sitting back in his chair as he read. Meacham finished the last part of the report, gathered up the rest of it, and carried it to Mrs. Biddle. They exchanged a few heated comments, then the woman took it.

Meacham went to a file cabinet and took out a cash box and a large box of envelopes. Keeler handed him the list of contacts and they began making up money envelopes for the contacts, Meacham counting out the money, Holcomb writing code numbers on envelopes, and Keeler checking both before sealing them.

Holcomb wrote the number on the last envelope and handed it to Keeler. ''It's Wednesday, Mr. Keeler. I could check on that feeler we had from Cicero, if you like.''

Keeler took the money from Meacham and counted it, thinking. Cicero was the code name for the doorman at the Hotel Lido, an ebulliently talkative man who was an outside intermediary for potential contacts. Keeler had conducted highly visible meetings with him in order to establish him as a channel of communication with the residency. Several valuable agents and other contacts had made their initial approaches through Cicero. Now another approach had been made by someone offering information. It had been a cautious approach, a note delivered by a street waif; the individual remained anonymous. But those who could provide valuable information were usually in a position that demanded the utmost discretion. It appeared promising.

And it could be a trap. The instructions were to park an embassy car outside the Kasmir Restaurant any Wednesday evening between eight and nine. A note with further instructions would be delivered by a waiter in the restaurant bar. But someone with a grudge, perhaps a Moslem fanatic who wished to avenge Western inroads in Iran, or some other enemy could be waiting outside the Kasmir as well.

With relatively limited experience, Holcomb was more industrious than cautious. But he had received the initial contact; by tradition, he should be allowed to develop it unless some compelling reason dictated otherwise. Keeler hesitated, putting the money in the envelope and sealing it, then replied, "Go ahead, then."

Holcomb smiled and nodded. "I'll see what we have there, Mr. Keeler. It might turn out to be nothing, but it could be a gold mine."

"It'll be a good bit of money out of your pocket if you loiter in the bar at the Kasmir," Meacham chuckled. "That's the most expensive place in Teheran. Where do you want to meet with Mueller, Mr. Keeler?"

"Let's use the Kardomah. I want to see Cheung

tonight, and you can call Mueller and give him the signal while I'm there."

"Shall I rejoin you and Chad to make the contacts?" Holcomb asked.

"No, I don't want two cars at the rendezvous. You take the envelopes for the contacts at the prefecture of police and deliver them after you've checked on the feeler from Cicero, then wait at the rendezvous off Shah Baz Square. Meacham and I will meet you there after I see Cheung, and we'll discuss what you turned up on the feeler."

Holcomb nodded, putting away the extra envelopes and the cash box. Meacham looked through the envelopes and picked out those for the contacts at the prefecture of police, dividing the envelopes into two stacks, then took his suit coat off the back of his chair as he stood up.

"I'm going up to the kitchen to see what they're preparing for dinner, Mr. Keeler," Meacham said. "Shall I call the garages and have a car sent around to take you home?"

"Yes, if you would."

"I'll pick you up at your house tonight, then."

Keeler nodded. Meacham shrugged into his coat as he crossed the room and went out the door. Keeler stubbed out his cigarette in the ashtray, then took his shoulder holster off the back of his chair and put it on as he stood up. "Holcomb, go by the wrestling club and pick up a few roustabouts when you go to check on Cicero," he said. "Send them along the street in front of the Kasmir before you park there."

Holcomb nodded. "Very well, sir. I suppose there are always some who fancy that they have a score to settle with us, aren't there?"

"It's always a good procedure to make allowance for that possibility," Keeler replied, crossing the room to the coat rack. He took his hat and coat, then turned back to Holcomb. "You'll also want to make certain at once that we aren't picking up a plant. Accordingly, your first interest should be why the prospect wants to run with us, not what he has to give us."

"Yes, sir."

Keeler put on his coat and hat as he went out the door into the basement hall, where a guard sat beside a table at the foot of the stairs. Keeler signed out on the register, then went up the stairs into a corner of the main lobby of the embassy. The expansive room was dark and quiet, the night duty officer sitting at the receptionist's desk and thumbing through a magazine. He nodded and spoke to Keeler as a guard unlocked one of the main entrance doors. Keeler went out and walked along the path to the drive at the side of the compound, where he waited for the car.

Dusk was settling and stars were brightening in the sky, the intense heat of the summer day fading as an evening breeze stirred. Security lights were on around the buildings and under the plane and locust trees along the walls. The clamor of the busy street in front carried across the hall. A black Humber sedan came along the drive and stopped beside Keeler, who opened the back door and got in.

A guard waved the car through the gate. As it turned onto the street, traffic surrounded it in a cloud of exhaust fumes and a bedlam of bells and horns. The congestion was made worse by teeming crowds that filled the sidewalks and spilled out into the streets, where bicycles and horse-drawn carts jostled with cars and trucks for space. On each side, tall buildings of European architecture mingled with pink ceramic and marble facings in neo-Persian style.

Keeler lived in Shemiran, a height overlooking the congestion and smoky haze of the city. The house was on a quiet street of large bungalows surrounded by walled, shaded gardens. Indistinguishable from the others on the outside, it was actually a closely guarded enclave. The guards and domestic staff, each carefully selected and exhaustively investigated, lived with their families in godowns behind the house.

The guard at the carriage gate shone a flashlight into the car, then saluted and opened the gate. The car pulled into the drive by the house, then Keeler got out and walked along the path. The house, furnished in modern European style, was quiet and softly lighted. The housekeeper met Keeler at the door, taking his hat and calling the maid as he went into the dining room.

After dinner, Keeler went to his bedroom. In the bottom of the wardrobe was a small compartment that held the gold coins from Moltke's house. Keeler took out one of the coins then went into the front room, where newspapers were stacked on the table by his chair. He sat down and read while he waited for Meacham.

When Keeler and Meacham rode back into the city, Teheran had settled into its evening ebb of activity. Businesses had closed, the noise had died away, and smoke from charcoal cooking fires eddied along the streets. At an intersection on a boulevard, Meacham turned onto a street that passed through an older part of the city and led to the Asian district, a belt of slums between the central business district and the corrugated iron shacks that housed the destitute on the edge of the desert south of the city.

They drove through a dark and cavernous maze lined with ancient, rickety structures of wood and sun-dried brick, the tires rumbling through holes and ruts. Shop doors were covered with heavy wooden panels, windows were shuttered, and the headlights shone on signs in Chinese and other Asian languages. Runners for opium shops and brothels lurked in doorways, watching the car pass. The heat of the day that lingered in the narrow streets intensified the odor of sewage in the gutters.

They passed a small café on a corner, Keeler looking through the grimy window at the handful of people inside. Meacham turned onto a cross street at the next corner, then he turned into a narrow, winding alley that came out beside the café. The beams of the headlights played over piles of rotting debris and rats scurrying over them.

Meacham turned off the headlights and drove along the alley at a crawl, then let the car coast to a stop beside a spindly staircase clinging to the side of the building in which the café was located. Keeler turned off the switch on the overhead light in the car. "Park here when you return from calling Mueller," he said, opening the door.

"Yes, sir."

The car moved out of the alley. When the sound of the engine faded, Keeler walked to the end of the alley, glancing along the street in both directions, then walked along the sidewalk to the café entrance.

It was the Café Canton, a small, dingy place that smelled strongly of soy sauce and burned grease. Several Chinese people sat eating at battered wooden tables, ignoring Keeler. A Chinese woman behind the counter glanced at Keeler then disappeared through a doorway covered with a ragged cloth. She returned a moment later and nodded to him, and he went back out and around the corner to the staircase in the alley.

When he knocked on the door at the top of the stairs, a panel in it opened, then closed, and the solid, heavy door opened soundlessly on well-oiled hinges. Silks rustled and the frangrance of incense blended with a delicate perfume wafted out over the stench of the alley. A small hand took Keeler's arm, guiding him inside. The door closed and lights came on.

A tiny, exquisitely beautiful Chinese woman stood before Keeler, dressed in a richly-embroidered costume. She bowed and silently motioned Keeler along the hallway. It's opulence contrasted sharply with the café and street, the walls alternating panels of rosewood and dark red velvet. Costly oriental carpeting was underfoot, and small bulbs in silver sconces shed soft light.

The woman had the attentiveness to her surroundings of those who are deaf. She moved gracefully along the hall in a whisper of silks, bowing and motioning to Keeler silently in elaborate courtesy. Stopping at a sliding door, she took his hat and put it on a low table by the door. She knelt and untied his shoes, slipped them off his feet, then slid the door open.

An aged Chinese man sat on one side of a low, lacquered table in the small room, his elbows resting on the table and his hands folded. His skin was the texture of ancient parchment, his temples and cheeks deep, dark hollows. Wispy strands of thin white hair hung down from his chin and upper lip. His fingernails were grotesquely elongated masses of scaly, yellow tissue, twisted and gnarled around his bony hands.

The old man inclined his head slightly and spoke in French, his voice a dry, husky whisper. "It has been several days since you last came to visit me, my friend."

"My work kept me away, Mr. Cheung. I would gladly come each day if I could."

"Yes, I understand. Sit."

Keeler stepped into the room and sat on the cushions on the other side of the table. The old man's eyes, almost hidden by the wrinkled folds of his upper eyelids, were cold and hard. The overlord of the district tong leaders, he ruled with ruthless, absolute power. Like others in similar positions whom Keeler had known, he had a dilettante's fascination with intelligence activities. When Keeler had arrived in Teheran, the old man had contacted him and offered his friendship.

As they talked, discussing the war, the woman brought a teapot and tiny, fragile cups. She poured the tea and sat next to the old man, her eyes riveted on his hands. Completely motionless, she looked like an elegant china doll, every hair in her elaborate coiffure in place, her dainty hands tucked into her wide sleeves. When the old man's forefinger moved, she picked up his cup and held it to his lips for him to take a sip.

During previous conversations, the old man had expressed extreme dislike for Russians. When the discussion had become more specific, Keeler had asked if the woman could read lips in French. The old man had explained that she had been uniquely beautiful as a child, and he had bought her from her parents to replace his ageing body servant. After her eardrums had been punctured and her tongue surgically removed, she had been trained to attend to his bodily needs with tact and skill. And she could read lips only in Cantonese.

The conversation turned to matters involving the Russians, to a man whom Keeler and the old man had discussed before. "This Yin Pui Hsieu works for Grotesmann, the director of the Teheran Hospital?" Keeler asked.

"Hsieu attended a university in Paris to become a doctor, and he works directly for the man Grotesmann," the old man replied. "After we talked the last time, I had a person speak with Hsieu about Grotesmann. And it is as you suspected. Grotesmann is a Russian agent."

"What did Hsieu say?"

"Grotesmann has boasted about being a communist in Holland, about the bombs and fires he set. He boasts about his friends at the Soviet embassy, and about what he does for them. Not long ago, he said that an important official was coming from Moscow to meet him."

"Did he name the official?"

"No. But he did say that another man has arrived from Moscow to join those who work for the man Vertinski."

"Did he say why more NKVD operatives are coming here?"

"No. He said that he is paid to do important work for the Soviet embassy. Sometimes he goes to other cities, and often he goes to a place in this city. That address is in this box."

A silver box covered with intricate designs was on the table. The woman's tiny hand darted out as Keeler reached for the box. She opened it, took out a slip of paper, and put it in front of Keeler. The address, in an older business district of the city, fit the pattern of places where the NKVD chose to locate their interrogation centers.

Keeler nodded as he put the paper in his pocket. "That is probably where the Russians take people for questioning. Grotesmann probably goes there to assist."

"A physician would know how to cause great pain," the old man said. "Hsieu has eight children, so I had the person who spoke with him give him a present in exchange for the information."

Keeler took the gold coin from his pocket and put it on the table. "I would also like to give him a present."

The woman picked up the coin and held it near the old man's eyes, turning it so he could see both sides. Then she put it in the silver box when he moved a finger and silently formed a syllable with his lips. He looked at Keeler, his thin eyebrows lifting. "You are very generous, my friend."

"My generosity has a purpose. I would like to know more about Grotesmann and everything he says. If Hsieu finds out enough of interest to me, he will receive one of those coins every six months."

The old man's head moved slightly in a nod. "I am certain that Hsieu will be pleased and very grateful, and a person will have him write down everything. When you come again, I will have what he has written."

"I will come again on Monday," Keeler said, glancing at his watch. "And now I must leave."

"Life is a burden to one your age," the old man murmured, his wrinkled lips twitching in a smile. "One your age always has too much to do, and too little time. But I will refrain from attempting to convince you that haste is futile when all paths lead only to the grave. I will look forward to seeing you on Monday."

"And I will look forward to seeing you," Keeler replied, standing up. "Good night, my friend."

The woman opened the door as he reached for it. He stepped out of the room and pushed his feet into his shoes as she followed him. She knelt to tie his shoes laces and handed him his hat, then they walked along the hall. Darkness closed in when she turned off the lights and opened the door. She put her hand on his arm and guided him out onto the stairway landing.

Meacham, dozing in the car at the foot of the stairs, sat up and started the engine when Keeler got in. He drove slowly out of the alley, glancing in both directions along the street, then turned on the headlights and accelerated, driving back toward the center of the city.

The streets became wider again when the Asian district was left behind. Meacham turned onto a boulevard and drove along it to a square, then he slowed and snapped off the headlights as he turned onto a dark side street. Security lights in shop windows dimly illuminated an embassy car parked at the curb. Meacham turned off the ignition and let the car coast to the curb behind it. Holcomb got out of the car in front and joined Meacham and Keeler.

Lighting a cigarette, Keeler listened as Holcomb related what had happened at the Kasmir Restaurant. A waiter had give him a note instructing him to call a telephone number and let it ring four times, then dial again and let it ring five times. Thirty minutes later, the waiter has given Holcomb a note instructing him to go to a car parked near the restaurant. A man named Farid Mokhtar had been waiting in the car.

Keeler had heard of Mokhtar, a lawyer and a member of the government of the shah who had been deposed when the Allies had moved into Iran in force. Having served in various government posts, the man had detailed knowledge of the inner workings of the Iranian government. He also retained substantial political influence despite his connection with the old regime. Shortly after the shah had been deposed, Mokhtar had become an advisor to Rashid al-Kharis, the drug dealer.

"He told me that Kharis was a close collaborator with the Germans in the past," Holcomb said. "That was before the Allies arrived, when the old shah was cooperating with them. But from what Mokhtar said, Kharis has continued collaborating."

Keeler rolled down the car window and tossed his cigarette out, shrugging. "I've heard that before, and I've heard the same thing about Mokhtar. Why does he want to run with us?"

"He gave me a lot of tripe about duty and country," Holcomb replied. "So I was suspicious at first. Then when I delivered the envelopes to the prefecture of police, I tossed out his name along with a few others. He dealt in drugs for a while after the old shah was ousted, and there are indications that Rashid put him out of business. It could be that he's been putting a good face on it and making himself useful to Rashid, biding his time until he found an opportunity for revenge."

"That's entirely possible," Keeler agreed. "Mokhtar is Persian while Rashid is an Arab, which would make Mokhtar even more resentful. That's good motivation for an agent if he has anything to give us."

"He gave me a sample of his wares. He said a German officer is arming and training the Kashgai tribe that Rashid is associated with—a man by the name of Lazich. Does the name mean anything to you, Mr. Keeler?"

The name was vaguely familiar. Keeler lit a cigarette as he thought about it, then he remembered; a major named Lazich was a staff officer in the SD. He took a drag on his cigarette and nodded, telling Holcomb about the man.

"That sort of thing would be consistent with SD operations," he said. "They often arm and train locals. What sort of arrangements did you make with Mokhtar about future meetings?"

"I'm to give him a signal by telephone, sir."

"Do so, and set up another meeting. Tell him we want to know all about Lazich and what he's doing. In the meantime, we'll query London and see if they can tell us anything about Lazich that will confirm what Mokhtar is giving us."

"Yes, sir. Shall I get a photograph of Mokhtar and have him write a biography in preparation to enroll him?"

"Yes. Pick somewhere less conspicious than the Kasmir for your next meeting. And if we enroll Mokhtar, it will be best to work with him through a drop. He's apparently aware of the danger, but dealing with that danger is another thing entirely. He isn't trained in tradecraft."

"Yes, sir. He's quite eager, so protecting him may turn out to be the major task in working with him. Shall I turn in my car and wait for you and Chad at the embassy?"

"No, there's nothing urgent at hand, and we'll take care of tidying up after the meetings. I'll see you tomorrow."

Holcomb nodded, glancing around the dark street as he stepped out of the car, closed the door quietly, and returned to his own. Keeler took a drag on his cigarette and flicked the ash out the window, thinking about Mokhtar. While working with him through a drop would be inconvenient, it would be much safer, eliminating the risk of personal contact with the residency.

There was also another reason for isolating Mokhtar from the residency. Rashid al-Kharis was a ruthless and vindictive man. If he discovered what Mokhtar was doing, he would not limit his retaliation to Mokhtar. Keeler thought about that danger, watching Holcomb's car disappear into the darkness along the deserted street.

The central business district was less deserted. A few windows on the street level were illuminated, the buildings above them dark, looming shapes against the night sky. A nimbus of light shone above the buildings ahead, brightening as Keeler's car drew nearer. Then Meacham turned onto a street of small cafés, taverns, and other places of amusement. The sidewalks were crowded with soldiers, and bursts of music came from the taverns.

A few blocks farther along, discreet signs shone over the doorways of restaurants and night clubs. The street was quieter, with civilians instead of soldiers on the sidewalks. Cars were parked at the curbs, the drivers talking while they waited for their employers. The Kardomah, a large restaurant with a wide, softly-lighted entrance, was on a corner. Mueller's car was among those parked in front of it.

Meacham turned onto the side street beside the Kardomah. He stopped the car at the curb, across the sidewalk from a side entrance to the restaurant. As he turned off the headlights and ignition, Keeler scanned the sidewalks and the cars parked along the street. Seeing nothing suspicious, he sat back in his seat and lit a cigarette, waiting.

A few minutes later, the side door opened and Mueller came out. A portly, graying man, he had the dapper appearance and air of self-satisfied aplomb of a successful European businessman. Meacham started the engine as Mueller glanced around and crossed the sidewalk, then got into the back seat with Keeler and closed the door. The car pulled away from the curb.

Mueller settled himself, urbane and self-assured as he smiled at Keeler in the dim light. "Good evening, Mr. Keeler."

"Good evening. Did you come to the restaurant alone?"

"No, I brought Celise with me. Some acquaintances are also at the next table, but I can be gone for a few minutes without arousing curiosity." He took a sheaf of papers from his coat pocket and handed it to Keeler. "This is what I received from Abadan yesterday."

Keeler picked up the flashlight from the seat and looked through the papers. The sondercommandos had been operating along the southern half of the railway, within easy reach of fighter aircraft from several bases. The attacks had been curtailed, but the sleeper in Abadan who had been identified by Moltke's driver had been activated. He was working the train yards, sending lists of cargoes and departure dates of trains to Mueller's cover address for transmission to Berlin.

As Meacham parked the car, Keeler took out his pen. In changing the list, a balance had to be made between discrediting Mueller with the Abwehr and tempting the Abwehr into ordering an attack on a train. Keeler marked out trainloads of munitions and petroleum on both copies of the list.

Handing a copy of the list back to Mueller, Keeler took out the listing that had come through Army channels. "These are sight reports on unit designations on vehicles that you're to send to Berlin. Space them out over a few days, and identify them as second-hand sight reports."

Mueller took the flashlight and looked at the list, then shook his head. "As second-hand sight reports? From this, it appears that some sort of offensive might be in the offing, and the Army would like to conceal their troop concentrations. But very little credence will be placed in second-hand sight reports, Mr. Keeler."

"The markings on that list include Army units that are in Egypt. Regardless of what the Army may think, I believe that the Germans would consider it very unlikely that they would be moved here. And if there is an offensive involving those units, then the Abwehr would have reason to be suspicous of you. Send them as second-hand sight reports."

Mueller nodded as he folded the list and put it in his pocket. "Very well, Mr. Keeler. Naturally, I'm grateful that your first concern is protecting my cover with the Abwehr."

Keeler took a drag on his cigarette, thinking about a plan he had been considering. Moltke's driver had told him about an agent who had a drop at the railway station, but he had been unable to locate him. If the Abwehr could be inveigled into sending something to Mueller, the courier trip would probably be used to send money or other necessities to the other agent at the same time. If the plan worked, surveillance could be maintained and the agent identified.

"I'd like you to be a few minutes late on your next schedule with Berlin," Keeler said. "Then use your alternate frequency and tell them that you're having trouble with the crystal for your primary frequency."

"Very well. Is it necessary for me to know the reason?"

"Not beyond the fact that I'd like them to send you a new crystal."

Mueller nodded. Keeler leaned forward and handed the flashlight to Meacham, who turned it on and looked through the envelopes, separating one. He handed it to

Mueller, then started the engine and drove back along the street. Mueller put the envelope in his pocket, looking at Keeler in the dim light. "Have I satisfied you about Celise, Mr. Keeler?"

"No."

"She represents no danger, Mr. Keeler," Mueller sighed. "She's only a sweet, young child who has suffered more than a thousand people should have to bear. My life is much richer through her, and she has found comfort and safety with me."

"We both know that you want to keep her. And we both know that having a woman living with you is a threat to your cover."

"Mr. Keeler, even if Celise became suspicious, she would never tell anyone. But I assure you that any suspicion on her part is impossible, because I exercise great care. She is of less danger to me in that respect than my servants."

"A woman living with an agent is a threat to his cover."

Mueller sighed and started to speak again, but thought better of it. As the car pulled to the curb by the restaurant, he glanced around the street and opened the door. "Good night, Mr. Keeler."

"Good night."

Mueller got out of the car and crossed the sidewalk to the restaurant door, then went inside. Keeler tossed his cigarette out the window and lit another. He watched the street for several minutes, looking for any suspicious movement; then he spoke quietly to Meacham. The car moved away from the curb.

After driving back the way they had come, Meacham turned into a residential district, apartment buildings lining the streets. The lights of a large gymnasium brightened ahead. Wrestling bouts, the national sport of Iran, were in progress inside. The gymnasium was filled with people, buses parked along the curbs in front and the roar of the crowd audible several blocks away. Meacham turned onto a side street by the gymnasium and switched off the headlights as he drove into the dark alley behind it.

A few minutes later, a man approached the car. Crouching by the rear door, he handed an envelope through the window to Keeler. He was a hotel clerk, and the envelope contained a list of guests who had registered at the hotel during the past week, as well as a list of those who had attended a political gathering there. After Keeler handed him his money envelope, he slipped back into the darkness.

Another man came to the car, the cutout for a clerk who worked in the Central Bank of Iran. He delivered a list of withdrawals and deposits made during the past week, took his envelope and one for the clerk, then left. The cutout for a clerk in the Iranian Parliament arrived, handing in a bulky envelope containing minutes of secret deliberations on bills before Parliament.

A team of surveillance agents had been assigned to watch Abolfazi, the apartment building owner who had been identified by Moltke's driver as an Abwehr agent. The man in charge of the team came to the car and reported on Abolfazi's activities. An agent who owned a photography shop delivered a large envelope containing the latest in a series of photographs for files that were being prepared on local politicians.

While others came to the car, delivering envelopes or whispering a mixture of gossip and information, the crowd streamed out of the doors on the other side of the gymnasium in a hubbub of noise. Bus engines roared and rumbled away. Then the noise faded into a gripping quiet, the lights in the gymnasium going out and the darkness in the alley becoming impenetrable.

Before the Allies had moved into Iran in force, most local politicians had openly supported Germany. Some, who could be identified by opinions they expressed during closed parliamentary deliberations, remained pro-Nazi. When Keeler had recruited an agent at the Central Bank, he had found that several pro-Nazi politicians were depositing amounts of money in the bank far in excess of their salary, bribes, and other usual sources of income. With ample funds to finance election campaigns, it was virtually assured that they would remain in office and continue to exert subtle pressures against the Allied war effort.

A German agent—possibly the one who had a drop at the railway station—was disbursing money among the politicians through a network of cutouts or drops that Keeler had been unable to trace. Among the mass of trivia, hearsay, and information Keeler's agents related, there was still no shred of evidence that a contact existed between any of the political leaders and a German agent.

The last agent, a janitor who worked at the airport terminal, told Keeler everything he had observed at the airport since their last meeting. He had an excellent memory, relating the information in chronological order. At the end of the long discourse, he confirmed what Cheung had said about the arrival of another NKVD operative. A Soviet transport aircraft had arrived from Moscow and taxied directly to a dark ramp. When a car from the Soviet embassy had gone out to the ramp, the agent had slipped out to watch. A single passenger had been on the airplane, and two NKVD operatives were in the car that met him and took him away.

As the agent took his money envelope and disappeared into the darkness, Meacham sat up in the front seat and yawned. "Well, everyone made the rendezvous tonight, didn't they, Mr. Keeler?" he commented. "It was a good night, wasn't it?"

"Yes."

"Shall we get on back to the embassy, then?"

"Yes."

Meacham yawned again, and started the engine. The air rushing through the car window was cool in the thick darkness of the hours before dawn. Keeler lit a cigarette, thinking about his conversation with Cheung and what the agent from the airport had reported. For some reason that remained uknown to him, NKVD activity continued to increase.

PART THREE

July-October, 1943

CHAPTER FOURTEEN

THE RECEPTION ROOM of the bordello was dark and crowded, with frenzied, tinny Eastern music blaring. Patrons were a moving mass of shadows silhouetted against the light on the walkways. Youths paraded on one walkway, their oiled bodies shining and women posed erotically on the other. Attendants mingled with the crowd, advising the patrons and guiding them and their choices to the rooms in the rear.

They gathered around Keeler and enquired in whispers about his preferences. The employee Keeler wanted to talk with, a Turk, emerged from a doorway on the other side of the room. A grossly fat man, with a fez perched on his gleaming, shaven head at a precarious angle, he created an eddy in the crowd as he crossed the room. The other attendants dispersed as he approached and motioned them away. He stood on tiptoe and spoke in a wheezing whisper over the clamor of the music, his thick, bulging body radiating moist heat. ''The man is here tonight, Effendi, as I told you he would be.''

''How long has he been here?''

"More than long enough to exhaust himself," the Turk replied. He chuckled softly, pointing toward a doorway. "Come, and I will show you where he is. He will be asleep now, and I arranged to have the door left open."

"Very well."

The Turk took Keeler's arm with his warm, pudgy hand and guided him along the rear of another reception room toward a second doorway covered with a bead screen. This room was for the more affluent and those with more exotic desires. Some on the walkways were grotesquely ugly, others rapturously beautiful. Some were costumed to cater to fantasies that ran the gamut of every perversion, teams standing in poses that suggested their specialties.

The bead screen opened with a soft clatter, and Keeler and the Turk went through it along a wide, dimly-lighted corridor where the walls were hung with heavy drapes between doors set in deep alcoves. The thick walls and the drapes absorbed sound, but a muffled pulse of throbbing music came from one room, while thin, wailing screams of agony came from another.

The Turk pointed to an alcove, stopping in front of it. "The man Pourzand is in that room," he wheezed softly.

Keeler took out a roll of money and separated several large bills. "I am grateful for your assistance."

The Turk took the money, smiling and bowing. "It is a pleasure to serve you, Effendi, and I look forward to serving you again."

Keeler stepped into the darkness of the alcove. As the Turk wheezed and puffed back along the corridor, Keeler looked at the thick door before him. Pourzand, a Belgian clockmaker and an NKVD agent, was the man Callaghan had described as also one of his agents. Approaching an NKVD agent was fraught with risks, but it had to be done.

Events of the past days placed Mueller in danger from the NKVD, and Pourzand was a potential source of information on how serious that danger might be.

The Abwehr had reacted as Keeler had hoped when Mueller had reported difficulty with the crystal in his radio set. A new crystal had been sent, along with a large amount of money for the drop at the train station. But instead of arriving by courier, a package containing both the crystal and the money had been mailed to Mueller's cover address from Tabriz, apparently by an agent who had slipped across the border from Turkey.

The instructions with the money had directed Mueller to place it in the drop and mail an envelope that had been enclosed in the package. The envelope had been addressed to a dentist in the city, a Frenchman named Broussard. Agents watching the drop had seen Broussard come for the money, then Keeler had placed him under surveillance. His movements had immediately revealed the network of cutouts and drops between him and the pro-Nazi politicians with large bank accounts.

Then Broussard had been abducted. The agents maintaining surveillance had described what seemed to be an NKVD abduction. Hsieu, the contact at the Teheran Hospital, had reported that Grotesmann had been hastily summoned away at the time of the abduction. There had also been activity at the building that Keeler had identified as the NKVD interrogation facility.

Abwehr agents assigned to different missions were kept isolated from each other. Under normal circumstances, Broussard would be unaware of Mueller's presence in the city, but then the delivery to Broussard would have been by courier. Broussard could have found out about Mueller through some other departure from standard Abwehr procedures. And if Broussard knew about Mueller, the NKVD would get it out of him.

How the NKVD had found out about Broussard was a puzzling, disturbing question. When a line of investigation was conducted into an area probed by another agency, telltale signs were almost always evident, and the NKVD was brutally clumsy. But there had been no evidence of NKVD interest in Broussard until he abruptly disappeared.

Keeler put an ear to the door. A scraping noise was faintly audible, rising and falling in a steady rhythm—a phonograph needle dragging through the groove at the end of a record. The door silently opened as Keeler turned the knob and pushed.

The phonograph was on the night stand by a small lamp, the record gleaming as it spun. The light spilled across the bed, where Pourzand lay sleeping with two boys. He was a small man of about fifty, with a flabby stomach, sagging buttocks, deeply set eyes, and a scattering of black hair on his white, knobby limbs. His thin, angular features were drawn in a petulant scowl as he slept.

One of the boys was only dozing. When he sat up, Pourzand opened his eyes and snapped to a sitting position with a snort of shock. Keeler pushed his hat back from his face and moved into the light. Recognition replacing Pourzand's alarm, he started to speak, but Keeler shook his head and lifted a hand for silence. Pourzand nodded and murmured to the boys as he nudged them off the bed.

He kissed both boys, patted their buttocks, then took money from his trousers to give them a tip. Keeler followed them to the door and bolted it as Pourzand gathered up his clothes and went into the lavatory. Keeler put a chair beside the night stand and sat down, lifting the phonograph arm and placing the needle on the edge of the record.

It was a French cabaret song that had been popular a decade before, in the halcyon atmosphere of Paris before the war. Keeler turned up the volume until it was blaring. A moment later, Pourzand came back into the room in his pinstripe suit. He sat down on the edge of the bed, adjusting his tie and radiating satisfaction over Keeler's interest in him.

A moment passed, Pourzand looking at Keeler in anticipation. Then he leaned toward Keeler and spoke in French over the roar of the phonograph. "You took me by surprise, Mr. Keeler, but this is unquestionably a safe meeting place. I am grateful for your discretion. Do you intend to make an arrangement with me?"

"If you wish."

Pourzand smiled and nodded, his dark, deep set eyes eager as he waited for Keeler to continue. Keeler took a drag on his cigarette and flicked ash into the ashtray on the night stand. Part of the record was scratched, explosive thuds coming from the speaker. The needle traveled on past the scratch, the music thundering and the female vocalist shrieking in nasal wails.

Pourzand's smile wavered, then returned as he leaned toward Keeler again. "Mr. Keeler, I know that you know about me and my associations," he said. "You must want information on something other than German agents. You have a large and efficient network to provide you with that."

He paused and sat back, looking at Keeler expectantly. Keeler picked a shred of tobacco off his tongue, and slowly exhaled. Then he nodded. Pourzand raised his voice over the music as he continued: "I am more than willing to make an arrangement with you, but I must work through a cutout. We both know what would happen if my other associations found out about this."

"There will be no need for regular meetings."

Pourzand pursed his lips and looked away, thinking. The light shone on his pale, thin face at an angle and made dark shadows in the deep hollows around his eyes as he pondered for a moment; then he nodded. "In that event, it should be safe for us to meet at my shop. There is an entrance from the alley, and you can come after dark."

"Very well."

"What sort of remuneration will I receive, Mr. Keeler?"

Keeler took a gold coin from his pocket and put it on the night stand. "One of those every three months."

Pourzand's eyes opened wide as he picked up the coin and looked at it greedily. "You pay well, Mr. Keeler."

"I expect full cooperation."

"You will have full cooperation," Pourzand said in satisfaction as he put the coin in his pocket. "And now I presume that you wish to know all the details about my other associations."

"Yes."

The needle was nearing the end of the record. Pourzand moved it back to the edge and began talking as the music blared. What he said reflected the pathetic, desperate vanity common to the foot soldiers of intelligence operations—the need to convince himself and others that he was at the hub of events. But for him it was more than hollow boasting; he had a significant position in the NKVD network. His control was Kurov, second in command to Vertinski. A telephone number for urgent calls had been assigned to him, the mark of a key agent.

Everything he related agreed with information from Hsieu, as well as with isolated facts from other sources. Naming all the operatives, he described the organizational structure and areas of responsibility within the NKVD residency. He told Keeler the location of the interrogation facility and other outside facilities. Then he began talking about specific assignments he had been given.

Repairing and servicing clocks took him to many places in the city, providing excellent cover. His control had given him a list of names and firms, ordering him to establish himself with them so he could collect information on their activities. When the sabotage operations on the railroad had started, the list had been expanded to include firms that could be a source of information on rail traffic.

There had been other assignments, virtually all involving people with Germanic surnames. Some had been eliminated from Pourzand's list, and put under full time surveillance by other agents. Others had simply disappeared, presumably because the NKVD had become sufficiently suspicious to have them abducted for interrogation. Most of them had been the flotsam of the war, the ripples from their disappearances quickly fading.

Pourzand put the phonograph needle back on the edge of the record again and again, continuing. Months before, Keeler had detected signs that Mueller had been investigated by another agency, and he waited for mention of his name. It was a brief, offhand comment when Pourzand finally referred to him. Wanting to avoid revealing specific interest in Mueller, Keeler interrupted Pourzand, asking why some of his investigations had been of short duration.

"In some instances, there was obviously nothing

suspicious about them," Pourzand replied. "At other times, things of higher priority arose."

"Give me some examples."

"Some time ago, I was ordered to drop Kern and Spengler. That was when the sabotage on the railroad began, and my list was expanded to include firms that use the railroad. I was investigating Mueller just before you came here, and I was ordered to drop him. The Polish resettlement camp at Kahrizak had opened, and I was ordered to see if any were German agents who were recruiting Poles."

"Did you go back to them later?"

"Sometimes, but not always. Mueller was left off my list, as was Kern and others."

Keeler nodded, lighting a cigarette. He had an impulse to probe deeper into the investigation of Mueller, but it was too dangerous. Like many of the best foot soldiers of the intelligence network, Pourzand was a grasping, avidly greedy man without principles or loyalties, which had to be taken into account when dealing with him. But he also had a cunning mind and might identify the common denominator in another approach to the subject of Mueller, even if it was indirect.

As he continued, most of the names Pourzand mentioned were familiar because they were people Keeler had himself investigated. Then he brought up Broussard. After Broussard had been abducted, Kurov had ordered Pourzand to keep in contact with people in the building where he had worked in order to find out if anyone suspicious asked about the Frenchman.

"Why?" Keeler asked. "During his interrogation, I am sure Broussard would tell them about all of his contacts."

Pourzand smiled slyly, nodding. "I asked myself the

same thing, and I quickly found the answer. I know the janitors and porters who work in that building, and one of them told me. The man took poison, and the interrogators could find out nothing from him."

"Are you certain?"

"Absolutely. A porter was in the hall when Broussard was brought out of his office, and he described the symptoms of cyanide poisoning. He was dead before they reached the interrogation center with him."

"But you didn't participate in investigating Broussard?"

"No, nor did any other agent in Teheran. Broussard came here from Shiraz two years ago, and suspicions about him arose because of something he did there or somewhere else."

"How do you know?"

"The porter who was in the hall described the men who arrested Broussard, and one of them was Vertinski. An arrest is made by the control in charge of the investigation, so Vertinski's presence means that another center was involved."

"It could be that Vertinski sometimes has occasion to work directly with some of the agents here, and acts as the control in some local investigation."

"No, never!" Pourzand barked irately, frowning and shaking his head. "If Vertinski ever worked directly with any agent in Teheran, it would be with me. He works only through the other operatives unless another center is involved. There are *no* exceptions, *none*."

Keeler nodded, putting out his cigarette and lighting another. His suggestion had wounded Pourzand's vanity, but the facts supported what he said. While his explanation was logical, it also resolved the puzzling and disturbing question of why Broussard had been abducted when there had been no evidence that the NKVD was investigating him. And the question of overriding importance had been answered. If Broussard had known anything about Mueller, he had not revealed it to the NKVD.

The intuitive urge to explore the subject of Mueller more completely continued to tug at Keeler's mind. Pourzand's remarks had brushed over something that gave Keeler the nagging, frustrated feeling of knowing two unrelated, unimportant facts that would form a vitally important whole if he could only identify and correlate them. He pushed the thought aside, as Pourzand continued talking.

He told Keeler about the recent arrival of additional NKVD operatives, naming several of them, but he knew of no reason for an increase in Soviet interest in Iran. His control had told him that an important official from Moscow would be coming, confirming what Hsieu had heard from Grotesmann; but Kurov had not told Pourzand the official's name, his position, or the purpose of his trip.

Hours had passed. Pourzand's eyelids had become heavy and his voice hoarse from competing with the music blasting from the phonograph. When he paused for a long moment, blinking sleepily, Keeler glanced at his watch and stood up. "That will do for now," he said. "I will telephone you to discuss arrangements for our next meeting."

Pourzand nodded, standing. "When you call, ask what time you can bring your watch to be repaired, Mr. Keeler. The time I tell you will be the time for our meeting."

"Very well. I would like to find out more about the official from Moscow."

"My weekly meeting with Kurov is tomorrow night, and I will ask him about it again. You will have full cooperation from me, Mr. Keeler."

Keeler nodded and put out his cigarette, pointing to the phonograph. Pourzand lifted the needle from the record and the sudden silence rang with the echoes of the music as Keeler crossed the room and stepped out into the alcove, closing the door behind him. He glanced out into the corridor. It was dim and quiet, the bead screen motionless. Keeler walked briskly along the corridor.

The embassy car was parked at the end of the street, Holcomb in the driver's seat. He started the engine as Keeler got in, then turned on the headlights and pulled away from the curb. "Did the man make the meeting, Mr. Keeler?" he asked.

"No, he must have changed his mind."

"That happens, doesn't it? I heard on the BBC a few hours ago that the Allies have invaded Sicily. That's good news, isn't it?"

"Yes. Was there anything in Mokhtar's drop?"

"Yes, sir. It's in the dash."

Keeler opened the glove compartment and took out a thick envelope. It contained a written report from Mokhtar, along with a tiny roll of film from the buttonhole camera that Holcomb had delivered to the agent two weeks before. Keeler took a flashlight from the glove compartment and leafed through the report.

Mokhtar had found a pretext to visit the tribe with which Kharis was associated. The report described a shipment of weapons and munitions the tribe had received from the SD, and included a list of the photographs on the film, which included several of the SD officers with the tribe. The report and film were a valuable addition to the information the agent had already provided.

Keeler put the report and film back in the envelope as Holcomb turned in at the embassy gate. He parked on the drive beside the chancellery building, then he and Keeler walked along the path and up the steps to the entrance.

A guard unlocked one of the double doors and held it open. The duty officer opened the night register as Keeler and Holcomb entered the lobby. "A priority message came in for you, Mr. Keeler," he said. "I notified your people, and they're waiting for you downstairs. And a mail plane arrived a few hours ago. The mail should be sorted out in a bit."

Keeler nodded, signing the register. Letters from Sheila usually arrived in groups of two and three each week, but mail deliveries were frequently delayed; it had been over two weeks since he had heard from her. He waited for Holcomb to sign in, then crossed the lobby and went down the stairs to the basement.

The guard sitting at the foot of the stairs sleepily pushed the register for the restricted area across the table. Keeler and Holcomb signed it, then walked along the hall. The beeping of code and a wavering whisper of Brahms filtered through the radio room door.

In a room at the end of the hall, one of the cryptographers was dozing in the chair at the desk, a tall, angular woman with sharp, pinched features, thick glasses, and gray hair. Meacham, napping at a table on the other side of the room, woke as the door closed. The woman also sat up, blinking and composing herself. "An operational priority came in over two hours ago, Mr. Keeler," she said accusingly. "London had been keeping a frequency open for an acknowledgment."

Smothering a yawn, Meacham separated the message from other papers on the table. Keeler read. It was a request for information on when and how direct action would be taken against the SD saboteurs; in effect, an order to take action. Keeler handed it to Holcomb and turned to the woman. "Please acknowledge, if you would, Mrs. Chumley. And advise them that we will respond within the hour."

"Very well, Mr. Keeler," she replied crisply. "Would you like to write that down so we'll have a file copy, or shall I do it for you?"

Keeler wrote the message on a pad and gave it to the woman, who then turned on the switches on the cryptograph equipment. Holcomb got out the folder on Mokhtar, then sat down by Meacham, taking the film and report from the agent out of the envelope. Both men silently waited for Keeler to say who would go with him, Meacham apprehensive and Holcomb eager.

Keeler lit a cigarette, looking at Holcomb. "Would you like to go on this one, Holcomb?"

Holcomb smiled widely, nodding. "Yes, sir!"

"You'll enjoy it, Clive," Meacham said enthusiastically. "We had great fun in Tabriz. Shall I get out the plan for the action at Tabriz, Mr. Keeler? That may save time in making up this one."

"Yes."

Meacham went to a file cabinet, looking over his shoulder at Keeler. "While you and Clive are gone, it'll only be necessary for me to do the sitrep and keep routine things in hand, won't it, sir?"

"Yes, but the information from Abadan that Mueller is transmitting to Berlin will take particular attention."

Meacham blinked, thinking for a moment as he thumbed through folders. "You said that war materiel should be eliminated from what Mueller is sending, didn't you, Mr. Keeler?"

"No, very little other than war materiel is being shipped on the railway, Meacham. Full trainloads of petroleum, munitions, armor, artillery, and things of that nature should be eliminated from the lists."

"What does that leave, sir?"

"Spares, foodstuffs, mixed loads, and so forth."

Nodding, Meacham brought a folder back to the table. Keeler sat back in his chair, taking a drag on his cigarette. "Are you quite clear now on what to do, Meacham?"

"Oh, quite clear, Mr. Keeler," Meacham replied. "You needn't have any worry at all on that score."

He chuckled confidently as he handed Keeler the folder. Keeler began studying its contents. Smothering a yawn, Meacham sat down at the table and gathered the papers on it into a neat pile. Holcomb unfolded the report from Mokhtar and began writing a summary for the daily situation report.

Keeler finished looking through the folder and put it aside. "The duty officer mentioned that a mail plane arrived a few hours ago," he said.

"Aye, one did and all," Meacham replied, looking up. "And it's about time. It's been a good while since I've heard from my Meg."

"Do you think they'll have the mail sorted out?"

"No, sir. I asked about it just a bit before you and Clive came in, and they were still working on it."

Keeler nodded, pulling a writing pad closer. He looked

at the calendar on the wall, where Holcomb had drawn circles around the dates on which the SD teams had met at a rendezvous with Faraj, then began writing the plan of action. The clamor of the cryptograph equipment across the room stopped as the woman finished encoding the message. She took the encoded copy to the radio room along the hall and returned a few minutes later. "It's almost four o'clock, Mr. Keeler," she said. "Will someone have the sitrep ready by transmission time?"

"We could do most of it now," Keeler replied. "Do you want to work on the sitrep when you're through there, Meacham?"

"Yes, sir. The action against the SD saboteurs will go in part one, so I suppose I should begin with part two, shouldn't I?"

"If you wish."

Holcomb looked up. "Bring all the folders, Chad," he said. "I'll work on part of it as soon as I'm through with this."

Meacham brought a stack of folders to the table and began working on the report. Holcomb finished with the report from Mokhtar, then took several of the folders and began working on the daily situation report.

When he finished the draft of the plan, Keeler pulled the pages off his writing pad, pushed the pad aside and lit a cigarette, glancing at Meacham. "I should think the people in the mail room have had time to finish sorting the mail," he said.

"Aye, they probably have, Mr. Keeler," Meacham replied, pushing his chair back and standing. "I'll step down there and ask."

He crossed the room and went out. Keeler handed the draft of the plan to Mrs. Chumley, who put down the book she had been reading and turned on the cryptograph equipment.

Meacham came back in with several letters, a beaming smile on his round, fleshy face. "Sure enough, here's a letter from my Meg," he chuckled. "And here's three letters for you as well, Mrs. Chumley. You always get a lot of mail, don't you?"

"I'd be grateful if you wouldn't bother with my personal mail, Mr. Meacham!" the woman snapped.

"I'm not bothering with it, Mrs. Chumley, I'm giving it to you. You didn't have anything, Clive. But here's one for you, Mr. Keeler."

It was a brown official envelope, not a letter from Sheila. Keeler noticed that it was thick. He put it down on the table and stared at it. Starting to open it, he changed his mind and put it back down. He put out his cigarette in the ashtray and immediately lit another one. Then he opened the envelope. It was from the office in London that processed the mail through the blind dispatch address, and contained his last two letters to Sheila and a note from a clerk in the office. The note said that Mrs. Sheila Conley had been killed in a bombing raid.

Meacham said something and Keeler looked up. Time had passed. His cigarette had gone out. The cryptograph equipment was clattering away. Holcomb was thumbing through folders and writing on his pad. Keeler put the cigarette in the ashtray and lit another one, then looked at Meacham. "Pardon me?"

Smiling happily, Meacham pushed his letter into the envelope. "I said that I'd read it again later, Mr. Keeler. My Meg always writes letters that are worth a second and third reading."

Keeler nodded. He looked down at the envelope and

pushed the two letters and the note back into it, then put it in his coat pocket. Keeler took a drag on his cigarette and exhaled, looking blindly down at the table.

He became aware that Meacham had spoken to him again. The woman had finished encoding the plan and was gone. Holcomb was writing busily. The room was quiet. Keeler put the cigarette in the ashtray.

''Pardon me?''

Meacham, his eyelids heavy with fatique, blinked sleepily. ''I only asked if you were going to do Part One of the sitrep now, sir.''

Keeler nodded. He picked up a pencil and pulled his writing pad closer, forcing himself to concentrate. Then he began writing.

CHAPTER FIFTEEN

WEHRMACHT ENLISTED MEN gathered around a coffee wagon on the train station platform fell silent and stood at attention, saluting smartly. Vorczek returned their salutes as he passed. Two Luftwaffe captains were outside the entrance to the waiting room. Vorczek exchanged salutes and nods with them as he went inside.

The lofty waiting room was filled with people milling about and with the echoes of blaring loudspeakers, the line at the military transportation kiosk curving halfway across it. Vorczek walked to the head of the line. As a corporal at the counter moved aside, the sergeant in the kiosk put down the corporal's papers and looked at Vorczek.

"I need motor transportation to Camp Quenz," Vorczek said.

"Very well, Lieutenant," the sergeant replied, reaching for a telephone. "A car will be in front of the station within a few minutes."

Vorczek nodded, turning away from the counter. He crossed the waiting room and went out the front doors.

Soldiers filled the benches that lined the wide entry off the sidewalk. Several started to stand as Vorczek walked toward a front corner of the entry, but he shook his head and motioned them to keep their seats.

The soldiers exchanged quiet comments, craning their necks to look at Vorczek's badges and insignia. Sondercommando officers were rarely seen, and a stir of interest had followed him all along his route. It was still very new to him, including the unaccustomed feel of the knee-high boots, jodhpur trousers, tight tunic, and the cap with a high peak and visor low over his eyes.

Two trucks pulled up, and some of the soldiers clambered into them with their duffel bags. Gears scraped and engines roared as the trucks drove away. Then an old Horsch touring car moved sedately through the traffic and stopped at the curb. The driver glanced around as he got out, then saw Vorczek.

He crossed the sidewalk, saluting. "Are you the officer going to Camp Quenz, Lieutenant?"

Vorczek nodded and returned the driver's salute. He gave his baggage tickets to the driver, then got into the car while the driver entered the train station, returning a few minutes later with Vorczek's baggage which he put in the trunk. They drove along the street, then turned onto a thoroughfare that led out of the city, turning into a road that twisted and curved its way up into the mountains toward Landsbach and the camp. Vorczek lit a cigarette and stretched out his legs, settling himself comfortably in the back seat and looking out the window. Officer training had been an acid bath, but it was now over.

The other students in the class had all been native-born Germans from well-established families. The curriculum had been based on a level of general education substantially above what he possessed. The philosophy of Aryan racial superiority had been a constant theme throughout much of the instruction, a philosophy that designated him as an outcast.

Niedersdorf had visited the academy three times, spending most of the day with Vorczek each time. Instead of the aloof senior officer of before, he had been a counselor and friend. Either through intuition or insight, he had known exactly how to put Vorczek at ease. He had explained that the citizens of expanding nations suffered hardships and needed reasons to persevere. Aryan superiority was a comfort to the masses, but indefensible as fact. Persians, among the most backward people in the world, were Aryans. But the fictions of the moment had to be observed; and after the war, Poland would need men who could act as a bridge of good will between Germany and Poland.

The talks with Niedersdorf had helped Vorczek look beyond the daily pressures and frustrations of the officer training academy. The visits by a senior officer from the Abwehr and a member of the General Staff had not gone unnoticed by the academy commandant, instructors, and students. Those who had previously regarded Vorczek's Polish accent as amusing suddenly found him an interesting acquaintance.

And the letters from Frieda, now his wife, came almost daily, filled with expressions of confidence that he would succeed. Her letters had become ecstatic after his graduation and commission became assured.

"Yes, Niedersdorf's visits had helped, as had Frieda's letters. But the reserves of determination required to complete the training had come from another source. In the back of a notebook, where he could look and remember when he felt himself faltering, had been the photograph that Kosanovic had given him—the picture of Stalin.

The road wound higher into the mountains, through misty veils of moisture and patches of drizzle of fog, turning into rain at the higher elevations. The rippled surface of Lake Quenz came into view, dull gray through the rain, then the slate roofs of Landsbach. The ancient town looked quiet and peaceful, dozing through another of the countless rainy afternoons of its centuries.

The driver shifted into a lower gear at the edge of town. The narrow, winding cobblestone streets were deserted, smoke from chimneys hanging low and eddying along them. The gasthaus could be seen ahead as the car went around a curve. Vorczek sat forward and pointed it out to the driver.

The gasthaus windows were shuttered, rainwater streaming from the eaves. Vorczek had a feeling similar to that of homecoming as he looked at it—a sense of returning to a place where at least he was known. He helped the driver take out the baggage and stack it beside the steps before the driver turned the car around and drove off.

The familiar daily routine of the gasthaus was in progress; the floor was damp from being mopped, while food cooked in the kitchen. Frieda came through the doorway from the kitchen, her sleeves rolled up and an old apron covering her dress. For an instant she failed to recognize him; then she raced to him, squealing in delight.

Herr Koehler came into the bar. "Anton!" he exclaimed. "By God, it's good to see you again! Here, Frieda, let me see him." He smiled up at Vorczek, shaking hands with him warmly. "By God, now here's a soldier! You certainly look well, Anton."

"I am, Herr Koehler. How are you?"

"Good, good, and seeing you makes me feel better." He chuckled, turning to the kitchen door. "Rula! Rula! Anton has come home!"

Frieda's mother came through the door from the kitchen, her face wreathed in smiles. "Welcome home, Anton! We were so pleased when we heard that you had finished your training."

"We knew all the time that you would, Anton," Koehler said heartily. "We had every confidence in you. Well, where are your things? You'll be able to stay upstairs with Frieda instead of at the camp now that you're an officer, won't you?"

"I believe so. I left my baggage on the steps."

"I'll help you carry it in, then. Your motorcycle is in the shed. I've been starting the engine every few days. And Frieda has kept the room ready for you, of course."

"August, give the young ones a moment to themselves," Frieda's mother chided. "Anton has just returned, and he must go to see his commander, but he wants a moment with Frieda."

"I know, I know," Koehler laughed, opening the door. "Let's all carry something, then it will be done and they can be alone. Here, you take this, Rula. And here's one for you, Frieda."

Koehler handed the smaller bags to Frieda and her mother, then picked up Vorczek's heavy duffel bag. Vorczek gathered up the rest and followed the Koehlers as they trooped through the gasthaus and up the stairs, laughing and talking in exultant satisfaction over his return. Then at last Vorczek was alone with Frieda.

Frieda sighed and murmured against his lips, then wriggled away from him and laughed breathlessly as she pushed her skirt down. "Your duty comes first, and you must see your commander, Anton," she said. "We can wait until tonight. Let me look at you again!"

"It's only a different uniform."

"But it's such a *magnificent* uniform, isn't it? Are you sure you will be able to stay here? I want everyone in town to see you!"

"I will ask Major Buehler," Vorczek replied, opening a bag to take out his raincoat and the rain cover for his cap. He pointed to another bag. "I brought you a small radio, some perfume and soap, and some gifts for your parents."

"My own radio?" Frieda gasped in delight, opening the bag. "And perfume and soap? That was so good of you, Anton." She took out the carton containing the radio, sighing happily, then looked at the other things. "Some of these are for my mother and father?"

"Yes, tobacco for your father, and handkerchiefs, lace, and a scarf for your mother."

Frieda pursed her lips. "That was very generous of you, Anton, and everything is so difficult to get now. But they won't have anything to give you in return, and we wouldn't want to embarrass them. I'll look at everything, then we will decide what to give them." She smiled brightly, standing on tiptoe to kiss him. "And I will put on some of the perfume for you tonight. Hurry back, Anton."

Vorczek kissed her, then shrugged into his raincoat and put the rain cover on his cap as he walked down the stairs. He went through the kitchen and out the back door to the shed behind the gasthaus. The motorcycle, a rare luxury, had belonged to a soldier who had been killed in Russia;

Vorczek had bought it from the family. He pushed it out of the shed and started the engine, then rode along the alley to the street.

The rain pattered down, the rear tire occasionally slipping on wet evergreen needles as Vorczek rode up the winding road to the camp. Platoons were marching in the rain on the parade ground at the lower camp. An intermittent crackle of small arms fire came from the rifle range at the upper camp. Vorczek parked the motorcycle in front of headquarters.

These surroundings gave him an even more complete sense of homecoming, of being where he belonged; everything was familiar and well-known. As he entered the headquarters building, Kosanovic and Oberg were working on training records on the table in the outer office. They whooped with delight, greeting him boisterously.

Hearing the voices, Buehler came along the hall from his office. Vorczek turned to him, bowing. "Good afternoon, Major Buehler."

"Good afternoon, and welcome back, Lieutenant Vorczek," Buehler replied. "It is good to have you back, and in that uniform."

"I am pleased to be back, sir. For a time, though, I wondered whether I would return in this uniform or that of a private."

Kosanovic snorted skeptically. "That isn't what we heard, Lieutenant Vorczek. The last time Colonel Niedersdorf was here, he said that you were doing very well at the academy."

"And you completed the hardest part first," Oberg added wryly. "I had far more difficulty with sondercommando training than I did with officer training."

"In any event, it is finished," Buehler said in satisfaction. He turned back to the hall, beckoning. "Come into my office, and let's sit down and talk, Lieutenant Vorczek. Is your wife well?"

Vorczek nodded, following Buehler. "She and her family are well."

"And as pleased as we are that you are back, no doubt. We have badly needed another officer, and it is very gratifying to have one of our own fill that need." He walked into his office, motioning to the chair by the desk. "Sit down, Lieutenant Vorczek."

Vorczek sat down as Buehler took his monocle from his eye and polished it with his handkerchief, sitting down behind the desk. They discussed the academy and the training, and Vorczek asked permission to stay at the gasthaus at night. Buehler consented, providing that Vorczek would be available by telephone. The conversation then turned to events that had occurred during Vorczek's absense.

The platoons that had been deployed to Iran to sabotage the Trans-Iranian Railway had been withdrawn through Turkey because of increased security on the railway and changes in priorities by the Abwehr. Traffic on the railway was being monitored through intelligence sources, with lines of communications being maintained to send a force back into the area if targets were identified that justified the effort.

Neumann was in command of a platoon en route to Russia to attack storage facilities at Shevchenko. Fremmel commanded another platoon that had been deployed to sabotage lines of communication and the port facilities at Tunis. Several squads commanded by sergeants had been sent to various other locations.

With no further deployments scheduled, Buehler told Vorczek that he would supervise the small arms range, assist Oberg with training records, and prepare for combat exercises to be conducted later in the month. Several secret contingency plans were in the safe in the outer office, ranging from plans for sabotage missions in support of an invasion of England to a plan to assassinate the leaders of enemy nations. Buehler told Vorczek to completely familiarize himself with all of them.

The notes of the bugle blowing retreat carried into the office as the flag was lowered for the day. Vorczek and Buehler went out and walked along the path in the rain. They exchanged salutes, then Buehler headed for the dining hall as Vorczek prepared to start the engine on his motorcycle.

Men walked along the street, darker shadows in the dusk and rain. The empty flagpole reached up above the bronze sondercommando statue, its long lanyards swaying and slapping in the wind. Bright lines stood out against the statue, names of men killed in combat that had been engraved into the plaque during Vorczek's absence.

The rain beat against Vorczek's face as he stood beside his motorcycle and gazed at the statue, thinking. The hearty greetings at the gasthaus and at the camp had been for an officer training academy graduate, not for him. Experience warned him against probing too deeply, to be content with appearances; but still he had a vague feeling of anticlimax.

A squad of trainees approached along the street. The lance corporal saw Vorczek and murmured a command; the men began marching with military precision. The lance corporal saluted as the squad passed and Vorczek returned the salute, watching them fade into the rain and dusk.

Then he shrugged off his depression. A hot bath, dinner and good wine were waiting at the gasthaus. Frieda would be passionate and fragrant with perfume. And he was prepared to avenge what Russian soldiers had done to him, his family, and his village. He started the engine on the motorcycle and rode back toward the town.

Later summer rainstorms lingered in the mountains, a period of wet, cool weather that warned of an early autumn. Vorczek rode up to the camp through the rain and darkness each morning, then returned to town after dark each night. He worked with new trainees on the small arms range during the mornings, helped Oberg make entries in training records during the afternoons, and studied the contingency plans at night. After he had thoroughly learned the details of the plans, he and Oberg made preparations for the scheduled combat exercises.

When the exercise was completed and Vorczek and Oberg brought the men back from the bivouac in the mountains, Fremmel had returned from Tunis and had added two captured flags to the trophies in the dining hall. He talked wryly about the long trip back and forth between Bremerhaven and the Mediterranean by submarine, a more grueling experience for him than combat. Then, on the following day, Neumann returned with his platoon and hung up a tattered Soviet flag.

With four officers to share the garrison duty at the camp, the workload was relatively light. The rainstorms passed, followed by sunny, balmy weather, and Vorczek settled into a comfortable routine. He helped Koehler in the gasthaus at night and talked and drank beer with the customers; on Sundays he took Frieda for rides along the lake on his motorcycle.

Radio Berlin announced that a combined British and American force had attacked Sicily and was being repulsed with heavy losses. The following day, a deployment order was received at the camp. A powerful radio station in Tripoli was beaming propaganda broadcasts at Italy; the mission was to destroy the radio station and attack the port facilities at Tripoli. Vorczek had ambivalent reactions over the fact that Buehler selected Oberg to command the platoon being sent. He had hoped to be sent to Russia, but he also considered himself next in line for a mission.

Three days after Oberg left, the telephone in the gasthaus awakened Vorczek during the early hours of the morning. The clerk at headquarters was on the line. An urgent message had come in from Berlin; Major Buehler wanted Vorczek to report to the camp immediately. Vorczek hastily dressed, then went out the kitchen door and mounted his motorcycle.

The camp was quiet, but the windows in the headquarters building were brightly lighted. Vorczek parked the motorcycle and went inside. Buehler, Kosanovic, Fremmel, and Neumann were sitting around the long table in the outer office.

Buehler held up a message as Vorczek entered. "Sit down, Lieutenant Vorczek," he said. "This is a deployment order, and you will command the platoon."

"Is Russia the location, Major Buehler?" Vorczek asked eagerly.

"No—Iran. Our intelligence reports have failed to show any valuable targets since we withdrew our platoons from there. But now we finally have one worth attacking."

Vorczek concealed his disappointment, but his disappointment changed to triumphant satisfaction when he read the message. A train was being assembled and loaded with munitions in the yards at Abadan. Replacements for part of the garrison at the port had arrived, and the soldiers who had been relieved would travel on a passenger train that would accompany it. The soldiers were Russians.

The trains were scheduled to leave Abadan in two weeks, giving ample time to reach the railroad. The platoon to be deployed would consist of three ten-man squads led by sergeants. The primary mission was to destroy the trains; the second was to mine the railroad tracks. A third mission was to capture as many personnel as possible from the passenger train and return them for interrogation.

Vorczek looked up and glanced around the table, smiling. "This is a good one, isn't it?"

"Yes, it is," Buehler agreed as the others nodded. "If you wish, we can have your platoon and all your equipment and supplies flown to the staging area near the Turkish border. Trucks are available there, and you can use them to continue on to your target. Or you can parachute in and make contact with an agent for transportation back to the Turkisk border when your mission is completed."

Vorczek took out a box of cigarettes and lit one, thinking, then shook his head. "No, I would rather avoid contact with agents, sir. And I will be taking heavy weapons, mines, and other munitions, so I would rather use trucks. We have good maps of the area, and I will travel on minor roads and only at night."

"It is your decision, Lieutenant Vorczek," Buehler said, nodding. "It will be to your credit if you can get the trucks back to Turkey, because it is very difficult to keep the staging area there supplied with equipment. But if returning in the trucks involves any risk to your mission or to your men, abandon them.''

''And I advise you not to load yourself down with mines, Anton,'' Fremmel added. ''When I commanded a platoon there, I found that closing the railroad for any length of time with mines is impossible. The engineers who maintain the railroad are experts. They can find and disarm mines in little more time than it takes to set them.''

''That is true,'' Buehler agreed. ''Your primary mission is to destroy those trains, Lieutenant Vorczek. Concentrate on that and attempt the other two missions only if you have time and opportunity.''

Vorczek took a drag on his cigarette, looking down at the message. He nodded. ''Yes, I will, Major Buehler. But I believe I can make time and opportunity for everything.''

CHAPTER SIXTEEN

THE SUN WAS a fiery disc in the brassy sky. Sweat streamed down Vorczek's face in the shadow of his helmet as he walked along the railroad tracks. The radio operator followed him, his black fatigues soaked with sweat and the long antenna on his radio pack swaying. Men crouched by the rails and burrowed in the gravel, planting mines. Grogan, a sergeant and squad leader, bustled about and snapped orders.

The air was breathlessly still, making Grogan's voice and the digging sound inordinately loud in the vast, parched landscape. Vorczek's men were spread out for miles along the tracks, too scattered for effective defense. The steely quiet felt tense, poised to erupt into the rippling thunder of attack aircraft sweeping in.

Vorczek took out his binoculars and looked down the tracks at a dark mass in the distance, almost lost in the shimmering heat waves. It was another squad commanded by a sergeant named Felfe; his men had finished planting their mines. Vorczek put the binoculars away and turned his attention to Grogan.

Grogan walked back and forth, checking as the men finished covering the mines with gravel. Vorczek turned and walked rapidly along the tracks, followed by the radio operator, Grogan and his men.

Felfe and his men in their black fatigues and helmets became visible to the naked eye, resolving into individual soldiers sitting in the brush. They rose, gathering up their weapons, then fell into line with Grogan's men behind Vorczek, who began trotting along the railroad tracks. The ties underfoot were too close for a comfortable step on each one and too far apart to step on every other one. The sweltering air burned Vorczek's lungs as he breathed deeply. Sweat poured down his face, his fatigues becoming sodden with sweat. The footsteps behind him became uncoordinated and began faltering.

Vorczek slowed to a rapid walk, turning and glaring at Grogan and Felfe, who bellowed in hoarse, panting voices at those lagging behind. They struggled to catch up, stumbling and weaving on their feet as they gasped for breath. The column closed formation again, and Vorczek picked up his pace.

Searing, agonizing pains stabbed through his chest. He became dizzy, the gray and brown landscape blurring and swimming around him. His toes caught on the edges of the ties, his steps becoming uncoordinated. Grogan and Felfe shouted breathlessly at their men and Vorczek slowed to a walk, waiting for the column to close together. Then he resumed trotting. Two taller hills came into view ahead, relief gave Vorczek renewed energy. He had risked disaster by keeping his men in the open during daylight hours; but now shelter was near.

He had taken other risks, and he had succeeded. Grogan, a demolitions expert, had been doubtful about setting antipersonnel mines under incendiary thermite mines. Because it had never been tried before, he had feared that the vibration of a train would detonate the antipersonnel mines, but Vorczek had ordered him to set several under the tracks. Trains had passed over them without incident.

Vorczek had driven himself and his men mercilessly for the past three days; but now twenty kilometers of the railroad tracks had been mined at intervals, a huge stretch. The delay fuses on the thermite mines, which would warp the tracks, would begin detonating within four days. and when engineers uncovered the first thermite mine and discovered an antipersonnel mine beneath it, they would become much more cautious.

Grogan and Felfe shouted at their men, pointing out the hills ahead. One was within a few yards of the tracks, part of it cut away when the railroad had been built. The tracks curved around a rocky bluff. Brushy terrain east of the tracks sloped down to a dry wash at the foot of another rocky hill.

The third squad was waiting in the shade of the bluff. It was commanded by a sergeant named Knuthe, who came forward as Vorczek approached. The men behind Vorczek collapsed on the ground in the shade, panting heavily. Knuthe and the other two sergeants gathered around Vorczek, discussing the tracks in the curve.

The track gauge was American standard. The sondercommando railroad manual stated that a full derailment would occur on a track of that gauge if a rail was moved four inches or more. Vorczek converted the measurements to the metric scale and marked a tie where the rail had to be moved.

"Everything must appear to be normal," Vorczek told

Grogan. There will be holes in the ties when you move the spikes, so fill them with gravel and color the gravel with creosote from the ties. If there are fresh hammer marks on the spikes, put creosote on them as well."

"I understand, Lieutenant Vorczek," Grogan replied. "I will make certain that everything appears normal."

"Do so, because it is very important," Vorczek said. "We will be far outnumbered, and we must have the advantage of surprise." He beckoned to the men. "Sergeant Knuthe, follow behind with four of your men and erase our footprints."

The squads gathered on the tracks. Vorczek walked down the sloped side of the roadbed and through the brush toward the dry wash. The squads followed him, the thick brush rustling as they pushed through it. Knuthe and his four men came at the end of the column and swept the ground with brush to erase their trail.

Vorczek's boots sank into the sandy soil, then he climbed the steep hill on the other side of the dry wash. Behind a long outcropping of rock near the top of the hill, the wind had scoured out a deep trench, which the men had covered with camouflage nets. Vorczek lifted an edge of the net and climbed down into the trench, which was crowded with weapons, equipment, and supplies. Two MG-42 heavy machine guns stood on tripods at either end, the camouflage netting draped across their barrels. Mortars were on their base plates by the machine guns, while rocket launchers leaned against the edge of the trench. Cases of munitions and food were stacked along the rear wall.

As the men climbed down into the trench, Vorczek told the sergeants to issue water and cigarettes. There was a bustle of activity, weapons clattering as the men stacked them. Grogan opened a can of water and filled canteen cups while Felfe doled out cigarettes. The radio operator brought Vorczek a cup of water and a cigarette, then sat down by his radio set.

The water was hot, with a metallic taste from the can. Vorczek sipped it and smoked his cigarette, looking out under the edge of the camouflage net at the railroad. The men, crowded together, dozed off. Vorczek told the radio operator to contact the lookouts down the tracks and the men at the trucks for a report.

The radio operator sat up and took the handset out of the pouch on the side of the radio set while Vorczek looked back out at the railroad, thinking about the trucks. They were almost fifty miles away, hidden under camouflage nets in a ravine near the road. and they were crucially important, a constant, nagging concern.

The radio operator put the handset back into the pouch. "The lookouts have seen nothing, and neither have the men at the trucks, Lieutenant Vorczek."

Vorczek nodded, wiping his face with his sleeve. The air was stifling, thick with the stench of sweat, tobacco, and gun oil. Vorczek ached with fatique. He leaned against the side of the trench and closed his eyes, trying to rest.

The radio set buzzed. Vorczek opened his eyes as the radio operator snatched the handset, he spoke into it and listened, then told Vorczek, "The lookouts report an observation aircraft, sir."

Vorczek took out his binoculars. A moment later the distant drone of an aircraft engine became audible. Then a small single engine airplane came into view, flying low over the tracks. Observation aircraft had been seen daily, a minor danger because they always passed at the same time. The numerous trains had been more of a problem, but the lookouts had provided warning. Occasional patrols by attack aircraft had posed the greatest hazard; but that danger was now past. The airplane disappeared down the tracks, and Vorczek replaced his binoculars in the case, leaned against the side of the trench again and closed his eyes.

When the sun set and a sultry breeze began swaying the camouflage net, Vorczek ordered the sergeants to issue rations, water, and cigarettes. The radio operator heated stew and handed a can to Vorczek with two slices of black bread. Vorczek ate, watching the tracks. Wispy clouds appeared on the horizon as dusk gathered, making details of the arid wasteland less distinct. The temperature dropped rapidly, the breeze becoming gusty and cold when the last light faded.

The men sorted out their blankets and lay down, but Vorczek still stood looking into the darkness toward the railroad. His fatigues were stiff with sweat and grime, and the stubble on his face itched, but his discomfort and weariness were overpowered by his anticipation of the next morning, when the train filled with Russian soldiers was due to pass. Knowing he needed rest, he wrapped his blanket around himself and lay down. He forced himself to relax; then he slept.

Trains came by during the night, and one passed near dawn, snorting and rumbling, awakening Vorczek. He folded his blanket and waited for daylight. The camouflage net rippled and swayed in the cold wind as the thick darkness began dissolving. The stars dimmed in the east, then the first gray light of dawn spread across the bleak landscape. The men stirred, shivering and holding their blankets around themselves. The wind died away as the sun peeked above the horizon. Vorczek ordered the sergeants to make coffee and issue bread and cigarettes. When the coffee began boiling, the radio operator brought Vorczek bread and a cup of coffee. Vorczek watched the railroad as he ate and drank.

The men settled down, talking quietly as they smoked their cigarettes. The last of the breeze died away, the sun inching higher into the sky. The air became warm, then hot. The radio set suddenly buzzed. Silence fell as the men sat up and watched the radio operator. He spoke into the handset, then listened, and told Vorczek, "The lookouts have sighted smoke from two trains, Lieutenant Vorczek."

Vorczek turned to Grogan. "Get your men and weapons ready to leave, Sergeant Grogan."

The silence changed into a flurry of activity as Grogan barked orders and the men scrambled about, putting on their helmets and gathering their weapons, carrying two machine guns, cases of ammunition and hand grenades to the end of the trench. Then everyone watched the radio operator as he knelt by his set.

Minutes dragged by. Then the radio operator murmured an acknowledgment into the handset and turned to Vorczek. "They are the target trains, Lieutenant—a passenger train and a freight train."

"Tell the lookouts I want a count and description of the cars as soon as the trains are close enough," Vorczek said. He turned to Grogan. "Make certain that the rails look normal, Sergeant Grogan, and remember that you are to disregard the first command to open fire. Good luck."

"And good luck to you, Lieutenant Vorczek," Grogan replied, his grimy, stubbled face flushed with excitement. He turned to his men, motioning impatiently. "Let's go! Move! Move!"

They scrambled out of the trench, stumbling and

sliding in the soft dirt as they ran down the hill with the heavy machine guns and cases of munitions. Felfe and his squad checked their weapons. Knuthe's men opened cases of ammunition for the heavy weapons and moved the camouflage net away from the mortars.

The radio operator said, "The passenger train has a flatcar with two machine gun turrets on it directly behind the engine tender, Lieutenant, twelve passenger cars and a caboose. The freight train has forty-six cars and a caboose."

"Tell the lookouts to rejoin the platoon when the trains pass them," Vorczek said. "Sergeant Felfe, take your men to their position. Sergeant Knuthe, the cabooses are your first target. If the radios in them are not destroyed immediately, we will have attack aircraft to deal with. Good luck."

Knuthe smiled in tense, contained excitement. "The radios will be destroyed immediately, Lieutenant Vorczek. Good luck to *you*."

Vorczek put on his helmet as he walked to the end of the trench, where Felfe's men were climbing out and running down the hill. The radio operator carried his set with him, guiding the long antenna to keep it from tangling in the camouflage net. He climbed out after the last of Felfe's men and positioned the radio set on his back, sliding his arms through the straps. Vorczek followed.

Vorczek heard a faint clanging as he reached the bottom of the hill. Grogan's squad was gathered around the tracks at the curve. Felfe stopped in the brush a hundred feet away and deployed his men in a line. As they scooped out depressions to lie in, stirring a haze of dust, Vorczek pointed out a spot for the radio operator. Grogan's men finished spreading the rails, then filed around the hill to climb up the other side.

Everything was silent and still. Vorczek took out his binoculars and looked along the tracks to the south.

Columns of black smoke rose in the distance, dancing in the quivering heat waves. Vorczek put the binoculars back in the case and glanced around as he called out, "Load!"

Felfe repeated the order in a ringing shout. The radio operator spoke into the handset. Bolts clattered, the men charging the firing chamber of their carbines. Vorczek took out his Luger and loaded it, then returned the pistol to his holster. When the smoke became visible to the naked eye, Vorczek knelt and looked over the brush.

The munitions train followed the passenger train at a distance of a hundred yards, thick smoke belching from the engines rising high into the still air. The machine gun turrets on the flatcar behind the first engine was wide cones of armor, with four guns on each. Russian flags fluttered on short staffs on the front of the first engine. Vorczek watched.

Time seemed to drag. Then the trains were suddenly near, the sound of the engines a deep, snorting roar over the rumbling clatter of wheels on rails. The ground trembled as the first train came into view. The cars were crowded with soldiers and others peered over the top of the machine gun turrets. The locomotive started into the curve.

The front of the engine dropped, a cloud of dust and gravel exploding in front of it. Heavy ties tumbled through the air and metal screeched against metal. Couplings slammed and jerked as the cars twisted sideways, derailing and jackknifing. The locomotive canted to one side and shuddered to a stop, steam bursting from it as its whistle screamed. Vorczek bellowed the order to open fire.

Felfe, his voice almost drowned by the whistle, repeated the order as the radio operator shouted into the handset. Carbines cracked, then the machine guns in the trench thundered. Streams of lead from both machine guns ripped into the top of the caboose, tearing the radio antennas off and shredding its roof. Rounds from mortars in the trench whined through the air, arcing toward the munitions train.

Geysers of dirt and brush erupted around the caboose at the end of the munitions train. On the second salvo, the roof lifted off and its sides buckled in a ball of fire and smoke. The machine guns worked back and forth on the caboose behind the passenger train, stitching rows of holes. Scattered, ineffectual small arms fire came from the cars; then the machine guns on the flatcar began firing.

A round from a rocket launcher roared across the dry wash between the turrets on the flatcar, detonating against the bluff on the other side of the train and bringing down an avalanche of rocks and dirt. Another rocket round whooshed overhead. One of the turrets exploded, armor plates and bodies tumbling. Men scrambled out of the other turret, staggering and sprawling as Felfe's men cut them down.

The scream of the train whistle faded, its tone descending to a sobbing moan. Puffs of smoke came from the other engine as it snorted and its drive wheels spun backwards. It began backing away, pushing the cars and the wreckage of the caboose. The engine leaped off the tracks, its boiler exploding and enveloped in a cloud of steam.

The doors on the car behind the engine flew open as the boiler exploded, guards jumping out. An incendiary mortar round detonated beside the tracks farther along the munitions train in a boiling cloud of white and yellow flames. As dirt and gravel sprayed around them, the guards ran into the brush toward the dry wash. Another mortar salvo whined through the air toward the munitions train.

Vorczek dropped flat as a bullet from the passenger train kicked up dirt beside him. The small arms fire from the passenger train was becoming concentrated. One of Felfe's men cried out as he jerked from the impact of a bullet and rolled over. The machine guns still chewed back and forth on the wreckage of the caboose.

Leaning toward the radio operator, Vorczek shouted; "Tell Sergeant Knuthe to suppress that small arms fire!"

The radio operator relayed the order. The machine guns traversed, their roar becoming louder and the muzzle blast a crushing pressure as they fired straight overhead. Glass flew from windows in the cars, the window frames bursting into splinters. The small arms fire from the train abruptly ceased. Soldiers leaped from the doors and windows.

Felfe's squad and the machine gun fire cut down some of the soldiers, but most of them reached the other side of the cars. As a jarring explosion shook the ground, Vorczek saw that a car on the munitions train loaded with bombs had exploded, a huge ball of flame floating upward as smoking debris rained down on a wide gap in the train. Other cars burned hotly, small arms ammunition exploding with staccato rattles.

The soldiers who had taken cover behind the passenger train began firing again. Bullets whined through the brush from the dry wash below, where the guards from the train had sheltered. Two mortar rounds fell into the dry wash; then the rifle fire from the guards stopped. A barrage of [illegible] ripped through cars of the munitions train. [illegible]wers of exploding munitions sprayed streaks of smoke into the air.

The small arms fire from the other side of the passenger train began growing in intensity. Vorczek turned to the radio operator and shouted; "Tell Sergeant Grogan to open fire!"

The radio operator repeated the order into the handset. Machine guns roared and carbines crackled on the bluff above the train. Black dots of hand grenades tumbled down and raised thick clouds of dust on the other side of the train as they detonated. Pandemonium erupted among the Russians as they darted about in terror, trying to find shelter from the deadly hail of bullets and grenades. Some of the Russians tried to get back into the train, but were cut down as the machine guns in the trench continued peppering the cars and Felfe's men fired rapidly. Then white cloths began flapping frantically in the dust swirling between the cars.

Vorczek turned toward Felfe and the radio operator, shouting; "*Cease fire! Cease fire!*"

The pounding of machine guns and spatter of carbines stopped. Vorczek lifted himself to his knees. Munitions on the freight train continued exploding, making the ground heave as waves of concussion pushed through the air; but there was a gripping quiet around the smoking, battered passenger train.

Vorczek cautiously stood up, looking around. "How many casualties, Sergeant Felfe?"

Felfe looked around at his men, then replied; "One dead and three wounded, Lieutenant Vorczek."

"Detail one man to attend to the wounded, and have the remainder fix bayonets." Vorczek changed to Russian, cupping his hands around his mouth and shouting at the soldiers on the other side of the train, "Come out with your hands on your heads, pig-shit!"

Bodies were draped over the couplings and littered the ground between the cars. Furtive movements in the thick dust turned into Russian soldiers who climbed over bodies on the couplings and hesitantly walked into the open, their hands obediently on their heads. Felfe's men walked toward the train, bayonets fixed. More soldiers came from behind the train, a trickle turning into streams.

A tense moment came when the growing crowd of Russian soldiers began recovering from their initial shock, looking at the handful of men in black fatigues. The flow of soldiers from behind the train slowed, then Knuthe arrived with his squad. Grogan and his men reached the train a moment later. The Russians, vastly outnumbering the sondercommando platoon, grumbled and muttered, but continued coming from behind the train, some of them wounded. Those who were unable to walk moaned and cried out.

Grogan and his men searched the train, finding others who were trying to hide. The mass of prisoners continued growing as Grogan's men chased them out of hiding. There were growing signs of resistance; angry, belligerent resentment swelled among them. Some refused to keep their hands on their head as they glared at the thin line of sondercommandos surrounding them.

Vorczek waited until Grogan's men finished searching. Finding a last half dozen hiding around the engine, the squad herded them to the crowd of prisoners. Vorczek walked toward them, shouting; "Silence, pig-shit! And keep your hands on your heads!"

The muttering among the prisoners grew louder. A

burly sergeant sneered and commented sarcastically about Vorczek's Polish accent in Russian. A corporal laughed raucously. The hubbub of voices among the prisoners abruptly died as Vorczek took out his pistol. The sneer on the sergeant's face changed to a look of alarm. Vorczek lifted the pistol, aiming at the sergeant's stomach, then squeezed the trigger. The heavy nine-millimeter bullet knocked the man backwards. He screamed in shock and pain as he fell. Vorczek swung his pistol toward the corporal, who darted behind another man, his eyes wide with terror. Vorczek squeezed the trigger. The man in front of the corporal shrieked as he pitched to one side and fell, shot through the chest.

The prisoners leaped and dodged frantically as the corporal ducked behind them. Vorczek fired. Another man fell. He fired again, and another fell. As the prisoners began spreading apart, the sondercommandos shouted and jabbed with their bayonets. Vorczek continued firing. Then two prisoners seized the corporal and threw him into the open, leaping back. Vorczek fired. The corporal screamed as he reeled backwards and fell.

The ground trembled as munitions continued exploding. Seven prisoners lay on the ground, four of them writhing and moaning, the only sound or movement by the passenger train. The prisoners were now silent and motionless, their hands on their heads, the thin line of sondercommandos around them unmoving.

Vorczek snapped the clip out of his Luger and took a handful of bullets from a pocket. "There is something you must understand," he said to the prisoners as he pushed bullets into the clip. "You are not prisoners of war. You are Russian pig-shit. I need very little provocation to kill

Russian pig-shit, so it would be unwise of you to try my patience again.''

A colonel started to protest, then changed his mind when Vorczek looked at him. Vorczek glanced around at the sondercommandos as he turned away from the prisoners. ''Separate the wounded from the others. Sergeant Grogan, look through the train and see if there are any papers that could be valuable. Sergeant Knuthe and Sergeant Felfe, come over here.''

Vorczek finished reloading the clip and snapped it back into his pistol, turning to Knuthe. ''It appeared that you destroyed the radios in the cabooses before a message about the attack could be sent.''

''I am sure I did, Lieutenant,'' Knuthe replied. ''That should give us time to escape.''

Vorczek nodded, glancing at his watch. ''Take Sergeant Grogan's squad and half of Sergeant Felfe's along with yours, and escort the unwounded prisoners to the trench. They will carry our wounded, as well as the supplies and equipment. Sergeant Felfe, take the rest of your men and the wounded prisoners, and have them load the wounded and dead into the train. Then shoot or bayonet the wounded prisoners, put them into the train, and set the train on fire.''

Vorczek took one of the Soviet flags off the front of the engine to hang in the dining hall at the camp. Walking back along the train, he looked at the dry wash below the munitions train. He saw the lookouts walking along the dry wash with the guards who had been on the munitions train. The guards were Americans, three of them wounded.

Grogan came out of the train with an armload of briefcases. "These are all I could find, Lieutenant. Those are Americans, aren't they?"

"Yes, they are," Vorczek replied, taking the briefcases. "Have the men take them over to the foot of the hill below the trench, and see what can be done for their wounded."

Vorczek took the knife out of the sheath on his boot and cut open the locked briefcases, then looked through the maps and the papers in them. Although he could read little Russian, he recognized the markings on the material that identified it as secret documents. He stacked the briefcases on the ground, then waited for Felfe and his men to finish loading the dead and wounded into the train.

Felfe and his men moved along the train with the wounded Russians, prodding them with bayonets. When they reached the end of the train, there was an outburst of shrieks. Shots rang out as some fled from the bayonets. When it was over, Felfe and his men heaved the bodies into the last car, then ran along the sides of the train and tossed incendiary hand grenades through the shattered windows.

Smoke billowed up from the train, blending with that from the exploding munitions. The swelling uproar of screams from the wounded quickly faded, the cars burning hotly. Vorczek looked up at the top of the hill. The dead sondercommando had been buried, two men smoothing the ground and hiding evidence of the grave. The others were loading the prisoners with the equipment and the supplies.

Grogan and the lookouts sat at the foot of the hill with the guards from the munitions train. The three wounded had been bandaged. The other Americans stood up with the sondercommandos as Vorczek approached. One was a sergeant and the others were privates, all of them pale and frightened. Vorczek nodded to them and looked at the wounded men. "Are they seriously wounded, Sergeant Grogan?"

"No, they will recover easily, Lieutenant Vorczek," Grogan replied. As the American sergeant spoke, Grogan said, "He says that all he will tell you is his name, rank, serial number, and date of birth, Lieutenant."

"That is more than I want to know," Vorczek said, laughing. "Tell him we do not have enough food and water to leave any for him and his men, but his comrades should be here shortly. And tell him that the next time he is in the line of fire from enemy heavy weapons, he should either surrender or flee instead of opening fire. What he did was foolish."

Grogan turned to the American, translating. The American shrugged and shook his head ruefully as he replied. Grogan turned back to Vorczek. "He says that he now knows that it was foolish, Lieutenant Vorczek."

The American saluted. Vorczek returned his salute, smiling. "Good luck."

Vorczek began climbing the hill, the sondercommandos following him. Near the top of the hill, Knuthe and his men formed the Russians into a column, the prisoners carrying the supplies, equipment, and heavy weapons.

Grogan and Felfe trotted ahead with the rest of the platoon to take their places in the thin line of sondercommandos on each side of the column of prisoners. Vorczek looked back along the column, beckoning; then the prisoners and sondercommandos followed him.

The escape route that Vorczek had picked out lay to the

west, across the parched wasteland to a dry, rocky river bed several miles away. A haze of dust rose as the prisoners pushed forward, leaving a wide trail of crushed brush and churned soil. The prisoners, soft and flabby garrison soldiers, began slowing after an hour, and Vorczek shouted back along the column. The sondercommandos began prodding the prisoners with bayonets to hurry them along.

When they reached the river bed, Vorczek stopped to let the men and prisoners rest for a few minutes. Logic would direct pursuers to the north, in the direction of Turkey. When the column began moving again Vorczek led it along the river bed in a southerly direction. A squad followed to smooth out footprints in patches of sand and to remove other evidence of the direction they had taken.

The river bed divided after several miles, the main channel turning to the southwest and a smaller one curving to the east, toward the railroad. Vorczek proceeded along the narrow tributary. A line of tall hills rose ahead after several more miles, the river bed turning into a dry creek that wound up the slopes to a gap in the hills. From the top of the hills, the railroad came into view in the distance to the east.

A smudge of smoke lay on the horizon to the north, dancing in the heat waves; whispers of thuds carried across the distance as munitions continued to explode. It was almost time for the observation aircraft. The sondercommandos hurried the prisoners as the squad behind worked frantically to hide the trail. Vorczek led them into the barren, rocky hills several miles east.

He had chosen a narrow, sheltered ravine to wait out the first flurry of pursuit and search. The sondercommandos cheered in relief as they reached the refuge. The column filed into the ravine, the squad leaders posting guards over the prisoners and organizing the men to put up the camouflage nets over the ravine. Vorczek walked back to a ridge overlooking the slopes leading down to the railroad and looked through his binoculars at the trail they had left behind.

The trail, visible at close proximity, faded into the surrounding terrain from a distance of a hundred feet. A night wind sweeping the soft soil and brush would make it virtually invisible, and it was improbable that a ground search would be made. Pursuers, would go to the north and west of the burning trains, while the trail was to the south and east.

The camouflage nets were up when Vorczek returned, the prisoners in tight rows along one side of the ravine. He ordered the sergeants to issue food and water, and to give each prisoner a slice of bread and a half cup of water. The prisoners devoured the bread and gulped the water, then watched ravenously as the sondercommandos heated their cans of stew over fuel pellets.

Vorczek ate, thinking about the battle. The mission had been an unqualified success thus far. At the cost of very few casualties, the trains had been destroyed, the railroad had been mined, and a huge number of prisoners had been taken. Within a day or two, he would lead them to the trucks. Then they could return to Turkey the same way that they had come, traveling unfrequented roads at night.

The main danger was that a prisoner would escape and lead the search to the column. Sitting crushed together in tight rows, their uniforms soaked with sweat, most of them dozed in exhaustion or stared dully into space, lacking the will to try to escape. But a few, most of them officers, were watching the sondercommandos and talking quietly among themselves.

When he finished eating, Vorczek told the sergeants to have their men tie the prisoners. The sergeants were doubtful that this would prevent them from escaping. "Keeping them from untying each other after dark will be the main problem," Knuthe said. "The guards will check them frequently through the night, but it will still be a problem, Lieutenant Vorczek."

"I will talk to the prisoners and tell them what will happen to them if they try to untie each other," Vorczek replied. "Have the men tie their thumbs behind their backs with string, then bind them in groups of five with rope around their necks. Put officers and enlisted men together in each group. I will talk to them when they are tied."

The men began collecting rope and pushing the prisoners to their feet as the squad leaders gave them instructions. A murmur of protest rose among the prisoners when the men began tying their thumbs, but faded as the men slapped and cuffed them.

The teeming activity in the ravine settled after a few minutes. Sitting together in tight groups with their backs together, the prisoners tried to get comfortable and to keep the ropes around their necks from choking them. The sondercommandos waited for Vorczek to speak to the prisoners.

Vorczek walked along the ravine, looking down at the Russians. "If one of you attempt to escape, everyone in his group will be shot," he said. "The guards will check frequently, and if a man is found with his thumbs untied, that will be construed as an attempt to escape. But if a man who unties his thumbs is reported to the guards, only that man will be shot, and the one who reports him will receive extra food and water."

Vorczek looked around at the prisoners. They looked back at him, their eyes dull. A Polish sondercommando was translating the Russian in a whisper. Vorczek paused. He waited for a moment, then continued: "Of course, one of you could untie another and then report him in order to get the extra food and water. All of you should be careful that does not happen, particularly you officers. I am sure you have had occasion to discipline these enlisted men, and they may retaliate against you."

Prisoners shifted and glanced at each other suspiciously as Vorczek paused again. He studied their expressions. Distrust had been shown among them, and they were frightened; but they were not completely demoralized. A sergeant with thick, brutish features was in the group directly in front of Vorczek, looking down at the ground. Vorczek leaned over him, suddenly shouting at the top of his voice. "You are not listening, pig-shit! When I talk, I expect pig-shit to listen to me!"

The sergeant straightened up with a snort of shock, his eyes wide. Vorczek seized the man's right ear and gripped it tightly, reaching for his combat knife. "This ear has offended me by ignoring me, pig-shit! Do you know what I do when I'm offended? *This*!"

The long blade of Vorczek's knife gleamed as he jerked it out of the sheath on his boot. The sergeant squealed, digging his heels into the dirt and pulling away. The other four men tied with him swayed and choked as the rope drew tight around their necks. The sergeant's squeal changed to a hoarse shriek of pain as the knife slashed through skin and cartilage. Blood spurted, the man's screams ringing through the ravine.

Then his screams choked off and his head snapped back as Vorczek put the blade against his throat. Blood poured from the stump of the severed ear. Trembling violently, he looked up at Vorczek, his eyes wild and glaring with fear. His breath came in shuddering gasps and he pushed back against the other four men, shrinking away from the keen blade.

Vorczek smiled, lifting the ear and holding it in front of the man's face. "Now eat it, pig-shit," he said softly.

A hiss of shock and astonishment passed through the others in the ravine, prisoners and sondercommandos. Then there was silence. The man's eyes bulged in horror. Vorczek pressed the knife harder, still smiling. Beads of blood appeared along the razor-sharp blade where it touched the man's throat. The man's thick lips parted, quivering. They slowly opened. Vorczek pushed the ear into the man's mouth.

Moist, clicking sounds came from the man's mouth, his lips sagging wider and twisting in a grimace of revulsion. Then he drew in a deep breath and closed his jaws. The cartilage grated audibly between his teeth, making him gag. Vorczek pressed the knife harder. The man gulped convulsively, swallowing, then clamped his jaws to keep from retching. Tremors raced through the man's body. He panted rapidly through his nose, his eyes closed and his lips a thin, white line. Vorczek waited for a moment, holding the blade against the man's throat. Then he wiped the blade of his knife on the man's sleeve and slid the knife back into the sheath.

Prisoners and sondercommandos alike were frozen in awkward positions, stretched, leaning, their necks craned, their eyes fixed on Vorczek in wonder and shock. They were as still and silent as statues.

Then Knuthe moved, breaking the silence. "By God, I'll bet the bastard wishes he had washed his ears this morning," he said, chuckling dryly.

The sondercommandos exploded into gales of uproarious laughter. Vorczek laughed, calling out; "Issue an extra rations of cigarettes, Sergeant Knuthe!"

Knuthe took out a can of cigarettes. The men crowding around him, he opened the can and passed out cigarettes as he crossed the ravine to Vorczek. He handed Vorczek a cigarette, and another man held out a match. Vorczek lit the cigarette, smiling.

The men moved away and settled down. Vorczek puffed on his cigarette and looked at the prisoners. What he saw filled him with deep, triumphant satisfaction. It was what he had seen in the eyes and on the faces of the people from his village they had been herded like animals along a road by Russian soldiers.

CHAPTER SEVENTEEN

THE ROAR OF the engines on the Douglas Dakota faded into silence, leaving a ringing in Keeler's ears. The airplane had descended from daylight into the early dusk of a windy, overcast day, and the airport lights shone through the small windows along the fuselage. A light over the cockpit door came on, casting a blinding glare and dark shadows back through the drab, austere interior of the military transport.

A few other passengers were scattered along the seats of canvas webbing over long aluminum frames at the sides of the fuselage. All of the other passengers were Americans, bleary from the hours of confinement. They began leaving the airplane, led by two medics carrying a man on a stretcher. Two military policemen pushed a large, belligerent-looking private in handcuffs ahead of them. A colonel clutched a briefcase as he went out.

One of the crewmen untied the cargo net over the freight at the rear of the airplane and helped Keeler drag out the four cardboard boxes that he had brought with him from Abadan. Meacham and Campbell came up the steps and into the airplane, accompanied by two soldiers. The soldiers gathered up the boxes, then Keeler followed them down the steps with Meacham and Campbell.

The wind gusted across the open expanse of the ramp in the twilight, keening around the dark forms of parked aircraft. A long row of hangars stretched away from the other side of the terminal, brilliant lights glaring.

The soldiers walked ahead with the boxes, trudging into the wind. Campbell's mustaches fluttered as he tugged his cap down tightly.

"Judging by those boxes, you must have been successful, Keeler," he said. "Were you, then?"

"Yes."

"That's good to hear, and you may be bloody assured of that. By God, we've had repercussions all the way from London on this. They're saying that the yards at Abadan are so congested with goods that the war may be over before they're cleared. I suppose you saw that, didn't you?"

"No."

"You didn't? I fancied the rail yards would be the first place you'd go to look for the bugger. Some want to blame the engineers because the railroad is still closed, but I can't fault someone for not wanting to muck about with booby-trapped mines. In any event, can I tell the brigadier that the matter's settled now?"

"Yes."

"Aye, well, how about other agents? How do we know another won't pop up as suddenly as that one did? That's the first thing the brigadier will ask me, Keeler, and you've got to give me something to tell him. Every time he sees me, he's at me like a badger. What can I tell him?"

"When the Army closes the Turkish border, the

Germans won't be able to maintain agents in Iran."

"Do you expect me to tell him that? We were just up there with everything we could muster, and a platoon of saboteurs got past us with God knows how many prisoners. Now haven't I cooperated with you? Haven't I kept the brigadier from writing through channels about his intelligence support? You must give me *something* to tell him, Keeler."

They were approaching flight operations. A staff car and a car from the embassy were among the other vehicles in the parking area. Meacham walked ahead to unlock the car for the soldiers to put the boxes in it. Keeler slowed and turned to Campbell. "The agent at Abadan had propaganda material among his things."

Campbell grunted and shook his head. "I mean something to tell him that will *pacify* him, Keeler, not just anything at all. After all, the bugger was a German agent, wasn't he? There's nothing remarkable about a German agent having German propaganda material, Keeler."

"There is when he is assigned to intelligence collection."

Campbell stopped, out of earshot of the soldiers. He frowned musingly as he thought about Keeler's words, then he shook his head again. "Keeler, you'll have to go into more detail. I know you're telling me something, but I don't know what the bloody hell it is."

"In the Abwehr, intelligence collection comes under the Operations Section. Distribution of propaganda comes under the Political Actions Section. Abwehr agents are virtually never controlled by both sections because of the possibility of conflicts in their instructions. This one was, which indicates that they're critically short of agents here."

Campbell brushed his mustaches, a smile spreading over his face. "By God, that *is* something to tell him, isn't it?" he chuckled. "And it has a very keen ring of insight about it. Incidentally, I sent over that list of known deserters from the Polish regiments that you asked for. You don't expect trouble from any of them, do you?"

"It's conceivable."

Campbell winced, then sighed heavily as he turned toward the staff car. "Aye, well, let tomorrow take care of tomorrow's problems, as they say. Good night, Keeler."

"Good night."

Keeler got into the embassy car. Meacham was racing the engine and holding his hand under the dashboard. "This heater doesn't seem to be working properly, Mr. Keeler, and it's quite nippy out tonight, isn't it?"

"Yes. Did we get anything from London on my request for a listing of graduates from the Wehrmacht officer training academy?"

"Yes, sir. They sent quite a long list. We've received a few other things, and Clive and I have kept it and all the product from the contacts ready for you to look through. Oh, and an envelope addressed to you arrived in the local mail yesterday. I opened it in the event it was something urgent, but the only thing was what appeared to be an old newspaper advertisement for men's clothing."

Meacham fell silent for a moment, then began talking again in a hesitant, cautious voice. "It's very good you found that agent in Abadan, Mr. Keeler, and I trust it'll lay to rest this bother about the railroad. And as I said, I can't express how grateful I am that you overlooked my mistake on that list of. . . ."

"I believe we agreed that you were to forget that, Meacham."

"Yes, sir, Mr. Keeler. I have, but I didn't see any harm in bringing it up in private."

"One cannot discuss what one cannot remember, Meacham. It's essential that Holcomb not be given further reason for suspicion, and that Beamish not have any inkling of what happened. The only way to do that is for you to put it completely out of your mind."

Meacham lapsed into silence again. Keeler took out his cigarettes and lit one. While he and Holcomb had been in Tabriz, the agent in Abadan had sent Mueller a list of scheduled rail traffic that included a munitions train accompanied by a passenger train. And either through inattention or because he had been drinking too much at the time, Meacham had allowed Mueller to transmit the list to Berlin without deleting the two trains.

When Keeler had returned, it had been too late to correct the situation without compromising Mueller with the Abwehr, while Meacham would have been recalled to London for disciplinary action if the facts had been presented candidly. Anticipating an attack, but handicapped by the circumstances, Keeler had done what he could to minimize the damage.

He had included an analysis in a daily situation report that led to the conclusion that the agent in Abadan had begun transmitting directly to Berlin by radio; then he had passed a warning through Campbell to increase the aerial surveillance over the railroad. He had waited for the blow to fall. It had come, sudden and devastating, with the trains destroyed, hundreds of Russian casualties, and the railroad closed by mines. In the ensuing upheaval, London had ordered action against the agent in Abadan.

The gusty wind blew drifts of sand across the road

leading toward the twinkling expanse of lights of Teheran. The headlights picked out a movement below the shoulder of the road—ragged robes whipping in the wind. A group of devout Moslems on their way to the holy city of Meshed had camped for the night by a large culvert.

At the embassy compound, Meacham parked the car on the drive by the chancellery building. Keeler and Meacham carried the boxes along the path and up the steps. A guard unlocked the door, then the duty officer opened the night register and pushed it across the desk as Keeler and Meacham crossed the lobby with the boxes.

Keeler signed the register and handed the pencil to Meacham. "I'll be down in a moment, Meacham," he said. "I have a call to make."

Meacham nodded, signing the register. He picked up two of the boxes and walked toward the basement stairs. The duty officer hesitated as Keeler looked at him, then stood up and moved away from the desk. Keeler pulled the telephone on the desk closer and dialed Pourzand's number. The telephone on the other end rang several times before Pourzand answered it.

"My watch needs to be repaired," Keeler said quietly in French. "What would be a convenient time for me to bring it to you?"

"Would eleven o'clock be convenient for you, sir?"

"Yes, I will be there at eleven."

"It is my pleasure to serve you, sir."

The line went dead. Keeler replaced the receiver, thinking about the conversation. Pourzand, his voice tense with contained excitement, had apparently found out something he considered important. Keeler pushed the telephone back across the desk, then picked up the boxes and walked toward the stairs.

Meacham and Holcomb came along the basement hall and took the boxes as Keeler came down the stairs. He signed the register, then walked along the hall to the room at the end. Meacham and Holcomb had put the boxes by the file cabinets and were making up money envelopes for the contacts that night.

The list of Polish deserters that Campbell had provided and the list of graduates from the Wehrmacht officer training academy were on the table, with a folder containing copies of statements made by American soldiers who had been guards on the munitions train that had been attacked. Folders containing material collected from agents during Keeler's absence were stacked on the table.

The only thing out of the ordinary that had occurred was another minor coup Holcomb had made through Mokhtar, who had somehow managed to find out the frequencies being used between Berlin and the SD officers with Kharis's tribe. It was a potentially valuable piece of information if the SD expanded their activities beyond training and maintaining friendly relations with the tribe. And it was another instance in which Mokhtar had apparently taken extreme risks.

"I sent a request to London for crystals for those frequencies," Holcomb said, sealing the last money envelope and placing it on the desk. "I could probably have got them from the people down the hall, but I thought you'd prefer to get them from London."

"Yes, I do," Keeler replied. "There's no urgency involved, so there's no point in revealing to outsiders that we're interested in those frequencies." He took a drag on his cigarette and exhaled musingly. "Mokhtar is beginning to worry me, Holcomb."

Holcomb nodded as he took the case box and envelopes

to a file cabinet. "It does seem to be getting harder to keep him reined in, Mr. Keeler. If Kharis becomes at all suspicious of him, there's little question that we'll lose our contact."

"I'm concerned that it might amount to somewhat more than that. Have you offered him a Z pill?"

Holcomb closed the file cabinet drawer and shook his head as he returned to the table. "No, sir. That would probably impress him more than the warnings I've given him, wouldn't it?"

"Hopefully; and if he has the courage to use the pill, it will reduce the likelihood that our connection with Mokhtar will be revealed. To further reduce that possibility, you'd better find a different drop and put a cutout between you and the drop. Arrange a personal meeting with Mokhtar to give him the pill and to tell him how to use it, then set up a new drop and the cutout as soon as possible."

"Yes, sir. You think we might be in some personal danger, then?"

"Of course. We always are, but avoiding unnecessary risks is simply good tradecraft. Kharis is a drug dealer, and drug dealers aren't known for observing the Marylebone rules of cricket." He stubbed out his cigarette in the ashtray. "Are you set up for a split rendezvous tonight?"

"Yes, sir. I was going to check Mokhtar's drop, then make my share of the contacts."

"We don't have very many tonight," Meacham said. "The only ones I have are the cutout for the clerk in Parliament and the man in charge of the surveillance team assigned to Abolfazi. I can give them a miss if you've something more important at hand, Mr. Keeler."

"No, there's no need for that. I want to meet with a

prospect, and I'll with you. You can let me off at the Shirivan just before eleven and make your contacts, then come back and wait for me."

"Yes, sir. It's a good while before eleven, so shall I sort out the contents of these boxes you brought from Abadan?"

"Yes, if you would. There's propaganda material and other things that would be of no use to London. Is there anywhere to store it until we have an opportunity to destroy it?"

"There's plenty of room in that building beside the garages, where we put the things from Tabriz. The head chauffeur said we can have the entire building if we need it."

Keeler nodded, turning to the material on the table. Holcomb gathered up most of the envelopes and left as Meacham began opening the boxes and rummaging through them. Keeler took out the list of Polish deserters, the list of Wehrmacht officer training academy graduates, and the statements from the American guards on the munitions train that had been destroyed. He spread out the papers and looked at them as he lit a cigarette.

The attack had been exceptionally effective, even for sondercommandos. The radio equipment in the cabooses on the trains had been destroyed before a distress signal could be sent. Approximately thirty sondercommandos had defeated more than ten times that number of Russian soldiers. A wide trail had led to the west for several miles; then the sondercommandos and their prisoners had simply disappeared.

The placement of antipersonnel mines as well as thermite mines along the railroad had aroused Keeler's interest. It was a different tactic, and any departure from proven methods was unusual for German forces. The way the sondercommandos had dealt with their prisoners had also piqued his curiosity. The Russians had been treated with a savage brutality that was uncharacteristic of sondercommandos, while the Americans had been treated with more than customary consideration.

The written statements by the Americans contained good descriptions of the German commander—a blond lieutenant in his early twenties, a little over six feet tall and weighing about two hundred pounds, a friendly man who had talked with the Americans. He had been addressed by name several times in the presence of the Americans. There was disagreement about the name, but all the different phonetic versions were distinctly Polish.

The names of all sondercommando officers, all unmistakably German, were known. The most logical explanation was that the Brandenburg Division had been assigned a new lieutenant whose name sounded Polish. But that did not explain the contrast in the treatment of prisoners. Then, reading through the lists of Polish deserters and officer graduates, Keeler found the same name on both lists.

Anton Vichai Vorczek.

Pulling a writing pad closer, Keeler wrote a short message to London, recommending that the name be added to the list of officers in the Brandenburg Division. He looked again at when Vorczek had deserted from Pahlavi, and at the date he had graduated from officer training. Vorczek's rise within the Brandenburg Division had been meteoric. His treatment of the Russian prisoners was evidence of what had provided the energy and determination for that rise. The man obviously had a lethal hatred for Russians. He was also an extremely dangerous man. Keeler added another sentence to the message, recommending that agents inside Germany be directed to obtain as much information about Vorczek as possible.

The Shirivan was a restaurant on the corner of a quiet street. Meacham pulled to the curb down the street, out of the light from the sign over the marquee. Keeler got out of the car, moving into the shadows of a doorway. The car pulled away as Keeler crossed the street. He stepped into an alley and walked along it to a recessed doorway. The ticking of clocks could be heard through the door; then they all began chiming eleven o'clock. The clamor of gongs swelled, then died away. Keeler tapped on the door, and it opened.

The darkness smelled of oily metal and Pourzand's cologne over stale sweat. The door closed behind Keeler and the bolts rattled into place, then Pourzand opened the door to the workshop at the rear of his store. A bright lamp beamed down on a workbench litered with tools and disassembled clocks. Cluttered shelves lined the shadowed walls. Pourzand sat on a stool in front of the workbench as Keeler sat down on a chair.

The glaring light shone down on Pourzand's face, making deep shadows in his cavernous eyesockets as he talked. Having indentified another NKVD agent in the city, he related the steps he had taken to locate the man. But it was only a preliminary; he had something important to report, and he was making the most of the moment, fleshing it out with trivia that contained interesting bits of information. Keeler smoked, listened, and waited.

The clocks in the shop chimed midnight, subsiding in a clucking whir of clockworks. A single clock that was out of synchronization with the others chimed. Pourzand frowned in irritation, but continued talking. Having exhausted the subject of the NKVD agent, he went on to a new assignment Kurov had given him.

Pourzand changed the subject again, his tone revealing that he was finally approaching his real reason for requesting the meeting. "I had a personal meeting with Vertinski three days ago, Mr. Keeler," he said. "I expected a call from you yesterday, because I mailed the signal to you immediately after the meeting."

"I was elsewhere," Keeler replied, taking a drag on his cigarette. "So you had a personal meeting?"

Pourzand smiled widely, nodding. "Yes, he wished to see me. Kurov arranged it then he took me to the Soviet embassy in a car. It was after dark, but the windows of the car had curtains to make certain that no one would see me."

"And what did Vertinski discuss with you?"

Pourzand's smile became wider, his deeply-set eyes shining. "He told me about the important official who is coming here from Moscow. He said that the official would present me with a medal for the excellent work I have done. He did not say when the man would arrive, but he told me his name. He said that I must not mention it to anyone, but I have no secrets from you, of course." He hesitated, licking his lips and prolonging the moment a breathless second longer before he finished. "His name is Andrei Aleksandrovich Kolesnikov."

Keeler took a drag on his cigarette and slowly exhaled, then nodded. "You have done well, Pourzand."

Pourzand licked his lips again, his eyes moving restlessly over Keeler's impassive face. "Are you familiar with the name, Mr. Keeler?"

"Why do you ask?"

"Because I am not, even though he must be very important from the way Vertinski spoke of him. I also do not know his official position, and one would wonder why he is coming here, wouldn't one?"

"He is undoubtedly coming here to present you with a medal, as Vertinski told you."

Pourzand blinked, then forced a hollow laugh. Keeler stood up, stubbing out his cigarette in the ashtray. Pourzand stood as well and moved toward the door. "Do you have an assignment for me, Mr. Keeler?"

"Continue looking for other NKVD agents, but be careful."

"I will," Pourzand replied, nodding emphatically. "I have no doubt about what would happen to me if Vertinski discovered my arrangement with you. Is there anything else?"

"When you find out the date of Kolesnikov's arrival, send me a signal."

Pourzand looked up at Keeler, his dark, recessed eyes probing and curious, then silently nodded as he opened the door. Keeler followed him into the tiny rear entry then stepped out into the stillness of the alley.

The door closed behind him. He stood and waited for his eyes to adjust to the darkness. The clocks in the shop struck one, a brief chorus of gongs. Then the clock with a different view of its position in the framework of time chimed a single bright, ringing note. Keeler walked slowly along the sidewalk, thinking about what Pourzand had said. He had known Kolesnikov's name for years. It had first found its way into the files in London on a long list of Stalin's trusted lieutenants, a faceless crowd that extended his reach and sting. The list had changed over the years as some enjoyed a brief moment in the sunlight and disappeared. But Kolesnikov had remained. He had been Stalin's eyes and ears in the OGPU, the Unified State Political Directorate, while that agency had been engaged in the collectivization of land, during which millions of dispossessed peasants had starved. Since the OGPU had proved an international embarrassment when the Soviet Union had sought admission to the League of Nations, it had been reconstituted as the GUGB, the Chief Directorate for State Security. Kolesnikov had remained in that organization during the great purges of the 1930s. When the war with Germany began, Kolesnikov was still securely in Stalin's favor, having survived the liquidation of several directors of the GUGB. He had been commissioned a lieutenant general and given command of a regiment of soldiers assigned the sole mission of protecting Stalin. Kolesnikov was the official charged with the responsibility for Stalin's safety. If Kolesnikov was coming to Teheran, then Stalin was coming to Teheran. And the only reason Stalin could have for coming to Teheran was for a meeting of heads of state.

The Shirivan was closed for the night. Meacham was asleep in the car farther along the street. Keeler woke him getting in, and Meacham shivered and grumbled about the inoperative heater as he drove along the silent, deserted streets to the embassy. They went in and signed the registers, then descended to the basement.

Holcomb was assembling material he had collected from contacts. Meacham went up to the embassy kitchen and returned with cups of tea on a tray and he sipped a cup as he wrote a memorandum on the surveillance of Abolfazi. Keeler looked through the material that Holcomb and Meacham had collected as he considered the full implications of what Pourzand had told him.

All the facts pointed to the conclusion that Stalin had decided that it was in his best interests to agree to the repeated requests from Washington for a meeting of heads of state. The NKVD networks in Iran had been manned with additional operatives and other preparations had been made, culminating in a visit by Kolesnikov to inspect security arrangements.

Only Moscow knew of the plan; Washington and London remained unaware. Keeler had struck gold, priceless intelligence. A meeting was going to take place at which agreements of far-reaching importance would be made. The opportunity to alter the circumstances that would influence those agreements was of incalculable value.

The Allies were unified against the Axis Powers, but their other objectives diverged. For months Stalin had been vehemently insistent that a western front be established in France to relieve pressure on his armies so they could drive into Eastern Europe. The planners in Washington, wanting to bring the war to a speedy end, were committed to Stalin's view. London agreed in principle, but they remembered the butchery at Gallipoli during World War I, the price of an amphibious landing on fortified beaches. And they also remembered the Crimea and other conflicts whose objective had been to contain Russian hegemony.

With armies locked in combat in Italy, the British wanted to push up through Italy and Austria, meeting the Russian armies in the Balkans and Eastern Europe. The Americans were pessimistic about Italy, where the Germans were retreating from one mountain range to another—battles fought for yards instead of miles. But German resistance in Italy could be broken.

If the planners in London knew that the heads of state were going to meet, they might decide that a decisive breakthrough in Italy before the meeting would be worth the sacrifice of divisions. When headlines proclaimed the breakthrough, Washington would be compelled to co-operate in order to share the credit. Then, when Roosevelt, Churchill, and Stalin met, Italy would be the answer to Stalin's western front.

But Keeler's information had been acquired through an unauthorized line of investigation, obtained through careful, deliberate penetration of an NKVD network, in direct violation of the limitations of the residency mission. It could not be attributed to any other source. The very nature of the information made the source immediately obvious.

Keeler stubbed out his cigarette in the ashtray. He would receive a written reprimand and a scathing lecture from Willoughby, damage to his career that could be eventually overcome. More importantly, he would be recalled immediately and reassigned elsewhere. Penetration of allied intelligence services was done only through means that could be denied, not by a field residency.

At whatever cost, London would not risk the slightest chance that the Soviets would discover the penetration. Pourzand would disappear. The meeting, which the Abwehr and SD were certain to find out about, would take place. And a new resident, unfamiliar with the area and the network, would face the hopeless task of providing intelligence support to the security forces.

Meacham shuffled a stack of papers and put them aside. "I suppose we could wait until we come in this afternoon to work on the sitrep, couldn't we, Mr. Keeler? Nothing out of the ordinary has happened, so it'll only be a routine report, won't it?''

Holcomb looked up from the papers he was thumbing through and Meacham smothered a yawn and looked at Keeler sleepily as he waited for a reply. Keeler hesitated as he lit a cigarette.

Then he nodded, taking a drag on the cigarette. ''Yes, we can wait until this afternoon to work on it. It'll be only a routine report.''

CHAPTER EIGHTEEN

NIEDERSDORF'S OFFICE WAS cold, the damp chill of early autumn that had settled over Berlin seeping in through cracks around the windows. He sat stiffly in his chair to keep from shivering as he watched Vorczek. The lieutenant sat on a chair beside the desk, reading a copy of Project Jael. He had changed completely since the first time Niedersdorf had seen him. From a gauche, clumsy corporal, he had turned into a poised, self-confident young officer. His hair was a blond bristle; his face and neck had a ruddy glow of vibrant, virile health. Even after days on a train, he was clean shaven and his uniform was immaculately neat. He also appeared comfortable in the cold office, relaxed as he turned the pages.

"I must apologize for the temperature, Lieutenant," Niedersdorf said. "But we have heat in the building only every other day now."

"I am warm enough, Colonel Niedersdorf," Vorczek replied, glancing up. He smiled. "It is much warmer in here than outside."

Niedersdorf smiled thinly and nodded, looking away.

After a moment, the lieutenant finished reading the plan and put it on the edge of the desk, sitting back in his chair. "As I mentioned, the staff has been working on the plan," Niedersdorf said. "If you are familiar with it, you saw that several changes have been made."

"A number of changes, sir," Vorczek replied, nodding.

"There will be further changes to incorporate recent developments, and the admiral may also have some suggestions. He wishes to meet you, so I will take you to see him when he finishes with Colonel Lahousen."

"I have been looking forward to meeting the admiral."

Niedersdorf nodded, thinking longingly of his quarters, a hot bath, and a drink. Hearing footsteps in the hall, he looked at the door as Lahousen passed. Suppressing a sigh of relief, he stood up. "We will see if the admiral is free now."

Niedersdorf walked briskly out of the office and along the hall, Vorczek following him. Canaris, sitting at his desk and poring over a stack of papers, looked up and nodded when Niedersdorf rapped on the doorjamb. Niedersdorf stepped into the office. "Admiral Canaris, this is Lieutenant Vorczek."

Canaris sat back in his chair as Vorczek marched across the office to the desk and snapped his heels together, bowing. His eyes moved up and down Vorczek, musing and analytical. "I am pleased to meet you, Lieutenant Vorczek."

Vorczek bowed again and stood stiffly at attention. "It is a pleasure and an honor to meet you, Admiral Canaris."

"I trust Frau Vorczek enjoys good health?"

"She is well, thank you, Admiral Canaris."

"When is the baby due?"

Vorczek blinked, surprised. Niedersdorf, unaware that

Vorczek's wife was pregnant, glanced between Canaris and Vorczek. The lieutenant smiled then and replied, "In about five months, Admiral Canaris."

"Please ask Frau Vorczek to send a note to Frau Canaris when the baby is born, so she can send a spoon. And your son Johann is well also?"

"He is well also, thank you, Admiral Canaris."

Canaris put out his cigarette in the ashtray, standing up. "I am sure you would enjoy some refreshment after your long journey, Lieutenant Vorczek. Will you join us, Franz?"

"Yes, thank you, Admiral Canaris."

Canaris went to the cabinet in the corner. Niedersdorf shifted his weight from one foot to the other, tensing his muscles to keep from shivering. The office felt as cold as his own, but Canaris appeared as relaxed and comfortable as Vorczek. The admiral returned and handed filled glasses to Nidersdorf and Vorczek, then lifted his in a silent toast.

Niedersdorf lifted his glass, then took a sip. The scotch had been finished months before, as had the other exotic liquors in the cabinet. The glass contained Steinhäger, Niedersdorf's favorite drink. The golden warmth trickled down his throat to his stomach, dispelling some of the damp chill of the room.

Vorczek drained his glass in a single swallow, then glanced between Canaris and Niedersdorf. He smiled, unabashed. "I beg your pardon, Admiral Canaris. Perhaps I am more accustomed to the barracks than to headquarters."

Canaris laughed heartily, the first time Niedersdorf had seen him thoroughly amused in weeks. He shook his head. "There is no need for you to apologize, Lieutenant Vorczek. A touch of the spirit of the barracks will serve to remind us of who we are, which will be good for me and my staff. Will you have another?"

"No, thank you, Admiral Canaris."

"Then sit down—and you, Franz." Canaris sat down, taking another sip from his glass and reaching for his cigarettes. "We have ample time to prepare for the mission you are to command, Lieutenant, and I want my staff to have the benefit of your experience. You will work with them and help them put Project Jael into final form."

"Yes, Admiral Canaris."

"The staff will also help you set up specific training objectives for your platoon. For example, we have recordings of the transmissions of your contact in Teheran. Your radio operator will become completely familiar with your contact's telegraphic rhythm, so the enemy will be unable to mislead you by attempting to impersonate him. Your demolitions people should practice setting charges with the type of explosives you are taking. Each man in your platoon must be thoroughly trained for this mission."

"Yes, Admiral Canaris."

Canaris took a cigarette from the box and sat back in his chair, picking up his lighter from the desk. "My staff has already made some alterations to the plan. You should review them as soon as possible so you will be prepared to work with them."

"Colonel Niedersdorf permitted me to read his copy of the plan, Admiral Canaris. I am familiar with the changes."

Canaris lit his cigarette and smiled as he exhaled smoke. "You are very enthusiastic about this mission, aren't you?"

"I am, Admiral Canaris," Vorczek replied, unsmiling. "I am prepared to excute any mission, as any soldier should be. But the opportunity to kill Stalin is more than I ever hoped for. I intend to succeed."

Canaris lifted his eyebrows and nodded. "I am gratified by your determination, but remember that Stalin is only one third of your mission," he said dryly. "You have had a long journey, Lieutenant Vorczek, so you may go to your quarters now. Tomorrow morning, Colonel Niedersdorf will introduce you to the officers you will work with. And I will talk with you again from time to time."

"Very well, Admiral Canaris," Vorczek replied, standing up. He bowed to Canaris and to Niedersdorf. "Good night."

Niedersdorf murmured a reply as Canaris nodded. Vorczek turned and left, his heels clicking on the floor. Niedersdorf stood up and put his glass on the edge of his desk. The warmth from the floor had faded rapidly. He thought about his quarters again, about a hot bath and a drink.

Canaris drew on his cigarette, looking up at Niedersdorf. "It appears that we will have a further complication on Project Jael, Franz. I was informed at OKW today that our comrades on the Bendlerstrasse are also sending a team on the same mission."

"Have we been ordered to collaborate with them, or simply to avoid a conflict?"

"Both," Canaris replied. "Our plans must be coordinated so there will *be* no conflict. At the same time, we must make provision for cooperation if both our forces suffer too many casualties and must combine their resources in order to complete the mission."

"Does the SD have a contact in Teheran?"

"Apparently they have what amounts to an advance party not far from there." Canaris chuckled. "They have some officers living with a nomadic tribe near Teheran, which will enable them to move their team into place quite easily. Emil has taken great interest in this, so we are compelled to be completely cooperative. I will have our liaison officer arrange a conference with the SD to work out the details."

"I trust that can be done soon, Admiral Canaris. This could seriously disrupt our preparations."

"I am sure the SD will be as eager as we are to proceed promptly," Canaris said. "I don't anticipate any delay because of this, so we will let the staff and Lieutenant Vorczek get on with it while we make arrangements with the SD." He puffed on his cigarette and exhaled slowly, staring into a dark corner of the room. "I was looking forward to meeting Lieutenant Vorczek," he said musingly. "And I wasn't disappointed. You did well in selecting him for officer training, Franz."

"Thank you, Admiral Canaris. I believe he will succeed in this mission, if anyone can. But it will be very difficult. And Keeler is in Teheran, of course."

Canaris smiled whimsically. "Yes, that is quite true, Franz," he murmured quietly. "Keeler is in Teheran."

PART FOUR

November, 1943

CHAPTER NINETEEN

SOLDIERS MOVED RAPIDLY and stamped out flames, extinguishing the fires that tracers from machine guns had ignited in clumps of the dry, brittle brush. The smoke from the burning brush, its scent blending with the penetrating reek of cordite, swirled in the cold winter wind gusting through the valley. Wounded horses screamed and thrashed, their sounds of agony stopping abruptly as soldiers shot them.

A line of pack horses was on the shoulder of the slope above the valley, wooden cases of supplies and munitions tied to the pack saddles. Keeler walked among the dead horses and looked at the stenciled markings on the cases. Holcomb, Callaghan, and an Army captain named Spencer prowled about in the valley, examining the bodies.

Keeler finished his perusal and joined them. The arid valley was drab and desolate in the flat, gray light under an overcast sky. The echoes of the roaring thunder of machine guns seemed to linger over the scene of slaughter where gouts of blood oozed from the gaping wounds of bodies in robes and Wehrmacht uniforms sprawled in the brush.

Spencer, Callaghan, and Holcomb were gathered around the body of an officer. They turned as Keeler approached. "This man was a lieutenant colonel, and there's another officer over there, Mr. Keeler," Spencer said. "And yet another one over there. They sent along a lot of rank for such a small party."

The face was partly visible. Keeler recognized it from the photographs Mokhtar had taken. It was Lazich, the SD officer who had been with the tribe. "Yes, it appears so," Keeler replied. "Would it be possible for some of your men to gather the bodies and weapons in one place?"

"Yes, of course, Mr. Keeler. Where would you like them?"

"Up there by the pack horses would be convenient."

"Very well. I'll have a word with Colonel Campbell about it, then I'll detail a platoon."

Keeler nodded, lighting a cigarette as Spencer walked away. Campbell was on the long, flat ridge at one side of the valley, where the soldiers had been deployed for the attack. Most of them were still on the ridge, clearing a landing strip for small aircraft. Spencer walked up the slope toward the ridge.

"Well, this was another smooth operation, Frank," Callaghan commented. "It went off without a hitch."

"You did more than your share, Charles. Holcomb, get set up to deal with the bodies, if you would. If airplanes are able to land here, we may be able to leave within a few hours."

Holcomb smiled wryly. "Let's hope they can, because I can well do without another drive like the one we had getting here."

"Not to mention the long walk that goes with it,

right?" Callaghan chuckled. "I'll give you a hand, Clive."

As they walked away, Keeler looked back down at Lazich's body. The contact with the tribe had greatly simplified the attack on the SD team being sent to Teheran. Mokhtar had found out where Lazich and the tribesmen intended to rendezvous with the team, and monitoring the SD radio frequencies, had provided the precise date that the team and their equipment would be dropped by parachute.

The tribesmen and the SD team had been completely relaxed, confident in the security of the isolated area. The attack had been totally unexpected and devastating. But the low hill across the valley was broken by ravines and gullies. In the confusion of battle, some could have escaped.

And there was an even more serious threat than that posed by the SD team. With the heads of state due to arrive the following week, Mueller had received instructions from Berlin to make arrangements for a platoon of sondercommandos. He had rented an empty warehouse near the edge of Teheran, where an ambush could be mounted. Sondercommandos were an elite force, far more effective than SD saboteurs. And ominously, the code name for the sondercommando platoon was "Anton."

The soldiers finished extinguishing the brush fires, then began unloading the pack saddles on the dead horses and carrying cases of supplies and munitions to the ravines across the valley to burn them. A platoon came down from the ridge, sent by Spencer to collect the bodies and weapons. As they carried out their assignment, Holcomb and Callaghan followed, emptying pockets, photographing faces, and taking fingerprints. Keeler walked up the slope to examine the belongings stacked neatly beside the bodies. Each man had identification tags. Their pockets contained wallets, pictures of relatives and friends, and other personal items. A map case was beside the body of a captain, the team commander. With Teutonic precision, he had documented the preparations for the mission in a notebook. His map case also contained a personnel roster of the team.

When the soldiers finished arranging the bodies, one long row in robes and another in uniform, they began digging two large pits to bury them. Keeler had the lieutenant in charge of the platoon send a soldier to count the dead horses, then took out the personnel roster and counted the bodies. There were forty-three dead saddle horses and thirty-six bodies of tribesmen. The roster listed thirty-two SD men. There were twenty-eight bodies in uniform. Seven tribesmen and four members of the SD team had escaped.

Acrid smoke from burning supplies eddied across the valley in the wind as Keeler studied the bodies again, considering those who had escaped. The four Germans were in an arid desert without food or water; but with assistance from the tribe, they could still be a threat. The seven tribesmen presented a problem of a different nature. Rashid al-Kharis would get a full description of what had happened. He might hear something that would make him look among those close to him for a traitor.

The smoke thickened as the soldiers set fire to the munitions they had carried across the valley from the pack horses, small arms ammunition popping. Holcomb and Callaghan bundled the belongings beside the bodies into empty cartons taken from the pack horses. When they had finished, the soldiers began dragging the bodies to the burial pits they had dug. Keeler carried one of the cartons up the slope with Holcomb and Callaghan.

The ridge was a high point in the surrounding terrain. Barren, rolling hills stretched away on all sides, fading into the hazy distance. Along the crest of the ridge, a wide swath of brush had been cleared for a landing strip. The soldiers were gathering around fires at one end of the ridge, laughing and talking as they sorted out their packs and weapons. Medics tended those who had been wounded. Campbell and Spencer sat by another fire with the platoon lieutenants.

Campbell turned to Keeler as he and the other two men put down their cartons and sat down by the fire. "We contacted the garrison, Keeler," he said. "They're sending an observation aircraft and one of those single engine transport aircraft. If the transport is able to land, we'll have you out of here promptly."

"Very well."

"The wounded will have priority, of course. But even if we have to trek back to the vehicles and spend the night getting back to Teheran, the trip has been well worth it, hasn't it?"

"Yes."

Campbell nodded in satisfaction, brushing his mustaches with a finger. "They'll think twice before they try that again! And now the dignitaries will be safe when they arrive, which is the main thing."

"Killing those horses struck a raw nerve," Spencer commented. "I saw a mare down there that's a twin of one I have at home."

Campbell sobered, nodding. "Aye, that was a sinful business, and I didn't enjoy it one bit. Do you own some

Arabs, then, Spencer?''

''Yes, sir. I have two, and two geldings that are first crosses.''

Callaghan chuckled, opening his canvas musette bag. ''Well, I have something here that I wouldn't trade right now for a herd of horses,'' he said. ''Who's for a drink of booze?''

''By God, I won't say no,'' Campbell replied jovially. ''This wind is cutting through me like a knife, overcoat and all.''

Callaghan laughed, taking a bottle of whiskey from the bag. He opened it and passed it around. The smoke from the ravines on the other side of the valley was thickening into billowing clouds and drifting across the ridge, the rattles of ammunition exploding punctuated by an occasional muffled thud of larger munitions. Keeler took a drink from the whiskey bottle and passed it on, listening to the conversation.

A committee comprised of equal numbers of American, British, and Russian representatives had been formed several weeks before to coordinate preparations for the momentous meeting. Keeler was a member of the committee, as were Campbell and Callaghan. The conversation turned to the committee, and to the fact that its final meeting was two days later. ''I'll be bloody glad to see the end of it,'' Campbell growled. ''I've had enough haggling with the Bolshies to last me for a lifetime.''

''I'm with you one hundred percent,'' Callaghan agreed. ''But when it started to get to me, I would just take a look at Frank. He certainly didn't let all of that nit-picking faze him.''

''Aye, well, the man's not human,'' Campbell chuckled. ''I daresay he's been neither happy nor angry since he was a schoolboy. We've just finished a completely successful attack on the enemy, but you would never know it. You might at least express some appreciation, Keeler."

"I'm most grateful, of course," Keeler said. "But the attack *wasn't* completely successful. Four members of the SD team and at least seven tribesmen escaped."

Campbell's smile faded. "Well, any soldier can tell you that it's well-nigh impossible to totally wipe out any force in this sort of terrain," he said. "And what can they do out here in the desert? They'll undoubtedly starve, particularly the Germans."

"The tribesmen will be back with their tribe before we're in Teheran. The Germans may die of thirst and starvation if they've become separated and lost, but they'll survive if they're with the tribesmen."

Campbell shrugged and looked away, disgruntled. There was a moment of awkward silence, then Campbell commented on a neutral subject. The conversation resumed, Campbell's aggravation fading as he talked with the others. Keeler lit a cigarette as he listened absently to the conversation and thought about the tribesmen who had escaped. Rashid al-Kharis would be enraged when he heard what had happened. Mokhtar had taken many risks. If the time came for him to use the cyanide capsule, he might hesitate too long.

The crackling of ammunition exploding in the ravine gradually faded. The morning hours slowly passed, the bleak, gray light remaining unchanged under the heavy overcast. During early afternoon, one of the soldiers saw the airplanes, dots on the murky horizon, flying at low altitude below the overcast as they searched the desert for the temporary bivouac. The wind carried away the sound of their engines until they were near; then it became a droning roar. The transport circled as the small observation aircraft descended toward the ridge.

After skimming along the landing strip, the airplane circled back around, touched down and bounced along the sandy, uneven ground, then taxied back to the downwind end of the strip as the transport descended. Soldiers carried the wounded on stretchers to the landing strip, Keeler following with Holcomb, Callaghan, and the officers.

The transport bounced along the landing strip, slowed and turned around, its engine snarling, then taxied back to a few yards from the observation aircraft and snapped around into position for takeoff. The pilots, both of them lieutenants, left the engines idling and climbed out.

The lieutenants exchanged salutes with Campbell and Spencer, the pilot of the transport talking over the noise of the idling engines. "I can take your wounded and the medics, Colonel," he said. "And one more man besides them, but I can't get airspeed on this dirt strip with any more weight than that. But I can make another trip before dark."

Campbell nodded, his mustaches fluttering in the wind from the propellers. He turned to Keeler. "It would make good sense for Callaghan to go on the first trip, Keeler. You have those boxes, and you and Holcomb will want to go together."

"Yes, that's right," Keeler agreed. "Charles, contact Meacham and ask him to meet us at the airport, if you would."

"Yeah, I sure will, Frank," Callaghan replied. "I hate to desert you, but I'll buy you a drink when I see you in Teheran."

"I can take one passenger, if that would be any help,"

the other pilot said. "Would you like to come with me, Colonel?"

Campbell shrugged and nodded. "Yes—the brigadier wants a report from me as soon as possible, so I will. Come on. Let's get our things, Callaghan."

They walked back toward the fire as the soldiers carried the stretchers to the transport. The pilot climbed and took lengths of cargo rope out of the rear of the airplane, handing it to the soldiers, who tied down the stretchers on the floor, then the medics climbed in.

Campbell and Callaghan returned with their bags, Campbell clambering into the observation aircraft as Callaghan got into the transport. The engine on the transport roared, then the airplane disappeared in a blinding cloud of dust. It came into view again when it lifted into the air at the end of the strip, followed by the other airplane.

It was quiet after they had gone. The wind swept across the ridge, carrying the haze of smoke from the fire in the ravines and smothering the voices and laughter of the soldiers around the fires. Spencer took a deck of cards from his pack, and he and Holcomb played whist with two of the platoon lieutenants. Keeler sat and stared into the fire as he smoked, listening absently to the conversation and thinking about Mokhtar.

The wind turned colder as the hours passed, the gray, dull light beginning to fade into protracted winter dusk. The transport aircraft reappeared suddenly, dropping out of the clouds a half mile away. Spencer carried one of the cartons down the strip with Keeler and Holcomb. The airplane landed and taxied back, then Keeler and Holcomb lifted the cartons into it and climbed inside.

There were no seats in the small transport. They sat on

the cartons and held onto the bare aluminum frame members at the side of the cargo compartment during takeoff. The airplane staggered into the air and picked up speed, banking into a climbing turn away from the ridge.

Hours passed. The cargo compartment was icily cold and enveloped in impenetrable darkness. Then the airplane began descending. The clouds outside the window shredded away and the lights of Teheran Airport gleamed in the night. The airplane touched down and taxied to a ramp.

The frigid wind sweeping across the open ramp, blowing tiny dry snowflakes, felt almost warm after the freezing cold of the airplane. Meacham was waiting with a car. Having expected Keeler and Holcomb back the following day, he had made preparations to meet the contacts that night. Back at the embassy, Keeler looked at the money envelopes on the table and went over the material that had accumulated during his absence while Meacham and Holcomb carried in the cartons. When they had finished, Holcomb looked through the material as Meacham brought in a tray of sandwiches and tea.

"There you are, Clive," he said. "They're only fish paste butties, but that's all I could get. And there's some for you, Mr. Keeler. Shall I make the meetings with the contacts tonight, sir?"

Keeler nodded. "Yes. I see that we aren't meeting tonight with the head of the surveillance team assigned to Abolfazi."

Meacham shook his head as he took a bite of a sandwich and went to the file cabinets. "I believe he's scheduled for tomorrow night or the night after, sir." He took the station roll out of a drawer and thumbed through it, then nodded. "He's scheduled for Thursday night. But I can give him a signal for tonight, if you wish."

"No, you have a full schedule tonight. Holcomb, call him and set up a meeting, if you would. Get a report, and set him up for meetings every other night for the next few nights. Also, give him the outside telephone number, in the event he needs to call us. Abolfazi could be an alternate contact for that sondercommando platoon."

Holcomb nodded, eating a sandwich. "Very well, Mr. Keeler. Shall I send any instructions to Mokhtar?"

"I'd like to order him under for a while," Keeler said musingly, lighting a cigarette. "But there's a chance that he may hear something about those four SD men who escaped. Send him instructions to put a message in the drop if he hears anything, but he's not to actively try to do anything else until further notice. He'll have to be very cautious for the next few days."

"Even he should realize that," Holcomb chuckled, pushing his chair back from the table. "I'll use the outside line to call the cutout for the drop and give him a signal, and I'll also call the head of the surveillance team assigned to Abolfazi."

Keeler nodded, thumbing through the papers on the table. Holcomb went out as Keeler opened the folder containing the file copies of the daily situation reports that Meacham had prepared during the past days. He read the reports, then looked through the folders of material Meacham had collected from contacts.

Holcomb returned and sat down at the table. "They're all set up, Mr. Keeler," he said, taking a bite of a sandwich. "The cutout for Mokhtar's drop will meet me behind the bazaar, and I'll meet the head of the surveillance team at the usual rendezvous. Shall I help you with the report on the SD team or anything?"

"No, I'll take care of it. You could get some rest before you go, if you wish."

Holcomb shrugged, taking a drink of tea. "I'm not all that tired, sir. This may be a good time to make the rounds of the coffeehouses, and I could check with Cicero and see if he's had any feelers."

"Very well. I'm sure you realize that you must be very careful for the next few days. If by some chance Kharis finds out about Mokhtar and our involvement with him, he will probably try to retaliate. You should also exercise additional care, Meacham."

Meacham looked up, his eyes wide. "Yes, sir. Do you think Kharis already knows?"

"I should think so. The tribesmen who escaped have probably rejoined the tribe by now, and Mokhtar reported that he believes Kharis has radio contact with the tribe."

"Well, I'll keep my head down for a few days, then," Meacham said. He gulped the last of his tea and pushed his chair back from the table. "I might as well be on my way. It'll take me a while to get set up, and I have a lot of meetings. Are you leaving now, Clive?"

"Yes, I'll go see what cars are available," Holcomb replied. "And I'll try to get one with a good heater in it."

"I have the best of the lot," Meacham chuckled, gathering up the money envelopes. "I won't let you have mine, but I'll rendezvous with you after our meetings and let you warm up before we drive back."

After they had left, Keeler pushed the plate of sandwiches and cup of tea aside and lit a cigarette as he placed the cartons in a row beside the table and opened them.

The items from the dead men's pockets were bundled in

handkerchiefs and pieces of uniform shirts stained with dried blood. The roll of film Holcomb had used to photograph the men's faces was in a corner of a carton, along with the sheets of paper he had used to take fingerprints. Keeler sealed them in an envelope, then began opening the bundles. After removing the money and other items of no intelligence value, he sealed the cartons with tape and took them and the envelope to the mail room where the clerk logged them in for shipment to London, making up a receipt. Keeler returned to the room and put the receipt on the women's desk, put up the plates and cups on the tray and carried the tray to the kitchen.

The night duty cook put the tray in a sink, then made a pot of coffee which Keeler carried down to the basement room. He poured a cup of coffee and lit a cigarette, then began writing the report on the attack on the SD team. When the report was finished, Keeler gathered up the material from contacts that was stacked on the table, filed them and began reading a series of area intelligence summaries that had come in from London during his absence.

The door opened as Keeler was almost finished. Meacham looked in. He glanced around the room and frowned worriedly. "Clive didn't come back here, did he, sir?"

"No."

"We were going to rendezvous, but he didn't show. I went over to the power plant, but he hadn't been there either. The head of the surveillance team assigned to Abolfazi was still there, so I took his report. I thought Clive might have picked up something urgent and returned here."

"He was going to rendezvous with the cutout for

Mokhtar's drop behind the bazaar. Did you check there?"

"No, sir. I didn't recall where he said they were going to meet."

Keeler stubbed out his cigarette in the ashtray, then put on his shoulder holster and suit coat, shrugging into his trench coat and putting on his hat as they went out.

It was snowing heavily. Waves of dry flakes swept through the air on the wind and turned into blinding clouds of swirling white as Meacham drove slowly. He turned onto a narrow street behind the bazaar, switching off the headlights, then stopped the car.

"I'll have to use the headlights, sir," he said.

"Very well."

He drove on, the tires skidding in drifts that were piling up, then slowed as the car approached the mouth of an alley. The headlights gleamed on a car riddled with bullet holes. Meacham slammed on the brakes and froze.

"Back the car out into the street and park it, Meacham."

Taking a flashlight from the glove compartment, Keeler got out and walked into the alley.

The alley reeked of cordite. The holes in the car had been made by automatic weapons. Holcomb was slumped over the steering wheel, enough of his face remaining to identify him. Mokhtar's head was on the passenger side of the front seat, along with the cutout's head.

Keeler reached through the broken window and lifted out the heads by the hair. He carried them along the alley and tossed them into a pile of refuse. The rats would dispose of them. Taking out his handkerchief, he wiped his hands as he walked back to the car.

Meacham cleared his throat. "Is he . . . there, sir?"

Keeler put his handkerchief away and lit a cigarette.

"Yes. Go to the embassy and awaken one of the cryptographers, and send a priority message to London. Advise them that Holcomb has been killed, along with the agent Mokhtar. Details will follow shortly."

"Yes, sir. Is there anything else?"

"Call Campbell, and ask him to send a wrecker and an ambulance driven by men who can be trusted to be discreet. The car will have to be destroyed. We'll have Holcomb buried in the garrison cemetery under a cover name unless London advises otherwise."

"Yes, sir. Are we going to do anything about this?"

"Our mission is intelligence collection, not conducting vendettas."

"Yes, sir."

Keeler got out of the car. Meacham drove away, leaving Keeler alone.

Thoughts of Clive Holcomb, the man, tried to intrude, but he forced them out of his mind and pondered. No assistance was available, because Kharis was too powerful for the police and too elusive for the Army. At the same time, Kharis could inflict little damage. The network of contacts was safely divided into secure, isolated compartments. He was limited to striking at the few visible elements of the residency.

An increase in security would be necessary. The rendezvous would have to be changed more often; some tactics for operations in enemy territory would have to be employed. But those measures would be a handicap and a drain on time and energy, and the residency had been reduced to two operatives at a crucially important time. The heads of state would arrive shortly. Four SD assassins were at large, and a platoon of sondercommandos was being deployed to Teheran.

The frozen, gripping silence of the deserted street was broken only by the moan of the wind and the whisper of the snow. The dark was absolute, no ray of light penetrating the thick, black night. The snow brushed Keeler's face with an icy touch as he stood on the corner and smoked his cigarette, waiting for Meacham to return with the wrecker and the ambulance.

CHAPTER TWENTY

THE CONFERENCE ENDED, a murmur of conversation swelling as people rose from their seats around the long, gleaming table. Callaghan and the security officer of the American embassy, a man named Hites, were on one side of Keeler. The security officer of the British embassy, a portly former policeman named Morton, was on the other side. The Soviet delegation was across the table—one of Vertinski's operatives, the security officer of the Soviet embassy, and six Army officers.

Waiters came through a side door carrying trays of sandwiches and cake, stacks of china and glassware, and beverages. The Russians gathered up their briefcases and left as the others crossed the room to the buffet. The large room had an atmosphere of subdued luxury, with deep carpeting, spotless pastel walls, and indirect lighting, dominated by a large American eagle emblem on the wall.

The chairman of the committee was an American brigadier general who had been wounded in Italy. Most of the military officers followed him as he limped toward the buffet. Keeler went toward the other end of the buffet with Callaghan, Hites, and Morton. Campbell emerged from the crowd of military officers, joining Keeler and the others.

He glanced at Keeler, putting sandwiches on a plate. "Have you found out any more about what happened to Holcomb, Keeler?" he asked. "All you need do is name the guilty party, and I'll see to the rest."

"No, I haven't learned any more."

"It looks as though your suspicion of robbery was right, Frank," Callaghan commented. "I haven't been able to pick up a word on it."

"That appears the most logical explanation. He was carrying quite a large sum of money that wasn't recovered."

Campbell frowned, nodding. "That sort of thing happens every night in this cesspool of a city," he growled. "But it does seem you would have a replacement without delay, Keeler, considering the fact that the Allied leaders are coming here."

"A new operative is more of a handicap than a benefit at first."

Campbell grunted, biting into a ham sandwich. "One can always look forward to a good feed here. Callaghan, I can't understand why you aren't as chubby as a tomato."

"You would if you ate here all the time," Callaghan replied wryly, putting sandwiches on a plate "You should see some of the crap they dish up."

"Oh, it couldn't be all that bad," Campbell chuckled. "This makes up to an extent for having to deal with those bloody Bolshies. But I suppose we're finally organized in spite of them, aren't we?"

Callaghan smiled and nodded. Keeler filled a cup with coffee and moved to one side. Morton and Hites joined the conversation between Callaghan and Campbell, discussing the agreements that had been made for security when the heads of state arrived. An attendant came out of the cloak room at one side of the conference room and spoke to an officer who glanced around, then pointed at Keeler.

The attendant approached Keeler.

"Mr. Keeler?"

"I'm Keeler."

"You have a telephone call, sir. It's a Mr. Bollinger."

The caller was Meacham, using the code name for an emergency. Keeler put down his cup and followed the attendant to the cloak room. A telephone was on a table at one end of the room, the receiver off the hook.

The attendant moved to the other end of the room as Keeler picked up the receiver. "Yes?"

"Something's happened to Tobias, sir," Meacham said breathlessly. "Our man who's watching that street said he saw four men taking Tobias out of his shop."

Tobias was Mueller's code name. Keeler glanced at the attendant and asked, "What did the men look like?"

"Our man didn't get a good look at them or their car, or Tobias either, but he believes he was injured. He's going to call back in a moment for instructions. Should I tell him to get more information, or should I go and investigate myself?"

Keeler hesitated. It sounded like an NKVD abduction, and there was a possibility that surveillance agents would be posted to see if anyone showed undue interest. "Neither," he replied. "Stay away from there, and tell our man to do the same. Telephone our man in the police, and tell him to find out what happened and meet us at the outside rendezvous. Then get a car and come here for me."

"Yes, sir."

Keeler pushed down the button on the telephone to break the connection, and dialed Pourzand's number. It rang several times, then Pourzand answered it.

"My watch needs to be repaired," Keeler said in French. "I must see you about it this morning."

Pourzand was silent for a moment, then he replied quietly, "That is impossible sir. I must avoid conflicts with other customers."

"I am aware of that, but I must have my watch repaired this morning."

"No, it must wait until a more convenient time."

"It cannot wait."

Pourzand was silent again, then sighed in resignation. "It must be at the outside place."

"Very well. At eleven o'clock."

Pourzand hung up. Keeler put on his coat and took his hat off the shelf, then went back out into the conference room. The four men, still conversing at the end of the buffet, fell silent as he crossed the room to them.

"I won't be returning with you, Morton," Keeler said. "I have a car coming for me."

"Nothing's gone amiss, has it?" Campbell asked. "Or is it something that we can assist you with?"

"No, thank you. I'll see you again soon."

The men nodded, then resumed their conversation. Keeler crossed the lobby and went out the front doors.

Several officers followed him and walked toward the cars parked along one side of the wide, paved courtyard in front of the chancellery building. It was another bleak, wintry day. And Keeler felt bleak. The increased security because of the trouble with Kharis was a handicap, made worse because time and effort were being stretched thin to cover what Holcomb had done. But Mueller's abduction was an even more severe problem, one for which the range of solutions was extremely limited.

The radio operator with the sondercommando platoon would be familiar with Mueller's distinctive telegraphic rhythm. It would be impossible to deceive him. And without Mueller to guide the platoon into an ambush, a powerful force of assassins would be at large in the city when the heads of state arrived.

A car from the embassy weaved through the traffic and Keeler stepped to the curb.

Meacham glanced in the mirror as Keeler got in, then accelerated rapidly and swerved the car into an opening in the traffic. "Our contact called back just after we talked, Mr. Keeler. I told him to stay completely away from there."

"Very well. Did you make the arrangements with Najafi?"

"Yes, sir. He said he'd go have a look, then meet us at the rendezvous. Who do you think might have done this, Mr. Keeler?"

"I don't like to speculate."

Meacham blew the horn as he pressed on the accelerator and passed a truck. "We're in a very ticklish situation now, aren't we, sir? Did you tell Charles and the others?"

"No. That would have revealed procedural matters and a key part of the network. It also would have been premature."

Meacham sighed worriedly and nodded, weaving through the traffic. He drove on along the boulevard to a narrow street that entered a park. The street turned into a traffic circle around a large fountain in the center of the park. Meacham parked the car at one side of the circle.

Several minutes passed, then another car came along the street, stopping a few yards away. Keeler got out and walked toward it. Najafi stepped out of the car, his swarthy face tinged with red from the cold. He pulled up the collar on his uniform overcoat as he walked toward Keeler, saluting. "Good day, Mr. Keeler."

"Good day, Najafi. What did you find out?"

"There were few witnesses, Mr. Keeler, and it happened very quickly. Four men went into the shop and attacked Mueller, then took him to a car in the alley. He was injured."

"Did you get a description of the car?"

Najafi cupped his hands together and blew into them to warm them, shaking his head. "No, only that it was a dark sedan. I believe it was the Russians, Mr. Keeler. The same thing happened today to a man named Keppler and one named Biehler, as well as one whose name I don't know."

"The Biehler who works at the meat market in the main marketplace?"

"Yes, that is the man, Mr. Keeler. It must have been the Russians."

Keeler took out a cigarette and lit it. On the day he had intercepted Moltke on the road to Turkey, he had questioned a driver in the convoy about Biehler. There had been no mention of Biehler's name, but the driver had positively identified him as a chemist who worked for Rashid al-Kharis, refining heroin from opium.

He suddenly knew what to do. He took a drag on his cigarette, shaking his head. "No, it appears to me that the drug dealers are having trouble with each other again, Najafi."

"The drug dealers?" Najafi replied doubtfully. "They

have gun battles and set bombs, but they don't do things like this."

"They abduct people when those people are important."

Najafi shivered, not wanting to argue the point. "If you think it is the drug dealers, then it undoubtedly is, Mr. Keeler. Is there anything else I can do for you?"

"Yes, I'd like you to drive Meacham back to the embassy. I'm going to see if I can find out what drug dealers are involved."

"Very well, Mr. Keeler," Najafi said, saluting as he turned toward his car. "I hope you find out what you need to know."

Keeler walked back to the car, motioning Meacham out. "Najafi will take you back to the embassy, Meacham. The drug dealers are having another war, and it appears that Mueller got caught up in it."

"Drug dealers?" Meacham exclaimed in surprise, climbing out of the car. "How on earth did Mueller get mixed up in that? Is that bugger Kharis involved?"

"I don't know, and Najafi didn't realize the problem. I'm going to see if I can find out who is involved, and perhaps I can get Mueller back."

"Let's certainly hope that you can, Mr. Keeler. I was just starting to do the sitrep when all this happened. Shall I go ahead and finish it? And shall I mention what happened to Mueller?"

"Yes. Advise them that the drug dealers here are in a war over territory, and it appears that Mueller was mistaken for a European who works for a drug dealer. Tell them that Mueller was abducted, and we're presently attempting to have him released."

Meacham disappeared along the street through the park. Keeler waited for a moment, glancing at his watch. Then he started the engine and turned his car around.

The outside rendezvous for meeting Pourzand was in the alley behind the Shirivan Restaurant. Timing his arrival for eleven o'clock, Keeler drove toward the restaurant. It was opening when he passed it, employees moving a folding wall of heavy wood panels from the entrance. Keeler turned onto a side street, then into the alley behind the restaurant. He approached the rear of the restaurant, slowing to a crawl. Pourzand leaped out of a recessed doorway and jerked open the back door, scrambling into the car and crouching down as he slammed the door. Keeler drove out of the alley onto the street.

"This is very dangerous, Mr. Keeler," Pourzand muttered resentfully.

"I know it is dangerous," Keeler replied. "What is Vertinski doing?"

"He is trying to protect himself," Pourzand sneered in disgust. "Kolesnikov said that there must be German agents here, and he demanded that arrests be made. Vertinski summoned me to a personal meeting and demanded that I give him the names of German agents. He was very angry and frightened, so I gave him some names."

"What names did you give him?"

"Biehler, Spengler, Dumas, and Keppler."

"Have other agents given him any names?"

"I have no way of knowing. But I was the only one who had a personal meeting with him, so I believe not."

Keeler slowed the car and stopped at the curb. Pourzand hissed in fright, lifting his head to peer around. Keeler turned and seized Pourzand's coat, then pulled him higher. "Tell me the names again."

"This is very dangerous! Someone could see me and—"

"*Tell me the names again.*"

"Biehler, Spengler, Dumas, and Keppler."

Looking into Pourzand's dark, deeply-recessed eyes, Keeler knew he was telling the truth. There was no reason why he would omit Mueller's name, if he had given it to Vertinski; and it was at least possible that another agent had talked. Keeler released Pourzand and turned back around, driving away from the curb. "What will you say when the men you named are interrogated and found not to be German agents?"

"I will say it was the interrogator's fault that they didn't confess. Vertinski doesn't care, because Kolesnikov measures results by how *much* is done, not by what is done. He is like any other Russian."

"Do you still have the telephone number to call in emergencies?"

"Yes. Why do you want to know?"

Keeler slowed the car and turned at a corner, driving back toward the restaurant. "I may want you to call Vertinski about a place where some German agents are meeting."

"You want me to tell Vertinski something that he will know is a lie?" Pourzand exclaimed. "There will be no such meeting! Vertinski will have me arrested when he finds out that I lied to him!"

"Men will be there, and they will have German propaganda material, weapons, and other German equipment."

Pourzand grunted skeptically. "Who will these men be?"

"That doesn't concern you. Your only concern is to devise an explanation of how you know about them. The Russians who attack them will think they are German agents, and Vertinski will be very pleased."

Pourzand was silent for several minutes, thinking. Then he chuckled. "He would also be grateful, because Kolesnikov would be pleased with him for finding some German agents. Are you certain they will have weapons and other things to make the Russians believe they are German agents?"

"Yes."

"Where and when will this meeting be?"

"I am not completely certain that I want to do this. If I do, I will call you. Stay near your telephone."

Pourzand murmured an affirmative, chuckling in satisfaction. Keeler drove past the restaurant and turned onto the side street, slowing to let Pourzand leap out, then turned onto the street again to a traffic square, and into the Asian district.

Keeler parked in the alley beside the Café Canton and walked around the corner to the entrance. The woman behind the counter looked at Keeler in surprise, then beckoned him and pulled back the ragged cloth over the door to the kitchen.

The kitchen, filled with steam and thick odors of cooking food, was torridly hot. Sweating Chinese men and women worked over piles of vegetables, ignoring Keeler. Motioning him to wait, the woman went through a doorway. She returned a few minutes later and led Keeler to a door that opened onto the alley.

Two stocky, stolid Chinese with clubs stood by the car, guarding it. Keeler climbed some steps and knocked on a door. The small, beautiful Chinese woman opened it, bowing gracefully, her delicate features composed in a tranquil half-smile and her almond eyes downcast. Keeler followed her along the hall to the sliding door. She put his hat and trench coat on the small table by the door, untied his shoes and slipped them off his feet, then opened the door.

Cheung sat at the low, ornate table, his elbows on it and his fingernails a bristling forest of yellow tissue around his folded hands. The wrinkles around his eyes and mouth deepened in a faint smile. "Come in, Mr. Keeler. This is an unusual time for you to visit me."

The woman closed the door behind Keeler as he folded his legs and sat on the cushions on the other side of the table. "Yes, it is. I hope I haven't inconvenienced you, Mr. Cheung."

"No, no, you haven't inconvenienced me, my friend. I enjoy your friendship, and our conversations are always very entertaining." His smile faded, his wise, hooded eyes moving over Keeler's face in the dim light. "I have heard that several people in the city were abducted today. And some say that the Russians did it."

"Yes. One of those abducted is a man named Mueller, who is important to me. I need to get him back."

"Would he be of any value to you after being questioned by the Russians?"

"They are abducting many people, which is keeping them occupied. They will not begin their interrogations until tonight or tomorrow."

The old man's lips twitched in a smile again as he shrugged. "Then he will be returned to you before he is questioned. We know from Hsieu where the Russians take people and my captains have many men. It would give me great pleasure to assist you, my friend."

"I am very grateful for your help, and this could be of some benefit to you as well. Also missing is a man named Biehler, a chemist who works for Rashid al-Kharis."

The old man hissed softly, nodding. "A man who can make heroin from opium is indeed very valuable. I would have to keep him hidden, because I have no wish for a war with Kharis, but that could be easy to do."

"I will point him out to your men. There will be many guards at the interrogation center, and I know that you would rather avoid bloodshed, if possible."

"If possible, yes. Do you have a plan?"

Keeler nodded, lighting a cigarette, then told the old man about his arrangements with Pourzand. "Those at the interrogation center will be the only men the Russians have readily available," he continued. "Most of them will be sent to attack the place where Pourzand sends them, leaving few guarding the interrogation center. I have German weapons I can give to a few of your men. They should be in a place where they can escape easily when the Russians attack."

"This man Pourzand," the old man murmured in his soft, dry voice. "Does he work for you first, or for the Russians first?"

"For money first, and I pay more than the Russians."

The old man chuckled softly. "Then he is a man you can trust. I know of a place that will be suitable. If most of the Russians are gone, forty men should be sufficient to attack the interrogation center."

"Yes, forty will be more than enough. I also need some things from Mueller's house. But the Russians may make enquiries about him, so I don't want to go there myself. If you will arrange to remove everything from his house, I will have Meacham meet your men at the edge of the city with soldiers and Army trucks. Then he can take everything to a safe place and pick out what I need."

"When do you want it done?"

"As soon as possible after nightfall."

"What should be done with the servants?"

"I would like to have them detained for a few days, and warned not to talk when they are released."

The old man nodded slowly, pondering. Keeler put out his cigarette in a silver dish on the table and lit another one. The door slid open and the woman entered with a tea tray. She poured tea into tiny cups and put one in front of Keeler, then held the other one to the old man's lips. He took a sip of tea and swallowed, still musing.

Then he sat up. "We will need ten men to act as German agents," he murmured, recapitulating, "in addition to the forty. I will send twenty men with four large trucks to your man's house, which will be enough to deal with the guards as well as to load everything quickly. Do you want the guards kept with the servants?"

Keeler nodded. "Yes, that would be best. I will keep Mueller at my house, and get some soldiers to protect him. I understand that he is injured, and there is a young Polish woman at his house. She can care for him if his injuries are not serious, so have your men turn her over to Meacham.

"Very well. I am very glad that you came to me for assistance. It pleases me to be able to help you, and I will also have the chemist who belongs to Kharis. But Kharis will blame the Russians instead of me."

"Yes, he must know who abducted Biehler."

"He must, and like most Arabs he is difficult to deal with when he is angry. He will probably seek revenge." The old man pursed his lips, his eyes moving over Keeler's face. "Some say that your man Holcomb was killed because Kharis is angry at you, my friend."

"He was. But Kharis could be kept too occupied with the Russians to cause me any more trouble. They would think that Kharis had instigated the attack on their interrogation center if some of his men were found dead there after the battle. That would insure a war between Kharis and the Russians, and neither of them would think of us."

The old man smiled, nodding. "Years ago in Paris, I knew a young man named Ho Chi Minh. He often said that the best way to conceal anything is to give everyone a reason to look elsewhere. I will have some runners or others who work for Kharis captured. My men will take them to the interrogation center and kill them with Russian weapons. We will drink our tea, then I will send for my captains and you can make your arrangements." He chuckled, his dark eyes twinkling. "This will be a very interesting night for you, my friend."

CHAPTER TWENTY-ONE

THE CAB OF the truck was cold, crowded and odorous. The four Chinese squeezed into the cab with Keeler were wearing ragged, dirty Arab disguises that stank. Keeler checked his watch again. Twenty minutes after ten. He had told Pourzand to make the telephone call to Vertinski at ten.

The truck was parked in an alley across the street from the blocky stone building that housed the NKVD interrogation center. Light leaked through cracks in shutters and gleamed through curtains, faintly illuminating two large, dark cars parked at the curb.

The driver of the truck was Yien, the captain of the group; the other three were his lieutenants. As the windshield began fogging up again, Yien grunted a syllable and one of the others wiped it with the edge of his robe. Keeler waited, trying not to think about wanting a cigarette.

A distant sound carried through the cold stillness of the night. Yien rolled down his window. Cars were approaching at high speed. Brakes squealed as two cars came into view and slid to a stop. Several men scrambled out, leaving the doors standing open as they ran up the steps in front of the building.

Wide doors at the top of the steps opened and other men dashed out, all of them armed. Keeler counted twenty-three. They piled into the cars, which pulled away at top speed, tires squealing.

Yien tugged at Keeler's sleeve. "How long they gone?" he asked in heavily-accented, broken English.

"Perhaps an hour or longer," Keeler replied.

"Plenty time," Yien grunted, then said something in Chinese as he opened his door and climbed out of the cab, followed by the others. Keeler slid across the seat and stepped down from the running board. More armed men jumped out of the bed of the truck, and out of the second truck.

Yien took Keeler's arm and nudged him toward the mouth of the alley. "You stay. Stay here. I call you."

Keeler watched as Yien and his men flowed out of the alley and into the street. Several at the rear carried six struggling Arabs who were bound and gagged. They disappeared into the shadows and silence fell. The minutes slowly dragged past.

The quiet was shattered as a satchel charge detonated in front of the doors with a thunderous roar. Dark red flame billowed up, the doors buckling inward and disintegrating. The concussion rocked Keeler, and glass rained down on the sidewalk from shattered windows. A wave of robed figures poured up the steps through the swirling smoke to the entrance of the building.

Echoes of the explosion blended into the roar of gunfire inside. Pistols cracked, Thompson submachine guns pounded, and Enfields barked. A spray of bullets came through a window and smacked into the wall several feet above Keeler's head, bringing down a shower of mortar and fragments of brick.

The gunfire diminished to isolated shots, then stopped. Light streamed down the steps from the gaping entrance as robed figures moved about inside. One came to the door and beckoned to Keeler, shouting. Several men ran up the steps from the sidewalk with the bound Arabs on their shoulders as Keeler crossed the street.

The lobby was a scene of mass confusion. Cordite smoke and dust hung in the air, and the floor was littered with debris. One guard near the entrance had been killed by the explosion; others scattered about the lobby had been shot. An Arab, released from his bonds, screamed as one man held his arms and another leveled a guard's pistol. The pistol barked and the Arab collapsed. Then they began untying another Arab.

Yien stood in a doorway across the lobby, beckoning and shouting. Keeler followed a crowd of men down to the basement level. One of Vertinski's operatives lay dead near the top of the steps and two guards were sprawled farther down.

The interrogation room was harshly lighted by bare bulbs in the ceiling. There was a chair surrounded by floodlights in one corner, and one with electrodes on the arms and seat of another. Implements hung on the walls. A heavy table fitted with restraining clamps stood in the center of the room over a wide drain ready to receive the blood, urine, and feces from the victim on the table.

A man with a large key ring was trying keys in a heavy door at one end of the room. At the other end, two men held a tall, thin European, waiting for orders as he cringed in terror. The man was Grotesmann, the director of the

Teheran Hospital. Recognition shone in his eyes as he saw Keeler. Yien looked interrogatively and pointed to Grotesmann. Keeler shook his head.

Yien barked an order. One of the men holding Grostesmann took out a knife. Grotesmann screamed wildly, struggling. His scream changed to a choked gargle as the knife flashed and blood spurted. The man at the door shouted in triumph as he unlocked and opened it a crack. Yien rapped out another order, and his men pulled the loose ends of their turbans over their faces as they headed for the door, followed by Keeler who tugged his hat down and pulled up his collar.

The door opened into a narrow corridor between rows of crowded cells. The air was thick with a foul stench of excreta. Some of the cell's occupants appeared to have been confined for weeks. Their gaunt faces and frail, ragged limbs were revealed by the light from the single bulb in the corridor. When the man with the keys opened the first cell, the prisoners wailed and resisted weakly as they were dragged out.

Keeler stood by the door and waved them past. As the prisoners realized that they were being released, they crowded to the door. Those in other cells screamed in pleading voices and thrust filthy, clawing hands between the bars, the noise swelling into a bedlam. When the first cell was empty, Keeler moved on to the next.

Some of the prisoners appeared to be guards or agents who had proven to be unreliable. Others had apparently been taken in random abductions. People from the Polish resettlement camp were among them, including a few women and two grimy, skeletal children. Some who had been injured crawled along the corridor. Two or three dead bodies were in each cell, bloated and discolored.

Prisoners who had been incarcerated more recently were in the farthest cells. Keeler saw Spengler and Dumas, then Biehler. He pointed him out to Yien, who barked an order, and Biehler shrieked and struggled as he was dragged out into the corridor, tied and gagged.

Keeler found Mueller in a corner of a cell. The suave, dapper Swiss businessman was gone, replaced by a battered, disheveled wretch in torn, filthy clothes. He was unconscious, his face waxen. Blood from a gash on his temple had dried on his face, and he was curled tightly into a fetal position. His features twisted and a soft sigh of pain came from his lips when Keeler turned him over to look at him. Two of Yien's men picked him up, and Keeler followed them along the corridor and up the stairs. Many of the prisoners had now reached the lobby, and they rushed outside as Yien shouted. The men carrying Biehler and Mueller pushed through the crowd, Keeler behind them. The trucks were parked at the curb, headlights on and engines idling.

Some of the prisoners fled into the night as they were herded to the first truck. Biehler and Mueller were also put in the bed of the first truck, then Keeler climbed in. Most of Yien's men got into the second truck, which swerved around in the street and took off in the opposite direction from the first.

The truck sped along dark streets, its canvas flap billowing over the mass of prisoners who swayed from side to side as it cornered abruptly, then raced through the city, turned in at an alley and stopped. Yien shouted from the cab at his men in the back. They pushed at the prisoners and forced them to jump out. When some tried to stay in the truck, they were dragged to the tailgate and thrown out. The truck jerked into motion again, rumbling along the alley and turning onto a street. Fresh air whipped through, wafting away the stench of the prisoners.

It drove along dark streets, avoiding the lighted boulevards until it reached the rail yards and stopped.

The men lifted the flap at the rear of the bed. The distant glow of floodlights around the locomotive sheds a half mile away gleamed dimly on an embassy car parked a hundred feet behind the truck. Keeler jumped down as the men lifted Mueller out. Meacham got out of the car, turning on a flashlight. As he shone it toward the truck, the men carrying Mueller grumbled angrily.

"Turn off the flashlight, Meacham," Keeler called. "They don't want to be seen."

"Sorry, sir," Meacham replied, complying. "Can I be of any help there?"

"Open the rear door of the car and turn off the light, if you would."

Meacham did as he was told. The men put Mueller in the back seat and sprinted back to the truck, shouting as they leaped in. The engine roared and the truck sped away, disappearing into the night. Meacham turned on the flashlight again.

He exclaimed happily, "By God, you got him back, didn't you, Mr. Keeler? But that's a very nasty-looking cut on his head."

"He also has other injuries," Keeler said, walking around the car to get in. "He may have some broken ribs."

"I told Colonel Campbell that Tobias might be injured, and he brought a doctor from the garrison. There's a bit of luck, isn't it?"

"Yes. Let's go."

Meacham started the engine and drove along the road

through the rail yards, relating recent developments. Campbell had provided trucks and a squad of soldiers. Cheung's men, in trucks filled with Mueller's belongings, had met Meacham and the soldiers at the edge of the city. Meacham had taken Mueller's things to the embassy compound, where he had collected Mueller's Afu radio set, code book, and schedules from their hiding places in the furniture.

"What about his car?" Keeler asked.

"They brought that as well, sir, and I had one of the soldiers park it among the others by the garages. His furniture and other possessions are in storage."

"Where is the Polish woman?"

"I took her to your house, along with the wireless and some other things. Colonel Campbell is there too, with the doctor and the soldiers."

"I suppose we have no use for her now."

Meacham nodded as he snapped on the headlights and turned onto a street. "But she has seen quite a lot now, hasn't she? In any event, I don't think she'll be any trouble. I expected her to be a handful when I untied her, but she was as meek as a lamb. I told her to sit out of the way in the dining room, and I daresay she's still there."

"Was there any reaction from London about Mueller?"

"Indeed there was, sir. They sent a redline priority message, asking for a full explanation and your plan of action. It came in several hours ago, and they've been holding a frequency open for a reply. Would you like to go by the embassy and see to that?"

"No. You can send a reply when we've settled matters."

Meacham nodded, turning the car onto a boulevard that led through the city. "Yes, sir. Was that sod Kharis involved in this, then?"

"He and a Chinese drug dealer are having trouble, and Mueller was taken by mistake. I'll give you the details later."

Meacham glanced at Keeler, then looked back ahead. "Mr. Keeler, I've been hearing all over the city that the NKVD has been abducting people," he said cautiously. "Doesn't it seem odd that the same thing could happen to Mueller at the same time?"

"No, there seems to be a lot going on just now. Besides Kharis' trouble with this Chinese, I heard a rumor that he's also managed to get into some sort of scrape with the NKVD. All in all, I believe he'll be too busy to give us any more trouble."

"Indeed?" Meacham exclaimed in relief. "By God, that's good to hear, and I hope that swine gets his just deserts."

"Emotion clouds the judgment, Meacham."

Meacham nodded, blowing the horn as he accelerated and passed cars. Hearing a soft whimper of pain from the rear seat, Keeler picked up the flashlight and turned it on, looking at Mueller who was still unconscious, his pale face twisted with pain and smeared with dried blood. Keeler turned back around in the seat and lit a cigarette, staring out the window.

The late evening traffic diminished to an occasional car when they reached the suburbs. Meacham turned onto the street where Keeler lived, then turned in at the gate in front of the house. Two soldiers were with the guard at the gate. An Army truck and a staff car were parked on the drive. The headlights glared on several more soldiers gathered around a kettle of tea on a kerosene heater beside the truck.

Meacham parked behind the staff car and called to one of the soldiers as he got out. "Sergeant, would you have your men give us a hand?"

"Yes, sir," the sergeant replied. "You there, come on."

Meacham opened the back door of the car and turned on the overhead light. "Where do you want him, Mr. Keeler?" he asked.

"There's an empty bedroom at the end of the hall."

"Very well, sir. I'll show you where it is, Sergeant."

The soldiers crowded around the side of the car, lifting Mueller out, then carried him to the house. Keeler followed them along the path and up the steps when Meacham held the door open as the soldiers shuffled into the house with Mueller. Campbell and another man in uniform were waiting in the front room.

Campbell nodded to Keeler. "Well, we were wondering when you would get here, Keeler. And this is Tobias, then? He appears a bit the worse for wear, doesn't he? This is Doctor Swann, Keeler."

Swann was a captain in the Medical Corps, a chubby man with a receding chin and hairline; he appeared disgruntled, resentful that Campbell had conscripted him to come to the house. Exchanging a silent nod with Keeler, he picked up his medical bag. The soldiers carried Mueller across the room and into the hall, Meacham and Swann followed.

The woman from Mueller's house sat on a straight chair in a far corner of the dining room, out of earshot from the front room. Her face pale and her eyes wide and frightened, she was watching Keeler as he glanced through the doorway at her. She quickly averted her eyes.

Campbell brushed his mustaches with a finger, moving

closer to Keeler. "I must say this is all very puzzling. Here we are preparing for the dignitaries to arrive, and I find myself detailing soldiers to move furniture and such. Is all this necessary?"

"Yes."

"I trust that we're not becoming involved in something that could reflect unfavorably on the Army. You didn't have that young lady in there kidnapped, did you? And that man Tobias—did you have to bash him about so much? The brigadier and I are more than willing to cooperate, Keeler, but all this seems a very strange situation."

"There will be no repercussions."

"Are you certain? Well, I'll accept your assurance, but I expect you to bear in mind how the brigadier feels about involving the Army in disreputable situations. I understand from Meacham that you'd like the men to remain here for the next few days."

"Yes."

"Well, I'll agree to it on a provisional basis, but I'll have to talk to their commanding officer." The soldiers tramped back along the hall, and Campbell turned to the sergeant as he came into the room. "Sergeant, you and your men may be staying here for a while. When I return to the garrison, you can send along one of your men with your vehicle. I'll see about rations and such for you, and you can bivouac out on the drive."

The sergeant stamped and saluted, barking a syllable in reply, then went out, the other soldiers following him. Campbell turned and watched the hall doorway impatiently, slapping his quarterstaff against his leg.

Meacham came into the room, his expression sober. He glanced between Campbell and Keeler and shook his head somberly. Keeler lit a cigarette, his eyes passing over the woman in the dining room as he turned away from Meacham. Again, she averted her eyes.

A few minutes later, Swann came in, shaking his head. "The man is seriously injured, Colonel Campbell," he said. "Beyond several contusions that can be treated easily enough, he has a ruptured gall bladder and possibly other internal injuries. It is vitally important that he be hospitalized."

"He must stay here," Keeler said, interrupting Campbell as he started to reply. "Whatever you need will be brought here."

Swann frowned, turning to Keeler. Then his frown faded and his expression became cautious. "You don't understand, sir. In order to treat that man's injuries, I must have hospital facilities."

"No, *you* don't understand," Keeler replied curtly. "He is going to stay here, and this is where you are going to treat him. I can appreciate the problems that may pose, but it won't be necessary to effect a recovery. You need only keep him alive for three days and administer drugs to make him fully conscious and alert for short periods."

Swann stared at Keeler in shock, his eyes wide. "Keep him alive for *three days*?" he stammered, appalled. "But I am a medical doctor, and I have a code of ethics! I can't deliberately. . . ."

"Again, you don't understand, Swann," Keeler said, interrupting him. "You have become involved with an activity that has its own code of ethics, its own protocol. Once you are involved, you leave everything else behind. To do otherwise, or to place yourself in opposition, entails extremely harsh penalties."

Swann blinked, puzzled and apprehensive. His eyes

moved to Campbell and Meacham, then back to Keeler. "What do you mean?" he asked.

Keeler crossed the room to Swann and stopped a foot from him. "I mean that if you cause further difficulty, I will destroy you," he said quietly. "Within the week, your commander will receive incontrovertible evidence that you are homosexual. If he decides to transfer you rather than to bring charges, you will go to the front lines in Italy. If you live to return to England, the Royal College will evict you and withdraw your authority to practice medicine."

"But—but how can you do that?" Swann stuttered. "It is absolutely false, because I have never even known. . . ."

"That is totally irrelevant, Swann. I can and I will do as I said. You have a choice; cooperate or be destroyed."

Swann wilted, his face pale. "But I can't remain here," he protested in a quavering voice. "I'm scheduled for duty. . . ."

"Meacham, please telephone Sir Matthew," Keeler said, turning away from Swann. "Ask him to call the garrison commander and tell him that Doctor Swann will be absent for a few days."

"No, no, there's no need for that," Campbell said quickly as Meacham started toward the telephone. "No need to involve the ambassador. Doctor Swann, as I told you, the brigadier has ordered in the most forceful terms that Mr. Keeler is to have full cooperation. He'll see that you are excused from duty. Now please do cooperate. Make a list of what you'll need, and I'll see that you get it."

Swann looked at Campbell, his shoulders slumped. Shrugging helplessly, he turned and walked back toward the hall, his slow footsteps loud in the silence of the room.

Keeler stubbed out his cigarette in an ashtray on a table and lit another.

Campbell turned to Keeler. "Keeler, there was absolutely no need for you to be so vicious with that man," he said indignantly. "I could have talked to him and explained that. . . ." His voice faded as he looked at Keeler. Then he brushed his mustaches with a finger as he walked briskly toward the hall. "Well, I'll just go and see what Doctor Swann requires, shall I?"

He went out, and Keeler took a drag on his cigarette and turned to Meacham. "You could go to the embassy and send a reply to that message from London, if you wish."

"Yes, sir," Meacham said. "What shall I tell them, sir?"

"Kharis and a drug dealer named Fung Ti Yien are having trouble. Yien set out to abduct a chemist named Biehler, who works for Kharis. The men confused Biehler with Mueller and took both of them to make certain that they had the right one. There's a remarkable resemblance between them, and the names sound similar to those unfamiliar with European names. I contacted Yien and arranged Mueller's return."

"Very well, sir. Shall I tell them that Mueller is injured?"

"Yes. Mueller resisted, resulting in the injuries Swann described. Tell them that we're concentrating solely on the sondercommandos, which will probably result in Mueller's death. And ask them to check Swann in the files, as well as with MI-5."

"Yes, sir. We have a few meetings with contacts tonight. When I'm finished with this, shall I have dinner at the embassy, make up the envelopes, and come back here to pick you up?"

"Yes."

Meacham went out. Keeler took a drag on his cigarette and flicked the ash into an ashtray. Feeling the woman's eyes on him again, he turned and looked directly at her. She avoided his gaze, touching her hair nervously.

Campbell came back into the front room, folding a piece of paper and putting it into his pocket. "Doctor Swann gave me a list of what he will need, Keeler. I'll have the soldiers bring it from the garrison."

"Very well."

"I've had a talk with Doctor Swann, and I think you'll find him most cooperative now. He knows to contact me if he needs anything else. If he needs any help with Tobias, the soldiers will assist him. And I'll have them take him his meals when they prepare their rations."

"Very well. I'd like to meet with you tomorrow and discuss a potential threat against the dignitaries."

Campbell blinked, then frowned in concern. "What sort of threat are you talking about, Keeler? Does all this business with Tobias have something to do with it, by any chance? I do wish you would be more forthcoming, rather than keeping me in the dark all the time."

"I haven't developed sufficient information for a meaningful discussion, but I should know more by tomorrow."

Campbell sighed heavily and shrugged, walking toward the door. "Very well, and I hope that further meetings of bloody dignitaries will be held elsewhere. When and where do you want to meet?"

"At the embassy, if it's convenient, at about three."

Campbell grunted and nodded as he went out. Keeler put out his cigarette and started to light another one. The woman's eyes were on him again, moving away as he looked at her. He put his cigarettes back in his pocket and went into the dining room. She looked at him, standing up as he entered the room.

"Erling has had an accident," he said. "I suppose you gathered that, didn't you?"

"Yes," she replied softly. "I saw him when the soldiers brought him in. May I go and see him now?"

"I would rather you didn't. And there would be very little point in it, because he's unconscious."

"Is he seriously injured?"

"I'm sorry to say that it is quite serious. I believe you should prepare yourself for the worst."

She looked away, clasping her hands together in front of her. For a moment he thought she was going to burst into tears; then he saw that she had complete control over herself. And he saw that the stark, lost expression in her wide blue eyes was fear, not grief. Knowing her background, he could understand her fear. The walls of the secure refuge she had found were disintegrating. Her survival was threatened.

Then he actually saw her as if for the first time. She was suddenly a human being and a woman instead of an anonymous form on the fringes of matters that concerned him. And he could understand why Mueller had stubbornly refused to give her up.

The photographs in the files failed to do her justice. They portrayed a beautiful woman, but she was bewitching. Her wide brow, full lips, and large eyes were individually attractive, but some magic harmony about her features melded them into a whole that was exceptionally lovely. She was tall and slender, moving and standing with feline grace.

The Soviet internment camp had left its marks—a scar

on her brow, a chipped front tooth, and other small signs. But they failed to detract from her compelling beauty. The strength of character reflected in her face had enabled her to put her past behind her, as it had enabled her to endure the events of the night without hysteria. Her dress was torn and smudged, she was frightened but in full control.

"I'm very sorry for what happened to you tonight," he said. "It was unavoidable, although that can be of little consolation. And while you must be curious, I'm unable to explain further. I'd like you to stay here for the present. You'll have the freedom of the house."

She composed herself with a visible effort. "Would it be possible for me to get some of my clothes and other belongings?"

"Yes. I'll bring them tomorrow."

"And I believe I left some things in the car. Is it nearby?"

"No, but I'll have someone look in it. If you'll speak to the housekeeper, she'll arrange accomodations. She's probably in the kitchen, and she speaks English."

Celise nodded, pushing at her hair again. "Yes, I've met her. I believe she's concerned about dinner."

"She frequently is, because my hours are somewhat irregular. Will you have dinner with me?"

His offer was impulsive, the words coming out before he had weighed their full implications. Rarely speaking impulsively, he was uncertain of his own motivation. Perhaps it was pity for her, or possibly an urge that surfaced from the yawning chasm that Sheila's death had created within him; he was unsure. But Celise responded with eager, anxious haste.

"Yes, thank you very much," she said. "I'll take your coat and hat, and I'll tell the housekeeper that we will have dinner presently."

Celise put out her hand for his coat. It trembled, her blue eyes desperately pleading, fearful of a rebuff. She was grasping for safety and security, trying to find a place for herself. He took off his trench coat. She folded it possessively over her arm and took his hat, then went to find the housekeeper. Keeler decided to take a bath and change clothes.

When he returned, Celise was in the dining room with the maid and the housekeeper. The servants, who had always communicated in subtle ways that they considered it an abberation for Keeler to live alone, were cheerfully following Celise's instructions as they prepared the table. Her appearance was much improved. The stains were gone from her dress, the tears sewn up. Her hair, a gleaming mass of the rich blend of yellows and browns of East European blondes, was pinned up on her head.

The sense that he had lost control over the situation was muted by the vibrant feeling of life that Celise radiated, a sparkling vitality. As she and Keeler sat down at the table, the servants left. "The housekeeper was concerned that the roast may be somewhat overcooked," Celise said. "But I tested it, and it seems just very nicely done and an excellent cut. I consider beef the foundation of the most enjoyable of meals when it is prepared properly, don't you?"

"Yes."

"We had a choice of Lebanese and Cypriot wines. Cypriot wines go well with a spicy dish, but they can overpower a meat served without a sauce. So I chose the Lebanese, even though it may lack body with a red meat. I prefer a subtle wine, don't you?"

"Yes."

The conversation lagged as they began eating. Celise seemed to be watching him without actually looking at him. The silence stretched out, the only sound in the room the clink of silverware against china.

When the silence began irritating Keeler, Celise spoke. "I noticed that you have a quite good selection of books. Reading is one of my favorite pastimes. Do you enjoy reading?"

"When I have time."

"Yes, that's one of the burdens of life, isn't it? One's time is absorbed by necessities. But I have been fortunate in that I've had the leisure to read. I noticed that you have a volume of Goethe, even though German writers may not be as popular now as they once were."

"Goethe could scarcely be considered a Nazi. I believe he did express admiration for Napoleon, though."

She smiled at him in surprise and delight, and it was like a sunrise on a radiantly beautiful morning. "Yes, in his *Weissagungen des Bakis*," she said.

Keeler shrugged, looking back down at his plate. "I'm not sure about the source. A teacher I had commented on it—a man named Milliard."

"Professor Ephraim Milliard?" she gasped. "Yes, he was at Eton, wasn't he? And you had him as an instructor? He is one of the most reknown Goethe scholars, and his monograph on the interpretation of *The Soothsayings of Bakis* is considered definitive. It incorporates the work of Doctor Viehoff, Professor Beaumarchis, and others, then goes far beyond them."

"I seem to recall that he had written something."

"Yes, it is a landmark study. I was learning English when I happened upon a copy of it in the university library, and I was having such a difficult time with the language. I asked my English instructor to assist me in translating it, and she refused—very wisely, of course, because that made me work harder. Did Professor Milliard discuss the meaning of *The Soothsayings of Bakis* with you?''

''If he did, I've forgotten it. Perhaps you'll refresh my memory.''

Celise nodded and resumed eating as she began explaining the debate among academics over the work. Some dismissed it as a hoax perpetrated by Goethe, because the work was in riddle form and phrased in deliberately obtuse language. Others saw in it multiple meanings conveyed through form and metaphor. Celise presented both viewpoints and discussed the work as a whole, then, began a detailed explanation of Milliard's interpretation of the first quatrain.

Displaying an exceptional memory, she recited lines of the quatrain and quoted scholarly commentary. At first she was concerned that she might be boring her host, glancing at him and weighing his reactions as she talked. Then her uncertainty gradually faded and was soon completely gone. Her beautiful features were animated and her hands moved gracefully to emphasize her points.

Her accent was more French than Polish, indicating that her English instructor had been French, and her command of English was almost perfect. The chipped tooth gave her a charming lisp, while her voice had a pleasant, melodious quality.

The housekeeper answered a knock at the door. Several soldiers brought in several large boxes and carried them to Swann, then left. The maid cleared the table and brought an ashtray for Keeler. Celise continued speaking, moving closer to him and touching his arm occasionally for emphasis. After another hour, she had finished explicating ten of the thirty-two quatrains.

The front door opened and closed, and Celise paused. Meacham stood in the front room, holding his hat and blinking unsurely as he peered into the dining room at Keeler and Celise. Keeler pushed his chair back from the table. "I'll be with you in a moment, Meacham."

"Very well, sir," Meacham replied, turning back to the door. "I'll be out in the car."

Keeler took a drag on his cigarette and stood up. "The housekeeper will show you to your room. You must be very tired."

Tiny lines of fatigue and strain had formed at the corners of her eyes and mouth, but she shook her head quickly. "No, I'm not at all weary. I always find discussions of literary works very stimulating. Perhaps you would like to resume our conversation when you return."

"It will be very late."

"That's quite all right. I enjoy music as much as I do reading, and I will listen to the radio while I wait for you. I'll get your coat and hat."

Keeler nodded and put out his cigarette in the ashtray. She stood up, her hand resting on the edge of the table. Their hands, brushing together, suddenly clasped in a tight grasp that was almost an embrace, a promise. A radiant smile wreathed Celise's beautiful face as she met Keeler's eyes, then she went for his hat and coat.

CHAPTER TWENTY-TWO

A DRAINAGE TUBE from Mueller's abdomen hung from under the covers on the bed, a thick stench rising from the putrefaction that oozed and dripped from the tube into a pan. He was unconscious, his breathing shallow and rapid. The dark circles around his eyes contrasted sharply with the lifeless pallor of his face.

Swann, his face haggard and his shirt dirty and wrinkled, leaned over the bed and thumbed back one of Mueller's eyelids. He looked at his watch and took Mueller's pulse, then picked up a clipboard from the foot of the bed and made a notation. He shook his head worriedly. "The inflammation is much worse, Mr. Keeler, and I'm concerned about the rate of change. Mr. Tobias has gone down very rapidly today."

"Tonight will finish what we have to do," Keeler said. "Then he can go to the hospital."

Swann put the clipboard down and crossed the room to a table. He shrugged, looking at the boxes and bottles of medicine lying there. "I'll do my best, Mr. Keeler. That's all I can do."

"That's all I expect."

"I'll give him more of the stimulant this time, but I'll space it out over several minutes. It places a heavy strain on the heart, particularly for someone in his condition, and too much at once could cause seizure. How long do we have?"

Keeler glanced at his watch. "About thirty minutes. Give me a hand, if you would, and we'll get prepared."

Swann and Keeler moved a small table closer to the bed. Keeler opened a box and took out an Afu radio set. He set it on the table and plugged the cord into a wall receptable as Swann took the antenna out of the box, unfolded it, and put it in place. Keeler plugged in the earphones and hung them on the head of the bed, then took the telegraph key out of the box, putting it on the table with the code book, writing pad, and pencils. He carried his chair and ashtray over to the table and sat down.

Swann opened an instrument sterilizer. He took out the parts of a hypodermic needle, assembling it. "I would like nothing more than to get Mr. Tobias through this so we can take him to hospital, Mr. Keeler," he said. "He's a very brave man. I'm sure he knows his condition, but he hasn't complained or objected at all."

"Perhaps he will make it. You've kept him going so far. I doubt that many doctors could have done as much."

Swann smiled, reaching for a small bottle of medicine and placing it on the table by the hypodermic needle. Three days of confinement with little sleep and a monotonous routine of activities had made him tractable, and Keeler had transformed their relationship into that of an operative and an agent. Swann had become dependent upon Keeler's approval.

Now the doctor sank into his chair on the other side of

the bed, wearily rubbing his face. He began dozing almost immediately. Keeler sat at the table, smoking his cigarette. He stubbed it out in the ashtray and lit another one, glancing at his watch.

The earphones on the head of the bed hissed with the characteristic sound of an open frequency. Swann snored softly, his stubbled chin almost touching his wrinkled shirt and saliva drooling from his lower lip. Mueller's breathing was a rasping whisper, the lamp on the night stand casting dark shadows in the wrinkles on his gaunt face.

Keeler looked at his watch again. Then he sat up and put out his cigarette. "It's time to get started, Swann," he said.

Swann woke with a jerk. He yawned. "How long do we have, Mr. Keeler?"

"A little over ten minutes."

Swann filled the hypodermic needle from the small bottle and took a cotton swab from a jar, then injected the drug into Mueller's arm. Seconds passed, then Mueller stirred. He grimaced, his eyes opening. Swann bent over him. "How do you feel, Mr. Tobias?" he asked in a loud voice.

The brisk physician's smile was incongruous on Swann's stubbled, haggard face; the code name confused Mueller, as it always did. He looked at Swann blankly, then his eyes moved to Keeler. The dazed confusion faded. He licked his lips. "Thirsty . . ." he breathed feebly.

Swann filled a paper cup, dabbed a cloth in the icy water in the ice chest on the floor, then returned to the bed. Mueller gulped the water and closed his eyes as Swann wiped his face with the damp cloth. Swann gently lifted him and propped him up with pillows.

Color came into Mueller's blanched face as he reacted to

the powerful stimulant. When he opened his eyes again, they were bright and clear. He looked at Keeler. "I would like to talk with you for a moment, Mr. Keeler," he murmured hoarsely.

Keeler glanced at his watch as he stood up. He moved his chair to the side of the bed. The doctor filled the hypodermic as Keeler sat down, leading over Mueller. "We don't have very long to talk, Mueller."

Mueller nodded, licking his lips and swallowing with a dry, sticky sound. Then he whispered, his voice a rasping wheeze, "Did you find out any more about what happened, Mr. Keeler?"

"No. It appears that you were simply caught up in an NKVD effort to abduct everyone with a Germanic surname."

"I am still worried about what might happen to Celise, Mr. Keeler. I must be sure you are satisfied that she was not involved in any way."

"I am, and she is safe and comfortable. Stop worrying about her and worry about yourself. We'll take you to a hospital if you'll hold on for a bit after tonight's contact."

Mueller grimaced impatiently, shaking his head. "Mr. Keeler, I know I am dying. My concern is Celise and what will happen to her."

"She will be safe. The only thing you need worry about is making this contact tonight."

"A final deceit and then a quiet, faceless departure, as it were, Mr. Keeler?"

"That is all we have, Mueller. Those who require medals, parades, and speeches have no place in our profession."

Mueller sighed, then smiled faintly. "Yes—but it is a wine like none other, isn't it, Mr. Keeler? I have no regrets, because my life has had dimensions that few could even understand. Do I have your assurance that you will do all you can for Celise?"

"Yes."

"Then I will let it rest. Platoon Anton should be at the location now, shouldn't it?"

Keeler nodded, standing up and going to the table to get the telegraph key. It was fixed to a short, thin board so Mueller could use it while lying in bed. Keeler placed it beside Mueller's arm. "Yes, the platoon should be in place," he replied. "If we can confirm that and convince them that they're safe, we can turn this over to the Army."

Mueller flexed his right hand, then tapped out a series of dots and dashes on the key. Swann returned to his chair beside the bed, holding the hypodermic needle. Mueller tapped on the key for a moment, then flexed his hand again and nodded to Mueller, who took the connector on the end of the telegraph key cord and plugged it into the radio set and turned up the volume. The hiss from the earphones became louder, broken by occasional crackling bursts of static. Swann injected more of the drug into Mueller's arm, then sat back down. The three men waited. The hiss and static from the earphones was the only sound in the room. Finally it changed to the solid drone of a transmitter tuning on the frequency, then to the rhythmic beeping of morse code. Keeler listened, and picked out the letters of the uncoded identifier, Anton.

When the beeping stopped, Keeler turned a switch to the "transmit" position. Mueller tapped on the key, sending his identifier. When he had finished, Keeler turned he switch back to the "receive" position and put a pencil and writing pad on the bed. As Mueller picked up the pencil, the earphones began beeping again.

The message was a long one. The color drained from Mueller's face and his hand became weak as he printed the letters. Swann injected more of the drug into Mueller's arm. His strength returned for a moment, then faded again as the message dragged on. Swann frowned worriedly, rushing to refill the hypodermic needle. He injected more of the drug into Mueller's arm.

Mueller's face became deathly pale, his lips pressed together in a taut, thin line from the effort of laboriously printing the letters. The message finally ended. Gathering himself for a final effort as Keeler turned the switch to "transmit," he tapped on the key to acknowledge the message and terminate the contact. This his eyes closed and he collapsed onto the pillows.

Swann lowered Mueller to a reclining position and got his stethoscope from his bag. Keeler turned off the radio set, removed the writing pad and pencil from the bed, and reached for the code book. Swann monitored Mueller's heartbeat as Keeler leafted through the code book.

The doctor straightened up and turned to Keeler. "I have to give Mr. Tobias a massive dosage of the stimulant, Mr. Keeler," he said worriedly. "His heartbeat has become very irregular."

Keeler glanced at Swann, then at Mueller. He turned his attention back to the message, creasing the code book open on a page. "It usually wears off fairly quickly. See how he is in a few minutes."

Swann sighed, hovering over Mueller. Keeler began decoding the message. It was apparent that the sonder-commandos were unaware that they had been led into a trap. The message began with a request for confirmation on when the heads of state would arrive at Teheran

Airport, as well as on their schedule of meetings, including place, date, and time. It ended with a request to cease contact by radio and to deliver the information in person to the warehouse after nightfall the following day. Keeler tore the pages off the pad and put them in his pocket as he stubbed out his cigarette and stood up. Swann still sat on his chair, his shoulders slumped in dejection. The dark circles around Mueller's eyes had deepened. He was barely breathing.

Keeler walked to the bed. As he looked at Mueller, memories of the dapper, congenial man Mueller had been before stirred in his mind; he shrugged the memories aside. "It appears Tobias has taken a turn for the worse," he commented.

"Yes, he has," Swann replied, a catch in his voice. He sat up and rubbed his face, sighing wearily. "I truly wanted to get him through this, but I'm afraid it's only a matter of minutes now."

"You did all you could. Tobias was willing to make a sacrifice, but it wouldn't have been possible without your help."

Swann sighed again, standing and walking to the table. "Yes, I understand that now, as I understand many other things. If you need me again, Mr. Keeler, I'll be glad to do whatever I can for you."

"I'll bear that in mind, Swann, and I'll probably call on you for help from time to time. Meacham will be in directly."

Swann nodded, gathering up his instruments from the table. Keeler went out. The smell of the floor wax and disinfectant in the hall was fresh and clean after the thick stench in Mueller's room. A murmur of voices came from the dining room. Keeler took out a penciled map of the area where the sondercommando platoon was located, unfolding it as he entered the dining room.

Meacham, Campbell, Spencer, and another Army captain named Wilkins were sitting at the dining table with two sergeants. Clouds of tobacco smoke floated in the air, the atmosphere was one of tense expectancy. The men turned as Keeler entered, the conversation abruptly ceasing. He crossed the room to the table, addressing Meacham. "Secure the equipment and give Swann a hand, if you would, Meacham."

Keeler put the map in front of Campbell. "I found out their location, as I thought I might. It's an area I happen to be familiar with, so I drew this up." He pointed to the map. "They're in that warehouse."

The other men craned their necks, looking at the map as Campbell examined it. "That makes the job much easier," Spencer commented. "The way you ferret out details never ceases to amaze me, Mr. Keeler. With that map, we can reconnoiter the area and secure the best positions."

"I doubt you'll have time to do that," Keeler replied, pulling a chair away from the table and sitting down. "My information indicates that they intend to leave at nightfall tomorrow."

The men fell silent again, exchanging glances. Campbell grunted skeptically. "I don't see why they'd risk moving about this long before the dignitaries arrive," he said. "How reliable is your information?"

"Highly."

Campbell brushed his mustaches with a finger, looking at the map again. He shrugged. "Well, there may have been a possibility of tipping our hand if someone was a bit clumsy in the reconnoitering. We'll just have to set up and do it tonight, gentlemen."

"In my opinion, just before daybreak would be best, sir," Wilkins said. "What do you think, Jack?"

"No question about that," Spencer replied. "Keeping sentries awake just before daybreak is always a problem."

"Just before daybreak it is, then," Campbell agreed, glancing at his watch. "That gives us a little more than eight hours. And you say there are thirty of them, Keeler?"

"Yes. Typically, a sondercommando platoon consists of two rifle squads of ten men each and one heavy weapons squad, but they may not be armed typically. I have reason to believe that they're commanded by a Lieutenant Anton Vorczek. He led the attack against the munitions train and passenger train full of Soviet soldiers a few months back."

"By God!" Campbell exclaimed. "That blackguard is the commander of this lot? It'll be a pleasure to put an end to him!"

"It will probably be something of an undertaking as well," Keeler said. "I don't presume to offer advice on a military operation, but Vorczek is a very resourceful individual. We certainly wouldn't want him at large when the dignitaries arrive."

Campbell laughed heartily, shaking his head. "Have no fear on that score, Keeler. I have two full infantry companies. Not one of those sods will get away. And as you said, this is a military operation, so you leave it to us." He chuckled, glancing at the captains, then turned to the door as Meacham came back in and crossed the room to Keeler, his face solemn. "Excuse me, sir," he murmured. "Tobias just passed away."

Keeler nodded and asked Campbell, "Would it be possible to have him buried in the garrison cemetery?"

"Of course!" Campbell replied emphatically. "That's the very least we can do after what that chap did for us, isn't it? Yes, and we'll have him fitted out with a proper headstone and all. What was the rest of his name?"

"Tobias will be sufficient."

There was a momentary silence, then Campbell nodded and shrugged. "Whatever you wish," he said. He turned to one of the sergeants. "Sergeant, go fetch some men to take him out, and Doctor Swann's things as well. Now Keeler, if you'll explain this map in detail, we'll get organized."

The sergeant went out with Meacham, the others gathering closer, and listening to Keeler. The warehouse was separated from adjacent buildings by wide alleys. A canal and footpath ran behind it. There was an empty building across the street. Keeler pointed out the approach routes through certain streets and along the canal that were out of sight from the warehouse.

When he finished, sitting back and lighting a cigarette, the officers discussed tactics. As they spoke, soldiers trooped into the house following the sergeant. Two took out a sagging body bag, while others removed boxes of medical supplies and equipment. Meacham, carrying the box of radio equipment, came through the front room with Swann.

Campbell nodded in satisfaction, folding the map. "Yes, we'll bring this matter to a very speedy conclusion," he said. "Incidentally, Keeler, I was talking with Callaghan today, and I happened to mention the outbreaks of shooting we've had lately in the city. He said that the NKVD and one of the drug dealers are in a fracas.

What on earth could be the reason for that?"

"The Soviets aren't in my brief."

Campbell put the map in his pocket. "Well, we have a lot to do, gentlemen, so we'd best be about it. Keeler, I presume that you're through with the soldiers now, aren't you?"

"Yes. What time do you plan to attack?"

"We won't set a precise time until everything is organized, but it'll be nearabout five. You're more than welcome to join us, but it'll be at your own risk, of course."

Keeler nodded, putting out his cigarette in the ashtray. The others gathered up their overcoats, caps, and quarterstaffs, and Keeler followed them outside. The drive beside the house bustled with activity, flashlights moving about in the darkness and soldiers laughing and talking boisterously as they loaded their truck and prepared to leave.

Meacham came back along the path and stopped at the foot of the steps. "You'll want to join Colonel Campbell when all the preparations are made, won't you, sir?"

"Yes. Find out where his command post is and come for me at four, if you would."

"Yes, sir," Meacham replied. "I'll see you at four, then, Mr. Keeler. Good night, sir."

"Good night, Meacham."

Meacham disappeared into the darkness. Engines started and headlights came on. The car from the embassy, two staff cars, and the truck left the grounds, the truck engine snarling, its tires grinding in the gravel.

Keeler looked up at the stars shining through a high, thin overcast. It was a bright, still night, a bad night for the attack. He turned and went back into the house.

* * *

The servants were putting the dining room back in order with Celise's help. Keeler sat down in his chair and watched her through the open doorway. She was beautiful, charming, and entertaining; but more than that, she was strongly self-reliant, as well as spirited and independent. She was a proud, sensitive woman, whose feelings were easily injured. Somehow she combined the mind of a dreamer with a firm, practical grasp of the realities of life.

Her shift in loyalties had been abrupt and complete. What had begun as a mutual satisfaction of needs had developed into subtle bonds at many levels. The facets of their personalities were uniquely complementary and their relationship evolved rapidly. Keeler had become far more than protection and security to Celise, while she filled the deadly silences in his life.

Now she walked into the front room, smiling. "Would you like a drink, Frank?"

Keeler shook his head. "That's a pretty dress."

He had brought her belongings—books, old magazines, and cosmetics, as well as dresses and undergarments, lacy, frilly things that had been a pleasure to touch because they had touched her.

She laughed and she spun on tiptoe, striking an exaggerated pose. "Do you like it? It was made by a local seamstress, and it is a fashion from years ago. But if you like it, I don't care about fashion." She looked down at it, adjusting the fall of the skirt. "Did you have time to look in the car again, Frank? I'm positive my sequin handbag is in it."

"I looked, but I didn't see it."

"Did you look under the seats and everywhere? It may

be in a door pocket. It's like a handbag I saw in a shop window when I was a girl, and I treasure it." She came over to his chair and sat on the footstool in one smooth, graceful movement, leaning against his knees. "May I look for myself, Frank? Would that be possible?" Reaching out quickly and smiling apologetically, she put a soft, perfumed finger on his lips as he started to reply. "No—I am being very foolish. You've been so busy, perhaps you'll bring the car and let me look for myself when it is convenient. Just tell me if you can stay home with me now."

"I'll have to leave at four."

"That is hours from now," she said, taking his hand and standing. "You need to sleep, Frank. Come."

Her smile and tone suggested more than sleep. He tightened his hand around hers and pulled her down to his lap. She glanced at the dining room to see if the maid and the housekeeper were gone. Her girlishly prim sense of propriety and attitude of gleeful conspiracy made any intimacy with her more piquant. Then she melted into his arms, soft, warm, and fragrant.

He held and kissed her, her lips damp and eager against his. She moved the tips of her fingers over his face with light, feathery touches, moving closer. Their kisses became more passionate, her sighs turning into urgent murmurs as her hips moved against him restlessly. He gathered her up in his arms and carried her to the bedroom.

She undressed in a provocative manner that made it a form of contact without touching, her hands moving gracefully and inviting his attention to her soft curves that were revealed as the garments slipped away. Sometimes she had been playful and inventive, and at others she had undressed hurriedly and thrown herself into his arms in an urgent frenzy of passion. Still other times, she had been timid and trembling as she waited for him to undress her, her kaleidoscopic moods and impulses making her completely unpredictable.

The dim light of the lamp fell upon faint, silvery scars from wounds inflicted in the Soviet internment camp. But she was young and healthy, and her body had recovered just as her spirit had. Despite the scars, she was strikingly beautiful and vibrantly alive. The light gleamed on her satiny skin as she walked toward the bed, her firm breasts quivering.

Her movements and ardent kisses communicated her desire to finish with preliminaries, her concern for the few hours until he would have to leave and for his need of rest. She writhed beneath him and guided him, the forceful movements of her supple body setting a rapid pace as he entered her. Her breath brushed his face as she whispered urgently, opening herself wide and digging her fingers into his back, and he plunged in a surging rush into gripping spasms of ecstasy.

Still clasped in each other's arms and her silky legs entwined with his, the relaxed aftermath of love led him to the threshold of sleep. Thoughts of Mueller tugged at his mind, but they were distant and unobtrusive. He breathed the fragrance of her perfume and of her body, her hair scattered over his face and his head resting against the yielding warmth of her breasts. Her voice was a medodious, soothing whisper. She had been reading Dante, and she mused softly about the *Divine Comedy*.

CHAPTER TWENTY-THREE

SLEEPY AND SILENT, Meacham drove toward the center of the city. The high overcast had cleared, and it had turned colder. The stillness of early morning gripped the city, an occasional furtive wild dog that had slipped in from the desert the only movement in the headlight beams.

The car sped along dark, deserted streets, then slowed as it approached a wide intersection congested with Army vehicles.

Meacham swung the car around in a sharp turn and braked to a stop, glancing at Keeler as he turned off the headlights and ignition. "Colonel Campbell's a bit touchy this morning, Mr. Keeler."

"Has something gone wrong?"

"No, sir. It seems the brigadier ordered him to stay here until the battle is finished, and that has him narked."

Keeler and Meacham got out of the car. The vehicles were rows of bulky shadows in the darkness. A small light gleamed over the rear door of a communications van. Men from the ambulances and searchlight trucks were gathered around the van, talking softly, their breath making clouds of condensation in the frigid air. Keeler climbed into the van, Meacham behind him.

It was warm, bright, and crowded inside. A corporal in full combat equipment sat against the wall inside the door, while a radio operator crouched beside his backpack radio set in a corner. Two men were at radio consoles opposite a lighted glass display marked with the area of the warehouse. Campbell stood in front of the display, his cap pulled down to his eyes, his quarterstaff clenched behind him, and his mustaches bristling belligerently.

He turned and nodded curtly to Keeler. "Well, we're about ready, Keeler, and I trust your information is correct. If it isn't, we'll look a right lot of bloody fools."

"If they weren't alerted, they're there."

"Alerted?" Campbell snorted indignantly. "We've spent hours making certain they wouldn't be, while you were sleeping, no doubt. I sent in pathfinders, and some of them watched for any movement from the enemy while others led in the men, a squad at a time. They haven't been alerted, so you can forget using that as an excuse if they aren't there."

Keeler moved closer to the display. Drawn in grease pencil, it was an enlarged replica of the map he had given Campbell, the warehouse outlined in red. The platoons of one company were indicated in green along the canal. The other company was in blue across the street from the warehouse, two platoons in the empty building and one at each end. Circles were drawn along the front of the empty building. Keeler pointed to them.

"Heavy machine guns," Campbell explained. "More are being placed along the canal now. The company by the canal will keep flares in the air and provide fire suppression, and the other will assault. When they have a foothold, two platoons of the company along the canal will support them, while the other two remain outside as pickets. I don't want you to be able to say that any of them got away."

"When will the attack begin?"

Campbell looked at a clock on the wall. "In a little over fifteen minutes. I'll be leaving in time to arrive there when the battle's finishing, in the event you and Meacham want to go along."

"London wants a priority message on the outcome, so one of us should go to the embassy when it's over," Keeler said. He turned to Meacham. "Would you stay here, Meacham?"

"Yes, sir," Meacham replied promptly. "As soon as the men here get word, I'll send the message."

"If those buggers are in that warehouse, the bloody outcome is foregone," Campbell grumbled. "So if your information is correct, you can send it now." He turned as one of the men at the radio consoles touched his sleeve, muttering something. "What is it, man? Speak up!"

"Message from Captain Wilkins, sir," the man said. "He reports that his machine guns are now in position."

"Chalk them in on the map, then," Campbell snapped, unfastening his overcoat as he moved to the end of the van. He shrugged out of it and threw it and his cap into a corner, then took a pistol belt from a hook on the wall. "I'll go down there now, and if by chance you're contacted by anyone from the garrison, I'm inspecting the access routes. Do you understand?"

The two men nodded. Keeler watched Campbell as he put on the belt. "I should think you'll get there somewhat before the end of the battle, if you leave now," he commented.

"It'll take us twenty minutes," Campbell growled. "It will hardly be my fault if two infantry companies can't root out thirty bloody Germans in five minutes. Beyond that, I'm not a bloody headquarters pansy. By God, I'm a soldier!" He clapped a helmet on his head and tucked his quarterstaff under his arm, stamping toward the door. "Let's go, men! Wake up and get a move on!"

The corporal and the radio operator scrambled to their feet and went out, the radio operator dragging his equipment. Campbell tramped down the steps after them, Keeler following him. The men beside the van snapped to attention and saluted. Campbell touched his helmet with his quarterstaff. The corporal led the way around the trucks to a street that led off to one side of the square.

Campbell's mood having changed abruptly, he chatted cheerfully with the corporal as they walked down a narrow, darker side street for several blocks, then turned onto a wide avenue where the brick and stone buildings on both sides became intermingled with warehouses.

A series of sharp cracks suddenly rang out. Magnesium flares glared in the sky overhead, slowly drifting downward. A spatter of small arms fire echoed through the streets, then was drowned in the pounding roar of heavy machine guns. The drumming thunder grew louder as others joined in. More flares arced into the sky. Campbell urged the corporal to a faster pace.

The shattering clap of exploding bazooka warheads joined the machine gun fire. The sound of the battle was smothered in echoes, seeming to come from all directions. Then it was concentrated straight ahead as the corporal led the way into another street. The machine gun fire stopped suddenly, small arms, crackling, then fading under the renewed roar of machine guns. The radio operator called out, "Colonel Campbell, sir! Captain Spencer reports that the first assault has fallen back with heavy casualties!"

"Tell him to hold the second assault and keep the enemy pinned down," Campbell replied placidly over his shoulder. "And tell him that I'll be there in a moment." He beckoned the corporal, starting to run. "Let's go give them a hand, Corp. Step lively, lad!"

They broke into a headlong run. Shouting breathlessly into his handset, the radio operator dashed after them, Keeler stopped and lit a cigarette, then walked on along the street. The three men swerved into an alley behind the building on the next corner and disappeared.

When Keeler reached the alley, the sound of gunfire was a crushing pressure of noise. The flares drifting down cast glaring light and impenetrable shadows. Stray bullets whined as Keeler headed toward the rear of the building opposite the warehouse.

A platoon was in the opening between that building and the one next to it, the men crouching low, holding their weapons. Their faces, blackened with burned cork, turned up toward Keeler in surprise as he passed. Bullets spattered against the side of the building. Keeler paused briefly, then continued on his way.

A burly sergeant stared at Keeler, startled. "Who the bloody hell are you?" he demanded.

"As you were, Sergeant," a lieutenant called out, his voice almost drowned by the gunfire. "I'm Weatherby, Mr. Keeler. Get over beside the wall, if you would. Please keep your head lower."

The lieutenant was little more than a boy, his smooth face smeared with burned cork and the white rings around his eyes grotesque in the glare of the flares. He held a walkie-talkie to his ear as he pointed to the side of the building. Keeler nodded and knelt. The whoosh of a bazooka blended into the roar of its warhead detonating. Keeler leaned forward and peered into the street.

The front of the warehouse was riddled with holes, sparks of gunfire jetting from its gaping windows. Of its three large doors, two were wide, dark holes. The bazooka was firing at the third. Keeler sat back.

The sergeant turned to the soldiers, his deep voice ringing out over the gunfire. "Fix bayonets!"

Steel whispered from sheaths and bayonets clattered into place. The lieutenant took out his pistol and snapped open the cylinder to check the bullets, then closed the cylinder and watched the street, boyishly solemn and intent. The machine guns stopped firing, leaving a tense, ringing silence.

The lieutenant leaped to his feet, beckoning. "Follow me, lads!" he shouted. "Step out lively, now!"

The sergeant repeated the order to charge in a stentorian bellow and seized the back of the lieutenant's pistol belt as he lurched to his feet, holding him back as the soldiers caught up with them, trotting around the corner. Small arms fire crackled, building up to a roar.

Keeler leaned forward, watching intently. Sparks flashed in the warehouse windows, bullets ricocheted, men fell. The lieutenant ran beside the sergeant at the head of the platoon, beckoning his men and firing his pistol. He weaved on his feet, then resumed running and firing. Suddenly he stumbled. The sergeant put an arm around him and held him up, dragging him along as he continued to fire his pistol.

Another platoon poured into the street. Campbell ran out of the front of the building, bellowing and firing his pistol, followed by Spencer, platoon lieutenants, and a wave of soldiers. The street was full of men, bayonets glittering in the light of the flares, some of the soldiers stumbling and falling as they encountered a withering hail of bullets.

The platoons converged in front of the warehouse and poured through the doorways. A dozen or more flares floated down, making the night suddenly as bright as day. Columns of men surged along the sides of the warehouse from the canal, whooping and shouting, bayonets shining. they streamed through the doors while other soldiers formed a thin line, surrounding the warehouse.

The firelight inside was intense. Flares popped, illuminating the interior with blinding light. Thick clouds of smoke billowed out of the gaping doors and windows. The small arms fire spread throughout the warehouse, then faded into shouts and the clash of steel against steel.

As the last scattered shots died away, engines roared in the distance, coming closer. Keeler lit a cigarette and walked out into the street, which was littered with flare parachutes and bodies. The ambulances skidded around a corner followed by the searchlight trucks. The ambulances slid to a stop and medics leaped out. The searchlights came on, casting a glaring light on the medics as they tended to the wounded. Men began straggling out of the warehouse into the street.

Keeler saw the sergeant who had shouted at him earlier. "How is Lieutenant Weatherby, Sergeant?" he asked.

"He's bloody dead, sir," the sergeant replied curtly. He pointed and shouted at a soldier. "Wilcox, are you asleep on your bloody feet? Assemble your squad and see to our wounded before these bloody clap mechanics kill the lot of them! Look alive, man!"

The aimless milling about turned into orderly activity as

squads and platoons began assembling. Soldiers continued coming out of the warehouse, some wounded and others helping them. Men in the street separated the wounded and the dead, medics hurriedly bandaging the wounded. One ambulance left. Stretcher-bearers quickly filled another.

Campbell came out, the shoulder of his jacket torn where a bullet had ripped through it. Spencer, Wilkins, and the radio operator were with him as he walked over to Keeler. "By God, that was a scuffle, wasn't it?" he commented. "Swining Nazi dog that he was, I'll have to give the commander of that lot credit for knowing how deploy men. An assaulting force is always at a disadvantage, and he made the most of it. But we got them all, didn't we?"

"The escape routes appeared to have been covered. Are you wounded?"

"No, but my jacket's ruined," he replied regretfully. Then he laughed. "I suppose I'd best put on another before I report to the brigadier, or he might take me to task."

Spencer turned to Keeler. "Your information was half the battle, Mr. Keeler. If it hadn't been so accurate, this would have been much more difficult."

Campbell chuckled heartily, nodding. "I've learned to expect that of Keeler," he said. "He's given to making one word suffice for a dozen, but that one word is worth a thousand from most. As soon as we're organized, Keeler, I'll have the enemy dead brought out." He laughed, brushing his mustaches. "And you can satisfy yourself that we got them all."

"Very well."

"If you wish, I'll get word to Meacham that he's to go

on to the embassy and send his message. You said your people want it right away, didn't you?''

''I'd rather wait until I see the sondercommandos.''

Campbell's smile faded. He looked at Keeler narrowly, then grunted, brushed his mustaches, and walked away.

Two more ambulances drove off. Trucks began arriving. The stars dimmed in the east as dawn touched the sky. The soldiers shivered in their light battle dress as they collected the machine guns and took them to the trucks.

Men began carrying bodies and weapons out of the warehouse, putting the dead British soldiers with those on the street, and laying the dead sondercommandos several yards away in the cold, wintry dawn.

Campbell walked back across the street to Keeler, the officers following him. ''Keeler, you always want the bodies searched and fingerprints taken and such, don't you?'' he said. ''I don't fancy spending all day here, so shall I detail some men to get started on that?''

Keeler hesitated. Two men had just brought the body of a tall, muscular British soldier out of the warehouse, clad only in quartermaster issue boots and underwear. Keeler took out his cigarettes and lighter as the body was carried to the row of British dead and put down.

He lit a cigarette and nodded. ''Yes, if you would,'' he replied. ''Sondercommandos won't have much on them, but we may find a few things. One of them escaped, by the way. I suspect it was Vorczek.''

Campbell stiffened, glaring at Keeler. ''*One got away*?'' he bellowed. ''Now what sort of bloody foolishness is this? How could you know before you even look at them? We had that warehouse surrounded all the time, so you tell me how one got away!''

Keeler took a drag on his cigarette and pointed to the body in boots and underwear. "He walked away in a British uniform."

CHAPTER TWENTY-FOUR

KEELER SMOKED A cigarette, listening to the soft, sibilant whisper coming through the open car window. The man who was making his report was in charge of the group of agents maintaining surveillance over Abolfazi, and Abolfazi had broken his usual pattern of activity. Previously, the agents had seen him periodically every day. Abolfazi had puttered around his apartment building, making minor repairs, gone shopping and visited his favorite bordellos and taverns. But now a full day had passed and no one had seen him come out of the building.

The man finished, waiting for Keeler's reaction. Keeler drew on his cigarette. "No one came out who could have been Abolfazi in disguise?" he asked.

"No, Mr. Keeler," the man whispered. "And we saw no one who could have been a European. But after dark it is more difficult to see everything. Perhaps I should send a man to enquire about an apartment?"

"No, that could make him suspicious. Send someone to break a hinge on a shutter. If Abolfazi comes out tomorrow morning to repair it, use the telephone number you have and call Meacham."

"And if he doesn't come out?"

"Keep someone near your telephone at all times. If you don't hear from me, meet me here at the same time tomorrow night."

The man murmured in reply and crept away into the dark. Keeler tossed his cigarette out the window and lit another, glancing at his watch. Almost a full day had passed since the attack on the warehouse, a full day since black sondercommando fatigues with lieutenant insignia had been found there.

Meacham stirred and pulled his coat closer, shivering. He spoke quietly. "It's possible that Abolfazi is simply ill or something, isn't it, Mr. Keeler?"

"Yes."

"And it was almost dawn when Vorczek got away from that warehouse. Could he have reached Abolfazi's place before daylight?"

"Perhaps. Let's go."

Meacham started the engine and drove out of the alley. As they moved along the dark streets toward the embassy, Keeler thought about the situation. Vorczek had to at least suspect that Mueller had led him into a trap, and it would make him wary, reluctant to contact another agent immediately. It appeared more probable that he would hide for a day or two, possibly in the Polish resettlement camp.

But he would need food and weapons. He also needed information that only a local agent could provide. Soon he would have to approach another agent. However, it was possible that the Abwehr had agents in the city other than Abolfazi, sleepers under deep cover. It was also possible that Vorczek was not alone, that the Abwehr and the SD had coordinated their plans, and Vorczek had been joined by the four SD men who had escaped in the desert.

Two guards were at the embassy gate when Meacham turned in from the street. One wrote the license number of the car on a clipboard while the other leaned in the open window. "Sir, I must ask you to park at the garages," he said. "We have orders to keep the drive clear of vehicles."

"At this bloody time of the morning?" Meacham demanded irately. "They're not due in until this afternoon, you know."

"I'm sorry, sir, but I'm only following orders."

Meacham grumbled under his breath, rolling the window back up. He clashed the gears as he drove away from the gate, then stopped by the chancellery to let Keller out before going on to the garages at the rear of the compound.

Four guards were on duty at the entrance instead of the usual two. Morton, the security officer, was talking with the duty officer. He turned as Keeler entered the lobby. "Good morning, Mr. Keeler," he said. "That was certainly a coup you scored, finding those Germans. I understand they put up quite a battle."

Keeler nodded as he signed the register. "Yes."

"The gunfire was very loud here, and everyone talked about it all day yesterday. Was it indeed an attempt to assassinate the dignitaries?"

"I didn't have an opportunity to question any of them. Are you up late or early?"

"Early," Morton replied wryly. "The additional guards from the garrison will be here today, and I'm sorting out the shifts. Incidentally, an unfortunate development has occurred that complicates security. Have you had an opportunity to read yesterday evening's newspaper?"

"No."

"The press somehow obtained the schedule of meetings, and they published it. As you know, the meeting on the second day will be here, so I've asked for more guards. I realize that you're far from having time on your hands, but I'd be grateful if I could consult with you if anything unusual arises."

"Yes, of course."

"Thank you very much, Mr. Keeler."

Keeler nodded, turning away from the desk. He crossed the lobby and went down the stairs to the basement, signed the register and went into the room. A long message was on the table in front of his chair. He sat down and unfolded it.

Months before, Keeler had recommended that more information on Vorczek be obtained, a recommendation that had been ignored until the code name of the sondercommando platoon had been revealed. Then an agent inside Germany had been ordered to Landsbach, the town near the base camp of the Brandenburg Division, to gather personal information on the lieutenant. The message was a digest of that information.

Meacham came in with a tray of tea and sandwiches. He put the tray on the table and munched a sandwich as he went to the file cabinets. "If we're going to the airport, we may not have time to do the sitrep this afternoon, Mr. Keeler," he said. "Shall we do it now?"

"Yes."

Meacham stuffed the rest of the sandwich into his mouth, took folders out of the cabinet and carried them to the table. "The sitrep has become quite easy for me to do, except for Part One."

"I'll do Part One."

Nodding in satisafaction, Meacham removed several of

the folders from the stack and pushed them across the table. Keeler finished reading the message and handed it to Meacham who took a drink of tea and sat back in his chair as he read. Keeler began going over the papers in the folders.

Meacham chuckled as he finished reading the message and put it aside. "Beamish let one past the bat when he didn't follow up on your recommendation, didn't he, sir?" he commented. "I wish I had been a mouse in the corner when Willoughby took him to task about that, which he no doubt did. But there doesn't seem to be anything of much use here."

"The fact that Vorczek has a pregnant wife is meaningful."

Meacham took a bite of a sandwich and chewed, lifting his eyebrows. "Why, Mr. Keeler?"

"A man with a pregnant wife won't usually behave in the same way as an unmarried man. He won't risk his life as readily, for example."

Meacham chewed musingly, then nodded as he took a drink of tea. He shuffled through his folder and began scribbling on a writing pad. Keeler began writing the first part of the report.

When they had finished their work, Keeler and Meacham left. The lobby bustled with activity, several sleepy maids dusting, polishing furniture, and cleaning carpets. Meacham went upstairs to his room as Keeler telephoned the garages for a car and went outside.

Keeler stood beside the drive waiting for the car, surrounded by the cold pre-dawn darkness. He suddenly thought about taking Mueller's car home so Celise could look for her sequin purse. He was about to head for the garages when headlights came around the corner of the building. He stepped back to the end of the path and waited to be picked up.

A blush of light touched the eastern horizon, brightening into the dawn when the driver turned in at the gate in front of Keeler's house. Celise always kept a light burning until he returned. The yellow glow in the window gave the house a cheerful, welcoming atmosphere as he walked along the path.

Celise was curled in a corner of the couch in her dressing gown, asleep. Waking her abruptly frightened her, stirring responses that had been seared deep into her mind in the internment camp. Closing the door quietly, he moved softly to the liquor cabinet and poured several ounces of scotch into a glass, then sat in his chair and lit a cigarette, watching her. She slept like a cat, her beautiful face composed and her breathing soundless.

Her eyes suddenly opened. She awakened with a quick yawn, a lithe, graceful stretch and shrug. She was almost purring with pleasure as she smiled radiantly at him. He took a drink of scotch and drew on his cigarette, smiling too. "I've told you that you needn't wait up for me, Celise."

"And I've told *you* that I want to. I enjoy our moments together, and I don't want to be asleep when I could be with you." Her smile faded as she looked away, smoothing her hair. "It's also more than that. I've had time to think, Frank, to look behind and to look ahead. You're my one chance for contentment, and I would be lost without you."

"You're also very important to me, Celise."

She slid off the couch and knelt beside a stack of magazines on the floor at the end of the couch. They were some of the ones he had brought to her from Mueller's house, a tattered assortment of old issues of English and European magazines that she enjoyed reading over and over. She thumbed through them and took out one, then crossed to the footstool in front of his chair. Her dressing gown swung open up to her smooth, shapely thighs. The top had gaped while she had been lying down, revealing the cleavage between her firm, rounded breasts. The alluring fragrance of her perfume and the scent of her hair wafted around him as she sat down and leafed through the magazine, soft and warm against his knees. She was vocal even when she was not talking, clicking her tongue, sighing, and murmuring to herself as she searched for a particular page.

The scotch was warm in his stomach, creating a faint haze of euphoria. Relaxing his defenses and the constant awareness of his surroundings was a luxury that Celise's presence turned into a keen pleasure. She radiated invitation to look at her and to touch her, to enjoy her. As he drank from the glass and stroked her silky hair, his worries about Vorczek seemed to recede.

She found the page for which she was searching and put the magazine on his knees. "Look, Frank. Isn't that beautiful?"

It was an old motoring magazine published years before the war, open to a picture taken in the Cotswolds of a village beside a tree-lined stream—thatched roofs and narrow, winding cobblestone streets. Green hills in the background were dotted with sheep. Mossy stone walls wandered over the slopes, and fleecy clouds floated in an azure sky. Keeler looked at it, nodding. "Yes."

"Look at this cottage just up the hill, Frank. It has a pretty garden, trees, and its own little lane that leads down to the village. Isn't it lovely?''

''Yes.''

She turned the magazine back around and studied the picture, then looked up at him. ''Take me to that cottage, Frank,'' she said wistfully. ''Give me that cottage, my books, and a radio, and I will be happy. I know that what you do will take you away, perhaps for months or years, but I will always be there when you return.''

''That picture was taken a long time ago.''

''But that village is still there, just as it has been for centuries. And as that village is to those hills, so I will be to you. You live in a dark world of deceit, where you can trust no one. But you can trust me, Frank. Do this for me, and I will be loyal to you as no woman has ever been to a man.''

Keeler drank the rest of the scotch and put out his cigarette in the ashtray. She had avoided discussing her family and her ordeal in the internment camp, telling him that the subjects were too painful to her. Gaps in information about someone close to him made him instinctively uneasy. But he had confidence in Celise, confidence that came from knowing her. During the time she had been in his house, he had studied her closely, searching for any indication of deception. And there was none. He was convinced that Celise was precisely what she seemed to be.

And she was telling the truth. Years of experience had taught him to detect lies and evasion. Her sparkling blue eyes were completely candid as she looked up at him. If he took her to a safe, comfortable place, he would have her loyalty and devotion for life. Her eyes reflected a deep, desperate need far more intense than the most fervent love.

Her hand was warm and soft as she rested it on his. ''I'll

always be there for you, Frank,'' she whispered. ''The time will come when you will be in an office in London. We'll have a house there and our cottage in the country, and your colleagues will visit. I'll make you very proud of me, Frank—they will all envy you. Then you'll retire, and we'll be the slightly mysterious couple who live in the cottage above the village. Take me away from here to England, and I'll make you happy for the rest of your life!''

Keeler lit a cigarette, looking away. Her soft voice had described a vision of happiness as hopelessly idealistic as the picture in the magazine. But it could be within reach. Agents were often moved from place to place by means of circumvented laws—dark cars speeding to waiting aircraft, flights from one point to another, delays in isolated private rooms. He knew the procedures well; a request from him would be regarded as having authority from London.

It would cause an upheaval in London, but the upheaval would pass, because human frailties were understood in his profession far better than most. It might even be viewed with some satisfaction, because those with established ties were considered more reliable. Ties with a Polish refugee would raise questions, but they could be answered. And Willoughby would find Celise charming. . .

''Tell me if you want to, Frank,'' she whispered, stroking his hand. ''And if you do, tell me if you will try.''

''I want to. And I'll try.''

Celise closed the magazine and stood up, walking back to the couch. ''Shall I prepare you something to eat?''

''No, thank you.''

''Come, then. Make love with me and sleep.''

She held out her hand and he put out his cigarette and

stood up, taking her hand. She laced her fingers between his as they went to the bedroom.

Her wide blue eyes smiled into his as he undressed her slender, shapely body. She lay next to him, her skin warm and smooth against his. Her responses followed the mounting desire within him, an echo of his swelling need for her. She sighed and gasped, her lips opening under his and her breath mingling with his. Trembling eagerly, she arched to meet him. The damp warmth of her body enfolded him. Time collapsed, seconds becoming an eternity of seething sensations gripping every fiber of his being. She shuddered and strained, grasping for the rising momentum of sensation until they surged together in wrenching spasms of ecstasy.

She gathered his head to her breasts, her heart pounding. The pulsing subsided to a rhythmic thudding in his ear as her breathing slowed, then she brushed her hair over his face. "Tell me again that you want to, and you'll try," she whispered. "Tell me again, Frank."

"I will."

She sighed, content, the tips of her fingers gently caressing his forehead as she began talking softly, relating the story of a medieval German romance, *Der Arme Heinrich*. Her voice faded to a whisper as she became drowsy.

Gray winter daylight came through the window by the bed, the screen of her fragrant, silky hair over his face diffusing the light and tinting it with warm shades of golden brown. Her slender body was warm, one of her smooth legs resting across his. The beating of her heart in his ear was an echo of his own heartbeat. He closed his eyes and, listening to the melodious murmur of her voice, he fell asleep.

* * *

The housekeeper tapped on the door, awakening him. Celise slipped out of bed and put on her dressing gown and slippers, and Keeler went to the bathroom to bathe and shave, then dressed and went into the dining room where breakfast was ready and Celise at the table. She poured the coffee as he sat down.

Her beautiful face drowsy and smiling, she was cheerfully talkative as they ate. Then the sound of a car engine carried into the house from the drive. Celise went into the front room with him and helped him put on his trench coat, buttoning it as he fastened the belt. Then she looked up at him as she handed him his hat.

"Tell me once more than you want to, and that you'll try."

"I want to, and I'll try."

She stood on tiptoe to kiss him, her soft, damp lips tasting of coffee. One nipple touched his palm through the silky fabric of her dressing gown, and she reacted with a soft gasp, a quick tremor, and a sultry smile of promise for when he returned.

CHAPTER TWENTY-FIVE

THE AFTERNOON WAS cold and blustery. Meacham huddled in the driver's seat with his collar up around his ears. His eyes were bleary red from lack of sleep. He put the car in gear as Keeler got in and drove through the gate and out into the street. ''The man in charge of the surveillance agents assigned to Abolfazi called, Mr. Keeler,'' he said. ''Abolfazi came out this morning and repaired that shutter.''

''Very well.''

''So he was probably ill?''

''Possibly.''

Meacham yawned and nodded, accelerating along the street leading into the city, then on to the airport road. Traffic was moving at a crawl. Civilians were gathering on the sidewalks, their robes and overcoats stirring in the wind. Soldiers moved among them and passed out small American, British, and Soviet flags. The traffic thinned out at the edge of the city, where formations of American, British, and Russian soldiers were marching along the airport road.

Meacham rummaged in a coat pocket and handed a piece of paper to Keeler. "Just at the last moment, a decision was made to issue airport passes, Mr. Keeler. Mr. Morton got ours, and this is yours."

They were stopped at a guard post beyond the intersection with the road to the garrison. A military policeman looked at the passes, glanced into the rear seat, then saluted and waved them past.

The airport teemed with activity. During the past two days, American, British, and Soviet military advisors and their staffs had been arriving. The Soviet foreign minister, Vyacheslav Molotov, had come with the United States ambassador to Moscow, W. Averell Harriman, the British foreign minister, Sir Anthony Eden, had arrived from London.

All the aircraft had been moved to the north end of the airport, leaving an open expanse in front of the hangers. The central hangar, flags and buntings over its main doors, had been prepared for an informal meeting and exchange of greetings between the three heads of state. Light artillery pieces were positioned in front, along with a military band and formations of honor guards.

Three limousines stood in front of the hangar, and staff cars were parked at one side. A Cadillac belonging to Shah Mohammed Riza Pahlavi was among the cars, Iranian officials mixing with the crowd of officers. Reporters and photographers, flashbulbs popping, were everywhere.

Meacham parked at the end of a long row of jeeps and trucks. The raw, biting wind howled across the open ramp as Keeler and Meacham walked toward flight operations where Callaghan was standing beside a staff car, talking with an American Air Corps captain.

He turned and waved as Keeler and Meacham approached. "Hello, Frank, Chad. This is a hell of a great day for the bigwigs to get here, isn't it?"

Meacham laughed and nodded. "If they're bringing this weather with them, they should have stayed away. How are you, Charles?"

"I'll be all right if I don't freeze to death. This is Jack Whittacker, one of the operations officers. Jack, Frank Keeler and Chad Meacham, passport control officers at the British embassy."

Whittacker, a tall, lanky man wearing a pilot's leather jacket and a crushed cap, smiled, exchanging nods with Keeler and Meacham. "Charles was asking if this wind will give the airplanes any trouble," he said. "And it won't, in case you're wondering."

"What if it gets any stronger?" Meacham asked.

Whittacker shook his head. "We'd have a problem if it was a crosswind, but it's blowing straight down the runway. They were supposed to get here at the same time, though, and it'll spread them out a little."

"Will it delay them?" Callaghan asked.

"No more than a few minutes," Whittacker replied. "We have inbound reports on all three, and they should all be here in a little over two hours." He glanced at his watch, turning away. "I'd better get back in there. I'll see you guys later."

As he walked away, Callaghan turned to Keeler. "Frank, that business with the sondercommandos was really something, wasn't it? Have you been able to pick up anything on the one who got away?"

"No. Have you?"

"If you haven't, you can depend on it that I haven't," Callaghan laughed ruefully. "Say, what the hell do you think that Vertinski is trying to prove? A bunch of his people had another big shootout last night down at the rail yards with some of that gang of drug dealers."

Keeler shrugged and shook his head. "The NKVD and what they do aren't in my brief, Charles."

"Yeah, my ambassador has been telling me twice a day to stay clear of that myself," Callaghan chuckled. "But I almost got into it last night, because I was down there for meetings with some of my contacts." He looked across the ramp and pointed. "I see George Campbell is over there with the brass."

Campbell was talking with a brigadier and looking across the ramp at Keeler and the men beside him. Exchanging salutes with the brigadier, Campbell turned and started toward them, his head down against the wind and his overcoat flapping.

"Callaghan, how are you? Meacham? Having a bit of a blow, aren't we? Keeler, I was just speaking with the brigadier, and he again mentioned what a fine piece of work you did in locating those Germans. And he wants to know when you'll have something on the one who got away."

"I don't know."

"Aye, well, you can understand his position, can't you? Here we are with the dignitaries arriving, and we have a German assassin running loose. Now that's bloody embarrassing! So when you think we'll be able to set that right?"

"I don't know."

"Well, I'm keeping two platoons on ready alert, and all I need from you is word on where to send them. Now the brigadier and I agree that we don't think it's asking too much for you. . . ." A resounding boom rang out, and he wheeled and stared at the artillery pieces. "By God! Did some fool fire one of those guns?"

Callaghan shook his head, pointing. "No, that was the power substation, George. What a hell of a time for that thing to go out."

Smoke billowed from the electrical substation behind the hangars and sparks darted back and forth between wires and transformers. The crowd of officers in front of the hanger hurried over to take a look.

"A bloody awkward time for that to happen," Meacham commented. "And it made quite a bang."

Callaghan nodded. "Yeah, a big transformer popping can sound like a bomb. Let's go down to ops and see what they're doing."

As they walked toward the flight operations building, a fire engine rushed along the dirt road behind the hangers, sliding to a stop by the substation. Men with chemical fire extinguishers leaped off it and sprayed the transformers and wires. In the distance, tiny figures climbed up and down the steep stairway to the control tower. Some men came out of flight operations to watch, Whittacker among them. He turned when Callaghan shouted to him and trotted over, saluting Campbell as he approached. "This is a hell of a time for something like that, isn't it?"

"Indeed it is, Captain," Campbell replied, touching his cap with his quarterstaff. "What do you suppose went wrong?"

Whittacker shrugged. "We've had trouble with it before, Colonel, and it was probably overloaded from all those lights they put up in that hangar there. But the people in the control tower can't get their backup generator started, which is more of a problem. The phones are still working, and they called and said that the fuel tanks are contaminated with water. Somebody's ass will hang over that."

"The radios in the tower are out?" Callaghan exclaimed. "Christ, will the planes have to divert to another airfield?"

Whittacker shook his head. "No, no, Charlie. Radios go out all the time, and there's a standard procedure. They'll just have to fly an extra loop around the field before they land."

"Yeah, but it is a standard procedure for Russians?" Callaghan asked. "The pilot in Stalin's airplane is a Russian, remember."

Whittacker chuckled and nodded. "He would know what to do even if he was a German. The tower has signal lights powered by batteries, and they'll use them. The planes will make a low pass, then fly a downwind leg east of the field and come on back around to land. That's standard procedure for both military and civilian aircraft of any nationality when they don't have radio contact."

Keeler turned to Whittacker. "How far to the east?" he asked. "And in what altitude?"

Whittacker glanced at him and looked back at flight operations. "A mile and at a thousand feet—that's standard international procedure too. There's my boss, so I'd better get back over there. But don't worry about those airplanes being able to land. Everything is covered."

He hurried back to the flight operations building. The other three men looked at Keeler in expectant silence as the wind keened around them, tugging at their coats. Keeler took out his cigarettes and lit one, sheltering his lighter in his hands, then looked out at the barren terrain east of the airport.

Campbell broke the silence, brushing at his mustaches. "Well, what is it, Keeler?" he asked. "Are we to understand that you think something underhanded may be afoot here?"

"All this seems too coincidental," Keeler replied. "And a large airplane at a thousand feet would be a very easy target for someone with a heavy machine gun or a bazooka."

Campbell nodded, narrowing his eyes against the wind as he followed Keeler's gaze. "Well, the road to the garrison firing butts and the artillery range is about a mile or so beyond the airfield. I have two platoons on ready alert if you want to look around over there. But I think you're jumping at ghosts, because those three airplanes are hardly going to line up like ninepins to be shot down."

Callaghan shook his head musingly. "I'm not so sure, George," he said. "They'll only be a few minutes apart, and those in the second and third wouldn't be able to see what happened to the ones ahead of them. The tower wouldn't be able to tell them to pull up."

"And our man may settle for Stalin's airplane," Meacham added. "That would be disastrous, because there'd be no way to convince the Soviets that we didn't have a hand in it."

"Yeah, you're right there, Chad," Callaghan chuckled, turning to the substation again. "That *seemed* to be a transformer popping, but it could have been explosives with a timer detonator. And it seems odd to have water in the backup generator fuel tanks at the same time."

"Well, let's have a look, then," Campbell said briskly. "My jeep is just over here, so let's be on our way."

Keeler walked toward the jeep with Meacham and Campbell as Callaghan ran to his car, took a bottle of whiskey and binoculars from the trunk, then squeezed into the jeep's rear seat next to Meacham. Keeler got in and closed the door as Campbell backed the jeep out and drove down the road.

Vehicles filled with Iranian officials were still arriving along the road from the city and stopping at the guard post at the airport entrance. A military policeman saluted and waved the jeep past. Campbell braked to a stop and called to him, "Corporal, do you have a telephone there?"

"Yes, sir."

"I'm Colonel Campbell, and I'd like you to get in touch with Captain Spencer at brigade headquarters. Tell him to assemble the men he has on alert and bring them out to the firing butts with all possible speed. I'll meet him there. Do you have that?"

The man nodded, saluting and Campbell drove on.

The garrison came into view from the top of the incline, a sprawling complex of tents, temporary buildings, and equipment parking areas. Campbell turned down a road. The jeep bounced and rattled up and down rolling hills. The terrain fell away into a long valley on the right, where another road led down to the small arms range below. Campbell braked to a stop.

"It shouldn't take Spencer very long to get here with his men," he said. "We're just due east of the airport, so we should begin here and work to the north, shouldn't we, Keeler?"

"Yes."

"Well, I do hope it'll be of some benefit. I'm always more than willing to cooperate with you, but I did want to see the dignitaries."

"It's better to miss seeing them than to take a chance on

seeing them shot down, George," Callaghan laughed, taking the whiskey bottle out of his coat pocket. "Care for a drink, Frank?"

Keeler shook his head, lighting a cigarette. "No, thank you. Meacham looks a bit chilly, though. He'll probably have one."

"Aye, I will and all," Meacham said eagerly. "By God, my feet feel like they've turned to ice!"

After he, Campbell and Callaghan had drunk, the three men began discussing the preparations for receiving the heads of state. Keeler, smoking his cigarette, listened absently, looking out at the stretch of land between the road and the airport.

The parched, barren terrain, a wrinkled maze of sandy mounds and gullies with steep banks, was dotted with clumps of dried brush. Open land and accessible to anyone, it offered innumerable places for concealment. There seemed to be furtive movements on the edge of his vision in all directions.

Campbell looked into the rear view mirror, then opened his door. "Well, here they are, so we can get started. I do hope that it won't be an absolute waste of time."

Keeler, Meacham and Callaghan climbed out and followed him around the jeep. Two large trucks raced along the road and slid to a stop.

Spencer climbed down from the cab of the first truck and saluted, approaching Campbell. "I came as quickly as I could, sir."

"You made very good time indeed, Spencer," Campbell replied. "Keeler seems to feel it would be advisable to have a look out that way and to the north to make certain that no one is hiding there. A hundred yards or so out should be sufficient. How do you want to proceed?''

Spencer looked out at the dry, broken terrain and said, ''We could probably cover it more thoroughly and rapidly by leapfrogging the men, sir. I could put out one platoon here, then the other two hundred yards ahead. When the first reached where the second began, they could move up ahead.''

''That sounds an excellent procedure, Spencer. Let's be about it and waste no more time than necessary.''

Spencer saluted and stepped back to the first truck. The driver handed down a walkie-talkie as Spencer gave his orders. After the truck had pulled away, men jumped down from the second truck as Spencer came up to it. The platoon lieutenant, a walkie-talkie slung from his shoulder, led the men off the road.

Keeler got back in the jeep with the others and Campbell drove along the road and parked on a high point. Callaghan handed the bottle around again. When the second truck had passed, Campbell drove to another vantage point.

Wild dogs scuttled across the road as the soldiers scoured the area, pushing through brush, clambering up banks, and sliding into gullies. After they returned, dusty and weary, the trucks moved ahead. Campbell fell silent as he drove but Meacham and Callaghan continued talking and passing the bottle back and forth.

A dot appeared in the sky to the north, slowly becoming larger against the clouds. Callaghan leaned forward from the back seat and tapped Keeler's shoulder as he pointed at it. Keeler nodded. It gradually turned into an airplane descending toward the airport. Callaghan watched it through his binoculars, then handed them to Keeler. "I believe that's Stalin," he said.

Keeler looked through the binoculars. The plane was an American B-24 Liberator, a four-engine bomber, with Soviet insignia. Its landing gear was down, its rate of descent tapering off into an approach to the airport. Keeler offered the binoculars to Campbell, who glowered resentfully as he took them, then looked at the airplane. Keeler got out of the jeep.

The others followed and took turns looking through the binoculars as the plane flew low along the runway, climbed again, its landing gear retracting, then turned east.

Campbell turned to Keeler, sighing in disgust. "Keeler, we've wasted our time in a futile search for. . . ."

He broke off and wheeled around as an Enfield cracked somewhere in the gullies. A truck was parked a hundred yards ahead, the men spread out beyond it. They began converging as a rattling fusillade of shots rang out. Spencer jumped out of the truck and ran to the side of the road, shouting into his walkie-talkie.

Campbell cupped his hands around his mouth and called, "What is it, Spencer? What is it, man?"

Spencer turned and replied, but his voice was muffled by the wind and drowned in the rumble of the approaching airplane. He ran back along the road and Campbell ran to meet him. The other truck moved along the road a hundred yards behind, soldiers running to meet it. The noise from the airplane grew to a battering roar. The ground trembled as it shot past overhead.

Meacham and Callaghan sprinted along the road behind Campbell. Keeler lit a cigarette and walked after them. The thunderous blare of the aircraft engines faded rapidly, carried away by the wind. The men's voices became audible as Keeler approached. Two men had been sighted, one in robes and the other in European clothing. They had disappeared into a gulley, leaving behind a bazooka and ammunition.

The soldiers searched the gullies as Campbell and the others conferred.

"Can we be certain this is the same man who escaped from the warehouse?" Spencer was saying. "This appears to be someone very familiar with the terrain. And who could the second man be? Couldn't they be local people?"

"They could be Moslem fanatics," Campbell replied. "We've had a dozen or more men turn up in the city with their throats slit by those sods. If they would do that, they would be more than ready to do this."

"There's also a strong pro-Nazi faction in the Iranian Parliament," Callaghan added. "I wouldn't put it past them to try something. And the whole schedule of events was published in the newspapers, so anyone would know when they were arriving. What do you think, Frank?"

Keeler took a drag on his cigarette, looking away. He knew it was Vorczek. In Vorczek's last message to Mueller, he had asked for confirmation on when the heads of state would arrive. His only conceivable reason for wanting the information was that he had a plan keyed to their time of arrival. He had never received the information from Mueller, but it had been published in the papers. The bazooka and ammunition suggested that Vorczek had contacted an agent in the city, but virtually any type of weapon was available through the black market. The fact that there were two men indicated either that Vorczek had an agent with him, or he had linked up with the SD men who had escaped. The plan had been a good one; Vorczek was a deadly adversary, and he would try again.

Keeler glanced around, shrugging and shaking his head.

"Well, we acted promptly and foiled the buggers, didn't we?" Campbell said. "And that's the main thing. Keep the men looking, Spencer, and I'll be back directly. I'm going to the airport and see if I can still get a glimpse of the dignitaries."

Spencer saluted and spoke into his walkie-talkie as he turned and walked toward the trucks. Campbell, Meacham, and Callaghan walked toward the jeep. Keeler tossed his cigarette away and followed them. A whisper of aircraft engines carried across the distance as a second plane turned east from the airport. An Avro Lancaster bomber, with British insignia passed overhead while Campbell was turning the jeep around; then a B-24 with American insignia flew over. From the garrison road, the distant slap of cannon firing salutes was audible. When the road between the airport and the city came into view, civilians were flowing out of the city behind soldiers, waving small American, British, and Soviet flags.

The informal meeting and exchange of greetings was over when they reached the airport. Keeler stood with the others and watched. The three limousines in front of the hangar were decorated with flags and bunting. Photographers forced their way through the crowds to the limousines, flashbulbs flickering. The wind made the brassy blare of the garrison band sound thin and wavering.

Churchill's bowler was visible through a sea of military caps. Roosevelt, in his wheelchair, came into view momentarily as did Stalin, completely surrounded by a large group of officers. They were escorted to the limousines. The officers stepped back, saluting, and the flags on the fenders of the limousines fluttered as they moved along the ramp toward the road.

Campbell tucked his quarterstaff under his arm and stamped his feet, saluting stiffly. Roosevelt was laughing and talking with Harriman and two American generals in his limousine as it passed. Churchill was in the next with Eden, chewing a cigar and listening as an aide read aloud from a paper. He glanced out and nodded to Campbell, then looked briefly at Keeler. Everyone in Stalin's limousine was staring straight ahead. Stalin's face was impassive, inscrutable.

The shah's Cadillac followed, then cars filled with senior officers, Iranian officials, news reporters, and photographers. A face in a car filled with Russian officers caught Keeler's eye, vaguely familiar and out of place in a uniform; then the car was gone.

Campbell smiled in exuberant satisfaction at Keeler and the others. "Well, this is a very monentous occasion, isn't it?" he said. "What do you think, Keeler? Even if you have to be a bit affected by this. We're at the very center of history in the making."

Keeler was lighting a cigarette. He took a drag on it and nodded. "Yes, we are," he replied. "History of one sort or another."

CHAPTER TWENTY-SIX

THE CRYPTOGRAPHER IGNORED the knock on the door as she thumbed through folders, filing material. Meacham glared at her over his shoulder, then went to the door and opened it a crack.

A voice murmured in the hall; Meacham turned and told Keeler that Morton wanted to speak with him. Keeler put out his cigarette and crossed the room to the door. The security officer moved back as Keeler stepped out into the hall.

He looked up at Keeler, smiling apologetically. "I'm sorry to bother you, Mr. Keeler," he said, "but something has come up that seems strange. I was in the kitchen a short time ago, and the head cook was complaining about some vegetables that had been delivered and that were getting in his way. When I saw the head steward in the lobby a few minutes ago and mentioned it to him, he said he didn't order any vegetables."

"Who delivered them?"

"I didn't ask, but the guards wouldn't have let anyone but the regular vendor through the gate. I realize it seems a very minor thing, but you did say that you wouldn't mind if I consulted you on anything out of the ordinary. . . ."

His voice faded into a faintly embarrassed cough as Keeler thought about what he had said. It did seem trivial, probably no more than a misunderstanding. But a vendor was a means of access to the embassy compound, and the meeting between the heads of state the next day would be held upstairs.

Keeler turned back to the door. "Ask the steward to go to the kitchen, if you would, and I'll be up in a moment."

Morton nodded, turning and walking along the hall. Keeler went back into the room and put on his jacket as he told Meacham what Morton had said. Meacham followed him out.

It was after ten o'clock, but the lobby and the hallway leading back through the building still teemed with activity. In rooms along the hall, senior officers were discussing the conference that had been held during the day and making plans for the subsequent one the following day.

The mood among the officers was subdued. Roosevelt and Churchill had met in Cairo before coming to Teheran, where they had agreed upon a planning and command staff for Operation Overlord, the invasion of France. The Soviets had dominated the conference that day, adamantly insisting that an early date be established for implementing Operation Overlord before other items on the agenda were discussed.

In the kitchen, the staff bustled about preparing food for the night shift. Morton, the head cook, and the head steward were at the table that the kitchen staff used for meals. The steward, Lummas, was an archetypal civil servant, gravely polite. The cook was a chubby, excitable man named Phillips.

The vegetables were in bags and boxes on the floor in front of the refrigeration lockers near the back door. Keeler questioned the cook about them and learned that they had been delivered by the usual vendor. He had arrived at about seven-thirty, as he normally did, and had parked his van outside the back door. He had taken about fifteen minutes to carry in the vegetables, which was a normal amount of time.

"How did he act?" Keeler asked.

The cook cleared his throat, pushing at his tall white cap, then shrugged. "Well, he seemed a bit quiet, now that I think of it. But I really wasn't paying much attention, Mr. Keeler. Like I said, I didn't really notice the vegetables until it came time to mop the floor."

Keeler turned to the steward. "It is normal for deliveries to be made without your knowledge?"

"Yes, sir," Lummas replied. "Vendors and merchants have standing orders for deliveries to the kitchen, garages, and the housekeeper, and I get a bill, later, which I match with the copy that was left by the vendor, and send them both in for payment. We've been laying in more stores than usual. That's probably why Mr. Phillips didn't question this delivery."

"Aye, that's right," the cook agreed, nodding rapidly. "I've been getting deliveries right and left from all the vendors. And I can use those vegetables, the way we're going through them with all these people here, but my bins are full right now."

"This could have been a simple mistake, Mr. Keeler," Lummas added. "That is our standing order for vegetables, but they came on the wrong day. I tried to call the vendor after speaking with Mr. Morton, but the only telephone number I have is for his warehouse. There was no answer."

Keeler lit a cigarette. The vendor could have made a mistake. Or he might have been used as a means of access to the embassy.

An intuitive urge to probe deeper tugged at Keeler, a warning whispering quietly in the back of his mind. He turned to Meacham. "Get the vendor's name and address, if you would. Take a car, get our man in the police, and question the vendor. If anything appears suspicious, have him taken in and call me."

"Yes, sir. If we take the man in, you want him taken to an upstairs room, don't you?"

"Yes."

"I see the obvious gap in our security, Mr. Keeler," Morton said. "And I'll correct it immediately, of course. The guards at the gate will contact Mr. Lummas before they let any vendor in, and so forth. Beyond that, should I alert the people in the building?"

"No, that won't be necessary."

"The name and address is in my office, Mr. Meacham," Lummas said. "If you'll come with me, I'll give it to you."

Lummas and Meacham headed for the west wing of the building as Keeler went back downstairs to the basement room. London had requested a detailed report on the incident at the airport, which he had been preparing. He hung up his coat and sat down at the table, glancing over what he had written, then he resumed working. An hour later, he handed the finished report to the cryptographer. There was a knock on the door as he returned to the table. It was the guard from the end of the hall; Keeler was wanted on the telephone in the lobby.

Several officers were standing near the receptionist's desk. Keeler moved to the other end of the desk and turned his back to them as he lifted the receiver. It was Meacham, calling from a restaurant. Music, conversation, and a clatter of dishware could be heard in the background as he spoke quietly.

"There's no telephone in the vendor's house, so I had to come here to call you, sir," he explained. "It appears that this is something very serious indeed. The man, his wife, and their children are all dead."

"How long ago did it happen?"

"Apparently not very long, sir. The woman's and the children's throats were cut. Our man from the police said that the blood hadn't completely congealed. The man was garroted, probably somewhat later than the others were killed. It appears that a local is involved, doesn't it, sir?"

"Yes. Have the man at the apartments taken in."

"Upstairs or to the downstairs room, sir?"

"Downstairs. I'll be there within two or three hours."

"Yes, sir."

Keeler hung up the receiver and beckoned to Morton, who was talking with the guards by the front doors. Keeler took him aside and quietly told him what Meacham had found. Morton's normally stolid face reflected shock as he listened.

He sighed heavily and shook his head. "I'm very sorry to hear that, Mr. Keeler. It removes all doubt about a mistake or misunderstanding, doesn't it? Do you think an intruder may be hidden in the compound?"

"I think it's more likely that he planted some explosives and left. If you would, call the garrison and contact

Colonel Campbell. Ask him to bring a team of sappers here as soon as possible."

"Yes, sir. Should I have the building evacuated?"

"No, that won't be necessary. I'll be outside."

Morton nodded, hurrying to his office. Keeler went back down to the basement for his hat and trench coat, then returned to the lobby and went outside into the raw, dark night. An icy wind keened around the building and the trees in the compound tossed and thrashed. Keeler walked down the drive to the gate.

Morton had already questioned the guards, and they were defensive, insistent that they had thoroughly searched the vendor's van and emphatically certain that no one but the vendor had been in it. The vehicle log showed that the van had been in the compound for about twenty minutes, which agreed with what the cook had said. Keeler walked back to the rear of the chancellery.

The old building had been renovated and expanded several times. The wing at the rear was of relatively recent construction, three stories high and built of brick, with the kitchen and pantries in an addition at one side. The rear wall of the building was broken by decorative horizontal bands of brick that jutted out a few inches at the second and third floor levels.

The main conference room was at the rear of the building, in the center of the second floor, three feet above one of the brick bands. Security lights in the flower bed below directed their beams up the wall. The beams failed to overlap in several places, leaving areas of shadow. One such area was directly beneath the conference room windows.

As Keeler stood looking up, Morton came around the

corner of the building, bundled in a heavy overcoat. "I contacted Colonel Campbell, Mr. Keeler," he said. "He will be over directly with the sappers."

"Thank you. We could use a few more lights back here."

"Yes, sir. Several have become inoperative both here and around the walls, but the shortages make it difficult to get replacements. I've had them on order for quite some time now. All the lights we do have are turned on."

"I see. Is there a ladder available that will reach the conference room windows?"

"Yes, I believe there's one at the garages. Do you want to have a look up there, Mr. Keeler?"

"No, but I'd like to have one for the sappers."

Morton crossed the flagstone courtyard behind the building to the garages and went into the head chauffeur's office. Two drivers came back out with him carrying a ladder. They set it down and went back toward the garages. When they were out of earshot, Morton spoke quietly. "Do you think some explosives may be hidden up there, Mr. Keeler?"

"It's a logical place."

Morton pulled his coat closer as he turned away. "I'm going to check the guards at the rear of the compound, Mr. Keeler. I'll be back directly."

"Very well."

Keeler walked along the building and stood at the corner beside the drive. A few minutes later, a jeep and a van entered the compound, braking to a stop in the courtyard. Campbell stepped out of the jeep. "Well, here we are, Keeler," he called. "And I trust it's something important. I'm always more than willing to cooperate with you, but I don't fancy leaving a good supper and coming out on a night such as this for nothing. Why do you want the sappers?''

''I believe we've had an intruder in the compound who may have left some explosives.''

''Bloody hell! That's a fine state of affairs, isn't it? Well, we'll see what we can do to put it right.'' He turned to the van. ''All right, Sergeant, let's get busy.''

A young sergeant got out of the van and nodded, closing the door. ''Very good, sir. Are there any suggestions as to what we're looking for and where it may be?''

''Start up there, if you would,'' Keeler said, pointing to the ledge below the conference room windows. ''It may be something on the order of a satchel charge or two with a timer detonator.''

''Aye, and we have a ladder there, don't we?'' the sergeant commented, walking toward the rear of the van. ''Very good. Let's get ready and have a look up there, men.''

Two more soldiers climbed out of the cab, opened the doors at the rear of the van and took out bags and tool boxes while the sergeant shrugged out of his overcoat and put on an oversize set of coveralls.

The three soldiers began selecting tools from the boxes. As Keeler and Campbell watched, Morton returned. He and Campbell talked quietly, discussing the situation; then Morton informed Campbell of the murder of the vendor and to his family.

Campbell turned to Keeler in outrage. ''A woman and three children with their throats cut?'' he exclaimed. ''By God, that's the very limit of infamy! Have you ever heard of anything as vicious, Keeler?''

Keeler took a drag on his cigarette, nodding. ''Yes.''

"Well, anyone who does something like that has no place among human beings," Campbell growled. "But at least we can find what's been done here, and undo it before it causes any harm." He turned to the van, calling, "Are you about ready there, Sergeant?"

"Yes, sir," the sergeant replied, stuffing tools into his pockets. He pulled on gloves and looked up at the ledge as he walked toward the rear of the building. "Let's get the ladder up there, men."

As the soldiers lifted the ladder, Campbell stepped closer to Keeler. "You aren't proceeding on the assumption that the person who got in here is the same one who escaped after the attack on the warehouse, are you, Keeler?" he asked quietly.

"Yes."

"Well, I don't want to try to tell you your business, but how would the know who the vendors are?"

"He made contact with an agent."

"An agent? A *German* agent? You mean to say that there's a *German* agent here? Well, what are you doing about finding him?"

"Meacham is having him arrested and taken to the prefecture of police. I'm going there directly to question him."

"You mean you've already found him? Well, that was quick work, I must say. I'd like to go with you! Anyone who would have anything to do with killing a woman and her children so brutally is a fiendish swine of the most foul sort. It would give me the greatest pleasure to see him get his just deserts!"

"Very well."

Campbell brushed his mustaches and grunted in grim satisfaction, looking back at the sappers. The ladder was in place, the wind pulling at the sergeant's coveralls as he climbed it. Keeler dropped his cigarette and stepped on it, then lit another as Campbell came closer to the ladder. The sergeant reached the ledge and took a flashlight from his pocket, looking back and forth.

"Well, do you see anything?" Campbell called impatiently. "Is there a satchel charge or something up there?"

"More than that, sir," the sergeant replied cheerfully. "I'd say it's about ten kilos of plastic high explosive, enough to put this wall right through the front of the building!"

"Perhaps we'd best evacuate the building, then."

The sergeant shook his head, taking wire cutters from a pocket. "No need for that, sir," he said. "The detonators are the type that are triggered by a wireless transmitter, and they're as stable as a rock when it comes to jolts and such. Heads up, Jip. There's two detonators, and I'll drop them down to you. John, fetch a bag from the van."

The sergeant worked with the wire cutters, neatly removing the detonators and dropping them to the man below. The other man returned with a bag, which he tossed up. The sergeant ripped tape loose and stuffed blocks of plastic high explosive into it.

Keeler looked at the soldier holding the detonators, then turned to Campbell. "Doesn't the signals company at the garrison have direction-finding vans?"

Campbell pursed his lips, thinking, then nodded. "Aye, and that's a good idea, Keeler. The signals people should be able to test those things and tell what frequency they're set on, then use their direction-finding vans to locate the transmitter. I'll stir them out tonight and get them posted. And when that bugger turns on the transmitter, we'll run him to earth once and for all."

Keeler took a drag on his cigarette, shaking his head. "Tomorrow afternoon will be soon enough. That's when the meeting is scheduled, so that's when he'll send his signal." He turned to the sergeant as he climbed down the ladder. "Is there a mark up there from a climbing hook, Sergeant?"

"Aye, a big, deep gouge, sir," the sergeant replied. "Whoever put that up there must have some arms on him. And he also has a pair of stones the size of footballs. I wouldn't like to have the job of climbing up there and hanging by one hand while I wired detonators with the other."

"He's a murdering Nazi blackguard, Sergeant," Campbell said sternly. "Regardless of that, I want you and your men to remember what I said about secrecy. Nothing you saw or heard here tonight is to be mentioned to anyone. This is a matter of the most confidential nature. Now take the fuses out of those detonators and let me have them. Keeler, we can take my jeep to question that foul swine. That's one trip I will certainly enjoy."

Keeler nodded, drawing on his cigarette. One of the soldiers held a flashlight while the sergeant removed the fuses and handed the detonators to Campbell, who put them in his pocket. Keeper dropped his cigarette and stepped on it as he followed Campbell to the jeep.

It was well after midnight. The street outside the embassy compound was dark and deserted. A cold draft blew in through the cracks around the windshield, making the cloth top ripple as they raced along the quiet boulevards to the Prefecture of Police. As they approached the building, Keeler pointed out a narrow street leading around behind it.

Police cars and vans were parked in the alley and halfway along the building, an embassy car waited beside the steps leading up to a door, the engine idling. As the jeep stopped behind it, Meacham opened the door and stepped out.

He nodded to Campbell in greeting, then looked at Keeler. "Everything is ready, sir," he said. "Will you need me?"

"No, I think not," Keeler replied, walking up the steps. "You may as well wait here, Meacham."

Campbell started to follow Keeler, then hesitated. "You aren't coming in, Meacham?"

"No, I believe I'll stay out here, Colonel Campbell."

Campbell grunted, puzzled, following Keeler up the steps. A small panel in the door opened when Keeler rapped on it. A flashlight shone on Keeler's face, then the panel closed. A bar slid to one side inside, and the heavy door groaned open. A policeman saluted as Keeler entered. Campbell followed Keeler along a vast, dim corridor as the policeman closed the door and replaced the bar. When they came to a junction of corridors, Keeler led the way down the one to the right where a policeman sat at a table at the far end, a light over the door beside the table.

The policeman stood up and silently saluted as Keeler and Campbell approached. He unlocked and opened the door, releasing a gust of dank, subterranean air. Steps on the other side of it led downward. Keeler started descending, Campbell behind him. The narrow stone steps were steep, the low stone ceiling and damp stone walls seemed to be closing in.

The steps spiraled into a turn to the left, illuminated by a small, weak bulb, then continued downward. Water dripped with clucking sounds, and a rat darted out of the shadows. The light at the next turn was burned out, leaving the steps in thick darkness. Keeler walked carefully as Campbell muttered under his breath.

Dim light brightened as Keeler and Campbell went down another steep flight ending at a cell-block, where a policeman sat at a table. The interrogation room was across the landing. The policeman stepped to the door and unlocked it. Keeler and Campbell went inside.

A bare bulb in the center of the low ceiling cast its harsh light on rusty implements hanging on the stone walls and cluttering the corners of the room. Abolfazi lay on a heavy table in the center of the room, stripped naked and his wrists and ankles in clamps. A pudgy man with olive skin and a neatly trimmed beard and mustache, he shivered with cold and fear as he twisted his neck to look at Keeler.

Najafi sat on a bench at one side of the room, the floor under his feet littered with cigarette butts. Dropping his cigarette, he stepped on it and stood up, saluting Keeler and nodding to Campbell, then moving away from the bench. Keeler nodded and sat down. Campbell looked around uneasily, sitting beside Keeler.

Brushing his mustaches with a finger, Campbell muttered, "Now I see why Meacham waited outside. By God, I thought medieval dungeons were a thing of the past."

"It is effective when there is little time."

"Effective?" Campbell said, lifting his eyebrows. "I should bloody think so! Only seeing this place should make anyone willing to tell whatever they know. Are you sure that is the man who killed that woman and her children, Keeler?''

''I'm reasonably certain.''

''Aye, well, it serves him right, then. A bloody torture chamber is just deserts for an inhuman swine of his sort, isn't it?''

Keeler lit a cigarette, gazing at Abolfazi. Najafi had hung his coat and cap in a corner and was moving toward the table, tucking his tie into the front of his shirt. Abolfazi looked up at him and murmured a question. The policeman ignored him, and rolling up his sleeves. Then he folded his arms and stood looking at the wall above Keeler's head, his face impassive.

Silence fell. The man on the table trembled as he twisted his head from side to side to look first at Najafi and then at Keeler. Keeler took a drag on his cigarette and spoke: ''How long have you been a German agent?''

Najafi translated in a flat monotone. Abolfazi gasped in shock and stuttered, asking a question. The policeman waited, his face wooden. Abolfazi licked his lips and murmured something, protesting and shaking his head. Najafi translated in an uninflected voice: ''I have never been a German agent.''

Keeler nodded. Najafi turned and took a flail and a mouth brace down from the wall. The flail slashed down, leaving raw weals on the smooth, olive skin. Abolfazi closed his eyes and opened his mouth wide as he screamed. The policeman popped the mouth brace into Abolfazi's mouth and worked the ratchet to spread it, then took a handful of small tools from a can and leaned over Abolfazi's head.

Abolfazi's hips lifted from the table and a thin keening came from his gaping mouth. Najafi put one tool aside and began using another. The man on the table uttered a wheezing scream, bouncing. Najafi looked through the tools again and selected a third. Abolfazi became rigid, his body arching up from the table as he screamed shrilly; then he fainted, collapsed limply.

Najafi removed the mouth brace and put it back on the wall, then dipped water from a bucket and threw it on Abolfazi's face. He stirred, moaning and whimpering. The policeman slapped him to bring him back to full awareness. Abolfazi blinked, groaning and holding his mouth open as he looked from Keeler to Najafi again. Najafi folded his arms and stood as before, looking at the wall above Keeler's head.

Campbell cleared his throat and plucked at Keeler's sleeve. "Are you *sure* that man is a German agent, Keeler."

"I'm positive."

Campbell coughed and brushed his mustaches, sitting back. "Aye, call, it serves the bugger right, then, doesn't it?"

Keeler dropped his cigarette, stepped on it, and lit another, repeating the first question. The policeman translated; Abolfazi lied again. Keeler nodded. Najafi pulled a large, wheel-mounted magneto out of a corner and wheeled it to the table.

Untangling the frayed wires, Najafi placed one alligator clamp on Abolfazi's nose and the other on the man's testicles, then rolled his sleeves higher and gripped the crank handle. The magneto squeaked, rattled, and scraped as it began turning slowly, then more rapidly, generating sparks. Abolfazi screamed and jerked convulsively.

Najafi threw his weight against the crank handle, turning it faster and faster. The magneto whined; sparks flashed and crackled. Abolfazi's shrill, ragged screams filled the room, his body drumming against the table. Blood covered his wrists and ankles where the iron clamps cut through his skin. Urine spurted from his penis and his bowels voided.

Campbell leaped up, his face ashen. "This smell is a bit much for me, Keeler!" he shouted hoarsely over the noise of the magneto and Abolfazi's screams. "I'll be with Meacham!"

Keeler nodded. Campbell went to the door and beat on it until it opened, then closed behind him. Abolfazi fainted again. The policeman released the crank handle and the magneto slowly wound down and scraped to a stop. Najafi threw more water into Abolfazi's face, then opened a bottle of ammonia to revive him.

Abolfazi continued to lie when he recovered consciousness. Taking toothed pliers and bottles of acid and caustic soda from a shelf, Najafi began on the soles of Abolfazi's feet and worked his way up to his gentials. Each time the man fainted, Najafi revived him and continued. At last Abolfazi broke, replying truthfully to Keeler's series of test questions. Then Keeler began questioning him about Vorczek.

Abolfazi said that Vorczek had come to his apartment building before dawn on the morning of the attack on the warehouse. Vorczek, having spotted the surveillance team watching the apartment building, had told Abolfazi and the two had left the building immmediately, Vorczek leading Abolfazi past the surveillance agents in the darkness. The next day had been the day on which Abolfazi had not been seen.

Abolfazi had taken Vorczek to a seller of firearms and other contraband, and had heard much of the conversation between the two. Keeler questioned Abolfazi closely to find out everything Vorczek had bought. Abolfazi named a bazooka with ammunition, high explosives, detonators of various types, a radio transmitter, and a roll of wire.

It appeared that Vorczek had made preparations to plant explosives at the embassy at the same time he was preparing his plan at the airport. He had wanted a map of the airport, as well as the names and addresses of vendors who delivered to the embassy.

The contraband dealer had delivered Vorczek's purchases to him on a dirt road outside the city. Vorczek had paid with gold coins. He had also given Abolfazi four gold coins. The interrogation was interrupted at that point, Najafi asking Abolfazi and apparently finding out where he hid the money in his house. Then Keeler resumed.

Abolfazi had seen no one but Vorczek, and Vorczek had said nothing to indicate that he had been joined by the four SD men. Abolfazi had, however, provided Vorczek with food and items of clothing, which he described. The food had been far too much for one man, as had the clothing. That, combined with the fact that the soldiers had seen two men at the airport, was evidence that Vorczek was not working alone.

Several hours earlier, Vorczek had come to Abolfazi's home and they had then gone to the vegetable vendor's house. After taking the man and his family captive, Vorczek had questioned the vendor about the procedures for making deliveries to the embassy. Vorczek had ordered Abolfazi to remain at the house and to kill the woman and children after Vorczek had left with the vendor. Then Abolfazi had returned home.

Keeler again went over the conversation Abolfazi had

overheard between Vorczek and the contraband dealer. Abolfazi was uncertain about how much explosives Vorczek had ordered, but the dealer had jokingly remarked how heavy it would be. That indicated a large amount, possibly more than Vorczek had used at the embassy and for the electrical substation at the airport. Abolfazi was also vague about the numbers and types of detonators.

Najafi translated in his flat monotone. Keeler pursued each lead, however, fragmentary, exploring in all directions, and one led to a conversation between Vorczek and Abolfazi. Vorczek had asked Abolfazi what he had overheard of Vorczek's conversation with the contraband dealer; then he had warned Abolfazi to tell no one about it.

Keeler went back and forth over Abolfazi's narration, feeling an intuitive need to examine it completely, which was vaguely puzzling because it was a pointless conversation. The warning was entirely superfluous, and Vorczek was not the kind of man who wasted time in idle talk. And the wire that Vorczek had bought from the dealer was puzzling as well. It was a tantalizing anomoly, an incidental and harmless item on Vorczek's lethal shopping list.

When the search for further valuable information became futile, Keeler ended the interrogation. Najafi took down a length of wire with a loop at one end and a wooden handle at the other. Abolfazi wailed in a pleading voice, trying to pull away, but the policeman slipped the loop over the man's head and around his neck, then leaned back against the handle.

The choked, gasping noises stopped, and the bulging eyes glazed. Najafi checked for a pulse, then smiled brightly as he began unfastening the clamps on Abolfazi's wrists and ankles. "Did you find out everything you wanted to know, Mr. Keeler?"

Keeler put out his cigarette and stood up. "I believe I found out everything he knew."

"I also found out something very interesting," Najafi chuckled. "He has four gold coins in a post in his bed, along with other money. But half of it belongs to you, of course."

Keeler rapped on the door, shaking his head. "No. Keep it all, and thank you for your help tonight."

Najafi smiled and nodded. "It was my pleasure, Mr. Keeler."

The key rattled in the lock, and the door groaned open. Keeler went out of the room, nodding to the guard as he saluted, then climbed the stairs and knocked on the door at the top where another guard opened it and saluted. Keeler nodded to him, passing along the dim, wide corridors to the alley door.

The wind outside was fresh and cold. The idling of the embassy car's engine was the only sound in the dark alley. The jeep was still parked behind it. Campbell and Meacham were in the front seat of the car. Keeler opened the rear door.

Campbell chuckled heartily as Keeler got in the car. "Well, well, here it is," he said. "By God, that smell took me so bad that I was about to lose my gorge, Keeler. But for that, I would have seen it through right to the end. Was he the one who killed that woman and her children?"

"Yes."

"Then it served the savage blackguard right, didn't it? There's justice if I ever saw it. Did you find out anything?"

"Nothing that would indicate what Vorczek may be planning to do next."

"By God, I can tell you that," Campbell laughed. "He's going to turn on his wireless transmitter, and then we're going to track the bugger down. I'll have the direction-finding vans and signals people out in force, as well as two companies of soldiers to block the streets and search for him. Shall I meet you at the embassy when we get set up tomorrow?"

"If you would."

Campbell nodded, opening the car door. "I'll get on back to the garrison and get some rest, then I'll begin organizing things soon as the others are up and about. We'll put a finish to that bugger tomorrow. I can feel it in my bones. Good night, then."

Campbell got out of the car and went back to the jeep. A moment later the jeep drove off. Meacham glanced at his watch and turned to Keeler. "We've missed our contacts tonight, Mr. Keeler," he said. "I suppose we'll just have to double up and make them all tomorrow night, won't we?"

"Yes."

"Very well, sir. Shall I drive you home, then?"

"If you would."

Keeler thought about telling Meacham to take him to the embassy so he could drive Mueller's car home and let Celise look for her purse, then decided against it. It was late, and he wanted to get home to Celise.

CHAPTER TWENTY-SEVEN

THE OLIVE DRAB Army van weaved through traffic and sped along the street ahead, Meacham close behind. Keeler watched the large hoop antenna on top of the van slowly turning, swinging parallel to the street. The van approached an intersection, its horn blaring, then whipped into a left turn. Gearing down and braking, Meacham blew the horn as he followed it into the street.

Another van had stopped up ahead, its antenna turned parallel to an apartment building. Meacham slammed on the brakes behind the one he was following as it slid to a stop, its antenna in line with the one on the other van. The rear doors of the vans flew open and soldiers leaped out, pointing to the building.

A third van skidded around the corner, Campbell's jeep following it, and stopped beside the other two. Men scrambled out. Campbell's jeep slid sideways and stopped in the center of the street. Jumping out, he fumbled with a walkie-talkie, extended the antenna and spoke into it.

Meacham looked at his watch. "They found it in about five minutes, Mr. Keeler," he said. "And apparently it's still broadcasting."

Keeler nodded, opening the door and getting out of the car. They were in a shabby residential area of apartments and small, dingy shops. People came out of the buildings, watching curiously.

Three large trucks swerved into each end of the street, blocking it, as other trucks raced through the intersections to block the other thoroughfares. Soldiers poured out of them, forming lines at the ends of the street to keep pedestrians from leaving.

Spencer and the signals officer Lieutenant Fuller, had joined Campbell at the jeep. The signals officer held a small meter with a stubby antenna at one end. He pointed to a dial on the meter and to the apartment building as he spoke to Campbell and Spencer. Keeler came over toward the jeep, Meacham following him.

Campbell turned to Keeler. "Well, we have him, Keeler," he said. "He didn't have time to get away, and we'll flush him out if we have to take every building apart. By God, I'm going to have done with that bugger once and for all!" He turned back to Fuller. "Now are you certain that transmitter is in that building?"

"Yes, sir," Fuller replied, checking the dial and moving the antenna up and down. "It's on an upper floor, or possibly even the roof."

Campbell grunted in satisfaction, turning to Spencer. "Spencer, put a platoon in there with Fuller and his people, and let's track down that transmitter. And put a platoon or two on the rooftops, because he may try to get away across the roofs."

Spencer saluted and turned away. Fuller started toward the apartment building, the soldiers from the vans joining him. A platoon across the street caught up with Fuller and his men, loading their rifles. Other soldiers dispersed along the street, looking for stairways to the roofs.

The drivers of the vehicles blocked in by the trucks began gathering in loud, angry groups. Pedestrians collected at the ends of the street where the soldiers stood, some complaining, others chatting or sitting on the sidewalk and waiting for the soldiers to leave. People stood in shop entrances or carried stools and chairs out on balconies to watch the excitement.

Keeler pulled up his collar against the wind and cupped his lighter in his hands as he lit a cigarette. The transmitter had begun broadcasting somewhat later than he had expected; the light was fading into dusk. And he knew that Vorczek was miles away, nowhere near the apartment building. It had been much too simple and easy; killing or capturing Vorczek would not be simple and easy.

Soldiers appeared along the roofs across the street. A growing uproar came from the upper floors of the building, muffled by the wind sweeping along the street. Soldiers ran along hallways, doors burst open, and people screamed and shouted excitedly.

A single shot rang out inside the building, followed by a burst of shots. Campbell and Spencer took out their pistols as they ran to the building and disappeared inside. The gunfire spread higher in the building, then shots were heard on the roof. Suddenly everything stopped. Keeler dropped his cigarette and stepped on it as he and Meacham walked toward the building.

The tiny, dirty entrance was crowded with people who pushed back as Keeler and Meacham passed. The stairway was rickety, the steps creaking underfoot and the bannister swaying from the vibration of their footsteps. The access to the roof was through a trap door in the ceiling of the top floor hall, a ladder leading up to it. The wind keened across the roof as Keeler climbed through.

The transmitter was in a corner of the roof, against the parapet overlooking the alley behind the building. Two men in robes were sprawled near it. Spencer, Fuller, and some soldiers milled about, examining the bodies and the transmitter while Campbell waited impatiently for Keeler. Keeler and Meacham knelt by the bodies and began searching them for identification.

The faces were European, darkened with a vegetable dye, and the men had been armed with Mauser automatic pistols in shoulder stocks. Neither of them fit Vorczek's description. They appeared to be two of the SD men who had escaped, but it appeared that they had disposed of all of their identification. Then Meacham found a photograph hidden in the tattered burnoose on the body he was searching.

It was the picture of a woman with the stamp of a portrait studio in Munich on the back, and it was inscribed to Otto. Otto Krueger was one of the SD men unaccounted for after the attack in the desert. Soldiers helped Meacham get soot from the chimneys to take fingerprints, then Meacham took out his camera and photographed their faces as Keeler looked at the transmitter. Glossy black wires trailed from it across the parapet to the electrical wires leading into the building from across the alley. The same kind of wire had been used to make an antenna—insulated field telephone wire, the wire that Abolfazi had mentioned.

Fuller came up to Keeler. "They probably got jolted a time or two while they were hooking up to the mains, Mr. Keeler. They would have blacked out half the block if they had turned off the electricity."

"Yes. That's new wire, isn't it?"

"Yes, sir. The way the loops lie indicates that it just came off the roll, but it's very poor wire for this sort of job. They would have done better by pulling down some of the copper wire hanging about up here."

Campbell snorted impatiently. "Well, whatever they used made the bloody thing work, didn't it?" he snapped. "Keeler, if you're quite through here, would you kindly tell me which of those men is the one we were after?"

"Neither."

Campbell slapped his quarterstaff against his leg and turned away, fuming. "Spencer, let's get these bodies out of here and return to barracks," he growled. "And I'd be grateful if you'd get the street cleared. In the event you don't know, the confusion your men are causing down there is just the sort of thing that brings complaints from the local authorities. I'd rather not have to explain it to the brigadier if I can avoid it. Keeler, I'd like a word with you."

Soldiers began carrying the bodies toward the trap door as Fuller and his men started unhooking the transmitter. Keeler took out his cigarettes as he stepped aside with Campbell.

The colonel pointed to the bodies as they were lowered through the trap door. "Keeler, if neither of them is the man we were after, then *who in the bloody hell are they*?"

Keeler lit a cigarette and took a drag, then replied; "Two of the SD men who escaped."

"Do you mean to say we're dealing with them as well now? Did they set the explosives at the embassy, then? I do wish you would explain, because this is becoming bloody confusing to me."

"Vorczek set the explosives. The SD men are helping him."

Campbell gripped his quarterstaff behind his back and sighed in disgust. "The brigadier had me in this morning about that sod, and I told him I was going to catch him this afternoon. Now I'm going to have to go back and tell him the bugger got away, and that we're dealing with more besides. But I must have something more than that to report. What do you think that swine will do next?"

"I don't know."

"Didn't you find out *anything* from that man last night? I mentioned that to the brigadier, incidentally, and got a very sharp reprimand for being present at such an undertaking. I did explain that I was there at your express invitation, but he was concerned that my presence might suggest that the Army would countenance such a proceeding. That aside, it appears to me you should have found out something."

"I found out what Vorczek bought from a black market dealer."

Campbell brushed his mustaches, frowning. "The explosives and such?"

"Yes."

"Well, what else did he get? If you found out what he has, you should be able to deduce what he'll do next. If you can't, you tell *me* what he has and I'll bloody well tell *you* what he'll do."

"Everything he obtained seems to be more or less accounted for by what he's done thus far. The only thing that seemed odd was some wire, and now that appears to be explained as well."

"You mean he's used everything he obtained?"

"As far as I know, but he may have had more explosives than I can account for. And I'm not certain about detonators."

"Aye, well, anything's possible," Campbell murmured. He pondered for a moment, his frown fading; then he shrugged. "The situation really isn't all that grim, is it? The dignitaries are leaving day after tomorrow, and it shouldn't be an impossible task to keep things in hand until then. What can that bugger possibly do between now and then?"

"I don't know."

"You always take a dim view, Keeler, and you won't commit yourself to anything unless it's graven in stone. What possible harm could he do if he's used all the materials he obtained? Your information on that satisfies me, and I'm sure it'll appease the brigadier. I would also like to tell him that you and I will meet with the Americans tomorrow to discuss security for the dignitaries' departure."

"Very well."

Campbell grunted a farewell, crossed the roof to the trap door and climbed down the ladder. Meacham stood waiting for Keeler on the deserted rooftop. A loose wire hanging from a pole snapped in the wind in front of Keeler as he walked toward the trap door. He was about to step over it. Then he stopped and looked at it, thinking.

Wires of various kinds could always be found on roofs of old buildings, particularly apartment buildings. Vorczek could have depended upon having wire available that was more suitable than that he had bought. Keeler dropped his cigarette and stepped on it, then studied the other wires as he walked on across the roof.

Dusk fell as Meacham drove to the embassy. The meeting had ended, and cars were streaming through the gate. Meacham drove into the compound and stopped on the drive beside the chancellery building to let Keeler out.

The lobby was crowded, the atmosphere gloomy. Keeler overheard bits of conversation as he crossed the lobby to the basement stairs; apparently the Soviet delegation had achieved its principal objective. An early date for the invasion of occupied France had been agreed upon, with only the composition of the invasion force and tactical considerations remaining to be resolved.

The daily situation report had been prepared earlier in the day. The cryptograph equipment clattered as one of the women encoded it. Keeler sat down and began writing a report on tracing the transmitter. Meacham came in with the film and fingerprint sheets, put them in a large envelope and took it to the mail room. Quiet fell as the woman turned off the cryptograph equipment, took the encoded report to the radio room and left for the night. Meacham returned with a receipt for the envelope and sat down, asking Keeler if he intended to go home for dinner.

Keeler put down his pencil and lit a cigarette. The contacts scheduled for a meeting the night before would be at the rendezvous, as well as those scheduled for a meeting that night. Dinner with Celise was always a keen pleasure, as was every moment with her, but there was a possibility that a contact would have information that could be developed into a lead to Vorczek.

He shook his head, picking up the pencil. "No, I believe I'll have a sandwich."

"I will as well, then," Meacham said, standing up. "With all these officers here, the schedule in the dining room is in such a mess that it isn't worth the bother of trying to get in. I'll go fetch some sandwiches."

Meacham went out and Keeler continued working on the report. As he wrote, he analyzed each fact and event for any significance that may have escaped him before, thinking about the events of the past days, searching for a pattern that might suggest what Vorczek would do next.

The only pattern was that Vorczek always had an alternative in the event that he failed in his primary objective. When the sondercommandos had been attacked, he had gotten to Abolfazi before dawn. He had known the route to the agent's apartment building, prepared to escape if his platoon was discovered. Preparations for planting the explosives at the embassy has been made at the same time as those for bazooka attack at the airport in case the first plan failed.

But what Vorczek had done before provided no clues to his next plan. The man who had attacked a train filled with Russians who far outnumbered his force was bold. The man who had escaped from enemy territory with a platoon of sondercommandos and scores of prisoners was a master of stealth and deception. The man who had planted anti-personnel mines under thermite mines along the railroad would do something unexpected.

Keeler finished the report and put it on the women's desk, then sat back down at the table, thinking again about the wire Vorczek had used with the transmitter. Vorczek was a man who left nothing to chance if he could avoid it, one who would make certain he always had everything he needed. But he was also not a man to waste effort; and more suitable wire had been available on the roof.

Vorczek had needed a variety of miscellaneous items. The explosives at the embassy had been taped to the ledge, but there had been no mention of tape during Abolfazi's interrogation. Vorczek had used a hook and rope to climb the wall, neither of which had been mentioned by

Abolfazi. They were common items which Vorczek had obtained one way or another; wire was also a common item, but it was the only one Abolfazi had known about.

Meacham came in with a tray of sandwiches and tea, put the tray on the table and took the cash box, station roll, and envelopes from a file cabinet. He and Keeler ate while they prepared the money envelopes for the contacts. When they finished, Meacham took the tray and dishes back to the kitchen. He returned and gathered up the envelopes, then put on his topcoat as Keeler put on his trench coat and hat.

When Keeler and Meacham reached the rendezvous, several contacts were waiting for them. They lined up and took their turn, cutouts passing envelopes through the window and agents whispering their reports. Meacham shivered with cold as he passed the money envelopes to Keeler to hand out. When those who had been waiting were gone, others arrived at regular intervals.

The surveillance agents who had kept watch over Abolfazi had been assigned to the Polish resettlement camp outside the city, looking for any indication that Vorczek was using the camp as a refuge. Using the cover of peddlers and tradesmen, they were moving in cautiously, because the NKVD had agents in the camp to monitor the Poles. They were working hard, still smarting over being outwitted by Vorczek, but none of them had heard anything about anyone who could possibly be he.

The agents were having more difficulty infiltrating the resettlement camp than Keeler had anticipated, because there were far more NKVD agents than before. It puzzled him, because few knew Vorczek's identity. While it was unlikely that the NKVD had put more agents into the camp specifically to watch for him, there was no other apparent explanation for the sudden increase in NKVD interest in the resettlement camp.

The clashes between Kharis's men and the NKVD apparently had produced an unexpected result. An agent who worked at the airport reported that a car from the Soviet embassy had brought someone under guard to an airplane the night before. He had slipped out to watch. The man had been Vertinski. By NKVD standards, it seemed a drastic punishment for becoming embroiled in warfare with a drug ring. The NKVD used methods that frequently involved them in confrontations with police authorities and others. But it was possible that the situation had irritated Stalin, the ultimate indiscretion.

When the last contact had left, Meacham backed the car out of the alley and drove away. Among all the trivia and information the agents had reported, there had been no word of Vorczek or the SD men. As Meacham drove back toward the embassy, Keeler looked out at the dark streets and thought about the three men. With Vorczek as their leader, they were a deadly menace. Keeler had hoped for even the most fragile hint that might indicate what Vorczek was contemplating. He knew Vorczek was near, a threatening, hostile presence in the dark, quiet night. And he knew Vorczek would strike again.

CHAPTER TWENTY-EIGHT

TWO MESSAGES WERE waiting for Keeler when he returned to the embassy. One referred to two officers in the Soviet delegation whose names were not listed on the Soviet Army rolls, and another who had the name of an officer known to have been killed at Leningrad. The message was a request for the real names of the three, if they could be identified, and for photographs. The second message requested a summary case report on Abolfazi.

On the day the heads of state had arrived, Keeler had glimpsed a face among the Soviet contingent that had been out of place. But it had been only a fleeting glance at a face that was vaguely familiar; he was unable to associate it with a name. Meacham put the envelopes from the contacts on the table. Keeler handed him the messages and began writing a summary of the agents' verbal reports.

Meacham glanced over the messages, frowning in perplexity. "Why would they send someone here under someone else's name, Mr. Keeler?"

"There are always criteria agreed upon in advance for conferences of this nature, including who may attend. It appears that the Soviets found the criteria cumbersome."

Meacham nodded. "These pictures they want aren't the sort of thing our photographer can do, are they?"

"No, but the public relations officer may be able to get what we need. Any number of photographers have been taking pictures of all the meetings, and he should be able to get copies."

"Yes, that's a good idea," Meacham said, putting the messages aside. "We have a meeting with Colonel Campbell this afternoon, and other things may come up. Should we do the sitrep now?"

"Yes."

Meacham took out the folders for the daily situation report, then began going over them. Keeler finished the summary of agents' reports and looked through the material he had collected at the rendezvous. It included reports on secret parliamentary deliberations and on private meetings between politicians, some of whom had remained strongly pro-Nazi even after the flow of money from the Abwehr had been stopped.

The Teheran conference had brought the movement more into the open. When the conference was over, the normal activities of the residency would resume, and one of the problems to be dealt with was pro-Nazi sentiment among politicians, because they hampered the Allied war effort in subtle but effective ways.

Keeler looked over the request for a summary case report on Abolfazi and began writing. Meacham began working on the daily situation report.

After an hour passed, Meacham began yawning. "Will you be going home directly, Mr. Keeler?" he asked. "It's past the time when we usually pack it in."

"No, I'll stay and work for a while yet. You go on upstairs and get some rest."

"I believe I will," Meacham said. "This is well in hand, and I'll be able to finish it off in good time. Shall I leave a note upstairs for the public relations officer about the pictures of the Russians?"

"Yes, if you would. But do tell him that we need photographs of all the delegations, not just the Soviets."

After Meacham had left, Keeler lit a cigarette and continued working on the report. He had solitude and hours of routine work to do while he considered the problem of Vorczek. The fact that he had made two attempts on the lives of the heads of state was a closely-guarded secret; release of the information could create widespread alarm. But the security had been increased as a result, which restricted Vorczek's options.

There were other limitations as well, personal factors that would restrict his choices. If an assassin had nothing to live for, he greatly increased his chances of success. But Vorczek had established himself in Germany, and had a pregnant wife. He would take risks, but they would be short of suicidal.

Keeler was certain that Vorczek's primary target was Stalin. His mission included the assassination of Roosevelt and Churchill, but Stalin would always be first in his mind. The other two were in danger only when they were with Stalin.

They would all be together only at the final meeting, and when they left. And they would be most vulnerable on the morning of their departure, as their limousines moved slowly along the streets. An attack from a roof with a rifle was an obvious danger, or explosives planted under the pavement. But Vorczek would avoid the obvious. He would do the unexpected.

As the hours passed, Keeler became tired and his thoughts more random. Something was trying to emerge from the jumble, but it remained tantalizingly elusive. Like a very faint star, it could be perceived only indirectly. Each time Keeler stopped work and tried to isolate it, it disappeared. It was complex, impossible to grasp without close examination.

Keeler felt the stir of movement on the floors above. Another day had begun. He finished the report on Abolfazi and began a proposal for political action to unseat pro-Nazi politicians. One of the cryptographers came in with a stack of coded messages from the radio room. Leaving the messages on her desk, she went up to the kitchen and returned with cups of coffee, put a cup on the table for Keeler, then turned on the cryptograph equipment and decoded the messages.

They were priority advisories, all concerning Vorczek. An agent inside Germany had obtained bits of hearsay about him in the town of Landsbach. There were descriptions of combat missions on which Vorczek had been deployed, along with other information that might provide insights into Vorczek's personality. There were extracts from sondercommando manuals, with analyses of how those procedures could be applied to the situation in Teheran. Keeler read through them all, then went back to the political action project.

A knock at the door penetrated the clatter of the crypograph equipment as the woman encoded the report on Abolfazi. She went to the door and opened it a crack, then called Keeler. It was the guard, saying that Keeler was wanted on the outside line in the lobby. Keeler pulled up his tie and put on his suit jacket as he followed the guard.

Winter sunshine glared through the windows in the lobby. The midmorning atmosphere was jarring to Keeler after the long, quiet night. The lobby bustled with activity. Keeler moved the telephone to the other end of the desk.

There was a long second of silence. He started to speak again. Then he heard Celise's voice hesitant and timid. "Is that you, Frank? It is Celise."

"Yes."

"I'm very sorry if I interrupted you in something important, Frank, but I was worried. You didn't come home last night or this morning, and I wondered if something was wrong. And I wasn't certain what number to call, but the telephone operator gave me this one. Are you angry because I telephoned?"

"No."

"I'm so relieved! I was worried and I had to call you, but I feared that you might be angry. Do you have a moment to talk?"

"Yes."

"You do? I'm very pleased, because I wanted so much to speak to you for a moment. I couldn't sleep last night, and I read for a while and listened to the radio. The BBC kept fading out, but the reception from the station in Stuttgart was unusually good. They played parts of *Der Ring des Nibelungen*, which I always enjoy, and. . . ."

Her melodious voice continued, the telephone accentuating her slight lisp and French accent. Her vivacious, scintillating personality also seemed to reach out and enfold him as though she were in the same room.

He could envision her beautiful face as he listened. It would be smiling and animated. She would be gesturing with her free hand and touching her forefinger to her lips as she searched for a particular word in English. The noises around Keeler faded into the background and his fatigue slipped away.

A door behind the desk opened, and the embassy public relations officer came out with a stack of large, bulky manila envelopes. Glancing at Keeler meaningfully, he crossed the lobby and went down the basement stairs. Two officers talking to a woman at the desk left.

The public relations officer returned and went back into his office. The woman at the desk began glancing up at Keeler curiously. He looked at his watch. Almost fifteen minutes had passed. "I must go now," he said, interrupting Celise.

"Very well, Frank," she replied. "I will tell you the rest in more detail when I see you. Will you be home for dinner?"

"Yes."

"I'll look forward to it—I've missed you! I don't want to be a nuisance, but I depend upon you so much. And I love you, Frank. Goodbye."

"Goodbye."

Keeler hung up, crossed the lobby and went down the stairs. The manila envelopes the public relations officer had brought were on the guard's table. Keeler took them into the room, sat down at the table and resumed working.

It was past noon when he had finished the project. The cryptographer returned from lunch, bringing coffee and sandwiches for Keeler. He ate as he opened the manila envelopes and took out dozens of photographs of the conference. He separated those of the Russians and discarded the others. Checking the list of the Soviet delegation, he found forty-six names, but there were only three men in the photograph of the Soviet delegation. Keeler studied each face, memorizing it, then began looking through the other photographs.

A face leaped out at him from the background of a picture taken at the airport on the day of the dignitaries arrival, the face Keeler had glimpsed in a car leaving the airport, one that had seemed out of place in military uniform. With a magnifying glass, Keeler examined it.

The man had aged since the last photograph Keeler had seen of him. It took him a moment to recall the name. He was Leonid Petrovich Polyakov, a senior official in Department Eight of the NKVD, whose mission was acquisition of technology. His presence raised the possibility that an NKVD agent had infiltrated either the American or the British delegation, and that Polyakov had used the conference for a personal meeting.

So the request from London was not entirely a routine query; the Soviet connections of some members of the American or the British delegations was conceivably a matter of intense interest. Keeler circled the face on the photograph, then looked through the others. He found two other men, immediately recalling their names—Boris Nikolaevich Pavlichenko and Nikita Sergeyevich Kruschev, members of the Politburo.

Meacham came in while Keeler was writing his reply to the query about the three Russians. "Didn't you go home at all, Mr. Keeler?" he asked.

"No, I wasn't tired."

"I'll wager you are now, sir. Are those the pictures from the public relations officer? And are these the ones they're asking about? Right looking lot, aren't they? Shall I make up an envelope to send them by pouch?"

"If you would."

Meacham went to a cabinet for an envelope. "I'll prepare this and take it to the mail room, then I'll go up to the kitchen and see about some tea, Mr. Keeler."

"Very well. You might see if you can get in touch with Campbell and find out when he'll be here for that meeting."

"I did that before I came down, sir. He'll be over at about three or four this afternoon."

Keeler nodded, lighting a cigarette, and went back to work.

The afternoon hours passed slowly. The elusive thought about Vorczek that had been just out of reach during the night remained buried in some inaccessible part of his mind. He finished the first part of the daily situation report with a carefully phrased comment on the rumor that Vertinski had been returned to Moscow, then he handed the pages to Meacham, who gave them to the cryptographer. She began encoding the report as Meacham put the teacups on the tray and left, returning a few minutes later to tell Keeler that Campbell had arrived. Together, they went upstairs.

Morton's tiny office was crowded with folding chairs and people. Hites, the security officer from the American embassy, sat near the door. Callaghan was in a corner, his topcoat open and his hat pushed back. Campbell sat beside the desk, arranging his notes. Morton placed folding chairs against the wall for Keeler and Meacham, then sat down behind his desk.

Campbell had spent the day discussing security arrangements. Additional guards would be placed around the airport before nightfall, with orders to shoot at any movement outside its perimeter. Barbed wire was being strung around the area. At daybreak, helicopters carrying soldiers armed with submachine guns would begin patrolling.

"That takes care of the airport," Campbell said, turning over a page of his notes. "In the city, the guards along the streets will be doubled, and we're changing the route. The limousines will leave their respective embassies to arrive at the main square on Posht-e-Adimi at the same time, then convoy to the airport from there. So if anyone has the idea of getting on a rooftop with a rifle, he's in for a surprise."

"That'll also take care of explosives under the street," Callaghan added. "If this can be kept out of the newspapers until tomorrow, those are two problems we can forget."

"That's quite true," Campbell agreed. "At the same time, though, we're taking measures in event the information does leak out. In addition to the extra guards, the route will be thoroughly inspected by American engineers and British sappers. And I suppose the Russians will have a look as well. As far as the airport road goes, every inch of it will be checked. Now, can anyone think of anything we've missed?"

The men exchanged glances and shook their heads. Campbell turned to Keeler. "Keeler, the brigadier asked me specifically to ask you if you can think of anything that's been left undone. I did explain to him that an intelligence officer has no particular expertise on security, but he was adamant that I ask. Do you see any shortcomings?"

"Do the limousines have to travel together?"

"Absolutely," Campbell replied, nodding emphatically. "Someone brought that up, and it almost caused apoplexy among the Soviets. I fancy they're unsure whether it's more prestigious to go first, second, or third, and they're afraid to ask Stalin. And if they guess wrong about what he thinks, then it's the salt mines, isn't it?" He leaned forward, brushing his mustaches and lowering his voice. "And if disaster strikes and the bugger is killed, then they'll be certain that we did it, won't they? No, we daren't touch that one, Keeler. Is there anything else?"

"No."

"Nothing at all? Are you certain?"

"Yes."

Campbell sat back in his chair. "Then I'll inform the brigadier that you consider the security arrangements completely satisfactory. He also asked me to find out when we will be able to lift the secrecy on this matter. Spencer is up for promotion, and a mention of his contribution in dispatches is just what we need to sew it up. So when will we be able to release the information?"

"Never."

"*Never*?" Campbell snorted indignantly. "You mean that we're to *keep* what happened here secret? That's the most unreasonable thing that I've ever heard, and I'm sure the brigadier will agree. If we get through this in good order, and you just said yourself that we will, he'll insist on its being made public."

"Then he should anticipate a very sharp reaction from London as well as severe limits on cooperation and exchanges of information with me in the future. It is the policy of the Service to indefinitely maintain absolute secrecy on Service activities."

Campbell sighed in disgust, gathering up his notes. "Aye, well, I should have known," he said. "I'll be happy to get back to soldiering and have done with bloody skulduggery! If there are no further comments, I'll tell the brigadier that we're set for tomorrow."

As the men began standing, Callaghan turned to Meacham. "Chad, I think we should have a party when this is all over, with a steak dinner and plenty of booze. How about you?"

Meacham chortled. "By God, I like the sound of that!"

Callaghan laughed, slapping Meacham's shoulder. Keeler and the others walked out into the hall. The final meeting of the conference had ended and the British delegation had returned to the embassy. Groups of officers were milling about in the lobby and talking, while others carried out luggage. Keeler and Meacham went back downstairs to the basement room.

Meacham reached for his topcoat as Keeler took his trench coat off the coat rack. "Shall I drive you home, sir?" he asked.

Keeler nodded, then thought again. "No, I'll drive Mueller's car," he said. "Where are the keys?"

Meacham took the keys out of a file cabinet. "We have only two meetings scheduled for tonight. I'll see to them if you wish, sir," he said, handing Keeler the keys. "And I'll call you if anything important comes up. Are you going to come by here tomorrow morning?"

"I still have that pass, so I may go straight to the airport from my house. If I decide not to, I'll call you."

"Very well, sir."

Keeler put the keys in his pocket and left the building. The sky was clear, the setting sun casting deep, dark shadows beside the chancellery as Keeler walked along the drive to the garages. Mueller's car was a large sedan, parked among the embassy cars. The head chauffeur and a driver, standing in front of the garages, spoke to Keeler as he passed.

Celise's missing purse had become something of a continuing joke, which Keeler was almost relucant to end. After looking in the car once more, feeling the door pockets and glancing under the seats, he got in, pulled out the choke and pumped the accelerator, then pushed the starter button. The engine groaned once, then stopped.

The head chauffeur came over as Keeler got back out. "Won't she kick over, Mr. Keeler?" he asked.

"No, it appears that the battery is dead."

"Aye, this cold weather will do that, sir. Shall I have the mechanic start her?"

Keeler hesitated, then he shook his head. "Thank you, but I won't bother with it just now. Could someone drive me home?"

The man nodded and touched his cap. "Yes, of course, Mr. Keeler. I'll have a driver and a car for you in just a moment."

Keeler put the keys back into his pocket and went out of the garages. The sunshine was without warmth, the cold of the approaching night already settling.

He pulled up his collar as he waited beside the drive. A few minutes later, a car crossed the courtyard and stopped in front of Keeler. He opened the door and got in the back seat. It moved along the drive toward the gate as Keeler looked out the window, thinking about Vorczek. The sense of foreboding would not be dispelled, and he could not silence the inner voice suggesting that Vorczek could have found a way around all the precautions.

CHAPTER TWENTY-NINE

KEELER WOKE SLOWLY. He usually emerged from sleep abruptly, fully aware of his surroundings. But his fatigue had overcome him. Now he was awakened by a train of thought that tugged at his mind arousing him gradually.

Celise was warm and soft beside him, her perfume scenting the air. She breathed slowly and deeply, almost soundlessly. Her smooth, resilent breasts moved, one of her nipples nearly touching his lips each time she inhaled. One of his hands rested on the satiny curve of her hip. Her hair was scattered over the pillow.

The previous evening had been pleasant—a hot bath, a shave and clean clothes, and a delicious dinner. Celise had been charming as always at dinner, and passionate afterwards. And all the while, Keeler had kept trying to isolate the idea about Vorczek that continued to nag at him.

But in the twilight between sleep and full consciousness, the thought was suddenly crystal clear. Confusing irrelevancies were swept away, leaving only the significant details.

The fact that Abolfazi had been under surveillance was

proof that he had been a loyal German agent. Vorczek had known he could trust Abolfazi and use him if he could outwit the surveillance agents. And Vorczek was a master of stealth. Avoiding them in the darkness had been easy for him.

Dealing with an agent under surveillance involved the further risk that the agent would be arrested and interrogated. The conversation between Vorczek and Abolfazi concerning the weapons and explosives had been seemingly pointless. But it had been purposeful. Vorczek had been finding out what Abolfazi would reveal, certain that he would be arrested and interrogated.

The information about the wire had been puzzling; there had been no need to obtain it from the contraband dealer. But the wire could have been for something else. Perhaps Vorczek had made a mistake in allowing Abolfazi to find out about it, only discovering his error when he questioned the agent about what he had heard. Then he had rigged the transmitter with the wire to conceal its real purpose.

And there lay the clue to his next step. Field telephone wire came in rolls hundreds of feet in length, as well as in small rolls. A large roll might be part of a weapon, Vorczek had one, as well as a magneto detonator and explosives.

Though Stalin was Vorczek's primary target, he would make every effort to assasinate Roosevelt and Churchill also. He would be willing to take certain risks, but he would also provide himself with a margin of safety and a means of escape. Those limitations, combined with the heavy security precautions, severely restricted Vorczek's options.

But there was one possibility that deftly evaded all security precautions. All three limousines could be demolished at the same time, and Vorczek would have a good chance of escaping.

Realization of what Vorczek's plan was dawned in Keeler's mind, jerking him abruptly wide awake. Vorczek would use the one place that everyone would suspect and no one would suspect, where everyone would look and no one would see.

The hands on Keeler's watch glowed dimly as he picked it up from the night stand. Then he relaxed and put it on his wrist; there was time. He quietly gathered up his clothes and closed the door softly behind him as he went out. The house was dark and quiet, the hallway floor cold under his bare feet.

He turned on a lamp in the front room and dressed, then telephoned the embassy and asked for a car to be sent to his house, speaking quietly to avoid awakening Celise. But she was in the hall doorway when he turned away from the telephone, taking out his automatic to check the bullets in the clip.

Her hair was tousled, her wide, frightened eyes moving from the pistol to his face. She pushed her hair back, clearing her throat. "What is it, Frank? What's wrong?"

He slid the clip back into the pistol and put it in his shoulder holster, then took two extra clips from a table drawer. "I have to go out for a while."

She hesitated, then nodded, tying the belt on her dressing gown. "There should be some coffee in the kitchen. I'll heat it for you."

Her slippers whispered on the floor as she went through the dining room, then the light came on in the kitchen. Keeler adjusted his tie and felt for the silencer in the pocket of his jacket. He put on his trench coat, then lit a cigarette and took a deep drag, planning what he had to do.

The prudent course of action would be to contact Campbell, but Vorczek might have the two remaining SD men posted to watch for any unusual activity. Even assistance in getting past the airport perimeter could serve as a warning, and Vorczek would escape again. The only way to kill Vorczek was to meet him on his own terms, with stealth. And Vorczek had to die.

Celise came in with a cup of coffee and put it on the table at the end of the couch, then brought his ashtray to the table. They sat side by side in a silence uncharacteristic of Celise. Keeler drank the coffee and smoked his cigarette. Celise held his free hand tightly, then lifted it to her lips, looking up at him. "This is the first time I've seen you check your pistol before you leave, Frank," she whispered, her breath warm against the back of his hand. "Whatever you do, please be very careful."

Keeler drew on his cigarette and nodded. "It isn't anything to be overly concerned about. However, there's a compartment in the bottom of the wardrobe in the bedroom, and it contains quite a lot of gold. If anything should happen, take the gold to the Café Canton in the Asian district. Ask for a man named Cheung and tell him that I sent you. He will see that you have any assistance you need."

She shook her head, squeezing his hand and pressing it to her forehead. "I don't want gold, Frank," she whispered. "I love you, and I want *you*."

"Shall I write it down for you? I want you to remember it."

"I will remember it."

Celise leaned against him, still holding his hand to her forehead. As he finished the cigarette and put it out in the ashtray, something about the rhythm of Celise's breathing made him look at her. She was weeping silently, tears streaming down her cheeks.

He put his hand under her chin, lifting her face. "I didn't intend to frighten you, Celise. I meant to tell you about the gold some time ago. Life is uncertain, and something could happen at any time."

She forced a smile, wiping her eyes and cheeks with her sleeve. "I am truly grateful that you're concerned about me, Frank. But when you leave here, please don't worry about me. I want you to think only of what you are doing."

"I will, but I'll be considerably more at ease in my mind when you're safe in England."

It took her a long second to fully realize what he had said. Then she gasped, her blue eyes widening, and a radiant smile spread over her beautiful face. She uttered a muffled cry of ecstatic delight, burrowing her face against his shoulder.

The sound of a car engine could be heard moving up the drive. Celise helped him button his trench coat and fasten the belt, then picked up his hat and handed it to him. She clung to him, lifting her lips to his. He held her and kissed her, caressing her through the silky fabric of her dressing gown. Then he left.

The sky was clear and the night was bright, but a gusty wind was blowing. The car raced along the deserted boulevards, then turned onto the street leading to the embassy.

Keeler sat forward and tapped the driver's shoulder as

he began slowing to turn in at the embassy gate. "Stop, please."

The driver glanced back, surprised. "Here, sir?"

"Yes."

The driver pulled the car over to the curb and Keeler stepped out. "I'll take the car," he said. "Please tell the head chauffeur that I will return it tomorrow."

The man hesitated, peering at Keeler in the dim light. "Are you sure it'll be all right, sir? I was only told to fetch you."

"Yes. Just tell the head chauffeur."

The man nodded, touching his cap. "Very well, sir. Good night."

"Good night."

Keeler pulled away from the curb, whipping the car around in a sharp U-turn, and headed for the airport road.

The airport road was dark and deserted. The headlight beams lit up the shoulders of the road, leaving clumps of brush below dark shadows on the edges of the light. The shoulders disappeared where a drainage culvert went under the road. Keeler controlled an impulse to ease up on the accelerator and glance at the culvert.

A bright nimbus of light rose in the night sky over the airport, and floodlights illuminated the guard post at the entrance where a lieutenant was on duty with six military policemen. The policemen stepped into the road as Keeler approached the guard post, waving the car to a stop. One of them took the keys and looked in the trunk and under the hood of the car while the lieutenant examined Keeler's pass and identification. The policeman handed the keys to the lieutenant, who saluted as he returned them to Keeler.

Lines of blue and white lights on the taxiways and runway stretched into the darkness, and red lights outlined the control tower. The three bombers stood on a distant ramp awash with brilliant light, the tiny forms of guards moving around them. Floodlights around the electrical substation silhouetted more guards.

The windows in the flight operations building were brightly lighted. Soldiers milled around vehicles parked in front of the temporary headquarters for guards at the far end of the terminal. More cars and trucks were parked on the near side of flight operations. Keeler approached slowly, then swung into an empty space.

He slid down in the seat and waited, glancing at his watch. Three minutes passed. The arrival of his car had apparently attracted no attention. He reached up and turned off the overhead light, then crawled over the seat and lay on the floorboards in the rear. He heard laughing voices as the aircrew returned to their pickup. Doors slammed, then the pickup drove away. Keeler wanted a cigarette, trying to push it out of his mind. Five more minutes passed. He quietly opened the car door.

Keeler listened for a moment, then crouched low and crept toward the rear of the building. He pulled up his collar to hide his face and tucked his hands into his pockets, moving rapidly and quietly.

Near a low mound, Keeler lay down in the brush and dead weeds. The lights of the city were a twinkling blanket to the west, across miles of thick, featureless darkness. Headlights moved along the road to the southwest, tiny in the distance, disappeared behind a rise, then came into view again.

Keeler lay there for several minutes, listening. Finally he heard a cough and a movement ahead and to his right. A flare blossomed in the sky to the north, casting a thin light. Voices murmured quietly to the left. Avoiding the guard posts, he slid along the ground for a few yards, crawled straight ahead.

The terrain sloped downward at a shallow angle, the soft, sandy soil covered with low scrub and brush. Aircraft engines filled the night as an airplane landed. Keeler lay motionless and waited until the noise faded, then continued crawling. Another flare appeared in the sky to the north. He lay flat again until the light faded.

Now the guards were behind him, keenly alert and under orders to shoot at any sound. A nervous guard could imagine a sound, or a capricious gust of wind might rustle the brush. Flares would illuminate him as rifles barked. Keeler felt along the ground for rocks and moved them aside as he kept inching forward.

The dry, scrubby growth began thinning out into dense clumps several feet apart. Keeler tried to keep stands of brush between himself and the guards. He came to the first barbed wire barrier, a loose coil stretched along the ground.

He lay on his back, gathered the barbed wire in his hands and lifted it as he slid under. Its metallic rattle sounded loud in the stillness and the sharp barbs stabbed his hands and snagged his clothes.

A wide swath had been cut through the brush to accomodate the second coil of barbed wire. A flare arced into the sky to the north as Keeler started to stretch out on his back. He huddled by a clump of brush. The flare's light was bright enough to distinguish nearby objects. His coat and hat were much darker than the sandy soil and the guards were only yards away up the slope. He pressed himself to the ground. A few yards further along, there was a depression in the ground making a pool of inky blackness. The flare sank lower and disappeared. Keeler crawled until he was across from the depression, then lay down on his back to slide under the mass of loose, tangled coils.

A flare rocketed into the sky with a solid thump no more than two hundred feet away. Keeler pulled the barbs loose and slid free. Rocks tumbled and knocked together as he rolled into the depression.

The flare ignited high overhead with a loud crack, casting glaring light. The noise from the wire and rocks had carried to the guard posts directly up the slope from Keeler, and another flare ignited almost directly overhead. He lay motionless, his face pressed into the dirt. Seconds dragged past, the flares slowly descending on their parachutes, then sputtering out as they neared the ground. A guard, still not satisfied, fired another flare which drifted down and went out, spreading an acrid odor of burning magnesium. Keeler waited several minutes longer, then pushed himself out of the depression, his night vision slowly returning after the glare of the flares.

A dry wash lay at the bottom of the slope below the guard posts. After Keeler crossed it, the terrain turned into a wasteland of mounds and gullies that stretched between the airport and the city. To the south, the airport road ran through the center of a wide expanse that had been bulldozed through the broken terrain. Keeler picked a route through the gullies, working his way to the west.

When he was far out into the cold, dark isolation of the parched wasteland, doubts began to form in his mind. Conclusions about what others might do in a given set of circumstances were often unreliable, because people were unpredictable. And a futile, dangerous search in one place while Vorczek struck in another would be the ultimate defeat.

He examined all the facts again, searching for alternative courses of action that Vorczek might have taken. There were none. More than that, he had a strong intuitive feeling that he was right. The doubts faded, replaced by a sense of certainty. He climbed a mound and looked at the airport lights to orient himself, then turned south toward the road.

The wind had become frigidly cold. Light touched the sky in the east, dimming the stars. The wind carried sounds of activity from the airport, aircraft engines spluttering and starting in the distance. Keeler looked to the south and saw vehicles moving along the airport road from the city.

Time was getting short, and other dangers were near. He took out his automatic and put the silencer on it, trying to walk quietly as he hurried along the gullies. Dawn spread across the sky and filtered down into the gullies. Keeler increased his pace to a trot.

The first helicopter took him by surprise, skimming fifty feet above and approaching upwind. He dived into a stand of brush and flattened himself to the ground. The sun was still below the horizon, the light on the ground a flat, gray twilight. The helicopter passed, its rotors thumping and flashing lights winking on the bottom of the fuselage. Keeler watched it and started to climb to his feet. Then, glimpsing another one approaching, he dropped to the ground again. It too roared past. He got to his feet and trotted on.

Then he slid to a stop, looking at some furrows dug into the side of the gulley. They had been made by men sliding down it sometime during the night. Deep footprints stretched ahead of him. He ran along the gully again, listening to the helicopters and looking ahead.

Two men crouched in a depression under an overhanging edge of one side of the gully. Keeler saw them as he looked around a curve. Glimpsing the light colored robes they wore, he ducked back, then leaned forward and looked again. They were about fifty feet away and looking in the other direction, watching for the helicopters. Keeler backtracked, thinking rapidly.

They had to be the remaining SD men, and attacking them increased the possibility of failure. If one fired a shot, it would be heard. But going around them would involve crossing the top of a mound with the helicopters nearby. Keeler pondered, listening to the rippling echoes from the helicopters. Then he lifted his automatic and thumbed the safety to the off position, moving forward again.

The silenced automatic thudded dully and rapidly. The two men snapped and jerked as the .445 dumdum bullets slammed into them, mushrooming on contact. The nearer man pitched forward and slid out of the depression. The other one lifted a Luger machine pistol and almost got off a shot, but the weapon dropped from his hands as another bullet ripped into his chest.

The sound of the helicopters was loud as Keeler sprinted along the gulley. He heaved the bodies into the depression and crowded with them. The hot, meaty odor of blood was thick in the enclosed space. The helicopters roared, approaching. One of the men moved. Keeler put the automatic to the back of his head and squeezed the trigger. The sound of the shot was drowned by the helicopters. The man's head bounced and flopped back to the ground, a mass of bloody pulp.

One helicopter roared past, a hundred feet away. The other flew across fifty feet away in the other direction. Keeler climbed the side of the gully, changing the clip in his automatic and watching the helicopters. They flew toward the airport, then swung north and circled toward the city. Keeler climbed higher and looked for the road, then jumped back down into the gully and ran ahead.

The jumble of brushy mounds and maze of gullies ended less than two hundred yards away, at the edge of the bulldozed terrain north of the road. But full dawn had arrived, a blush of color from the rising sun spreading across the sky. It was almost time for the limousines to leave the embassies.

The helicopters returned, the sound of their engines pounding in Keeler's ears as he raced along. The soil had eroded away from the roots of a large clump of brush on the edge of the gully. He scrambled up the bank to it and pushed in among the overhanging roots, panting for breath as one of the helicopters passed directly overhead, creating a choking cloud of dust. The other helicopter flew past several yards away, and Keeler slid back down into the gulley. He ran while the roar of the helicopters was loud enough to smother the noise he made, then slowed to a trot when it faded.

The gully led into a wider one behind a mound facing the road across the bulldozed expanse. Keeler climbed the side of the mound. The helicopters were circling near the airport, and two others were hovering to the north. Climbing higher, he saw still other helicopters east of the airport. Keeler crawled through the brush and looked across the level expanse at the road which seethed with activity, soldiers marching along it and forming into lines along either side. A group of American and British engineers were checking the shoulders and the slopes below. Russian engineers followed them, and vehicles sped along the road to the airport. In the distance, civilians were being held back by soldiers.

The culvert was diagonally to Keeler's left. He crawled toward it through the brush, which was dense enough to hide him from the road but not from the air. The helicopters were miles to the north, making another sweep from the city to the airport.

Where the brush ended, there was a bare stretch where he would be in clear view. He started to turn back toward the gully, then stopped. The American and British engineers had reached the culvert. They examined it closely, then went on. The Russian engineers then dug rocks and dirt out of it and a small man crawled through it. They too went on.

The maze of possible routes for the limousines in the city narrowed to one out here. For an assassin, the airport road was the only choice. The culvert was a likely place to conceal explosives, an obvious danger, so obvious that it drew attention away from its surroundings. Keeler was certain the explosives were buried either under or near the culvert.

A growing sense of urgency gripped him as he returned to the gully, looking at his watch. When he was past the bare stretch on top of the mound, he climbed out of the gully again and crawled through the brush. The culvert was opposite him, across the level area. The clumps of brush and rocks between the mounds and the road offered many places of concealment, but none that would provide Vorczek with an escape route after the explosion.

Keeler crawled closer to the edge of the mound. The minutes until the limousines would come along the road were passing rapidly. Then a gleam among the rocks and brush caught his eye. It was a shiny line, the weak, thin sunlight reflecting from a short length of field telephone wire. When the wire had been laid in the dark, part of it had missed being covered with dirt, or else the wind had blown the dirt away. Keeler glanced between it and the culvert, and saw another short length of wire angled between the culvert and a point twenty or thirty yards to his left. He picked out several large rocks off to the left to use as a point of reference, then slid back from the edge of the brush.

A bullet struck the dirt a few yards from Keeler with the impact of a sledgehammer, and he heard the crack of a rifle. Another bullet struck closer; a third clipped through the brush over his head. Then bullets peppered the mound, thudding into the dirt. Bits of brush rained down on him as bullets whined overhead, the crackle of rifles becoming a roar. Keeler flattened himself against the ground as the hail of bullets pounded around him. A wild dog suddenly squealed in agony behind him; it had made a movement in the brush that a soldier had seen. The rifle fire diminished and stopped as it yelped, rolling down the hill. The dog's cries faded as it died. Keeler crawled toward the gully which continued along the rear of the mound, then turned sharply to the right and opened out into a wide hollow between that mound and another one. Keeler knelt and peered around the curve; he had found where Vorczek was hiding. The rocks he had picked for a point of reference were directly in front of the hollow, a perfect place for Vorczek's purpose.

A thicket provided concealment, as well as a full view of the road from a safe distance. Vorczek could watch the limousines approach from his hidden vantage point, and the gully behind the hollow as an avenue of escape he could use in the confusion following the explosion.

A large mound rose a few yards behind the hollow, providing cover as well as elevation for shooting down into the brush at the front of the hollow. Keeler climbed it.

The road came into view. It was ominously quiet, empty of traffic. The wind had driven soil into drifts against thicker clumps of brush. Keeler tried to keep them between him and the road as he crawled up the slope. Then the brush turned into a dense thicket, a strong stench of dogs coming from it.

A wild dog den was in the center of the thicket, a wide opening with a tangle of brush forming a roof. Paths had been worn through the undergrowth. Keeler forced his way along a path and through the den, then along another path. The helicopters approached. Keeler retreated into the den and lay motionless. When the helicopters had thundered past, Keeler crawled along the path again and up the slope.

The undergrowth on the crest of the mound was almost impenetrable. Keeler twisted and wriggled through, working his way across. Nothing moved on the road below. The soldiers stood stiffly at attention, the atmosphere expectant.

Keeler snapped the clip out of his automatic and checked it, then he pushed it back in and checked the bullet in the firing chamber. He thumbed the safety to the off position and slid to the edge of the mound above the hollow. He looked down. There was no sign of Vorczek.

The shoulders of the mounds on each side were bare slopes, with no place where Vorczek could be concealed. The wires led to the hollow; it fulfilled every requirement for Vorczek's purpose. But he was not there.

Keeler kept staring down, the evidence of his eyes battling with his total conviction that Vorczek had to be hidden there somewhere.

The soldiers along the road stirred as the officers shouted a command. They presented arms. A line of staff cars came into view, followed by the three limousines, flags fluttering, then more staff cars.

Keeler's numb bewilderment changed into an imperative urge to do something—anything. But if he tried to slide down the mound and run to the wires to rip them loose, he would be cut down by rifle fire long before he could reach his objective.

The staff cars were approaching the culvert. Suddenly the ground near the front of the thicket in the hollow moved. Keeler stared as a square section of dirt slowly lifted. Vorczek had dug a pit and covered it with a trap door, which was now opening. Keeler could see Vorczek's arm and shoulder.

The staff cars were driving across the culvert at a slow, deliberate pace. As the front edge of the trap door lifted higher, Keeler glimpsed Vorczek's blond hair. Vorczek lifted out a magneto detonator. His head came into full view as he checked the contacts on the detonator and started to lift the plunger.

The first limousine approached the culvert. Keeler aimed his automatic at Vorczek's head and squeezed the trigger. Dust exploded in front of the trap door. The bullet had missed. Vorczek snatched up the detonator and ducked down into the hole, the trap door slamming closed.

The first limousine over the culvert. Keeler aimed at the trap door and squeezed the trigger three times. The bullets pounded into the trap door, making it bounce as dust billowed up. The breeze swept the dust away; the door slowly opened again.

The second limousine was approaching. Vorczek stood up. Fragments of dumdum bullets had ripped into his head and neck, which were streaked with blood. He held the detonator, the plunger raised. The muscles in his arms knotted and his face contorted as he summoned all his fading strength.

The three limousines were now centered on the road above the culvert. Keeler fired. The bullet struck Vorczek in the forehead. His head snapped on his neck, the back of his head exploding and spraying blood and brain tissue across the ground. The detonator tumbled harmlessly from his hands as he collapsed.

Keeler's need for a cigarette was a raging hunger, a tormented craving. He lay with his face buried in the dusty shoulder of his trench coat, the butt of his automatic resting loosely in his hand, enduring the gnawing desire for a smoke as the minutes slowly dragged past.

Engines roared as airplanes taxied along the runway and lifted into the air. Trucks came along the road to pick up the soldiers. Traffic began to move normally again. Keeler fumbled his cigarettes and lighter out of his pocket, lit a cigarette and took deep drags on it as he put his automatic and silencer away.

Then he slid down the slope to the hollow. Vorczek was sprawled on the edge of the hole, his eyes glazed, one muscular arm still reaching toward the detonator. Keeler looked down at him, smoking his cigarette.

It burned down, and he lit another, drawing on it as he knelt by the detonator, unfastening the wires from the contacts and grounding them together. Then he stood up, gazing at Vorczek again. He turned away and began walking through the brush toward the road. A car veered onto the shoulder, dust boiling up as it slid to an abrupt stop. The door opened and Meacham got out. He came around the car, his topcoat blowing in the wind. Then he lifted an arm and waved. Keeler took a drag on his cigarette and waved back.

PART FIVE

December, 1943

CHAPTER THIRTY

"THE SERVICE CAN be very unfair, Mr. Keeler," Meacham said, shaking his head as he finished reading the message. "Merely thinking about what would have happened if you had failed to stop Vorczek makes my blood run cold, but you didn't get any credit for it. And now this."

Keeler shrugged absently, sketching a rough map on a writing pad. "By definition, what an intelligence service does is secret, Meacham. It or its personnel come to the attention of the public only when someone errs or something goes awry."

"But you would think that someone in London might have thought to send you a note of congratulations," Meacham replied, handing the message back across the table. "And now they're recalling you for transfer, just when you have things nicely organized. That doesn't seem right."

Keeler put the paper aside and continued sketching. "We have to expect frequent transfers, particularly during wartime."

"Well, I shall certainly be sad to see you go," Meacham

said glumly. "I find working with you very agreeable indeed. And we're due two other operatives, aren't we? I wonder who they'll be?"

"It's difficult to say."

"The career force is still spread very thin, so both of them will probably be wartime augmentees, won't they?"

"Very probably."

Meacham grimaced, shaking his head morosely. "It'll certainly be difficult to become accustomed to that again. It's been a very pleasant experience to work with a career officer, and I've learned a lot from you, Mr. Keeler." He stood up and stepped to the file cabinets. "I suppose I'd better start on the sitrep."

"Very well."

Meacham took some folders out of a cabinet and returned to the table. Sighing heavily, he began going through them. Keeler finished the map and drew lines on it, indicating the various possible routes for Celise's journey to England.

The transfer was timely, opening up the possibility of being able to take her with him instead of sending her alone most of the way. The furor in London would end after she was questioned and investigated; then he would make quiet arrangements to ostensibly legalize her presence in England. During his briefings for his next assignment, he could find time to look for a house in the country.

Better arrangements could also be made for Sheila's son. As a temporary measure, the Conley boy was now in a boarding school. The reports from the school indicated that he was amiable and well-behaved, if somewhat puzzled over the abrupt changes in his life. Celise had been delighted when she had heard about him. A home would be a better environment for the boy, and he would provide companionship for Celise.

Meacham glanced up at Keeler. "At least it appears we'll have time to see to things, doesn't it?" he commented. "Nicholson received notice one day and had to leave the next, but they've given you several days. You'll be able to make arrangements about your house and all your belongings."

"Yes."

"And we still have a few loose ends, don't we? One that comes to mind is poor Mueller's things out in the storage building. What do you intend to do with them, Mr. Keeler?"

"Najafi can take care of them."

"Yes, I'm sure he'll be glad to," Meacham chuckled. "Some of those things are quite nice, aren't they? And quite expensive. My Meg would like to have that furniture, but getting it to England would be a problem. And I certainly wouldn't mind having that car. It's a very nice car, isn't it?"

"Yes."

"I thought someone was trying to steal it once, when you were gone and I was meeting with Mueller. It's certainly a car that catches one's eye, and probably far better than any I'll ever to able to own. If I could get into the career force I might, though, because the pay scales are far more generous than they are for wartime augmentees, aren't they?"

Keeler nodded absently; then he thought about what Meacham had said. He lit a cigarette, looking at Meacham. "What made you think that someone was trying to steal the car, and when did that happen?"

"It was while you were in Abadan, seeing to that agent

down there,'' Meacham replied, thumbing through the folders. ''But the man wasn't trying to steal it, Mr. Keeler. He was sort of lurking around beside it, as though he were hiding from someone. I saw him as I was driving along the street to the restaurant for a rendezvous with Mueller. He was gone by the time I passed the car.''

''What did he look like?''

Meacham stopped shuffling the folders, his smile fading. ''Is it important, Mr. Keeler? I would have mentioned it to you before, but I didn't think it was anything to be concerned about.''

''What did he look like?''

Meacham shrugged and cleared his throat, looking away guiltily. ''It was dark, of course, and I didn't get a good look at him. And as I said, he was gone by the time I reached the car. But he was in European clothes, so he must have been an Iranian. I don't know what a European would be doing lurking around a car or hiding from someone. . . .''

''Where was Mueller's driver?''

''He wasn't in the car, so he must have been with some of the drivers of the other cars. You know how the drivers will sometimes go for a drink together or something to eat. . . .''

''What other cars were parked near there?''

Meacham pursed his lips, thinking for a moment; then he shook his head. ''I'm sorry, Mr. Keeler, but it's been so long ago that I can't remember. And I didn't really look at them, so I'm sorry but. . . .'' He broke off, then continued: ''Well, I *do* recall that a car from the Soviet embassy was parked around the corner, one of those large sedans. The reason I remember it is because you were so emphatic that nothing was to be done that would make the NKVD suspicious of Mueller. But it was gone before Mueller came out for our meeting. And that's the only car that I can positively recall. . . .''

His voice faded. Keeler took a drag on his cigarette, looking down at the table. Meacham went back to his folders.

Keeler became aware that time had passed when Meacham said something to him. His cigarette had gone out. He put it in the ashtray and lit another one, looking up. ''Pardon me?''

''I only commented on the fact that I've become quite familiar with all of the sitrep, sir. I'll do Part One as well, if you wish.''

''Very well.''

Keeler stared down at the table. Meacham's voice penetrated his awareness again, and Keeler looked up. Pages that Meacham had written were stacked by his writing pad. Keeler's cigarette had gone out. He put it in the ashtray and lit another. ''Pardon me?''

''I only said that I shouldn't have any trouble with the sitrep on this change of personnel, sir. When Nicholson left and before you came, the home office often got very narked about it, even with Holcomb helping me. That shouldn't happen this time, because I can do it all very well on my own now.''

Keeler nodded, taking a drag of his cigarette. He forced himself to concentrate, to think about what he had to do. He pushed his chair back and stood up. ''I'm going out for a while.''

''Very well, sir.''

Keeler started to leave, but Meacham's voice stopped him at the door. He turned back. ''Pardon me?''

''I only asked if you were taking your coat and hat, sir.

It's very nasty out today, and you'll want them if you're going outside."

Keeler took his hat and coat, putting them on as he went out and walked along the basement hall. The guard caught up with him on the stairs, saying something. He returned and signed out on the register, then went on up the stairs.

Morton spoke to Keeler in the lobby. Keeler was unable to concentrate on the words—they were only meaningless sounds. But he nodded, which appeared to satisfy Morton, who smiled and said something else as he walked away. Keeler crossed the lobby and went out the front doors.

The wind was bitterly cold, moaning around the building and driving tiny, stinging snowflakes through the air. The bare trees tossed against black clouds scudding across the sky. Keeler's coat whipped around his legs and broken, withered fragments of autumn leaves around his feet as he walked along the drive toward the car parked beside the garages.

He stood behind the car and looked at it. The head chauffeur came out of his office, shivering with cold and pulling his coat closer. Asking something, he pointed to the car. It seemed to satisfy him when Keeler shook his head. He ran back to his office. Keeler did not move.

Time passed. The wind howled and tiny snowflakes rattled against the car. Then, concentrating on what he had to do, Keeler examined the car. It took him only a moment to locate what he was looking for. He realized then how willingly he had joined in a conspiracy to deceive himself. He had managed to completely disregard the obvious.

Her attempts to get access to the car should have made him suspicious. Now, once suspicion was aroused, facts leaped together to form a conclusion. The evidence was damning. It was mountainous, overwhelming.

Months before, Mueller had been monitoring the frequencies used by the SD saboteurs operating along the railway in Northern Iran. Then a Soviet regiment had attacked one of the teams. Later, the Abwehr had ordered Mueller to place money in a drop for the agent Broussard, the dentist. Subsequently the NKVD had abducted Broussard.

During the first meeting with Pourzand, something he had said about Mueller had been vaguely worrisome. The necessity to avoid showing interest in Mueller had prevented Keeler from pursuing it, and it had seemed unimportant. But someone loitering around Mueller's car while a car from the Soviet embassy had been parked nearby had seemed unimportant to Meacham.

The words that Pourzand had used were buried under events since Keeler's meeting with him in the bordello. It took a moment for him to isolate the memory, then it was clear in every detail. The blaring music, the foul odors of the place, Pourzand's pale face and deeply set eyes. And his precise words:

"*I was investigating Mueller just before you came here, and I was ordered to drop him. . . .*"

The comment had troubled Keeler because of the time to which it referred, the time when Mueller had employed Celise as a maid. It had been at that same time that Pourzand had been ordered to drop Mueller.

Pourzand had reported something about Mueller that had made Vertinski deeply suspicious and Vertinski had planted a key agent in Mueller's household. It had been a coup, one that had produced results—the whereabouts of SD saboteurs so they could be attacked, the fact that

Broussard was an Abwehr agent, and undoubtedly other information as well.

It had also been the cause of Vertinski's downfall. Vertinski had identified Mueller as an Abwehr agent, but not as a British agent. That had led to a series of events that Vertinski had not anticipated when Mueller had been arrested. The agent who had been planted on Mueller had disappeared into thin air, along with Mueller, his servants, and his belongings.

Vertinski's recall to Moscow had not been because of the war with Kharis. He had been recalled because he had somehow lost a valuable agent. And she was extremely valuable, because the NKVD had managed to recruit her without creating the gaps and ripples in her background that betrayed most agents.

The reason for Mueller's abduction was explained, as well as other things. The surveillance agents looking for Vorczek in the Polish resettlement camp had discovered increased NKVD activity there because Vertinski had placed more agents in the camp, exhausting every possibility in his frantic search for the missing agent.

Pourzand had insisted that Vertinski had no direct contact with agents, but he had been wrong. Vertinski had been the control for the valuable key agent. The means of contact between control and agent had been the car, which had disappeared along with everything else when the agent had vanished.

The drop was inside the right front fender of the car, a metal box the size of a tobacco can. It contained an encoded message, the letters printed in Celise's neat hand. The probable time that the message had been prepared made it likely that it related the fact that Mueller was the contact for a sondercommando platoon enroute to Teheran.

Vertinski would have delayed ordering Mueller's abduction if he had known about the sondercommandos. Some unknown event had prevented him from receiving the message. One small incident had influenced major events, perhaps altering the course of history.

And for himself, that incident had placed into motion a sequence of events that had led to ignoring the glaringly obvious. But the self-deception had been easy, because Celise was so convincing. And she was convincing because she was truthful. Circumstances had trapped her in the secret war, and she wanted out. She had become involved in a twilight world of spies, a dark, hidden world of subterfuge, intrigue, and violent death. And she wanted out because she belonged to the daylight world of bright sunlight and clear skies, of fresh breezes sweeping across open fields. She was not meant to be a participant in the secret war.

He looked at the message, wishing he had given her an opportunity for her small and innocent treachery. She would have searched for her sequin purse and given up, resigned and disappointed. Later, she would have left him for a moment, perhaps to speak to the cook, and the message would have been gone.

Suspicions would have arisen even if Meacham had said nothing about the man beside the car. Her questioning in London would have revealed small anomalies. But he would have helped her explain them away, because she could have satisfied his suspicions, because she was always telling the truth when she spoke about her love and her need for him.

But the message from the metal box was concrete evidence, not a suspicion. Far more than his network had been penetrated. Contamination had invaded *him*, its tendrils rooted firmly in the innermost recesses of his life, tainting even his most private and secret thoughts. And it had to be exorcised.

He tore the paper into fragments. The wind snatched them and they were gone. Something of himself was gone as well. A searing sense of loss blended with grief over what he had to do. For a moment his eyes stung and his face was wet, his breath catching in his throat. He took out his handkerchief and dried his eyes and face. Then he went to get a car.

The raw, bitterly cold weather had emptied the streets. Vendors had remained at home, small shops were closed, and the sidewalks were almost deserted. The wind howled around the car as Keeler drove home. Stopping a short distance from his house, he took out his automatic and loaded a round into the firing chamber. Then continued along the street to his house.

Celise was in one of the back rooms, replying from down the hall when he called to her. "Frank?" she exclaimed in a surprised, pleased voice as she hurried toward him. "Are you home for the day?"

"I want you to come with me in the car."

"Come with you?" she gasped ecstatically, smiling radiantly. "You mean you've already made arrangements for me? But you said I could take my clothes and all my books, and I haven't packed anything or. . . ."

Her voice as well as her smile faded. He shook his head. "It isn't that. I want you to come with me in the car."

She looked at him, perplexed. Then she knew. Her wide blue eyes became stark with sorrow and fear, the color draining from her beautiful face. She nodded tautly as she turned to walk back along the hall. Keeler pushed his hands into his pockets and waited, looking out a window at the bare trees whipping in the wind.

Her footsteps returned a few minutes later, slow and dragging. The housekeeper was with her. Her voice carried into the front room as she asked Celise about something to do with dinner. Celise replied softly, her voice almost inaudible and her lisp pronounced. She said she didn't know.

But she knew. She came into the front room, wearing her chesterfield coat and tying a scarf over her head. And she knew. She knew that her life was measured in minutes. She knew she would never again enjoy dinner, listen to a familiar selection on the radio, or read a favorite book. Keeler held the door open for her and followed her out.

The highway to Damavahr led out of the city to the west. As Keeler drove through the city and turned onto the highway, Celise trembled from more than fear. Realizing that he had left the heater off, he turned it on. The last buildings on the outskirts of the city disappeared behind them. Keeler slowed the car and turned onto a dirt road leading into the desert.

They passed a cluster of shacks beside a spring in a vast, arid valley. The road led up the other side of the valley, then curved around jagged, rocky peaks overlooking the lifeless expanse behind.

Miles of desert stretched out ahead, a desolate place of snakes, scorpions, and wild dogs. Gaunt outlines of barren, stony ridges rose against the cloudy sky beside valleys where the parched brown brush thrashed in the wind. The road climbed around a ridge. There was a dry wadi below it on one side. Keeler stopped the car and parked at the side of the road overlooking the wadi.

Celise opened the door and stepped out. "They said that my family would be tortured to death if I didn't cooperate, Frank," she said quietly, pushing her trembling hands into her coat pockets. "They took me out of the internment camp and put me in a cell. Several men came to talk to me. They said that my family would be treated well if I cooperated, but if I didn't they would die horribly."

"I don't want to know."

"But you must," she protested, her voice almost breaking. "Above all people, you must know. I know I've betrayed you in a way that hurts you more than any other. And I want you to understand—to know there was nothing I could do. I would have told you, but I knew what it would mean to you. So I hoped the danger would pass. . . ."

Her voice faded as she turned, looking out over the wadi. Then she continued, the wind almost smothering her words. She talked about her family and the internment camp. Keeler wanted to end it, to be finished, and yet he wanted to delay. He listened as she related what had happened and talked about events after she had arrived in Iran.

"Erling was such a kindly man," she said. "It was almost impossible for me to believe that he was a German agent. Then after the men took me to your house, I understood. And I also realized that Vertinski had made a serious mistake. The first time I ever heard of you was when Vertinski told me about you. He talked about you at length and said that you were a dangerous man. And to an enemy, you are. . . ."

Her voice faded again. The wind pulled her scarf away from the side of her face. She untied the knot and pulled the scarf tighter under her chin, her hands shaking. Then she pushed her trembling hands back into her pockets. Keeler cupped his lighter in his hands and lit a cigarette.

Celise glanced at him and began speaking again. "After I was brought to your house, I became truly alive for the first time since the Russians and the Germans invaded Poland," she said. "And I had time to think. All the letters from my mother were on the same kind of paper and in the same ink, and said very little. I realized that they must all have been written at the same time, that she has probably been dead for years." She turned and looked at him again. "And I fell in love. At first you were only a way of escaping Vertinski. And then I realized how deeply you needed me. I have been wanted many times, but never before have I been truly needed. And I fell in love with you, Frank."

Keeler looked away, taking a drag on his cigarette. Celise turned back, gazing out over the wadi. Dark clouds rolled past overhead as the cold wind whipped the sparse brush along the sides of the road, stirring up whorls of dust. The silence dragged out, seconds turning into a minute.

"I know that I've betrayed you, Frank," Celise said at last. "But I came to you as I was, not as what I chose to be. If this can be allowed to pass and be forgotten, you will never have reason to distrust me. I told you before that you would have nothing but loyalty from me, and it remains true. And you need me, Frank. Without me, you will have no one. You truly need me, Frank."

She looked at him, waiting. He knew that the story she had related was true, but it was also irrelevant. Against her will, she was an NKVD agent. But she was still an NKVD agent. It would be like having a tumor within him, a tumor always on the verge of turning into virulent cancer. He shook his head, dropping his cigarette and stepping on it.

Her eyes filled with tears as she started to say something else; then she stopped herself. She lifted her chin and stepped to the edge of the road, pulling up her collar and holding it with one hand. Her face averted, she waited.

Keeler took out his automatic and held it at arm's length, sighting down the barrel at the back of her head. His thumb rested on the safety, pushing it down. His finger tightened on the trigger. His hand shook. He was unable to pull the trigger. The wind rustled the brush at their feet and tugged at their coats as they stood motionless, the pistol aimed at the back of her head. Her last words still echoed in his mind, somehow robbing him of control over the finger that rested on the trigger. Those words also contained a raw, keen insight.

Obsessive secrecy had become his way of life, as well as a wall of isolation. Contact beyond that wall had become increasingly difficult and infrequent as the years had passed. His communication with others was limited to those who were capable of reaching him, and they were few.

Celise was one of the few. In her love and need, she had reached out to him. If what she had been would be like a tumor within him, it was deeply embedded. It had become a vital part of him. He needed her. He was physically incapable of killing her. He was unable to pull the trigger.

Lowering the automatic, Keeler pushed the safety on and put the pistol back in his holster. He took Celise's arm. She uttered a gasping sob, her knees folding, and she almost fell over the edge. He helped her back into the car, then got in.

Celise huddled against the door, her face ashen and her teeth chattering. As he took out a cigarette, his fingers shook and broke it in two. He took out another one and got it lit. Celise tried to compose herself, her hands shaking uncontrollably as she straightened the scarf on her head.

Then the chilling moment of terror began to pass. Strangely, it had brought them closer together. Celise's lips were still pale and stiff as she tried to smile, but her eyes reflected a deeper knowledge of him than before. Keeler rolled down the window to let the cigarette smoke out of the car. He collected his thoughts, analyzing the situation and the courses of action open to him.

Then he took a drag on his cigarette and flicked the ash out the window. "When we get to London, you'll be questioned," he said. "Obviously, it will be necessary to reconstruct some facts."

"Yes, Frank."

"You'll have to write down everything, beginning with the first contact from the NKVD in the internment camp. Then I will write a new history for you, and you will have to memorize it. The one I write will replace the one that you wrote. It will become the truth."

"Yes, I understand."

"I will have some of my men keep you awake for several days and nights while they question you. When you give a wrong reply, they will touch you with an electrical contact. After a time, you will feel uncomfortable if you even try to remember what actually happened. Then what I wrote will become the truth."

"I understand."

"It will cause you distress, but a doctor will be in attendance to ensure that your health isn't endangered. It is necessary because it is essential that we alter your memory of your past."

"I won't mind, Frank. I want to change that past, and it will be over within a few days."

Keeler nodded, tossing his cigarette out the window, then lit another as he started the engine and drove back the way they had come.

Celise reached out and rested a hand on his arm. "I didn't know that you love me, Frank," she said quietly. "I knew that you needed me, but I didn't know that you love me. You do, don't you?"

"Yes. Some time ago, we discussed a story about a man named Heinrich Von Aue."

"*Der Arme Heinrich*?" Celise replied, sitting up. "It has always been one of my favorites. It is a very old story—I first read it when I was studying medieval literature. Would you like to discuss it further?"

"Yes, please."

She cleared her throat and adjusted her scarf, composing herself and collecting her thoughts. Then she began telling the story. After a few minutes, the normal healthy color had returned to her face and the quavering tremor in her voice was gone. She was engrossed in the story, smiling, gesturing, and touching his arm as she talked. He was engrossed in the pleasure of listening to her as he drove out of the desert.

EPILOGUE

CALLAGHAN REALIZED HE had dozed off for a few minutes. It was nearly dawn. Both the rain and the motorway had been left behind. The car was on a two-lane highway.

The first light of the new day was touching the horizon in the east. They were traveling along a narrow highway that curved through rolling hills. Stars twinkling between the broken clouds overhead slowly disappeared into the gray light of dawn. The light began filtering across the hills, turning dense shadows into copses of trees and quenching the yellow spots of light in farmhouse windows.

As Callaghan sat up, Conley glanced at him in the dim light. "Are you back with me, Charles?" he asked, chuckling. "I lost you to the sandman for a bit there, didn't I?"

"Yes, I dozed off for a while," Callaghan replied, laughing. He stretched, then he looked at Conley again; his eyelids were heavy, and lines of fatigue were etched into his round, amiable face. "If we're going to stay on this highway much longer, I could take a turn at the wheel," he said. "You must be pretty tired yourself."

Conley smiled and shook his head. "I'm somewhat tuckered, but I'll do, Charles. There's a place just a few miles farther on where I always stop, and we'll both feel more lively after a good breakfast. I've driven this route so many times, though, that I could come near to driving it in my sleep."

"I'll bet you could. You came home during all the holidays from school and so forth, didn't you?"

Conley nodded. He began describing his school holidays and other times when he had returned home. An avid hunter, he had spent most of his holidays hunting in the surrounding region. As he related amusing incidents that had occurred during hunting trips, he talked about a time during which the events of World War II had been history. The long story that had filled the hours of the night was left behind, a part of the past as the new dawn brightened.

Shades of pink touched the folds of the clouds drifting overhead, then the sun edged above the horizon and rose over the England of travel agency posters, washed clean and fresh by the rain. Mossy stone walls outlined green fields that shimmered with raindrops drying in the morning breeze. The highway led past small villages, clusters of wattle and daub cottages with thatched or slate roofs. Farmhouses, their outbuildings huddled around them, dotted the rolling hills.

Shortly after sunrise, they stopped at an old inn for breakfast. It was at the end of a narrow, tree-lined lane, a picturesque, half-timbered building with low, deep doorways and leaded windows. As they got out of the car, yawning and stretching, Conley led the way to an iron gate in the stone wall at one side of the inn. The gate opened into a shaded flower garden where spring flowers made a riot of color under gnarled, ancient trees.

The kitchen door was ajar. Conley called out as he walked toward a table and chairs in the center of the garden. "It's Conley, Mrs. Forbes! I have a friend with me!"

A woman inside the kitchen greeted Conley as he and Callaghan sat down at the iron Victorian lawn table whose ornate designs were blurred by coats of white paint. The pleasant disorder of the flower garden gave it a relaxed, restful atmosphere, rusty tools in corners and old wooden buckets used for flower pots slowly decaying and breaking apart.

The woman, plump and middle-aged, came out. She put snowy linen and sparkling china on the table, then brought out coffee. It was hot and strong, delicious with thick cream. The piquant, appetizing aroma of frying ham wafted out of the kitchen and blended with the fragrance of the flowers. When the coffeepot was empty, the woman refilled it, then brought out breakfast.

The eggs, from the henhouse behind the inn, were flanked by generous slices of ham and links of small sausages juicy and spicy with sage and pepper. The potatoes had been parboiled and diced, then fried with onions into tasty patties. The toast, thick slices of homemade bread browned over a wood fire, tasted faintly of hardwood smoke and was covered with a cloth to keep it hot while it soaked up the rich creamery butter.

Almost uncomfortably full when he finished, Callaghan argued goodnaturedly with Conley over who would pay the bill while the woman refilled their thermos bottle. Then they drove on, passing small, sleepy villages and farms that were stirring in their centuries-old pattern of life. Conley had to stop the car for a herd of cattle crossing the highway from one pasture to another, then stopped again while a flock of sheep flowed around the car.

It was nine o'clock when they reached their destination, a somewhat larger village with the ruins of an old mill beside a millpond shaded by towering oaks. Conley waved to two old men who were fishing in the millpond. They lifted their caps. Turning off the highway, he drove across a square and along a street through the village. When the car passed the last scattered houses, the street became a lane with a stone wall along one side. A stream splashed along the other side, ducks and geese waddling along its grassy, shaded banks.

A hundred yards from the village, Conley turned in between the bulky, weather-stained gateposts flanking a carriage gate in the wall and onto a long gravel drive which divided at the house, leading around to the front entrance and back to a carriage house that had been converted into a garage.

The large, old house was Tudor, with mullioned windows in its half-timbered bays. An array of short wave antennas and a dish satellite antenna set off to one side were jarringly anachronistic. Conley drove past the house, where trees and the roof of a pergola rose above a hedge enclosing the flower garden. Conley parked the car, and he and Callaghan went through a gate in the hedge.

He was sitting in the pergola and reading the paper. He had not aged as much as Callaghan had expected. His white hair was full and thick, while the lines and creases in his face were those of a mature but not an old man. He came out of the summerhouse to meet them, his posture straight and his step firm.

His expressionless, aloof reserve was as Callaghan had expected; he was an extremely private, undemonstrative man. In making the introductions, Conley addressed him as his father. He acknowledged the introduction with a silent, unsmiling nod, but his handshake was firm and warm. Callaghan spoke as they shook hands. "I'm very pleased to meet you, Lord Keeler," he said.

"Frank," Keeler responded quietly, pointing toward a lawn table and chairs on the flagstone patio in front of the pergola. "Let's sit over there."

The sun was warm, Callaghan took off his topcoat and Conley shrugged out of his trench coat. Keeler was wearing a dark suit with a white shirt and tie, as formally attired here at home as elsewhere. Conley disregarded his reserve, speaking to him in a respectfully affectionate vein while Keeler murmured and nodded tersely in reply.

Then Conley commented on the physical resemblance between Callaghan and his father: "From a picture I saw once, I'd say he's much like his father when he was younger. Do you think so, Father?"

Keeler hesitated. Looking at Callaghan reflectively, he almost smiled, the wrinkles at the corners of his eyes deepening. Then he nodded. "Yes, he is, George," he replied. "The likeness is even closer than a photograph could suggest."

Callaghan handed the carton of cigarettes to Keeler. Nodding in thanks, he took out a pack and opened it. He had emphysema, with slow, audible breathing and a dry cough. When he lit a cigarette, a spasm of coughing seized him. He controlled it, then took a deep drag and asked Callaghan about his father.

It was almost a monologue as Callaghan talked about what his father was doing. Whenever Callaghan paused, Keeler murmured a terse question that provoked a lengthy response. He showed no reaction; his lined, craggy face was immobile, his eyes completely expressionless. Like two discs of glass, they seemed totally devoid of depth.

Keeler suddenly looked past Callaghan, toward the house and his eyes glowed with life. Conley exclaimed in delight as he got up from the table and walked rapidly toward the house. Keeler and Callaghan also stood up.

To an even greater extent than Keeler, she had somehow avoided the ravages of age. Wearing a yellow spring dress trimmed with frilly white, her long, thick silver hair arranged on top of her head, she was strikingly attractive. As she and Conley embraced and kissed, it seemed incongruous when he addressed her as "Mother." Shapely and beautiful, she looked like a woman of forty with prematurely white hair.

It was only when she and Conley approached the table that Callaghan saw the network of fine lines and wrinkles around her eyes and her mouth. But they were obscured by her dazzling smile and the vibrant force of her personality. Her large blue eyes sparkling and her perfect teeth shining, the years had passed over her lightly; in every way that mattered, she remained a young, beautiful woman.

She was engagingly cordial when Conley introduced her to Callaghan, her accent and her slight lisp charming. Callaghan took her warm, slender hand, replying to her greeting. "It's my pleasure, Lady Keeler," he said.

"No, please!" she exclaimed, laughing. "Let's not be formal. I am Celise, and you are Charles. And you are the new officer in charge of passport control at the American embassy, Charles?"

Callaghan hesitated, then nodded; it was her term of reference. "Yes, that's right."

"And you are our son's good friend as well. He's spoken of you so often, and I've hoped for the opportunity of meeting you." She turned to Keeler. "Frank, I asked the housekeeper to prepare lunch in the morning room. That will be pleasant, don't you think?''

Keeler nodded, lighting a cigarette. ''Yes.''

''Then I'll leave you to your discussion for now,'' Celise said, turning back to Callaghan. ''And I'll look forward to talking with you at lunch, Charles.''

Keeler coughed, shaking his head. ''Why don't you join us, Celise? And after lunch, ask the housekeeper to prepare a guest room. You will be able to stay for the night, won't you, Charles?''

Callaghan was surprised and pleased; it was an unusual distinction, the remote, aloof man's circle of close associates was extremely limited. Conley and Celise exchanged a glance, also startled, then smiled at Callaghan. He replied, ''I would certainly like to. I don't have to return to the city tonight, sir. But I didn't come prepared to stay over.''

''We can provide everything you'll need. You'll be able to remain tonight, won't you, George?''

''Yes, sir,'' Conley replied. ''I'll only need to make a couple of telephone calls to let the staff know.''

''Very well. It may be useful to Charles to have our perspective on some of the problems his predecessor experienced. We'll go over that this afternoon or after dinner.''

''Yes, sir. I'm sure he'll find that very useful.''

Taking a drag on his cigarette, Keeler held a chair for Celise. When she was seated, Callaghan and the others sat down at the table. Celise leaned over and put a hand on Callaghan's arm. ''Tell me about your father, Charles,'' she said. ''We were all very distressed when we heard that he had suffered a heart attack. How is his health?''

Callaghan again began talking about his father, and her

beautiful face and wide blue eyes reflected concern as she listened closely, then asked Callaghan about his wife and children. It appeared to Callaghan that she remembered every single fact that Conley had ever told her about himself and his family; that his two oldest sons were at Yale, that his wife collected etchings. Beyond her remarkable memory, her interest in him and his family was more than flattering. He had met other skilled hostesses with highly-developed social and conversational skills but he had never encountered anyone who could compare with Celise.

During the conversation, it became evident that intelligence activities were openly discussed in her presence. An hour after she had joined them, they were talking about the assistance Conley had given Callaghan in escaping from Iran during the revolution led by Khomeini. Conley minimized his part in it, shaking his head at a remark that Callaghan made. "I daresay you could have managed on your own, Charles," he said. "In any event, I had to get out myself, didn't I?"

"Yes, but you could have done it a lot easier without me," Callaghan replied. "It was touch and go for a while, wasn't it?"

Conley chuckled wryly. "Indeed it was. I never thought I'd be pleased to see Afghanistan, but I was then. Iran was a shambles, and it has steadily become worse ever since."

Celise nodded emphatically. "It certainly has. But it was hardly orderly when I was there during the war."

"I should think not, Mama," Conley said, laughing. "After all, refugees from all over were pouring into Iran. But it would have been much worse if the Allied armies hadn't been there."

"Yes, it would have," she agreed. "But only in some

ways, George. One of the problems in Teheran was the criminal element, which the military could do little about. After I met your father, though, I was quite content. And I must say that Teheran at its very worst was a virtual paradise compared to the Soviet internment camp at. . . ." Her voice faded. Frowning in perplexity, she tried to complete the sentence. "The Soviet internment camp at. . . ."

She suddenly winced in pain, the color draining from her face. As Callaghan watched, she seemed to age decades within a second. Pale and haggard, the lines and wrinkles on her face were suddenly much more pronounced. An essential part of her personality seemed to be visibly disintegrating.

Her eyes, fixed on some distant point beyond the horizon, were somehow also turned inward; they mirrored stark horror at something within herself. Conley looked at Celise in helpless bewilderment.

Keeler sat forward and put his hand on hers. "The Soviet internment camp at Krasnoyarsk," he said. "In the Siberian highlands."

"The Soviet internment camp at Krasnoyarsk," she repeated, her eyes still blank as she echoed his flat, uninflected tone. "In the Siberian highlands." She blinked, her eyes focused again. Drawing a deep breath, she swallowed, trembling. Then she turned to Keeler. "What is wrong with me, Frank?" she asked plaintively. "Why does that happen?"

"As I've told you," he replied, patting her hand, "you have an exceptional memory, so you become distraught when you forget something. It creates such a strong conflict that you have difficulty dealing with it. But the things you forget happened a long time ago, Celise. It is perfectly reasonable to forget things that happened so long ago. You remember the internment camp now, don't you?"

"Yes."

"Then there is no reason to be upset."

As he sat back, stubbing out his cigarette in the ashtray and taking another one from the pack, he glanced meaningfully at Conley. Conley leaned forward, smiling anxiously. "Yes, that was a long time ago, Mama. Anyone could forget something that happened so long ago."

Turning to him, Celise sat up and smiled wanly. Callaghan quickly added his reassurances. Celise smiled at him as well, now faintly embarrassed and regaining her composure. The conversation began with a rush, everyone speaking at once. Keeler lit his cigarette and looked away, listening.

The lingering tension from the awkward moment rapidly faded. Through a chance comment that Celise made, Callaghan discovered they shared an enjoyment of Benoit's novels. Celise recalled even the minor characters in the novels, old friends of hers. Then the conversation turned to early American literature. Celise playfully chided Conley for his lack of interest in books, then began talking about one of her favorite American works, Longfellow's *Golden Legend*. Her wounds from the secret war were now safely hidden once again; she was youthful, beautiful, and charming. Conley smiled affectionately. Callaghan watched her and listened, fascinated. Keeler smoked and coughed as he looked away, listening.

the unexpected peace

jack kelly

As combat raged in the Philippines the bloody Pacific war was coming to a close. But for the men of the 306th Infantry the war was just beginning.

The raw replacement troops were sent into the Philippine hills to flush out the remaining Japanese, and they had to struggle against the jungle and their own inexperience as well as the enemy.

When peace was declared the job of the 306th wasn't over. They enforced the peace while withstanding the attacks of a desperate, unsurrendering enemy that had sworn to destroy *all* Americans—at *any* cost!

LEISURE BOOKS 2003-3/$2.50

THE SCORPIO CIPHER

RALPH HAYES

Rosenfeld was the man who invented America's greatest weapon—the deadly laser cannon.

Now Rosenfeld was the captive of Iranian zealots who were determined to learn the secret of his design.

Gage was the man the President sent into Iran to get Rosenfeld out.

It wasn't routine—even for Gage, whose assignments were never routine. Rosenfeld was held under heavy guard. Rosenfeld was being tortured by a twisted master of pain.

And Gage was supposed to take Rosenfeld's place!

LEISURE BOOKS 1060-7/$3.25

the commandos

elliot arnold

SABOTAGE IN THE ENEMY'S CAMP!

They were expert dealers in death, men who would stop at nothing to destroy the enemy. When American Alan Lowell led an expedition to capture a Nazi garrison on the Norwegian coast, he encountered an unexpected complication in the beautiful Nicole, mistress of a Nazi captain!

If their liaison were discovered, it would mean death for Nicole—and untold disaster for the commandos' mission!

Price: **$2.75**
0-8439-2009-2
pp. 304

Category: **War**